SOUL
STRIPPER

SOUL STRIPPER

KATANA COLLINS

APHRODISIA

KENSINGTON PUBLISHING CORP.

www.kensingtonbooks.com

APHRODISIA BOOKS are published by

Kensington Publishing Corp.
119 West 40th Street
New York, NY 10018

ISBN-13: 978-0-7582-9011-3
ISBN-10: 0-7582-9011-X
First Kensington Trade Paperback Printing: June 2013

eISBN-13: 978-0-7582-9012-0
eISBN-10: 0-7582-9012-8
First Kensington Electronic Edition: June 2013

10 9 8 7 6 5 4 3 2 1

Printed in the United States of America

For Sean

Acknowledgments

When I set out to be a writer, I made a goal for myself that I would be a published novelist before I turned thirty. And I am thrilled to say this book is scheduled to come out less than a month before my thirtieth birthday! As exciting as this is, goals are rarely accomplished without the help of others. And this dream of mine would certainly not be a reality without the help of so many.

Tremendous thanks to everyone at Kensington who worked so hard for this book to hit the shelves. And to my editor, Martin Biro, for taking a chance on me as a writer. For believing I had the talent. And for pouring so much of yourself into all you do. You are an inspiration to watch.

My gratitude to all the ladies and gentleman at the NYC chapter of Romance Writers of America—especially Lise, Shara, Teresa, Mageela, and Leanna. Each meeting was just the boost I'd need to put myself out there. To my critique group—Krista, Derek, and Shauna—you guys are all so talented and always the kick in the ass I need.

Lots of love and thanks to my canine "assistants" Red and Bebop, who offer kisses and snuggles late into the night as I'm writing—there will be many Milk-Bones waiting for you! To my sister, Bridget, for teaching me to believe in real-life fairy tales. To my brother, Bo, whose imagination never ceases to amaze. And to Mom and Dad—for always filling my life with books, dreams, and inspiration.

And last but not least, my husband, Sean. Thank you does not even begin to cover it.

PROLOGUE

She lay on top of his body, her bare breasts pressed against his tight muscles. His breathing was steady against her chest. She lifted herself up quietly so as not to wake him. She hadn't known her date for long, but he seemed nice enough.

She walked to her bathroom, not bothering to turn on the light. A candle glowed on the sink, and she ran the faucet to splash some water on her face. A tendril of red, curly hair fell over one shoulder, and she could taste something bad in her mouth—what was that? Morning breath? She grabbed her toothbrush, which hadn't been used in ages. Every now and then to spruce up before a date, but really—she had no need for one other than keeping up appearances. She scrubbed the bristles against her teeth, the action feeling foreign, and stared at her reflection.

It was dark, but her succubus vision was sharp.

There was something next to her mouth—a crease? It couldn't be. Succubi don't *get* wrinkles. She closed her eyes and shifted, thinking about what areas she wanted to change. Where there would normally be a tingle—some shiver of magic running through her body—she felt hardly anything. A few goose bumps rose on her arms. When she opened her eyes, the crease was still there, though slightly less visible. She spit the minty foam into the sink and tossed her toothbrush down, bringing her face in closer to the mirror to investigate.

She was naked with the exception of the beautiful anklet dangling just above her foot—a gift from the man lying in her bed, fast asleep. Her breasts brushed the cold porcelain of her sink, making her jump back slightly. She closed her eyes and shifted into clothes. The power was still there, though barely. She looked down, now wearing a sheer camisole and panties. It wasn't what she had in mind, but at least it was something. Her head was spinning and she was dizzy, faint from the energy spent.

The light behind her clicked on and she jumped, turning to find her date standing behind her. His eyes, which had been so kind only hours before, now seemed like empty, bottomless holes. "Trouble sleeping?"

She shook her head, fiery hair tickling her collarbone. A pull came from deep in her gut, feeling his aura's shift from earlier in the night. It was red—a purplish red. She sent him the sweetest smile she could muster and casually tossed her hair behind her shoulder. "Not at all. Just wanted to freshen up before round two." She reached for the sink, grabbing her porcelain hand mirror from the vanity and slowly brought it to her face. She kept one eye on him and managed to act as though she were looking at her reflection.

His chiseled jaw clenched, and his face twisted into a sadistic smile. "Come now, Savannah. We both know there's not going to be a round two. I can smell your fear." From behind his back, he pulled out a knife with a serrated blade. He moved quickly, lunging at the succubus, but even in her exhausted state she moved faster.

She smashed the porcelain mirror against the counter, the

glass shattering, leaving her with the pointed shard of the handle. She swung the shiv toward him, just barely missing his arm. They each stood in a crouched position, ready to strike.

He laughed at her. His head tipped back, the low chuckle escaping his throat like the soft rattle of a dangerous snake. With no warning, he threw his knife, the blade slicing through her bare foot, staking it to the hardwood floor.

She screamed, her body crumpling into a heap, and yanked the knife away. She sat there, blade in one hand, shiv in the other, waiting for her foot to heal itself. Waiting for regeneration that didn't come. He cackled above her. She looked up to find him standing over her, another knife in his hand.

He knelt, eyes cold like stone. "You're waiting for something that's not going to happen, hun. You are practically human. Nothing's going to heal itself this time."

Her breath became shorter—panic. She had not felt true fear in such a long time. Not since she was human. She forced her breathing to slow down. Forced herself to stop the tunnel vision from closing around her. She still held two weapons, his knife in one hand and her shiv in the other. She would not go down without a fight. The small tingle of power coursed through her veins, reminding her she still had a touch of magic left—she would find the right time to use it.

She swiped the knife across his bare chest, and the blade slid into his tender flesh. He fell back, a scream echoing in the bathroom. In the moment it took him to gather his composure, she leaped over his body, running to the bedroom. Her leap was not high enough and he raised his knife, cutting her deeply behind the knee.

Both legs were damaged. She could hardly stand; most of her weight rested on her hands, leaning on the dresser. She had lost the knife somewhere along the jump, but the shiv was still clenched so tightly in her fist that her palm was bleeding. The blood from her knee traveled down her leg, over her calf, and as it dripped across her beautiful anklet, steam rose with a sizzle, as though the anklet were absorbing the blood. The blood that hit the anklet dropped to the floor, still steaming and sizzling, creating burn marks like a chemical spill.

He walked slowly toward her, knives dripping with blood. His, hers—did it matter? "It's over, Savannah."

She shook her head, eyes wide and wet. "Why?"

His eyes creased, and he smiled in that evil way again. He shuddered with pleasure as her body trembled in fear before him. "You kill for a living. And now, so do I."

Adjusting her body, she forced herself to stand so that she was leaning only against one arm—the shiv stretched out in front of her. "Then come and get me, fucker." Despite her tough exterior, her heart hammered against her ribs.

He ran toward her. As he did, she shifted into a serpent with her last remaining power. Her fangs sunk into his abdomen just before his knives slit her throat. A handful of scales fluttered to the floor and a fang ripped out of her mouth as she choked on her own blood. She fell to the ground, transforming back into her human form. A bloody goddess with lifeless eyes.

He chuckled softly and licked the blood from his knife, his body radiating with the power of fresh blood and a new kill. Her magic entered his body with her blood, slithering down his throat like a fine cognac. He bent down and ran his hand down the length of her lifeless body. Using the edge of the knife, he gathered a pool of blood on the blade and scraped it across two small test tubes. "I'd fuck you one last time, but I fear it would somehow wake you," he whispered to himself. "Such a waste." His fingers trailed down her hips, across her ass, and down her thighs until he reached the anklet. He ripped it swiftly from her. body, pocketing it before taking off.

1

The smell of coffee always turns me on.

Well, it might not be the coffee as much as it is my manager *at* the coffee shop. Drew. I liked to repeat his name in my head. Drew. *Drew*. *An*drew Sullivan—one of the best men I've ever met. Which might not be saying much for him considering the degenerates I hang out with. I wiped down a table with a few stains, thinking about those dimples of his. He always had the faint aroma of coffee on his clothes. And under his cotton T-shirts, I could see the slightest ripple of muscles. Long and lean. The muscles of a soccer player.

I stood there wiping the same spot over and over, my nails scraping against the tabletop. I imagined Drew's lips gently brushing against the dip in my neck. His growing erection pressing into me as he tenderly nibbled the soft skin above my collarbone. *Monica, Monica,* he'd moan. . . .

"Monica?" His smooth voice snapped me out of my dream. "I think that table's clean." His lips curled into a playful smile, eyes sparkling with mischief. He turned his attention back to the faucet, wrench in hand, fixing the constant drip that had been annoying all the baristas over the past week.

"Oh. Right, of course. Sorry, Drew. I'm sort of lost in my own thoughts today." My eyes traveled to his tight ass; his signature dirty towel was hanging from the back pocket of his jeans. Disoriented, I turned to move on to my next task and slammed into a customer closing in on the table I just cleaned. His iced coffee spilled onto my chest. Ice dribbled down my white T-shirt, and cold coffee covered my now-tight nipples.

"Oh shit." I looked up at the regular customer whose caffeinated beverage I was now wearing. He looked angry—which for anyone else might have been a problem. But for me? This was an easy fix for any succubus over a century old. That's what I am—a succubus. And whatever notions you have in your head about succubi are probably wrong. Just because I am a minion of Hell doesn't necessarily make me an "evil" being.

I used to be an angel and am apparently the *only* angel-turned-succubus known within the demon realm. I guess this sort of makes me a celebrity. They call me the golden succubus—the nickname makes me cringe. It's a bit too reminiscent of a particular "golden" sex act.

I looked up at the angry man standing over me and felt the tingles as my succubus magic handled the situation. My bottom lip pouted naturally when I spoke. "I am just *so* sorry." As I took a deep breath, his eyes fixed on my nipples pushing out my wet T-shirt. "I'm such a klutz!" Running my fingernail along his forearm, his face softened.

"It's really no problem." He flashed a smile after licking his lips. "We should really get you out of that shirt." He lifted a hand to his mouth, and I noticed a wedding band on that ring finger of his.

Fucking men.

I opened my mouth to answer, but before I could, Drew

stepped between us, his eyebrows low over his eyes. "You can go have a seat—we'll bring you another coffee."

"*Iced* coffee." The married man smirked and looked past Drew, meeting my eyes.

"Iced coffee? What's the matter—can't take the heat?"

"It's Vegas, man. Who drinks hot coffee in the middle of the desert?"

Drew's mouth tipped into a barely visible smile. "*I do.*"

The customer ran a hand through his dark brown hair. "Fine, whatever man."

Drew was still standing protectively in front of me, and I touched his arm lightly, an attempt to break him from his aggressive stance. As he rocked back on his heels, Drew's face cracked into a friendlier smile—one that was much more appropriate as the owner of the coffee shop. He clapped the man on the bicep in that weird way men do to each other. "Just messin' with you, man. Have a seat. I'll get your iced coffee."

Once the customer was out of earshot, Drew swiveled around, his smile entirely gone, replaced again with the anger I had seen a moment ago. He leaned down, his face suddenly close to mine. "Do you have to come on to every friggin' customer?" He grunted and pushed past my shoulder, heading back behind the counter.

"*Me?* I don't know if you saw the whole thing, Drew—but that guy came on to *me*. Not the other way around." I was whispering so not to create a scene in the crowded café.

"You don't even realize how much you flirt."

I paused, taking in his vibe. "We're not talking about *him* anymore, are we?"

He snorted and slammed some of his tools around, not answering right away. After a few seconds of silence, he stood with his hands on his hips, not meeting my eyes. "That was a long time ago, Mon. Trust me, I'm not exactly sitting at home pining away over you."

"Six months is not that long ago." Ever since I started working for him here at the coffee shop, I knew he was bound to ask me out at some point. He managed to hold out longer than most men—almost two years after we first met, he invited me to dinner. And I for some stupid reason still have a conscience—that little bit of angel left in me—and had to say no. I couldn't take that risk with Drew's soul.

He sighed. "It is in the dating world. You should know that."

I resisted the urge to roll my eyes. "Whatever. I'm happy you've moved on." I swallowed. His lips pressed together and one eyebrow twitched into an arch. Maybe he knew I was bluffing, maybe he didn't. It didn't exactly matter anymore. We held each other's gaze for seconds too long. I broke the eye contact first and joined him behind the counter, pulling out a new cup of ice for the customer's replacement coffee.

Drew cut me off, taking the cup from me. "Why don't I refill this for you? You're still a little bit—eh—indecent." His eyes flicked toward my breasts.

"Oh. Right." I glanced down at my shirt. Brown stains covered my hard nipples. "And—I really am sorry. About spilling the coffee," I clarified quickly. "I feel off my game today. Spilling stuff, drifting off, daydreaming . . ."

Drew smiled at me, turning back into his normal self. "It's fine, Monica. Really." He tossed me the hand towel that was hanging in his back pocket.

I smiled back. "Well, feel free to take the refill out of my hips—oops, I mean, *tips.*" I smirked, exaggerating the flirting.

He rolled his eyes. "There you go again." He smiled, lines creasing around his mouth. "I have an extra shirt in my office, if you need it."

I headed to the bathroom. "No, it's fine. I think I have one in my bag."

I shut the bathroom door and slid the lock to the left. Can't have anyone walking in while I'm shapeshifting. In actuality, my shapeshifting is just a mind-trick on mortals and immortals. A mirage of sorts. I took a look at the reflection in the mirror. My dark blond hair still looked in place, parted on the side with a slight curl at the ends. But my shirt was a mess. I focused—closed my eyes. A familiar prickle surrounding my body as I shifted into another clean, white shirt.

The idea of stealing souls for Hell makes my stomach twist. Even though I am technically a demon, you could say I sort of play for both teams whenever possible. Ethical souls are the nutrition. They're like eating fresh vegetables and free-range chicken. The bad souls, well, they're the fast-food equivalent. I'm essentially sustaining my existence on this mortal plane on a diet of chocolate and potato chips. My body certainly craves something better, but I allow the indulgence only when absolutely necessary.

I looked away from the mirror. I wasn't always such an immortal vigilante. There was a time I accepted my fate as a succubus. A time in my existence I wasn't exactly proud of.

Maybe I should try a new hair color—go blonder—surfer bleach blond . . . like Drew's new girlfriend, Adrienne. Ugh. I couldn't even bear the thought of it—Drew with a girlfriend. A *blond* girlfriend. It was just so . . . so . . . obvious. I mean, okay, my hair was blond, too, but mine was natural. I hadn't changed my looks much since my angel days, partially because I liked my cherub features but also because the art of shifting takes a lot of power. It simply takes less energy to adjust the looks I already have in people's minds rather than create a new vision entirely.

I thought again of Adrienne and her platinum blond hair. The sort of white blond that looked as though it had been singed at the bottom—brittle and crisp. It just screamed Pamela Anderson. Sighing, I walked out of the bathroom to finish up my closing shift duties.

I finished cleaning the tables and restocked the sugar, and as

I carried another bag of arabica coffee beans to the front, I inhaled their scent and thought of Drew. That sweet smell that hits you at the back of the throat. That scent will get me through the end of my night job. The strip club doesn't always have the nicest men . . . or the nicest smells, for that matter.

"Aren't you going to be late for the club?" Once again, Drew snapped me out of my thoughts.

Nine p.m. Which meant yes . . . I was going to be late. I flashed him a smile. "Yes, probably. With any luck, I'll be fired." I laughed to myself at the thought. Lucien would never dream of firing me. I'm his best dancer and the closest thing to a sister that he's got. As my ArchDemon, Lucien is in charge of Nevada and the entire Southwest region. He may seem threatening to most, but when he pitches his fits, I only ever see a petulant teenager stomping his feet and raising his voice.

Drew took a few steps closer to me and placed his rough hand on my elbow. They were the hands of a carpenter. A hard worker—rough and masculine. "Maybe you should quit. I could give you a raise here." His green eyes grew wider with hope—and perhaps a slight hint of desire.

My mouth tipped into a sad smile. "You can offer me a thousand dollars per night?" *Not to mention the easy access to men's souls.* The strip club is the best way to meet bad boys and avoid the good ones. The degenerates that come into that club give me just enough energy to keep running. I glanced back up at his green eyes, his warm breath tickling my lips. Drew's soul was clean. Pure and totally Heaven-bound. Sure, he was quite the flirt—even with a girlfriend. But that alone doesn't warrant a one-way ticket to Hell. He deserved better than me. Even still, when he was this close to my body, my ethical stance became fogged.

Drew chuckled, and his laugh reminded me of water bubbling over a fountain. "No, I definitely can't offer you that."

His hand was still on my elbow, and his fingers moved in gentle circles over my skin. "But I can give you unlimited coffee and an extra two dollars an hour."

"That's a *tempting* offer," I teased, "but somehow I'm not so sure I can sustain my life on coffee."

"I could find other ways to keep you happy here." His breathing became more shallow and his face lowered closer to mine. I knew he was just reacting to my succubus pheromones. It wasn't Drew talking—it was simply his carnal desire coming through. No man can resist a succubus in heat. And though I rationally knew this, I still couldn't pull my gaze away from his. I could feel the need from deep within my body, an itch to have sex with someone so deliciously pure and good. I looked down at my nails and they were glossier, with a sheen most women paid good money to get. My powers were running low, which meant only one thing—I needed to sleep with someone tonight. Everything about me was designed to draw in humans. I'm like a shiny, intricate spiderweb, waiting to catch my prey. As my body requires a recharge, my hair gets shinier, my eyes become more vibrant, and I emit a pheromone unlike any a human has ever produced.

We stayed there, eyes locked, as the bell above the door chimed. I sensed Adrienne's aura before even hearing her acrylic heels clacking against the floor—another succubus perk. Being able to sense most auras—human and demon. I quickly broke away from Drew's grasp and grabbed my bag.

"Well, hey there, handsome!" Adrienne came up behind Drew and wrapped her orange, faux-tanned arms around his shoulders. Her platinum hair fell into her eyes, making her black roots even more painfully obvious. *Ugh, a typical Vegas girl,* I thought. Which was admittedly ironic, since *I* was the stripper out of the two of us. Her aura shone as a bright red. That usually meant one thing—adultery. I'd seen her aura just

the other day and it had been green. She must have recently finished the deed. I inhaled, and though I couldn't smell the stench
of sex on her, there was something different about her scent.

Drew's face faltered and he withdrew his hand from me as if
my touch burned. His eyelids drooped in that way that a man's
does after watching golf for a few hours.

"Hey, back at you, gorgeous." His voice sounded genuine,
for the most part. It strained a little bit on the word *gorgeous,*
but that also might have just been my imagination.

Without thinking, I groaned. Adrienne darted an agitated
look in my direction and Drew's head dropped to the side, his
eyes rolling at me in a chastising way that made me feel like a
teenager.

"Oh, um, sorry. I can't find my costume for tonight. I
thought I had it in my bag." Adrienne narrowed her eyes at me,
obviously not buying my story. Maybe I'm not as smooth as I
thought.

Drew sighed. "Don't mind Monica, babe. She's our resident
cynic here at the café."

I shrugged at Adrienne. "Well, I'd better get going. See you
tomorrow, Drew." I rushed past them, bumping her shoulder
in the process.

But before exiting through the door, I saw the married man
from earlier. The one whose coffee I spilled. His eyes went directly toward my tits, acting as though if he just stared hard
enough he'd develop X-ray vision. I ran up to him, grabbing
my card from the bottom of my bag. "Here," I said, handing
him the card. "If you're interested, I'll be dancing there tonight."
It simply had my stage name, *Mirage,* listed with the strip
club's name and information.

His eyes sparkled and he licked his lips as he glanced down
at my card. "Oh, I know this place," he said.

I looked back again at Drew to find him staring at me. His

lips were pressed into a thin line, eyebrows knitted in the center. *Good,* I thought, *be jealous.* I turned and headed for the exit, glancing over my shoulder one last time to look at Drew. Instead, I found the married man staring at my ass. Sometimes it was just too easy being a succubus.

The itch between my legs simply would not go away. As I drove down Las Vegas's dusty roads, I knew I had to take care of my desire, and soon. I hoped the married coffee shop guy would show up, or I'd be forced to sleep with one of the other regular assholes who frequented Hell's Lair. That's the name of the strip club—real original, huh? I shifted myself into my stripper look while driving, which was becoming increasingly hard to do as my powers lessened. I made my hair a dark brown—almost black—as I tried to decide which costume to wear tonight. Schoolgirl seemed too obvious. Cowgirl was *so* overdone here in Nevada. And dressing like an angel hit a little too close to home for me. Maybe a 1950s housewife character tonight? Or even better—I'll go vintage chic. Classy but naughty. I shifted into a tight black dress that was backless but left something for the imagination. Underneath, I put on lacy black underwear that was styled in a retro fashion, with thigh-high stockings that had a seam running up the back of my leg and a garter belt. As the finishing touches, I added a pillbox hat, black elbow-length gloves, and a long cigarette holder. Like the one Audrey Hepburn had in *Breakfast at Tiffany's.* I had to make my shift gradually so that the other drivers on the road didn't notice anything funny. Luckily, Lucien's club isn't in the heart of Vegas. Being off the beaten path makes it a little easier to not only attract the scum of the earth but it is also perfect for bringing in the immortal crowd.

I parked and ran inside, feeling completely out of place. The costume didn't even look like a stripper's costume. Grabbing one last look at myself in the full-sized mirror at the entrance, I had to admit it was unusual for a dirty strip club but still incredibly sexy.

I walked into the dark, smoky club and saw a few of the girls dancing on the stage. Hell's Lair was frequented by both mortals and demon-folk, and the seats around the stage reflected the lowest of low from both worlds. The floor was slick with oil, grease, and probably bodily fluids that I didn't let myself think too hard about. To the right and left of the stage were two bars. I crossed next to the crowd of men who were circling around the stage, each turning to look at me as I made my way past them, the smell of my sex hitting their noses—among their other regions. I nodded at T, our bartender and bouncer, and he winked in my direction. T got his name because he wears jewelry like Mr. T, and although he has a similar coloring and height, that's where the resemblance ends. Where Mr. T had muscles, T simply has fat.

Standing in front of the stage entrance blocking my way was Lenny, the annoying new manager Lucien had hired to run the place. He stood there, arms crossed over his man boobs, tapping his foot with his eyebrows knitted together. I inwardly rolled my eyes. He's shorter than me, probably somewhere around five foot four, and his greasy black hair combed over his balding scalp resulted in a zebra striping pattern along the top of his head. His belt was cinched tightly around his hips, and his belly spilled out over top. I could guarantee that at some point during the night, his shirt would come untucked, revealing his dimpled belly fat.

"You are late! Again!" He pulled out his clipboard and scribbled something down.

This time I rolled my eyes so that he saw me and brushed past him to go backstage.

He followed at my heels like some sort of balding, ugly

puppy. "Monica! *Monica!* Are you even listening to me? I'll fire you if you continue this pattern."

At that threat, I twirled around to face him. A slow smile spread across my face. I spoke quietly and calmly—and continued to give him a biting smile through my gritted teeth. "No. You won't fire me, Lenny. You can't and you *know* it. Now get the fuck out of my dressing room." I sat down at my mirror and dabbed on some lip gloss.

His chin dropped to his chest, creating even more jowls. "You're on in fifteen minutes," he muttered, dragging his feet behind him.

For tonight's music, I chose an old jazz tune with a lot of bass. The curtain opened and the spotlight warmed me. I started center stage, and as the first beat began, I smoked my cigarette from the long holder, taking the time to inhale deeply and slowly. The smoke streamed from my lips and swirled around the top of my head. After slipping the gloves off one at a time, I tossed them into the audience. As I slowly pulsated my hips to the rhythm, the dollar bills shot high into the air like statues in my honor. Starting with an older gentleman to my left, I allowed him to unzip my dress and peel it down over my body. His knuckles shook nervously as they brushed the smooth flesh on my back. When it reached my ankles, I opened my legs to him and stuck my hip in his face. Giving me a shy smile, he tucked a twenty into the garter belt. I danced away, moving on to the next man in the crowd, but not before I let my fingernail travel down the older man's cheek.

I stood at the edge of the stage, moving my hips in rhythm to the music. At the back of the crowd, I met eyes with a sexy man. Despite the dark bar and bright spotlight, I could see him clearly. Thank you, succubus vision. He had dark brown hair that tickled the tops of his ears and thick eyebrows that sat low over his eyes. I held his gaze for a few moments. He broke eye contact first and turned to leave the club. Some men just can't handle a forward woman.

Pivoting, I found my next tip, and that's when I noticed him against the edge of the stage. There, in the front row, was my married man from the coffee shop. His knuckle was raised to his lips, and low and behold—he had no wedding ring on his finger. Tsk, tsk. My lacy panties grew even wetter. He was no Drew, but he was definitely hotter than most of the men in this joint. Not to mention the most nervous. The beat wore on, the neon lights hit his eyes, and I sauntered over to him, crouching down so that my breasts were in his face. I was sure he could smell my sex from where he stood below me. I took another drag from the cigarette and blew it into his face. He drank in the smoke—and his eyes flashed with lust. I was his cocaine—his drug of choice, sweeter than any alcohol, more addictive than nicotine, and far more dangerous than any hallucinogen. I passed him the cigarette and he took a drag as I unhooked my corset, letting the straps drag over my arms and fall to the floor. My nipples puckered as the men around me gasped.

Through my peripherals, I saw more dollars fly into the air. I winked at my married man and continued on to collect the rest of the money. I moved fluently around the stage and finished my dance in nothing except heels, thigh-highs, and the pillbox hat.

After my set, I quickly shifted into my original dress, sans the panties and corset, and headed back out to the club. Every man I passed called out to get my attention. Propositioning voices circled around me as I walked straight for my married man. I was done waiting. I needed my fix now. The needy feeling was not one I ever got used to—an itch that is so uncomfortable, if we wait too long, it actually becomes painful. With the types of men I sleep with, I'm lucky to make it forty-eight hours before I need to find my next fix.

Ignoring everyone else, I plopped myself down on his lap.

His eyes darted around the club. "My name is Erik." I smiled to myself watching him glance nervously about.

"Really?" It was less of a question and more of a bored statement. No need to feign any interest. "Well, Erik, I don't give a fuck what your name is." I took another drag of my cigarette and looked into his mundane brown eyes. "Buy a private dance."

"Oh, um, well . . . I-I don't know about that. You see, I'm a newlywed and I was just curious about this place . . ."

"Erik, please." I rolled my eyes. "You knew what you were getting into by coming here. Especially after a personal invitation from me." I lowered my face so that my lips brushed his as I spoke. "So . . . buy a fucking private dance. Now." I paused once more, giving a second thought to how forceful my voice was. "Unless, that is, your wife satisfies you fully."

If the stress lines around his face were any indication, I'd bet that he was sexually frustrated. But for a moment, his face softened at the mention of his wife. I thought he was going to push me off his lap. Go running back to his wife for some plain old meat-and-potatoes missionary sex.

Instead, he simply nodded, drool practically dripping from his lips. "She's a prude. Only ever cares about her work."

I sighed. Men are such shits. In the couple of centuries that I've been around, that's never changed. I guess I couldn't be too annoyed by him though—it was that lack of morality that would give me enough energy to survive the next couple of days up here on Earth. I grabbed his hand, leading him to the back room. I yelled to Lenny as I passed the pot-bellied manager. "Gotta private one here, Lenny." He marked something on his clipboard.

I shut the door behind me. "Money first, *Erik*."

"Right. Uh, how much again?"

"Four hundred dollars. Plus tip."

"Four hundred? Dollars?"

"Plus tip."

He gulped. "Wow, I don't know that I have that much . . ."

I slipped my tongue in his ear. "Trust me. I'm worth it. What I'm about to do to you would typically cost much, *much* more." I pressed my breasts into his back.

"You're killing me. . . ." He groaned and exhaled between barely open lips. It was unclear whether he was referencing his wallet or his libido.

Ha. "Oh, sweetie. If you only knew." I nibbled his earlobe.

He reached into his back pocket, opening up an expensive-looking leather wallet. A few wallet pictures of a baby fell to the floor. I bent to pick them up and studied the beautiful child smiling back at me. She couldn't have been more than six months old. A knot formed in my throat, and I instinctively placed a hand on my stomach. "Is this your daughter?"

Erik grabbed the photograph and tucked it into the folds of his wallet. "Nah. It's my brother's kid."

My eyes narrowed as I studied his aura. No shift in color— he was telling the truth. I sighed, my tense shoulders relaxing.

He handed me the cash without any more debate, plus an extra twenty. Cheap-ass. You don't come to a strip club with several hundred dollars in your wallet and plan on leaving here innocently. It definitely made me feel better about what was to happen. Nevertheless, I always marvel at how easy it is to get men to cheat on their wives.

He sat in a chair in the middle of the room. I slowly undid the buttons of his shirt and slid it down over his shoulders. Surprisingly, he had an amazing body. Much more fit than I thought he would be. Grabbing his bottom lip between my teeth, I sucked on it while undoing his belt and lowered his pants. They dropped to the floor with a clunk.

"What do you have in those pockets? Rocks?" I smirked, tilting my head to the side. He was already hard, standing at full attention.

I left him in the chair, his pants pooled around his ankles, and danced around him, lifting my leg over his shoulder. It offered him close-up view of my sex peeking out from under the black fabric of my dress. "You want to taste me, don't you, *Erik?*"

He cleared his throat, allowing his eyes to travel up my thigh and land on the glistening flesh between my legs. "Uh-huh." His eyes were wide and dazed.

"So? Go ahead. Give me your best tongue."

He flicked his tongue out, lightly brushing over my skin. The contact made me moan softly, yearning for more. He slowly ran his tongue along my lips and into my folds until finally covering my clit with his mouth, sucking. I grabbed his hair and pulled him into me harder. Two fingers entered me. I was so wet, I begged for a third. He quickly obliged, pulsating them in and out with a "come hither" sort of movement. My muscles tightened around him. It wouldn't take long for me to come.

"Just your tongue. . . ." My voice was hoarse and breathy. He followed my orders, removing his fingers and delving his tongue deep within me. In seconds, I was coming on his face.

As my tremors finished, I grabbed his hair and pulled his face back so that he could see mine. "How'd I taste?"

"Amazing." His voice was gruff. The shy stutter was completely gone, replaced with lust.

"Tell me I taste better than your wife," I demanded.

"You taste so much better than my wife. She's nothing compared to you."

I turned around and had him unzip my dress, slipping the soft fabric off my body. The movement made my already-hard nipples even tighter. Naked, with the exception of my thigh-high stockings and heels, I straddled him.

"Wait." Concern suddenly filled his eyes. For a moment, there was hope for his soul. "Don't we need . . . protection?"

I laughed a sultry, throaty chuckle. "Not with me, baby.

That's not an issue. Relax. . . ." I dropped to my knees and low-ered my mouth to his cock, running my lips along his shaft and twisting my tongue around his tip. I loved the feel of a cock slamming into the back of my throat. I increased my pressure and speed until he was ready for me.

I sat up, facing away from him in the reverse cowgirl posi-tion, and lowered myself down. It felt incredible having him fill me entirely. He sat there, not moving at all. And it figured. For four hundred dollars, of course he expected me to do the work. I lifted myself up, enjoying the sensation of his dick pulling away from me, and just before I lifted up entirely, I came back down hard. He groaned and grabbed my breasts, tweaking my nipples. I continued bouncing on him, feeling his size grow larger as he got more and more excited.

"You like that?" I asked, much louder than before. "You like being fucked by someone other than your wife?"

"God, yes," he cried out.

"Tell me!" I turned so that I could face him and grabbed his face roughly with one hand. "Say it again." I continued fucking him hard, squeezing my muscles as I reached his tip. My wet-ness grew with each thrust—so much so that I could feel it dripping out over my lips.

I slapped him across the cheek, perhaps harder than I in-tended to. "I *said*, tell me!"

"I love being fucked by you. You're so much better than my wife."

My itch raged on, worse than before, almost unbearably so. It wouldn't be relieved until he came—my release would come when he did. I could tell by his suddenly larger girth stretching my insides that he wasn't going to last much longer. I rolled my hips in circles over him, and his velvety tip rubbed just the right areas. The swelling felt amazing. He grabbed my ass and pulled me down onto him hard. His body trembled and his juices filled me. I groaned in delight at both his release and the life I was sucking from him. The orgasm was good, but the high from his soul was even better.

In a flash, I saw a movie reel of his life. Like a flipbook, I caught a quick glimpse of what was to come in Erik's life and what the world would lack by my stealing a portion of it. I saw him playing catch with a little boy, signing divorce papers, and finally . . . I saw him sitting quietly in a rocking chair, eyes closed. I exhaled, and it wasn't until that second that I realized I had been holding my breath. You just never know until that moment what exactly you're taking from your conquest. Knowing he was going to die peacefully in his rocking chair allowed my stress to melt away.

Seconds later, my human form radiated with life—*his* life. Muscles deep inside me tensed, and the sweet release of my own orgasm squeezed every last drop from him. With a forefinger, he flicked my clit and I screamed as the tremors rolled through my body again.

Pulling away from his body, I could feel his cum dripping down my thighs. I put my other leg back up on his shoulder. "Lick me," I demanded.

"But, I-I—" he stammered, staring nervously at his juices combined with my own.

"Shut the fuck up and *lick* me." I spoke through clenched teeth.

More hesitantly than before, he brought his tongue to the dripping area between my legs, tentatively licking.

"Harder!"

His tongue stiffened, and the tension built inside me once again. My muscles pulsed, squeezing the cum out of me and onto his tongue.

"How do I taste *now?*"

"Still amazing," he said. He slapped my ass, squeezing my cheek with one hand.

His sudden force caught me off guard, and I moaned as my

body convulsed in yet another orgasm. After, I leaned down and licked the juices from his lips.

We finished dressing and he came up behind me, kissing my neck. "That was amazing." He reached in front and caressed my breast through the material of my dress. "*You* are amazing. I had no idea it could be that great." He tucked another hundred dollar bill between my cleavage. "Can I see you again?" He was speaking fast, and I could see the effects of succubus sex affecting him already. It acts as a sort of high, making my victims more manic and stronger than they normally are. One of the many ways we succubi keep them addicted, coming back for more.

I rolled my eyes, and even though he couldn't see me, he probably sensed my annoyance. "Well, of course we'll *see* each other again. You're in the coffee shop every fucking day."

He turned me around so I was face-to-face with him. I didn't realize before how tall he was. My eyes were about level with his pecs. "That's not what I meant." He brushed a piece of hair from my face.

"I-I know." I stammered slightly, feeling uncharacteristically bad for the man. "But I try to keep my two lives separate. My dancing life and the café life. Inviting you here was a . . . a momentary lapse in judgment."

He tilted my chin toward his and gave a small tug on my almost black locks. "I like this look. Is it a wig?" Then with the same hand, he cupped my jaw. For a second there, I really thought he was going to kiss me.

"Something like that," I replied.

"So, I can visit you here at the club?"

I nodded, sadness washing over me. Leaning in, he brushed his lips against mine. It was so intimate. So atypical for me. Intimacy was not something I experienced on a sexual level. It had been decades since I had felt that sort of sexual affection and actually acted on it. My stomach clenched; a rush of sorrow flooded me for . . . everything. For his wife. His deceit. Because of me, he would die a week sooner than he should have; I stole part of this man's soul and suckered him into cheating on his wife. Okay, well, maybe I didn't sucker him, but I certainly offered temptation. He may have gone his entire marriage without any infidelity if it hadn't been for me. Maybe I was the reason he'd be signing those divorce papers in the future. I needed to get away from him—away from this club.

I broke free from his kiss and headed toward the door. "I'll see you around, Erik." It was the first time I said his name without dripping sarcasm.

As the door clicked shut behind me, I instantaneously felt Lucien's presence. Seconds later, he stood before me. And he did not look happy.

"My office, Monica. Now."

2

The scowl Lucien sported was definitely his *don't fuck with me* glare.

"Hey, boss," T shouted over the hum of bar noise. "You ain't heard from Crystal lately, have you? She was supposed to swing by and pick up her last paycheck a week ago."

Lucien's glare shifted from me to T, and in an instant Lucien held the three-hundred-pound man by the shirt and kicked the stool out from under him so that he was dangling by his collar. His power crackled around us, sucking the oxygen from my lungs. In a low voice, he snarled, "Shut your fucking mouth about my girls. Let's not broadcast to the whole motherfucking bar that she's no longer here at the club." He let go of T's shirt, shoving him to the bar, knocking over an empty pint glass. He snapped his fingers, pointing in the direction of his office. "Monica," he whistled as a gesture for me to follow him.

A sarcastic laugh caught in my throat and I crossed my arms, eyebrows raised. "Excuse me?" I tapped my foot, waiting.

He growled and slowly turned back to face me. "I'm *sorry*," he said with sarcasm that would put mine to shame. "Monica, would you mind joining me in my office for a moment."

"Please?"

His jaw clenched and he spoke through gritted teeth. *"Please."*

"Well, of course." I smiled at him as I sauntered through his office door. Once we were both inside, I lit another cigarette sans the vintage holder. "So what the Hell was that little display out there about? Where's Crystal?"

I watched as he fiddled with his pen, a nervous tick he's had since the day we met, flipping it back and forth over his fingers. "Don't you worry about Crystal. Just needed to remind T who the boss was around here."

I rolled my eyes at that. "Right. As if you let any of us forget."

"Only you, my *love.*" I smirked at him in a prepubescent way while narrowing my eyes. He ignored my childish reaction and went on with our meeting. "I need to talk with you about your performance lately. You know I'm judged on the souls you acquire, too, right?" Lucien folded his arms and sat on the edge of his desk. "And why are you smoking those things? They're disgusting."

I shrugged, feeling a bit like I was a schoolgirl being yelled at by the principal. "I'm immortal. It's not like a few smokes will hurt me." I ashed the cigarette onto his rug defiantly.

He snorted in disgust. "Yes"—there was no hesitation in his voice at all—"but it does affect the mortals who surround you. Secondhand smoke and all. For someone who used to be an angel, you don't have much regard for those humans you *claim* to care so much about." He paused, staring at me with cold, dark eyes. "Besides, you were immortal as an angel—and you didn't smoke then."

I sighed. "Things were different back then." I didn't take another drag, but I didn't put the cigarette out, either. He was right and I knew it, but that didn't mean I had to admit it in front of him. "I assume this D.A.R.E. lecture isn't the only reason you wanted to speak with me? You mentioned my performance. . . ."

"Yes, right." Lucien leaned closer toward me, and even though we were only a foot away from each other, I could feel his presence thicken the air. He was sexy if you went for that sort of look, I suppose. Black hair pulled into a short ponytail at the nape of his neck, dark eyes, olive skin. He looked Romanian or of some sort of Eastern European descent.

His voice, sharp with authority, snapped me back to reality. "I know your reasons for choosing the souls you steal. I get it, I do. But we both have a job to do here. And the execs down in Hell are beginning to notice a lack of . . . success . . . in my jurisdiction. Especially now that a couple of my succubi are MIA."

"What? Who?" I asked, growing concerned. I hadn't heard anything about that. A surge of panic caught in my throat. "Kayce?" I thought of my best friend and fellow succubus.

He held up a hand to quiet me. "Kayce is fine. Don't concern yourself about the missing succubi. But, while I've tried to be supportive of your reasons, when it comes down to your ass or mine, I choose my own, got it?" We both knew this wasn't true. Lucien had a sort of big brotherly love for me. If we were a majorly dysfunctional family, that is. He had definitely chosen my ass over his in the past.

"Erik wasn't that big of a loser. And I did get him to cheat on his wife."

"And you look stronger than I've seen you in months."

I glanced in the mirror and saw how bright my shifted image was, suddenly ashamed that only seconds ago I had been bragging about my conquest. I looked to the ground, hiding my eyes from Lucien. "There has to be a loophole, Lucien. There has to be some way to regain the magic that allowed succubi to enter a man's dream and steal his life that way." I thought of all the stories Kayce told about succubi several centuries ago. We didn't use to require physical sex with anyone to steal their souls. Until Saetan discovered that by actually having sex with our conquests as opposed to entering their dreams, we got the job done quicker and more effectively. Lust in the flesh is much more dangerous than lust in your fantasies. I shut my eyes and imagined how amazing and easy the job would have been, not having to wear the sin of my job like a halo around my body.

"Monica, you need to let that go. That's the old way things were done, and it's been a long time since a succubus has entered a man's dreams. Saetan changed the rules; the magic just doesn't work that way anymore. Besides, don't feel too guilty about Erik. He was destined to cheat. It was in the cards already; you just sped up the process."

That did make me feel better. A little.

Lucien went on, not even noticing that I was still standing in the same position, frozen. "So, Erik was a better catch than you normally get. Kudos. But most of these losers you sleep with are already Hell-bound. Saetan practically has their souls in the bag already. He doesn't need your help corrupting them. Now, a guy like Drew, however there's where He could use the help." He smiled at what he knew was a jab in my gut.

"Leave Drew out of this." I snapped at him a little too quickly and his eyebrows arched in amusement. I looked away for a brief second, studying the awful carpet in Lucien's office. I continued more calmly, "I'll never sleep with the good guys. I refuse."

"Never say never, Mon. You've done it before, you'll do it again. Even little corruptions can help our team gain power."

I folded my arms across my breasts, the cigarette still burning, getting closer and closer to my fingertips. "I think you're missing the point, Lucien. It would be sentencing them to an eternity in Hell. I can't do that to the men who are Heaven-bound."

"Christ, Monica. It's been over two centuries since you were an angel. When are you going to get over this whole ethical inner battle of yours? You're on our side now. Start playing for our team, or you're going to begin to feel the penalties. I can't protect you from everything."

I walked over to him and put out my cigarette on his desk. His glare deepened. Staring at me over his rigid brow bone, he growled. An actual growl like he was some sort of vampire or something. I almost laughed, but I knew that would have been a huge mistake. Despite his growl of a threat, I lowered my voice and leaned in close to his face. "Lucien, I'm not going to change. Get over it. Just because one of Saetan's minions managed to lure me into bed back in my Cherub days doesn't change the fact that I'm still an angel at heart."

An angel having sex with anything Hellspawn is a big no-no. But apparently, angels simply having sex isn't necessarily a big deal. Who knew? I just learned it the hard way.

With his long finger, Lucien reached over, lifting the bottom of my dress revealing my sex, still glistening. "Yeah, you're a real angel, huh?" He smirked at me as if he'd won some sort of small victory.

I slapped his hand away, heat burning my cheeks. I knew it was silly—a succubus feeling embarrassed about sex, but I couldn't help it. I turned away from Lucien's gaze, unable to match his stare. "Without the evil, there would be no good to measure by." This was the mantra I told myself over and over to justify my actions in any way I could.

He touched my chin, pulling my gaze back to his. "Monica, you know I don't like pressuring you into anything you don't want to do. But at some point this starts to reflect on my abilities as your boss. I just need you to step it up a *little* bit. A good boy every now and then—maybe one a month—and it will keep the authorities down there"—his eyes flicked to the floor—"off both our backs."

He was being reasonable—I knew that. But I still couldn't

forgive him for bringing up Drew. I pivoted on my stilettos and walked toward the door. "Anything else?" I peeked back over my shoulder and saw frustration in his furrowed brows.

"Yes." His glare softened, though only a little. He walked back to his desk, picked up a file, and riffled through his papers. "There was some British guy out there looking for you not too long ago. His name was, um . . . Willis, maybe? William?"

"Wills?"

He nodded. "Yeah, I think that was it. He looked familiar."

"Why didn't anyone tell me this sooner?" I asked, my voice so shrill, it could shatter glass.

He shrugged, looking at me over some paperwork. "Damn, calm down. Maybe if you hadn't been *late* to work, someone would have had time to tell you. Then afterward you were a bit occupied." He gestured to the back room where Erik and I had our private time.

"Were you listening to me? When I was with Erik?" I leaned into the doorframe and crossed my arms.

He smiled back playfully. "Yes. Though don't let that go to your head. The whole goddamn club could hear you."

Despite our playful banter, I stood there in his office, stunned. Wills was here—in my club. I hadn't seen him in years—decades. Since I lived in London in 1939. Wow, he must be ancient by now. . . . What the Hell was he doing in Vegas, and why was he looking for *me?* Poor old coot must have Alzheimer's. But more importantly, what was he doing still alive? I slept with him continuously for quite a long time. I *saw* him die in my visions on the battlefield. I must have taken years and years off of his life . . . and yet, he's here in Vegas. And I look exactly the same—not a day older than I did in 1939. Shit. I really should adjust my looks at least every few decades. If he hadn't seen me dance, I could just change my looks altogether. At least I have the dark hair tonight. I'll have to tell him I'm Monica's granddaughter or something.

Lucien coughed. "Is there anything else I can answer for you, Monica?" He was practically reading my thoughts.

"Can I sit for a moment? Collect myself before I go out there and explain to Wills why I still look exactly the same as I did back in the 1930s?"

He was already submerged in whatever he was reading, barely noticing I was still in the room. "Yeah, yeah, whatever." He gestured to a seat with his pen. "Just not too long."

I sunk into the chair near the door. Focusing on my breathing, I studied Lucien's office closer. Such a typical, boring office. Like the kind a CPA would have. Faux wood paneling straight from the seventies. Gray carpet. Cherrywood desk with a gold nameplate and one of those Newton's Cradle desk toys with the five silver balls that swing and strike each other. I had heard a rumor once that those toys actually started swinging on their own when they sensed another higher immortal's presence. I just threw it into the rumor mill along with the claim that stones could trap power and tin foil hats prevented mind reading.

"Hey, Lucien, is it true what they say about those desk toys?" I nodded toward his. "Does it really start to swing in the presence of a higher immortal?" I mean, why else would he own one, right?

He didn't look up at me from over his laptop. "Yes. It's true." There was a soft *ding* from his BlackBerry signaling that he had a new message. He looked down to read it, a look of concern flashing over his face briefly.

"Really? Why isn't it swinging when I'm present, then?"

He sighed and slapped his pen down onto the desk hard enough to let his annoyance be known but not so hard that the pen broke. He rose from his chair and walked over to me as he spoke. "Because it's linked to me, therefore it calibrates higher immortals based on my power gauge. I swear, you're like talking to an inquisitive toddler sometimes."

Lucien grabbed my elbow, forcing me to my feet and leading me in the direction of his door. "Why don't you go have a quick nightcap before looking for your Brit? It will help you think."

He opened the door and escorted me out. His fingers unclamped from my elbow, and I noticed just the slightest bit of perspiration breaking out along his hairline. "You sure everything is okay, Lucien?"

"Yes, yes. Fine. I'm just . . . stressed." But his words didn't match the cadence in his voice. "Go home. I'll see you tomorrow . . . *on time.*"

And with that, he shut the door in my face. I leaned my ear against the door to listen for anything dramatic. Partly because I was concerned for Lucien's well-being and partially because I was nosy. I heard a familiar *crack,* the sound of Lucien teleporting to another location. I listened for another ten seconds just to be sure he had actually left and let my cheek rest on the cool door.

From behind me, there was a familiar, warm accent. "Monica? Monica Lamb? That's you, isn't it? I'd remember those legs anywhere."

3

I took a deep breath, my hand still resting on Lucien's heavy, wood door. I cleared my throat, preparing my little speech about who I was supposed to be. "I'm sorry? Were you . . ." I turned to make eye contact with my old flame, expecting to see a bag of wrinkles. Instead, Wills—*my* Wills from London— stood before me. He must have only been thirty at the oldest. The air sucked out of my diaphragm. I couldn't speak, and it felt like that time I was swing dancing and my partner dropped me on my back, knocking the wind out of me.

"Wills . . ." I managed to whisper, frozen where I stood.

"There you are, Pocket." He smiled, and these charming little wrinkles formed at the corner of his eyes. I hadn't heard that nickname in decades—it sounded like a foreign language. If it was at all possible, he was even more handsome now than he was back in 1939 when we first met. He stood at about five foot ten with his hands stuffed deeply into his perfectly pressed gray dress pants. He was wearing a very proper suit vest with his grandfather's signature gold pocket watch clipped to his vest. The watch itself was the same, but I recognized the chain as being new. An updated chain on an antique watch. His chestnut brown hair was parted perfectly on the left side and hung just slightly over his hazel eyes. Decades ago he had one crooked tooth, but it appeared he had that fixed, because the row of teeth in front of me were perfect in every way.

"I realize you probably expected me to be in my grave by now." He rocked back on his heels and pulled his hands from his pockets, putting a finger to his lips. "Well, I'm a . . ."

"You're a demon." I stood there, shocked. The bar was full of demons, and Wills's aura certainly wasn't overly strong. But his demon signature was definitely there. Standing in front of me. "How? How did this happen? You were the perfect mortal—Heaven-bound and everything."

"Yes, yes." He rolled his eyes. "I was a good little British boy." He paused. "Until *you* came along." The accusation was like a knife in the gut, and my immediate instinct was to defend myself. Before I could, he gestured to the bar stool. "Come, sit, Monica, sit. Let me tell you what happened."

I let him guide me to the seat. He gestured to T, "One scotch and water, please."

"Make that two, T," I said, still staring at Wills's face. "Please," I added as an afterthought.

"Actually, that one I ordered was for you." He winked at me. It was the same wink from decades ago. "See, Pocket? I still know you after all these years." He chucked me under the chin and laughed.

"Uh-huh," I said, feeling rather numb. My drink arrived, and I pulled the glass up to my lips. Not so much because I wanted a drink; mostly I just wanted something else to focus on. The ice clinked against my teeth as I took my first sip.

"Well." He took a sip of his own drink and savored the flavor before continuing, "As you recall, I joined the war. Initially my father had arranged it so that I wouldn't have to fight— being the wealthy family we were, he could certainly afford the payoff. But I felt like only half a man. It was such a cowardly way to live my life. To turn my back on my country—on every country, for that matter. So I ran away and joined the fight. That was—let's see . . . forty-two. It was awful. More horrible than the most horrible story you've heard."

"I know." I interrupted him. "After you joined, I became a nurse in the war. I was stationed in France." I stared into my glass. "I guess I was hoping that somehow I'd find you."

He nodded. "Ah. So you know what it was like."

"Yes, I know."

There was a moment of silence as we both remembered the atrocities of the time. "So, one day a giant piece of shrapnel caught me right here." He gestured to his stomach. "Bloody thing essentially cut me in half. I lay there on the battlefield in a pool of blood. Some of which was mine, and some was my friends' I fought alongside. I was screaming for the medic until I could feel my body twitching, my vision becoming a darkening tunnel."

I had known this much already. Our last night together, I had seen him dying in battle in my last vision. It's why I joined—with a slim hope I might be able to save him and defy fate.

Wills continued speaking, having no knowledge that I knew how he had died. "And all of a sudden, this woman was cradling me. And as she ran her hand from my forehead down to my wound, the pain disappeared. *You don't have to die here, like this,* she said. *We can take your pain away and give you immortality.* The numbness felt so damn good after feeling so much pain. I wasn't thinking clearly. Out of nowhere she pulled a piece of paper and told me to sign in blood. Wasn't hard to do since my damn hand was covered in it, anyway. And I signed my soul away."

I gasped. "Oh, Wills," I wanted to cry. I wanted to find that demon—the one who stole Wills's soul—and rip her limbs from her body. It was low, preying on the men who lay dying, battered, and twisted on the field. Offering them no pain and more years. What man would say no to that?

I took Wills's face in my hands. I touched his cheeks, his eyelids—I ran my fingernails over his eyebrows and ran my other hand through his soft brown hair. He grabbed my hand and kissed my palm. "Why didn't you come to me sooner?" I asked, a pleading tone to my voice.

He shrugged uncomfortably. "I didn't know where you were, whether you were alive or dead. After the war, I thought it would be easier to stay away from all my family and friends. Everyone thought I had died, and it just seemed easier to let them believe that. Mourn my loss and move on. I never really cared enough for my family to reunite with them, and I had no idea what had become of you. I tried to find you in London. I searched for years and then gave up, not knowing your true nature."

I nodded, my gaze falling somewhere past his shoulder. "It was a bad time."

He nodded with me in agreement. "It was. I didn't come to America until a decade ago. And then one day, about six months ago, I saw you. At first I thought I was hallucinating. I followed you to some little coffee shop. I sat out on a park bench and watched you through the window. As I watched, I thought maybe you were some sort of relative of Monica's. A niece or a granddaughter. I came every Thursday morning, sat on that park bench, and watched you. It wasn't until one day when you passed by me, talking on your cell phone. You were wearing this short skirt, and as you walked a little gust of wind blew your skirt up, revealing the birthmarks on your inner thigh. Two distinctive spots. And I just knew. You weren't a long-lost relative of Monica's—you were her. And after some research, I discovered who—or should I say *what*—you really were. I should have known sooner, really. Looking back at our years together. Of course you were a bloody succubus."

I shuddered when he mentioned the marks on my thigh. They weren't birthmarks, but I always just let everyone assume they were. I raised my fingers to my cheek, and it was only then that I realized I was crying. Silent tears streaming one after another down my face and neck, falling into the cleavage of my dress. "Wills." I spoke softly, dropping my head. "I'm so sorry."

"Shhh." He wrapped his hand around the back of my neck and pulled me into him. My cheek pressed against his vest, staining it with makeup and tears. "I'm not here to get an apology. It just took me this long to gather up the courage to approach you." He pulled my face away from his body, his large, soft hands cupping my jaw firmly. And he kissed me. I pulled away at first, stopping the kiss out of habit.

"Monica," he whispered, "I don't have a soul to steal anymore." He kissed my jaw. "I don't have a life to lose years off of." He kissed my temple. "You don't have to protect me from you." He kissed my eyelid. "Now kiss me. I've waited almost sixty-five years for this day."

I wrapped my lips around his, memories rushing back with each moment. His kiss—so foreign and yet so familiar at the same time.

"May I walk you home?" he asked.

I nodded, smiling. My Wills—ever the gentleman. "Well, this is Vegas, not London. We drive out here."

He smiled, too. "I know that. I just meant—can I make sure you get home okay? No funny business. We'll have plenty of time to get reacquainted."

"So . . . you don't want to . . . *you* know?" Oh Hell, I mentally smacked my head. I sounded like a friggin' fifteen-year-old.

Wills laughed. "Of course I want to ... *you* know. I just don't want to *you* know"—he wiggled his eyebrows— "tonight. Let's get to know each other again."

I cleared my throat and finished the rest of my drink in one swift swallow. The amber liquid coated my throat and burned just enough to feel good. Turning my head so that he couldn't see me, I swiped the remaining tears from my face and shifted my makeup back in place, and then turned my hair slowly back to its normal blond color. "Well, in that case, I'll have another." I slid my empty glass to the end of the bar as if I were some starlet in an old western movie. T, however, just barely catching my impulse, reached out a hand to grasp the glass just before it slid off the bar entirely. The alcohol was taking its effect already. My head spun around the seedy bar. "I was trying to channel Mae West," I said, a bit of embarrassment rising to my cheeks.

He nodded. "Seems like you managed to channel your inner Annie Oakley instead." A smile quirked the corners of his lips.

I pushed him playfully, and in doing so he grabbed my hand and pulled me in for another kiss. "Let's just stay here, right like this for a while," he said softly, his lips still on mine.

All I could do was nod, not breaking my mouth away from his. It's not exactly how Mae West would have handled the moment, but hey, she was one of the most notorious succubi in existence. I can't hold myself to her standards.

"I met Mae West years ago," I said between kisses. "She was a total bitch. I'd rather be Annie Oakley than Mae West any day."

Wills smiled during our kiss, and I realized my lips were on his teeth. He sighed. "Yep. Same ol' Monica."

We clinked glasses as soon as T refilled our scotch. Wills kissed my nose. "Lunch tomorrow? We have much to figure out. For now, we drink." He lifted his glass higher. "Cheers."

4

The next morning, I crawled into work with one of the worst hangovers of my life. Normally, I would just shift myself into looking amazing even if I felt like crap, but I was so worn down from those scotch and waters (how many *did* I have?) I could barely muster up a clean shirt and a ponytail. Hangovers were pretty rare for me; after a couple centuries of drinking, you sort of learn how to hold your liquor. Oh well, at least Drew would believe me this time when I told him I wasn't feeling well. Normally when I claim to be sick, I come in looking perfect.

The bells above the door dinged as I dragged my feet into the coffee shop. In my brain the ding sounded more like a friggin' fire alarm. Made me want to rip that fucking bell off the door. I groaned.

"You're late." It was stated as a greeting, not as a condemnation.

What else is new? I sat down on one of the bar stools in front of the espresso bar and slammed my head down onto the hard, ebony wood. "I know." I spoke into the bar.

A rough hand brushed the back of my head, stroking my

hair. "Rough night, huh? See ... this is why I quit drinking. Too many bad mornings. You can always join me at my next AA meeting." He chuckled softly.

I managed a nod, my forehead wrinkling up and down against the wood grain of the bar. There was some rustling and clanking of coffee cups and the familiar sound of espresso grinding and milk steaming. One last clank happened right next to my head, and I could sense Drew standing above me.

"What now?" I snapped. So, I can be a bitch sometimes. I'm a succubus—what do you expect?

"I made you your favorite. Mocha caramel latte. Triple shot. If this doesn't wake you up, you're a lost cause." I could hear the smile in his voice.

Well, shit. Now I *really* felt like a bitch. "I can tell you *now*— I'm a lost cause."

"I've just never seen you look so—tired before. It's kind of cute."

"Shut up." I didn't feel so bad about my short temper suddenly.

A damp rag slapped my arm. "Just drink up. Then get to work."

I pulled myself off the bar. I raised the coffee to my lips, took a sip of the delicious, perfectly mixed latte, and moaned a contented sigh.

"That good, huh?" Drew smiled, still putting away clean dishes. I simply closed my eyes and took in a long, deep breath. Drew continued talking, "So, what the hell happened? Booze? A man? Did you decide to take the café's customer service to a whole new level? I could just as easily have given him a few coupons for free iced coffee."

His voice had a playful tone, but there was something deeper than that. He refused to look at me ... kept looking down at those dishes. His tone suggested something. A hint of—what? Jealousy maybe? An accusatory tone? In my current state, the last thing I wanted to do was defend my lifestyle. A lifestyle I had no choice in, *anyway*.

I slammed my coffee mug down onto the little plate with a loud clank. "I should go put my stuff away and start my opening duties." I stood up from my stool, and though still a little dizzy, I powered through and walked toward the back room to my locker.

"Whoa, Monica." Drew tossed his rag down and walked briskly over to me. "What the hell's your problem? It was just a joke."

I swung around, my shoulders rising to my ears dramatically. "Was it? Just a joke? You were clearly aggressive with him last night. You saw me give him my card. And what? You think just because I'm a stripper I also jumped straight into bed with him?" Okay—so that's exactly what happened. Drew didn't need to know that.

He stayed quiet another moment, lips pursed, eyes assessing. "Yes. Okay, yes." He spoke calmly, but there was a danger to his words. Shaking my head, I turned to walk back to the lockers again. He reached out for my elbow and stopped me, but I didn't turn around. "You know what? Sometimes after you leave for your club, I debate firing you. It would force you to actually do something more with your life. You could have an actual career—not as a barista. Not a stripper. But as long as you're here, it'll never happen." He let go of my arm. "And sometimes, it just disgusts me."

I turned around, my eyes narrow slits. "I disgust you?"

His jaw clenched, and he rubbed a hand across his blond stubble. "No. That's not what I meant and you know it." He took a step back and raised one hand defensively. "Just answer me something."

I tilted my head in response.

"Why do you work here? You clearly don't need the seven

dollars an hour if you make one thousand on an average night at the club." He took a step closer to me.

He knew the answer to this question. He *had* to know the answer. I swallowed, a lump forming in my chest, and held his gaze. He licked his top lip, his tongue running along a thin scar on the right side.

"Well?" His hands clapped down to his sides.

He was close enough to touch, but I resisted. Just like I always do. "I like it here. It feels like—home."

He nodded slowly. "Home?"

I nodded, too. "Yes." I played with my purse strap between two fingers. "I need something other than the strip club to keep myself sane." *I need you.*

A small smile touched his lips, and he lifted a hand to my face, wiping his fingers against the right side of my mouth. "You had a little bit of foam."

Instinctively, I darted my tongue out, tasting the remnants of caramel mocha.

Drew sighed. "I just worry about you, I guess. Working in a place like that."

I nodded and took a step back, reality beginning to set in again. "I'm not yours to worry about."

His eyes looked back and forth between mine, thoughtful. "So you keep reminding me."

I smiled at him, headed back to the barista bar, and let my head fall into my hand. "I honestly don't know why I'm so hungover—I don't think I had that much to drink. But you're right. I did meet someone . . . or I guess re-met someone. He's an ex—it's been years since we've seen each other, and he was there at the bar. Without any warning, just suddenly in front of me." Drew gave me a look, eyebrows wiggling. "Nothing happened," I said through a smile. "We drank, we kissed, and he walked me to my door. That was it."

"That's nice—sounds like a good guy. Not taking advantage of the situation."

"He's definitely a good guy." I took another sip of my latte, which was now cold.

Drew held my gaze for a few seconds before I stood, picking up my bag. "Well, you're not paying me to sit here and gossip with you."

"Who said I was paying you for this?" He turned and headed back to the dishes left in disarray around the counter. "Oh, and Monica?"

"Hm?"

"You look really nice today—dark circles aside."

Dark circles?! I glanced in a mirror before heading to the back. He must have just been teasing me. There were no bags under my eyes. But as I looked closer, there were a few fine wrinkles at each corner. I gasped—dark circles would have been better. Those go away once you get some sleep and hydrate. But wrinkles? I hadn't seen a wrinkle on my face *ever*. I ran to my purse and dug around the bottom until I found an old makeup compact. It was dirty from being in the bottom corner of my bag for so long, unused. I opened it and the inside was cakelike and clumpy. I was pretty sure it had spoiled, but it would do for now. I put a little under each eye and stepped back to examine. It definitely looked a little better. I closed my eyes and mustered up as much energy as I could to flatten my ponytail and lessen the wrinkles with my power. A familiar tingle brushed along my body like a gently breeze, and when I opened my eyes, I definitely looked more like myself—but those wrinkles were still there. My energy should have been strong—replenished since Erik and I had sex just last night. After work, I'd just have to find another conquest a little sooner than I had hoped.

A couple of hours into my shift and I was ready to collapse. There was actual sweat breaking out across my hairline. *Sweat!*

I haven't sweat in—I don't even know how long it had been. I barely even glisten when I walk around in this Nevada heat—let alone in an air-conditioned coffee shop.

"You don't look so good," Drew said from behind me.

I swung my rag over my shoulder and leaned on the table I had just finished wiping down. "Well, someone's whistling a different tune. Wasn't it just"—I checked my watch—"four hours ago you were telling me how beautiful I looked?"

He laughed and stuck both hands in his pockets. "I believe my exact words were 'nice.' I said you looked nice today."

"Well"—I took the rag from my shoulder and ran it between two fingers—"if we're going to get technical, your exact words were actually 'really nice.' Regardless, are you saying I'm *not* beautiful?"

"You *know* that's not what I'm saying." He spoke through a smile and lifted his coffee cup to hide it.

"Oh?" I turned my back to him and bent over the table, wiping it down even though it was already clean. "Do I?" I didn't bother looking back at him—I knew where his gaze would be.

"Seriously, though, Monica . . . if you need to take a break, feel free to go sit down. You seem tired." His fingers grazed my arm in an attempt to get my attention.

As our skin made contact, I heard it . . . a specific *zap* sort of sound and a tingly feeling that I've felt many times before. Somehow with our contact, I had just stolen some life from Drew. Probably not much. But even the tiniest bit would be too much. It was definitely not supposed to happen with non-sexual contact. I sucked in my breath and stepped away.

He withdrew his hand and cradled it in his other. "Ouch! I've always said there was electricity in you," he said, clearly thinking it was just a typical shock.

I took a deep breath—maybe it *was* just static electricity. I'm so tired today, it's possible that I just mistook normal shock for my powers. Deep inside, though, I knew better than to chalk it up to some sort of coincidence. Something was definitely off about me today.

Drew's eyebrows knitted together in the center of his forehead. "You sure you're okay? You just turned very white." I took a step back from him, getting out of arm's reach. His eyes, initially on me, traveled past mine and over my shoulder. I turned slowly, and standing behind me, practically breathing down my neck, was Wills. I touched his arm in lieu of a normal hello.

Fucking demons. They're so good at sneaking up on people.

I looked back over at Drew. "You know, maybe I will sit down for a bit. You don't mind, do you?"

He gave me a nod. "Of course not." Looking over at Wills, he stuck out a hand. "I'm Drew, by the way." Then, responding to Wills's grim scowl, he qualified himself by adding "Monica's . . . boss."

While that might have appeased most men, Wills was no longer your typical mortal man. I was sure he could see right through to our chemistry. "Wills," he said simply while grabbing Drew's hand and giving it one formal pump.

After a thirty-second staredown, Drew gave me a look that seemed to say, *Who* is *this guy?* and left us alone.

After Drew walked away, Wills's demeanor changed instantaneously, a wide grin spreading across his face. He kissed both of my cheeks and my nose. He looked around the cafe with an annoying British haughtiness. "This is where you spend your days, is it? I've never actually been inside. It's a bit—cheery for the likes of us, isn't it?"

"I know you're still fairly new at this demon thing, Wills, but we don't exactly all spend our days in a damp cave."

"Let's go get some lunch." He took my hand in his, pulling me toward the door. "We have so much to discuss and figure out about, well, about us."

"Wills—I'm working. I can't just leave."

His face dimmed, looking around again. "It's a coffee shop. I think they'll manage without you for an hour."

"It's my job. I can't just walk out on my job." I glanced at the clock on the wall. "I have a few minutes though, if you want to sit with me on my break."

He pulled out his gold watch from his suit vest pocket and glanced at the time. "Of course."

"You should order something. Drew hates it when people use tables but don't order." Wills snorted but walked over to the counter and ordered tea.

I ran to the back to undress my apron and grab the coffee I had stashed back there. When I came back out, I saw Wills sitting in the darkest corner of the cafe, his back to everyone, looking at the wall. I joined him in the empty chair.

"So, what happened back there?" I gestured with my head over to Drew.

He cocked his head to the side. "What?"

"Oh, come on. . . ." I rolled my eyes. "I thought you two were gonna poke an eye out with your little testosterone sword fight."

He laughed at that, then half stood up from his chair and leaned over the table to kiss my forehead. "Same old Monica. A little cruder—but it's all there."

"I'm only cruder these days because it's more acceptable for a woman to speak her mind." He didn't respond. Just sat there looking at me with a lopsided grin. "Whatever. Just know nothing is there between Drew and me."

His lips pressed together. "Mm." He took a sip of his tea. I almost laughed as the dainty china touched his lips. Knowing Drew, he probably gave Wills the most feminine teacup we had as some sort of mind game.

I changed the subject. "I still can't believe you're here." I shook my head. "And how you managed to not approach me for months—I'll never understand how you did it."

"Well"—the corners of his lips twisted up ever so slightly—
"I wasn't sure it was you for quite a while. I just thought I was
observing your granddaughter or something. And then, even
when I suspected it was you, I wanted to make sure I was correct. Didn't want to approach a stranger speaking of World War
Two and demons and such."

"That's true." I yawned widely, throwing my head back in
doing so.

"Why are you so tired? How long has it been since . . . well,
you know." He looked at me, his eyes crinkling with concern.

"I should be fine. I, hm, how should we word it delicately. . . .
I 'recharged' last night." I used air quotes around the word.

"Last night?" he snapped.

"Before we met—before I even knew you were there."

The hardened stare softened. "Well, that's . . . good."

"Good?" I didn't want him to be enraged with jealousy, but
I didn't want him thinking it was good, either.

"I mean, not ideal—bloody Hell, Monica, I don't know.
I wish that as a demon I could recharge you. But, it's good
you're . . . er . . . *charged*." He smiled as he used the word.

"You're enjoying this way too much," I said through a
chuckle.

His smile dropped and he ran a finger along the lip of his
teacup. "Trust me"—his voice was softer—"I definitely don't
enjoy the idea of you being with other men." He looked up at
me with sad eyes. "But I understand. It's just part of the demon
deal."

I grabbed his hand from across the table and nodded. "Un-
fortunately. Speaking of—what exactly were the terms of
your—uh, contract? With the—uh, you know who." I looked
around the café without moving my head. After the first couple
scotch and waters last night, I had completely forgotten to ask
him what his job was for the big guy downstairs.

He shrugged. "I'm not exactly powerful. I do kind of clerical work, I suppose you could say. With my financial background, I'm a sort of accountant for the underworld. It was boring as a mortal, and it's just as boring as a demon."

"Wow. That sounds—painful." I laughed. "Of all the badass jobs to get—you definitely got the vanilla pudding job of our realm." I spoke in a whisper so soft that only an immortal ear could hear us.

Wills laughed loudly and tilted his chair back on the hind legs. "Well, not all of us can have sex for a living." He spoke loudly, and there was an edge of hostility to his voice. A bitterness that cracked in the back of his throat.

A mother at the table to our left glared at us, her eyes lowering. She handed her son a coloring book and scooted her chair closer to him. "Hey, listen, Wills . . . if we could keep the demon talk to a minimum around the café, I'd appreciate it. I try my best to keep the two lives separate."

He nodded. "Of course, sorry." His eyes darted over to Drew, who was taking an order from two college-aged kids. "So—he doesn't know?" His head jerked toward Drew.

"No."

"Okay."

There was silence at our table for what felt like hours. I checked my watch, not to see the time as much to find an excuse to leave the conversation. "Well, I should get back to work."

Wills nodded and stood. Holding my face between his hands, he pulled me in for a soft kiss. "I've missed you so much."

"Me too, soldier. Me too." I kissed him again.

"You never knew me as a soldier."

"No. But in the war, I always looked for you. Every time a soldier was rushed in, I ran, half hoping it was you, but always feeling somewhat relieved when it wasn't. I might not have known you as a soldier . . . but you were still *my* soldier."

He gave no response, just stood there studying me.

The silence made me uncomfortable. "I work tonight. How

about dinner tomorrow?" I shifted my weight to the other foot.

A smile crept over his face. "Perfect." And with that he walked quickly toward the door.

He has a very distinct walk with the best posture I've ever seen. It's sexy, but in a distinguished way. I watched him as he walked past the café's long storefront window. He brushed shoulders with another man. Dark brown, trim hair. Dark, low eyebrows. I *know* that guy. He was in the back of the club the night before. I ran to the window to get a better look, but he had already passed the coffee shop by.

I put him from my mind. Just a coincidence. Tossing the dirty rag over my shoulder, I went back to work. I walked to the back room to get some more coffee filters, and as I swung open the door to step down the stairs, my knees gave out on me. There in front of me as I went crashing to the floor was Drew carrying a big bag of espresso beans. He landed on his back. I landed on his stomach. And Illy beans flew into the air and sprinkled down on us, pelting our bodies like raindrops. Drew was chuckling despite the mess and the lost espresso product surrounding us.

We were nose to nose, breathing heavily after the crash. His hands had somehow landed on my hips, and he started laughing.

"Ugh," I said. "Sorry. Guess I was just rushing too much."

I heard a clacking sound and saw Adrienne's plastic platform heels before I looked up and saw the rest of her. "Oh, I'm sorry." Her voice dripped with snark. "Am I interrupting anything?"

Drew kept laughing. I guess he felt as though we clearly had nothing to be guilty of—I, on the other hand, could feel the flush rising to my cheeks. He was right, of course. We did nothing wrong—but if that was the case, why was I blushing like a teen caught parked at Make-Out Point?

"Trust me, babe." He got to his feet and lifted me up as well. "I wish this was as bad as it looked." He leaned in and kissed her lips, to which she grunted a response.

Bad answer, Drew, I thought.

"You know I'm not nearly suave enough to pull off any kind of sordid affair. Especially not with this one." He grabbed my head and gave me a noogie.

Drew has never *ever* in the history of us ever given me anything resembling a noogie. We have a special sort of affection, yes, but it's less brotherly and more Gatsby-esque. Forbidden yet classy. What the Hell was wrong with me today?

"You're bleeding all over the floor," Adrienne said, her nose wrinkling in disgust. "I'm getting out of here." She lifted her ten-dollar Payless shoes and clomped out of the room on her tiptoes—like she feared them being *ruined* by a little blood. *Bitch, please,* I thought, *my blood is worth more than those shoes will ever be.*

"Oh, my God," Drew said, looking down. "She's right, your shin is gushing."

"Oh." I didn't even feel the pain until they mentioned it. "That. It's fine, it'll stop in a second." And normally, I'd be right. Our bodies regenerate very quickly. I shut my eyes and waited for the wound to stop bleeding. I made sure to shift it so that it wouldn't close up too quickly—that type of thing tends to freak mortals out. Normally this task would take no effort at all. I opened my eyes even more exhausted than when I had sat before my break and looked down to find the cut bleeding even more. I had never before stood in a pool of my own blood. The crimson sight and coppery smell hit the back of my throat, and a wave of nausea wrenched my stomach. A tunnel of black closed in around my eyes, and the last thing I saw before I blacked out was Drew's arms reaching out to catch me.

5

London, 1939

It was 1939, and I was a singer at the Shim-Sham Club. It was actually now called the Rainbow Roof—but I hated that name. Shim-Sham was far better. I sat in Soho Square smoking a cigarette, wearing a lovely belted navy dress. It had been a gift from one of my most recent conquests. It was a beautiful dress, expensive and elegant. It clung to me like a sticky reminder of my torrid affairs. The fog around London seemed to envelope me, combining with my cigarette smoke like a giant, hazy hug, and I breathed it in, letting the smog and mist fill my lungs.

I looked down past my pleated skirt and saw that my thigh-high stocking had slipped down and was gathering in a pool of wrinkles by my ankle. Pressing the burning cigarette between my lips to free my hands, I flipped my skirt up past my knees and tugged the stocking, stretching it back up to its place.

"Well," said a delicious voice above me, "this might be the most inappropriate thing I've seen all day."

"Not to worry," I said, the cigarette bouncing with each word, "the night's still young." When I looked up into the young man's eyes, I saw naivety and a flicker of lust. Even as a young

succubus, I could sense the raw emotions. "Sit," I continued, "share this cigarette with me."

"I don't smoke." He stood a little taller—as if this fact made up for the bulge in his pants.

"Mm." I narrowed my eyes, assessing the man. He was handsome. More than handsome. The sight of him made my bloomers damp. He was way better than the cigarette, I decided. I put the smoke out on the ground and stepped on it. "There, now I don't, either. Come. Sit."

He hesitated—eyes darting around to see who could be watching—and then sat. At a respectable distance. He swallowed, and I saw his Adam's apple bob up and then down.

"Nervous?"

"Well, shouldn't I be? I've never sat with a prostitute before."

I should have been offended, but I'd been called much worse. "I'm not a prostitute," I said. At least it wasn't a total lie. That wasn't my official profession, though I suppose it could be argued that succubi are whores of the highest caliber.

His face turned crimson and he immediately looked me in the eye. "Oh, I apologize. I-I-" He dropped his head into his hand, swiping his palm across his carefully combed hair. "Bloody hell, I shouldn't have said that. What was I thinking?" Though embarrassed, he looked relieved. After he finished stumbling through an apology, his chest collapsed as a breath he had been holding escaped his lungs. "Well—what do you do, then?"

I laughed to myself. I had heard this question a million times and not once had I ever answered it truthfully. I leaned in closer to him, the stink of smoke still on my breath, and pressed my lips to his ear. He shuddered at the intensity . . . a good kind of shudder. "I'm here to steal your soul," I said in a husky whisper.

And then—he laughed. I suppose it did sound a bit ridiculous. "Okay, then. I get it, you're wicked. But what do you do to make money?" He leaned back on the bench and threw his arm behind me. He was letting his guard down around me—never a good thing, darling.

"I'm a singer," I said.

"Really?" He perked up. Singing could be a respectable job, and considering his suit and pocket watch and hair that was perfectly placed, that's what he looked for in a woman. Someone respectable.

"And a dancer," I said a bit quieter.

His muscles tightened and I could feel him sit up straighter. He glanced over at me. "Ah," he said. "Maybe I will take one of those smokes after all." He smirked, his eyes looking at me but his head still facing forward.

"Why don't we share one?" I lit my cigarette and passed it to him. He inhaled—much too deeply for a first-timer—and exhaled with a cough. I laughed. "Awww"—I combed my fingers through his hair—"that was cute."

He was still coughing. "I can't help it," he said when he finally caught his breath. "I'm an innocent man."

I glanced back down at his crotch, which tented his pants. "Oh," I said, "I don't know about that." And I ran my fingers down his chest to his stomach, then slid my hand in his pocket. With a firm hand and wide eyes, I gripped his erection. Looking back to his face, I smiled. He was larger than I had expected. "Lust is a deadly sin."

"But it's not nearly the worst of them."

"Are you the one to judge that?"

A pause. "Maybe I am."

"What's the worst sin, then?" I asked through a smile and rubbed him through the pocket. With the pad of my thumb, I circled over his head, and my body quaked as the tiniest bit of moisture soaked through the pocket onto my skin. If we weren't in such a public place, I would have loved to take him into my mouth, taste all he had to offer.

He groaned, and his head fell back on the bench as I stroked his shaft. He grabbed my hand to stop me. "What is your name?"

"Does it matter?"

"It does to me." His eyes were burning through me.

"Monica," I said quietly.

"Monica," he repeated. I loved the way my name sounded coming from him. "I'm Wills."

"Nice to meet you, Wills." I started stroking his length again, taking my time getting from base to tip. He grew harder and harder in my hand. Every now and then his cock would twitch; it occurred to me for a moment that Wills might still be a virgin. After a few minutes, I felt that familiar pulsation through the fabric. His breathing grew labored and he groaned. A sticky dampness covered my hand as I pulled it out of his pocket. I wiped my hand on my skirt. The surge of power I received from Wills was like nothing I had ever felt before. I was sure my skin was radioactive with his innocence—and just from a simple hand job. A quick flash of his life reeled before my eyes. It was a dull life; he both lived and died in a dreary, brown office.

"Can I hear you sing sometime?"

I laughed at him. "Cut to the chase, Wills. You don't want to hear me sing. You want to see me dance." My voice had a bitterness to it that I couldn't seem to shake.

He shook his head. "I'd rather hear you sing. I'll even leave before you dance."

"You want to hear me sing? No one ever comes to hear me sing."

"I do. I will." He stated the words simply. "Then, I'd like to take you to dinner."

I shook my head. "No, you don't."

He smiled, and he had one crooked tooth in the front. "Yes, I would. You're not as devilish as you think, Miss Monica." He stood up from the bench and removed his jacket. Slinging it over *his arm and placing it in front of his stained pants, he stood tall, waiting for my answer.*

"Your parents will kill you," I said, not sure if I meant for his pants or taking me to dinner.

"Probably. They'll get over it, though."

I took a deep breath and stood as well, straightening my skirt. "Shim-Sham Club tomorrow night. I go on at eight fifteen. Maybe after, we can grab something to eat. Maybe."

"You mean the Rainbow Roof?"

"Yes. Right. Rainbow Roof."

He gave one sharp nod, took my hand, and brushed a light kiss on my knuckles. "Until tomorrow."

6

I woke up to the sound of beeping and the smell of industrial cleaning agents. My eyes fluttered open, and the light was blinding.

"There you are." I recognized Drew's voice immediately. "I didn't have the new boyfriend's number to call, so I waited."

"The new who?" I put a hand to my head, putting the pieces together. I was in a hospital. Drew was with me. . . . I had a boyfriend? Oh, right. I have a boyfriend now. Sort of.

I sat up, immediately dizzy. "He's not new." My voice sounded gravely in my head. "He's an old boyfriend. A very, very old boyfriend."

"Okay," Drew said. "Either way, I didn't have his number, so I sat with you."

"It's in my phone," I said. When he didn't say anything more, I fell back onto the pillow. "How long have I been out?" I put a hand to my head, which was now only slightly throbbing.

"Oh, maybe forty-five minutes." He coughed to hide his

smile. "The doctor said it was better that you were out during the stitches."

"Stitches? I needed stitches?"

"On your leg. I have to say—I wouldn't have guessed you to be the squeamish type around blood."

"Yeah, me neither."

A pregnant pause hung in the air. "Well, let's get you home."

"I'm allowed to go home?"

This time he didn't try to hide his laugh. "Yes, Monica. They rarely keep people overnight for a few stitches."

I glared at him overdramatically, then sighed. "Okay, then. Let's go home."

As we walked out to Drew's car, he held my arm to steady me. I could feel the ache deep in my bones; the itch was raging. My powers were very low, and being this close to Drew made the sexual urge so strong that it physically hurt. His skin burned on mine. I could feel his heart beating against my body, and his other arm snaked around my shoulder. I took a deep breath and let my head fall onto his chest. "This is nice," I said. I could always blame what I said on the painkillers.

His arms clenched around me. Nervous. I was making him nervous. The tightness only reminded me of how hard and defined his muscles were beneath those clothes. A flare of heat shot between my legs and up through my torso. "Even though the doctors told me it was just a simple case of fainting, there was a part of me that worried you wouldn't wake up. Irrational, I know." He looked down at me, the slightest hint of a smile twitching at his lips. "But when you care for someone, irrational thoughts pop up now and then."

"Isn't that the truth." After a moment, I added, "So, you care about me, do you?" My crooked grin was tilted up toward him, and his smile grew wider.

"Oh, c'mon, now. No fishing for compliments. You're my

best friend—you know I do." He gave my shoulder a little squeeze and then released me to open the car door.

"I'm your best friend?" I asked, my words starting to slur. "We hardly see each other outside of work."

He shrugged as he balanced my arm, lowering me to the seat. "Guess I'm sort of a loner." Once I was in the car, he reached over me and pulled the seat belt across my body to the buckle. In doing so, his hand accidentally brushed across my breast. He jumped back as though my nipple had burned him. He mumbled something in the form of an apology.

"I could have done that, you know," I said, referring to buckling myself in.

"Really? I'm not so sure you could. Not after all those Vicodin."

"You totally copped a feel, dude." Man, maybe I *was* high.

He immediately pulled back and put his hands on his hips. "It was an accident."

I nodded. *Shit, why'd I have to tease him.* "Of course."

"Touching your breast was just a perk—um, an *accidental* perk." He walked around the other side of the car and slid into the driver's seat. "Quite the perky perk." He turned the key and the car growled to life. "Guess God decided to throw me a bone for helping ya out." He glanced over at me, a contented smile relaxed onto his face.

"I think God threw *me* a bone," I said, my eyes drifting to his crotch.

He shifted uncomfortably in his seat, probably adjusting himself.

After a few moments of silent driving, Drew spoke up again. "You might want to call in tonight at your—um, other job."

"Oh, right. Yeah, that makes sense, I guess. Not many guys get off on seeing stitches."

"God, I hope not. I can call the club for you."

I nodded, feeling my eyelids getting heavy. After another minute, I could barely keep my head off the back of the seat.

"Painkillers are working, I see," Drew said. Only in my ears the words sounded deeper and stretched out.

I had my hand in front of my face, fingers splayed out. I was staring at my hand as though it held the answer to the universe. Drugs don't normally have much effect on me—I had to admit, this was sort of fun.

To my left, I could hear laughter. Who was laughing at me? I was going to have to kick someone's ass. My head felt heavy, like a bowling ball. I couldn't lift it to see where the laughter was coming from. My chin flopped over to my shoulder, and I was again looking at perfection. My Drew.

"Drew," I said.

"Mm?"

"Dreeeeeeew."

He laughed in response. I'd let it slide. Just this once. "Andreeeeew."

"What is it, Monica?" He put his hand on my knee, and if I could feel anything but numbness I was sure I would have felt the excitement between my legs.

"Drew. What do you see in Adrienne?"

I could hear a sigh come from my left. "You don't know her like I do, Monica. She's really very sweet when she wants to be. When she opens herself up to being vulnerable—she really is a lot like you sometimes. I think you two could be friends, even. It's like she . . ."

And that's about the point I fell asleep. Maybe even by choice. I sure as Hell didn't want to hear any more. Don't even know why I asked.

7

Twelve hours and a blissful night's sleep later, light spilled in through my bedroom window, washing over me. I stretched, my nude body gliding over the silky sheets. I was moist between my legs and could feel the swelling and throbbing of my clit. Eyes still closed, I slid one hand down, lightly tickling my breast, abs, and thigh along the way. My other hand pinched my left nipple, and I moaned at my own pleasure. The flesh was soft and smooth between my legs, and I inserted two fingers as deep as I could, crying out at the sweet release of my touch. I thought of Drew, his lips on my neck, nipping at my earlobe. No, wait—I should be thinking of Wills. *Wills* licking me down between my breasts, lapping at my nipple. Oh well. Hell—why can't they both be here? It was my fucking fantasy.

I imagined both men in my bed—teasing me, licking me. At my service. I thought of their lips trailing down my neck and body and brought myself to climax with two men's faces flashing in my mind.

I imagined myself collapsing onto Drew's body, sticky and sweaty once we had all finished. I was lying on my stomach, and I could feel the weight of Wills lying down on top of me like a Monica sandwich. I felt lips on my shoulder. On my neck. On my ear. On my cheek. Which was weird—in most of my fantasies, they ended after everyone came. Cuddling is not typically fantasy material. The weight on my back felt all too real—

I opened one eye and found myself staring at a curtain of jet black hair. There was someone lying on top of me—but whereas in my dream it was hard pectoral muscles, here I felt soft breasts and a slim stomach against my bare ass.

"Well, good morning, star shine."

The voice was familiar, but I screamed and jumped out of bed anyway, grabbing my sheets around me. I took a moment to gather myself. "Kayce! Fuck!" My best friend sat on her elbow, spread out on the bed.

She laughed and lit a cigarette. "Ha, *fuck* is right." Her voice was raspy, as though she had been to a party the night before. But I knew better; that was just her voice. She sat up in my bed and tucked one foot under her. "Want one?" She held out the pack to me. "Looks like you may need it after what I just saw."

I hesitated, thinking of what Lucien had said the other night. But no mortals were around . . . and she was right. A cigarette would take the edge off. I looked down at my naked body wrapped in the sheet. "Why am I naked? Drew took me home last night." I paused and then added, "And why the Hell were you lying on top of me?"

Kayce shrugged, a small smile teasing her lips. Her eyebrows arched as she handed me the lighter. When she didn't bother answering, I lit up, making eye contact with my best friend's almond brown eyes. "What the Hell, Kayce. What did I tell you about teleporting into my apartment?"

"I *didn't*." She took a drag and blew the smoke high into the air above her head. "You left the damn door unlocked. What have I told you about doing that?"

I shook my head at her. Kayce seemed so tough sometimes but still got caught up in such mortal practices—like locking doors.

"Did you hear what I said? Drew brought me home last night. I was tanked on painkillers. I guess he forgot to lock the door behind him."

Kayce's face crinkled. "That doesn't sound like Drew. He's Mr. Protective." She took another drag of her cigarette. "Painkillers? New addiction?"

"No, not quite." I lifted the sheet to show her my stitches. "Addiction to masochism? Also no." I handed her the cigarette and went to the bathroom to brush my teeth. Even though I don't need to, I've always liked the way my mouth feels after. All minty fresh and shit.

"How the Hell did that happen?" Her voice raised an octave, shrill enough to match the mating call of the stray cats outside.

"It's a long story. I'm fine now. Besides, Kayce, we're immortal. We don't need to lock our doors. If I wanted to, I could shift into a three-hundred-pound man and kick the shit out of any intruder."

She made a *pffshh* sound through her teeth, similar to the noise a leaky tire makes. "Yeah, right. You'd have to sleep with someone much better than the trash who hang out at your club to have enough force in your reserves pull that off. Someone like . . ."

"Don't say it, Kayce. . . ."

"Drew."

I groaned. "In *theory*, Kayce. Hell." I ignored her comment about Drew. "Besides, I can sense most immortals who come within fifty yards of my home. They're the only real threat. No need to ever lock my door."

"Really? You can *sense* when another immortal is near?"

Her tone was biting and sarcastic. Behind me, I could hear the rustle of her standing up.

"What?" I asked through a foamy, toothpaste-filled mouth.

"If your senses and powers are as strong as you think they are, why are those stitches still in your leg? Just heal yourself." She stood there haughtily, sucking on her cigarette. "And while we're at it, why don't you go ahead and retrace the events of this morning."

"Ummm, OK." I matched her cynical tone. "I was sleeping. Then masturbating. Then your annoying ass came in and fucked with me."

Her weight was on one foot and she jutted her hip out like some Renaissance-styled sculpture. She cocked her head and smiled sarcastically. "Close, but not quite." I wanted to smack that smug little smile off her face. "I was watching you for almost twenty minutes before you woke up and noticed me. And even that was only because I took a little action."

I stared at her, foaming toothpaste gathering at the corners of my mouth. "Twenty minutes? Could you be any creepier?! Besides, what does that prove?" I asked again, spitting into my sink. "Outside of you being a voyeur—" The toothbrush dropped from my grip, clinking next to the drain. "Oh, my Hell. I couldn't sense you! Kayce, why couldn't I sense you?" I could feel the strain in my throat as my voice became more shrill. For a second, I had a glimmer of hope—was I no longer immortal? Maybe Hell had released its hold on me and I was getting another chance at mortality.

"I don't know." Kayce's smug look faltered momentarily, showing her concern for the situation. "I just figured you were low on your powers. Maybe the painkillers threw you off your game? How long has it been since you had sex?"

"The night before last. And he was a *good* guy, too. Had a wife and everything." I put the toilet seat down so I had somewhere to sit. "You know, I knew something was off yesterday. I was way too tired for having just had sex. I figured I had just pushed myself too hard and with Wills being back in town . . ."

"Wills? The guy from World War Two?" Kayce's eyes widened. "Holy shit, that's awesome! Is he just a bag of wrinkles now?"

"No," I said, still sitting on the can. "No, he's actually a demon now. Sold his soul back in the day on the battlefield."

Kayce paused, forehead crinkled in thought. "That's a bit odd. Do you think he has something to do with this?"

I shook my head. "No, he's a lower-level demon. His powers were barely even a blip on my radar. He doesn't have the abilities for something like this."

"Okay," Kayce said. "Who else did you come in contact with last night?"

"Seriously? I was at Hell's Lair—there were a ton of people there."

"Who did you talk to, though?"

"Lucien and I had a long conversation. There was Lenny—he was pissed I was late again. T, as usual. And then Erik is the guy I had sex with. And of course I was around Drew and Adrienne—"

"You don't think Adrienne has some sort of power over you, do you?"

I thought for a moment. "I never got any power readings from her. Her aura was bright red, though."

Kayce tsked. "No shit? She's banging some other guy? Poor Drew. Oh well . . . he's an idiot if he thought someone like Adrienne would ever be faithful."

"He's not an idiot," I said. "He's just trusting." My stomach growled a long, low grumble. "Holy shit." I brought my hand to my abs. "I'm hungry." I smiled at the thought. "I'm *actually* hungry."

"Hello! Monica, reality check here. Try doing something succubus related. Try shifting into your clothes for today."

I stood up from where I was sitting on the toilet, closed my eyes, and imagined myself in a leather skirt and bra. My stomach growled, but nothing else happened. "Wow." I stared at my reflection in the mirror. "I don't have any sort of glow, either. I just had sex two nights ago with a guy who had an affair—I should still be emulating that."

"This is terrible!" Kayce exclaimed, throwing her hands up in frustration. "How are you going to get around without your succubus powers?"

"Calm down. I'll get around like any other human."

"But you're *not* human, Monica. And scary things that go bump in the night might be coming after you."

"You are awfully melodramatic today." I laughed. "We'll go see Lucien after I eat some breakfast!" I was more excited than I wanted to admit about feeling this hunger thing after so long. I mean, we succubi eat and enjoy food. But I hadn't actually felt hungry in quite a long time. I went to my closet and pulled out a pair of jeans and a fitted, black backless shirt. I looked up at Kayce. She was biting her nails and her eyebrows were furrowed over her eyes. I decided to change the subject—for her sake. "You're looking awfully good, though. Get lucky last night?"

"You know it," she said, lowering her fingernail from her mouth.

"So, who's the guy you bagged?"

She rolled her eyes and plopped down on my bed. "Ugh, I fucked the geekiest comic book nerd last night. Total virgin. We had to be quiet all night so not to wake his mom, but it was worth it." She gestured to her body. "Got a good glow from it."

Kayce had chosen a gorgeous body as her mortal persona. Asian, with jet black, waist-long hair and enormous coffee-bean eyes. Comic book readers were her main target—and a good one, too. Typically a pretty wholesome crowd. She tended to hit the con circuits, scouring the fans for those virgins.

Over an hour later, I was putting the finishing touches on my makeup. I forgot how much time regular women put into their appearance. Shit, it almost wasn't worth it. Drew's face flashed into my mind. Then again, some men make it worthwhile, I suppose.

I was gathering items from my nightstand . . . my phone, keys, and some extra cash hanging out on the side table. Under my keys was a yellow envelope, the type you get with a greeting card at Hallmark. My name was written on the front in a cursive script. I pulled the card out, and on the front was a group of cartoony gravestones and at the top *Happy Halloween* was written in sparkly orange lettering. This was weird for a few reasons: (1) It was April. (2) Who the Hell sends Halloween cards? It's not a greeting card sort of holiday, is it? I opened the card, and in the same cursive, loopy handwriting, a short note was written.

Monica—
Olly olly oxen free.

And that was it. That's all it said. A strange saying from a children's game that I never quite understood, anyway.

From my living room, Kayce shouted something at me. I shoved the cryptic note into my purse and ran out there to meet her. "What did you say?"

"I said: I'm bored! Let's *go.*"

"Ok, okay." My keys were already in hand, and as we left my apartment, I hesitated a moment, the tip of my key touching the lock.

"Yes," Kayce said. "Lock the damn door, Monica."

I didn't bother arguing this time. Especially in light of the weird note that was definitely not on my nightstand the prior morning.

My ponytail swung back and forth across my shoulders as

we walked out of my building. My phone buzzed, and I looked down to see a text from Wills:

Your boss called me last night after he took you home. Told me about your accident. You ok? Still up for dinner tonight?

I texted him back: **Let's do drinks instead. Later tonight. I've got some errands to run first.**

I waited for his confirmation and then tossed my phone back into my purse.

"I wouldn't mind getting a bite to eat, either. One of the best things about being a succubus—I can eat a whole box of doughnuts and not worry about my hips. You on the other hand, should probably order egg whites. Just in case."

I paused a moment, imagining bland egg whites. Then I imagined myself with an extra fifty pounds. My stomach growled again, and I shot Kayce a look. One breakfast wouldn't kill my figure. "Egg whites? Only if they come on the side of my pancakes. Where do you feel like eating? A diner?"

"Anywhere close. Let's grab bagels at your coffee shop."

I stopped midstep. "You *cannot* be serious." Kayce stood there staring at me. "Kayce! I can't let Drew see me like *this!*" I gestured up and down my body.

"Oh, for fuck's sake. Monica, you look *fine*. He'll love the 'wholesome' look anyway!"

"Fine. But if Adrienne is there all dolled up, we are turning around immediately!"

"Fair enough." Kayce picked up her speed. I had to take twice as many steps just to keep up with her.

The bells atop the door jingled as we walked in. Sitting at the front table was Erik. I began to wave, but his wide eyes made me pause. Sitting next to him was, I assumed, his wife. She was dressed in a very plain but expensive-looking suit, reading her buzzing iPhone. She looked up upon hearing the jingle of the door, but her eyes barely gave me a second's glance before she went back to her phone, her mousy brown bob falling in her eyes as she lowered her head.

"Yum-*my*," Kayce whispered to me when she saw Erik. "Was that your last fix?"

I nodded, taking Kayce's arm in mine and dragging her to the front. Glancing back over my shoulder, I could see Erik's hungry gaze watching Kayce and me walking together.

"Hey, *Drew*." Kayce nudged me in the ribs.

"Hey there, Kayce. Been a while since we've seen you around here." He stood behind the counter wiping down a mug like some sort of Old West bartender.

"Hmm, missed me?" She leaned forward and winked at him. Seeing her flirting with Drew made me sort of want to grab her hair and shove her face in the coffee grinder. I know it's just in our succubus nature to flirt with everyone, but he was *my* desire and she knew that.

"And look who I dragged with me." Kayce tugged my elbow closer to the bar area and she took a step back.

Hmm, okay, she's safe from the coffee grinder. For now. "Hi," I said quietly.

"Hi back." He tilted his head to the side and smiled. "How ya feeling?"

I practically melted into a puddle right there on the floor. Normally, my succubus magic helped prevent my usual stuttering. Today, however, there was no such magic to help. We stood there like idiots, locked in each other's gaze.

"Much better, thank you. Thanks for—you know, helping yesterday." Another growl from my stomach broke the silence. "Oh, right," I said, shaking my head to help wake me up. "Kayce and I were gonna get some breakfast. Got any bagels left back there?"

"Sure do." Drew smiled and threw a hand towel over his

shoulder. "Feel like having some eggs too? I can whip some up on the griddle in the back. A healing lady needs her strength."

"Oh, no. That's not necessary. . . ."

"That would be great." Kayce and I had spoken at the same time; me, not wanting to be too much trouble, but Kayce letting her big eyes and gluttony do the talking.

"I'll be back in a minute. I think I have some leftovers from my breakfast earlier." Drew slipped into the back, and I turned to glare at Kayce.

Her eyes widened and she shrugged. "What? It's free food."

I shook my head. "You're one of the highest paid demons in our realm, yet you're fine taking money from a hard-working guy like Drew?!"

"Excuse me. Could we not advertise my wealth to all of Vegas, please!"

I sighed. "Are you ever going to be able to tell me what exactly you do for a living?" Kayce was always so elusive about her job, as in *if I told you, I'd have to kill you.* Part of me thinks this is her idea of a joke, but then I'll get a glimpse at her temper and be reminded to never push the point too far. To my knowledge, no one in our inner circle except for Lucien knew what she did. I was pretty sure it was something dark and dangerous. Every now and then, Kayce would get this look in her eyes and you just knew—this was not a woman to be fucked with. No matter how often she rationalized it, though, it always hurt that she didn't trust me enough to reveal what she did.

She shrugged, and for a moment I thought I saw a flicker of sadness in those dark eyes. "I hope I never have to," she said quietly.

"Fucking Hell, Kayce." I shook my head at her.

A deep voice came from behind me. "You should watch that language, lady."

I recognized Erik's voice and responded without even turning around. "You shouldn't be talking to me with your wife only a few feet away."

"She left already. For work." There was a bitterness when he said *work*.

"Shouldn't you be leaving, too, then?"

"In a minute." He leaned against the counter, forcing me to make eye contact. "I just thought I'd come over and say hi . . . maybe you can introduce me to your friend here."

Kayce smiled and ran her tongue over her scarlet lips. Always the attention whore.

"Of course. Kayce, this is Erik. Erik, this is Kayce. My lesbian lover."

Kayce cleared her throat, and when I looked over, standing in front of me with two plates of scrambled eggs and toasted bagels, was Drew. His mouth hanging slightly open.

Erik leaned in, not even noticing Drew. "Really? Well, maybe later you two can make me a sandwich."

Kayce grabbed a plate from Drew and took Erik by the arm. "Why don't you keep me company while I eat breakfast." Erik happily followed at her heels under the Kayce spell.

"Wasn't that the guy you spilled coffee on?" Drew pointed at Erik as he walked away from us.

"Um, yeah. That's him."

"He's not harassing you, is he? Because I do have the right to refuse service to anyone." He pointed at a sign on the wall that stated just that.

"No, no. It's not a big deal." I paused, taking as delicate a bite as I could from my bagel. "By the way, what I said just then . . . about Kayce and me, it was just . . . I mean, it's not true or anything."

Drew shrugged. "I figured. Though I don't think talking about lesbian sex is the right way to deter a man like that. Or *any* man, for that matter." He grabbed a fork, taking a bite of my eggs. "Unless, you don't *want* to deter him."

I smirked. "He's not my type."

"Oh yeah?" An eyebrow arched over his green eyes. "So what is your type? Oh, I almost forgot—*Wills* is your type, right?" Leaning on his elbows across the counter, he took another bite of my eggs.

I decided to ignore his pointed question. He was the one with the girlfriend, after all. "Ahhh," I cried, "those are my eggs." I jutted my bottom lip out in an exaggerated pout.

"I made 'em." He chuckled. "Nor have you paid yet. So I think maybe I could claim them as my own."

"You'll have to fight me for 'em." I held my fork up, en garde, like a sword. "And I'm pretty feisty."

He laughed in that bubbly way I love so much. "Oh, I know that. Believe me." He set the fork down next to my wrist. "You look nice again today, by the way. Different than usual." His eyes trailed from the top of my hair down my body, taking my new look in. He quickly returned his gaze to mine, cheeks flushing.

My face went hot at his compliment. The heat traveled all the way down my body stirring up a tornado of emotions. "Really? I feel like I'm . . . um, a bit casual today."

"You are," he said, holding my eye contact. "That's what I like about the look. It's like yesterday, except you don't seem quite so exhausted. You look more . . . relatable. You're normally so put together. It's intimidating."

I smirked as I took another bite, stifling a girly giggle. "Are you telling me *I* intimate *you?*"

"Of course not," he answered. "I'm clearly too masculine to be intimidated by *anybody.* Obviously, I meant other men who don't have the overflowing amounts of testosterone that I do." He posed exaggeratedly in a muscle man way. "So . . . you didn't answer my question—what's your type?"

"Mmmm," I hummed in response, leaning in closer to him. "I thought you answered that for me already."

His gaze shifted down to my breasts for a moment, and he quickly looked back to my eyes. "How's the leg?"

"Oh, fine." I took another bite of my breakfast. "Thanks for calling Wills last night." Drew nodded but said nothing else. "Also, um . . . I had no clothes on when I woke up this morning. I don't imagine you as the kind who would take advantage of a sweet girl hopped up on painkillers, but . . ."

Drew tossed his head back and laughed. "The second I got you into your apartment, you stripped off your clothes. I tried not to look, but, hey—I'm only human." I smiled at that. Deliciously human. "I put a protein bar and a glass of water by the bed, then left you to rest."

"Did you lock the door behind you?"

"Of course." He held up a set of keys. "Here's your spare set back."

"So, you snuck a peek, huh? Like anything you saw?"

His eyes lowered and his chest rose and fell with heavy breaths. His lips parted to speak when Kayce came up behind me, slapping my ass as she walked up, interrupting the moment. "Eat up, lady. We've got some errands to run."

Damnit, damnit, damnit. I forked a few mouthfuls in one bite and swallowed quickly.

"Errands, huh?" Drew pushed off of the counter and grabbed another coffee mug to dry. "You should come to this couples' night thing I'm going to tonight."

Kayce nudged me. Still chewing, my mouth full of eggs and bagel, I shook my head to say no as I swallowed the food down.

Even though I opened my mouth to speak, Kayce cut in before me. "She'd love to go." She shot me a look, eyes narrowed.

I took a deep breath. "What time is it? And where?"

He smiled wider, dimples creased so deep I could hide loose change in them. "It starts at eight p.m. at my church. Bring Wills."

"Oh," Kayce and I said in unison.

"Um, well, I have some plans tonight . . . but maybe we can

hang out another evening." I pushed my half-eaten plate away, getting ready to leave.

"Oh, c'mon, Monica. My church isn't that bad. We're very progressive. Mostly we just volunteer with youth groups and discuss passages that we still find relevant in everyday life. No exact interpretations of the Bible, no judgments. Nothing like that." He set the mug down on the counter in front of me.

Kayce looked skeptically at Drew. "You don't really strike me as the churchgoin' type."

He shrugged. "It's a sense of community. I found them when I joined AA."

My concern had less to do with judgmental hypocrites and everything to do with my whole minion of Hell situation. I literally could not step on holy ground without experiencing excruciating pain. Not since I fell from grace. And I was pretty damn sure Wills couldn't, either. Even with my new current situation, I couldn't be sure that I was exempt from that pain yet. I desperately wanted to visit a church, but my body writhing in pain would probably not make the greatest first impression on this group. "I suppose Adrienne's going to be there with you, huh? She doesn't exactly look like she belongs in a church, either." I sounded a little harsher than I meant to.

Kayce looked at me without moving her head and, covering her mouth with her coffee mug, whispered softly, "Bring it down a notch, Mon."

He stepped back from me—a slight gesture, but it didn't go unnoticed. "I'm actually the one who put the event together." He spoke quieter. "I'm not going as part of a couple. . . . I'm going as the coordinator, so, no, Adrienne won't be there." He turned his back to me and finished the thought without eye contact. "I guess I just thought maybe you would enjoy the night. Hang out with people outside of your stripper friends and patrons." My face felt hot as he said that. "I'm assuming that's why Mr. Three-way over there was over here just now.

He looked at you like he's seen you naked." His voice was more bitter.

Shit. "I'm sorry, Drew. I-I—" My stuttering threw me off, "I just get a little freaked out by churches. What's the address? If I have time, maybe I'll swing by."

He turned back around, with a hint of a smile . . . but still not quite his normal jovial self. He wrote down an address and handed it to me, our fingertips brushing in the process. My body trembled at his touch. "I hope to see you there."

I pocketed the address and turned to leave the store. Erik was there waiting for me. "I thought you were leaving," I said, exiting the coffee shop. I didn't even bother making eye contact with him. "And I thought we made an agreement. No contact outside of Hell's Lair."

"I know, I know." He put his hands up in front of him as if saying *stop.* "I bought this the other day—not sure why I bought it. I just liked it. Then last night, I found it in my pocket and it made me think of you. It's the exact color of your eyes." He handed me a dark blue smooth stone. It shimmered in the light and was about the size of a quarter. It had a little bit of dust on it—red dust. Like it came out of the Red Rock desert or something.

I reached out to take it from him, then held it in the palm of my hand. I'd never seen a stone quite like this before. It had the look of lapis lazuli but with more shimmer. I held the stone back out to him. "I can't take this," I said.

"Please," he said. "I want you to have it. It's a rare stone and nonrefundable. Besides, I can't give it to my wife—it's definitely not her style. She'll know something is up. I'm not even sure why I bought it. I guess I was just drawn to it or something."

I was about to say that that wasn't my problem, but the fact was there was a beauty to it that I just loved. And I thought back to his wife sitting at the café table—her mud-colored hair, her boring gray suit that didn't even fit well, her plain white-gold chain that hung around her neck. He was right, she'd never wear something like this stone. And I wanted to keep it. It was just my style. I thought it weird that he so easily found something that was perfect for me, but the man had money. And I had expensive tastes. So perhaps it was just circumstantial luck. It did match my eyes—a dark, ocean-like blue. I figured there was no harm in keeping it. I slipped the stone into the pocket with the address Drew gave me. "Thanks, Erik. I'll see you around." I brushed past him and out the door.

Kayce and I sat in my car, silently driving down the dusty road to the strip club. Lucien was almost always there. I pulled into my usual spot and saw Lucien's SUV parked on the other side of the lot. Demons aren't really the environmentally conscious kind.

The door creaked behind us as we entered. The club during the day seemed even seedier than at night. The slick floors, though recently mopped, still had a layer of oil on them from the sweat of the dancers and patrons. "Lucien?" My voice trembled, though I wasn't quite sure why.

The club had a faint odor of rosewater. I walked closer to his office door, which was cracked open.

"What are you doing here?" a gruff voice said from behind me. I jumped and turned around, face-to-face with Lenny.

I rolled my eyes. "I'm looking for Lucien. Is he here?"

"He's in a private meeting in the back room. The door is locked with an enchantment around it. You can wait in his office if you want."

My fingertips sprawled out over his office door, and with a light push, it opened. I walked inside, pretty used to entering his office whenever I wanted. Behind his desk in the window he had a new quartz I had never seen before. It was large, probably half my size. The Newton's cradle was swinging wildly from side to side, a heavy *click* sounding out each moment the swing-ing ball made contact with the center balls.

"What in the . . ." My words trailed off. I thought back to our conversation the night before about the Newton's cradle signifying a higher immortal. I looked over at Kayce, who had already plopped down in one of Lucien's plush chairs. I ges-tured to the Newton's cradle. "He must be having a meeting with some of the higher-ups."

Kayce pulled out a nail file and nodded. "Any idea how long we're gonna have to wait?"

I shrugged and walked over toward the quartz. I wondered what it was doing here. It wasn't here two nights ago. Maybe he requested it and that's what the meeting was about. I didn't know much about quartz and crystals and stuff. I knew they held some sort of magic, but you had to be a powerful demon or succubi in order to cast the spells. I reached out my hand to touch the smooth stone.

"Monica, no!"

It was too late. I brushed my fingertip over the sharpest point of the crystal like Sleeping Beauty over the spindle. With a scream, I pulled back my hand, holding my throbbing finger. Blood trickled down, over my palm. I stared at the cut for a few seconds. "Oh shit. Not again."

Kayce grabbed a tissue from Lucien's desk and wrapped it around my finger. "You have to be more careful." She froze, applying pressure to my wound. "Does this mean . . . could you die? Are you no longer immortal? I mean, you had to get stitches in your leg!" The blood drained from Kayce's face, leaving it a pale cream color.

A loud crack sounded from behind me, and I immediately felt tingles traveling up my spine as if someone were playing it like piano keys.

"Hello, Monica. It's been a while, has it not?"

8

"Jules." A sharp breath pierced my lungs. "Yes, it has been a while." I pivoted slowly so that I could face him. He wasn't exactly an ArchAngel yet—but he was well on his way to that status. I guess we both sort of were before I fucked things up. He was a mentor of sorts back in my angel days. He looked exactly the same—of course. None of us changed. Unless we were transformed from angel to succubus, that is. His wavy blond hair hung about midway down his neck; strands twisted around each other, curling over his ears. His angular features were masculine as ever. A strong nose, chin dimple, high cheekbones, and full lips were enough to make any girl swoon.

Back in the day, the two of us were not only colleagues, we were friends. One might have even called us best friends. I looked down at my finger, the sight of blood making me queasy all over again. "I need to sit down," and I plopped into a chair that suddenly appeared behind me. Having him there before me as I bled all over Lucien's seventies-inspired carpet was a bit much to handle all at once. I closed my eyes and took deep breaths so not to pass out again.

Ireland, 1740

"*Why the frown?*" *His touch at the base of my chin was cool and refreshing.*

My eyes were wet as I looked up into his bright blue eyes. "I—" The words wouldn't come. I lowered my gaze away from his, burning inside despite his cool hands. "I'm just feeling confused, I guess."

"Is that so?" He didn't force me to meet his eyes again, just left his fingertips grazing the skin on my neck. "Confused about what?" His fingers twirled around a lock of my hair.

My face flushed, and I could feel the heat rise up through my torso and spread throughout my sternum. "I've just been having these . . . feelings lately. Sinful feelings."

"Monica." Julian chuckled, "Love is not sinful."

"This is more than love, Jules. It's . . . I mean, it's . . . lust." We both knew lust was one of the most dangerous of the deadly sins. My head jerked up to look into his eyes. His face had lowered much closer to mine. "Julian . . ." I breathed. His name was a whisper on my lips.

"Lust can sometimes simply be a product of love. Humans who are married on Earth lust over each other—this is not sinful."

"We are married to God. We are not human."

He shook his head. "God understands love, whether it's coming from his children on Earth or his subjects in Heaven. If anything, loving another unconditionally shows God that you truly understand Him."

"So angels are allowed to have relationships?"

He nodded, eyes thoughtful. "Many angels have received blessings to stray outside of Heavenly relationships as well. As I said—God does not punish love."

"Relationships outside of Heaven? As in, relationships with humans?"

Again, Jules nodded, observing my reaction.

I thought about this, pulling my knees close to my chest. I hadn't been human for long, and that had been centuries ago. I had never known love in a romantic form.

"There is so much to teach you, Monica." He lowered his lips to mine, covering them in an all-encompassing kiss. His mouth moved around mine gently. I tried to stop the kiss, first by pulling away from his grasp, but his large hand cupping the back of my head and fingers entwined in my hair prevented my escape. He just pulled me in for more. It felt great; amazing even. I'd had many dreams about this exact moment.

Only this time, this time it was wrong. If only Julian had presented me with this sooner. His lips continued to devour mine, and his hands danced around all my naughty parts but never once touched them. He touched my sternum, my neck, my back, my stomach—waiting for permission to move to other areas. Permission that would never come.

"Jules—"

"Monica," he groaned, his lips still touching mine as he spoke.

"Julian, no! Stop!"

He immediately pulled away. There was no coaxing, no bargaining like the men in my human days. He stepped back swiftly, hands immediately down at his side. "Monica, what's the matter?" Concern washed over his face, his mouth curving into a frown.

There was no easy way to say this. "There's someone else."

He took a moment to let that sink in, eyes examining me in a cool manner. "Who is it?"

I didn't answer. I didn't need to. After a pause, his eyebrows twitched with realization and his face creased with worry. "Monica . . . you have to be careful."

"You just said God does not punish love!"

*"I know, and that's true. But it has to be true love. And the
repercussions if one of you is unfaithful are truly terrible."*

*"I would never be unfaithful, Jules," I answered. And part
of me wished it had been Julian I had fallen for first. It was too
late now.*

*Julian smiled sadly and cupped my face with one hand. "Oh,
seraphim. I know that. You are not whom I worry about.
Though it would be wise to get the relationship blessed by San
Michel before moving forward. You must be careful. While love
is not punished, lust alone is." He winced as though the thought
of this pained him. "As your mentor, I can only do so much to
protect you." He leaned in, his lips touching my ear. "And I
don't know what I'd do if I lost you."*

"Here." Jules's voice sounded more gruff than I remembered in my dreams. The tunneling vision surrounding my eyes
came into focus again as I woke up out of my faint. "Let me
help." He took me by the wrist and applied pressure to the
wound. "I'm not allowed to heal you, but this should speed up
the natural process your body will take."

"Thanks, Jules," I whispered.

Julian looked at me, taking in my haphazard appearance. "I
like the new look. You seem more . . . natural. Than your usual
stripper costumes, that is." I opened my mouth to throw a re-
tort back at him, but he cut me off before I could. "So, what's
going on here?"

"Well"—between my teeth, I chewed the fleshy corner of
my mouth—"we were hoping you could tell us."

"Lucien's not here?"

"He's in the back, in a meeting. We don't know how long
he'll be."

He nodded. A moment of sadness flashed across his cherub
face.

"Do you know what the meeting is about, Jules?" My eyes narrowed at him. He seemed to know more than he was letting on. But that was typical of angels in general.

He and Lucien worked together a lot as the demon and angel in charge of Nevada. True that Jules wasn't *quite* Lucien's equal yet in terms of status, but he'd get there soon. Many would think this would make them enemies—in actuality their jobs crossed paths often. The two considered each other an integral part of the world. Without good, there would be no evil. Without temptation, there would be no salvation. And so on and so forth.

Whatever it was Julian knew, he quickly brushed it aside. "So you have lost your powers, then?" He asked looking at me.

"Yes!" I started, "How did you kno—"

"You're bleeding." He gestured to my hand, his face serious. "The main question we need to answer is why. Obviously, Lucien will be able to help more with this than I."

The *click-clicking* of the Newton's Cradle was so loud, it sounded like a thunder crack every second. I walked over to his desk, picked it up, and allowed it to calibrate to my powers—which at the moment were virtually nonexistent. I could still hear and see supernaturally well. But that was about it. Basically one step above mortals. I slipped the desk toy into my bag, which muted the noise at least a little bit.

"Can't you help me?" I looked up at Julian. He was still a do-gooder—an angel who got his rocks off on helping people. "I mean, I'm not really a succubus anymore—am I? Not without my powers?"

Kayce looked at me in shock. "Monica, why are you in such a rush to change this? Isn't this, like, your dream?"

"What are you talking about?" It was hard for me to focus on anything other than the damn clicking coming from inside my purse.

"This is your chance"—Kayce walked toward me—"to live

a fucking normal life—to have sex with whomever you want without repercussions. Don't you get it? You and Drew can be together now."

I froze, stunned. To my right, I heard Julian intake a sharp breath, wincing at Kayce's bad language. Or maybe at the thought of me having sex with someone.

He leaned into me, his breath like a cool autumn breeze on my neck. "Take care of yourself, Monica. I'll check in on you soon."

Another crack sounded through the air and Julian was gone. From deep inside my purse, the clicking of the Newton's Cradle abruptly stopped, silencing Lucien's office. Within seconds, the clicking resumed.

"Well, well, well, what do we have here?" Lucien stood in the doorway, arms crossed. He sniffed the air, his mouth tightening at the scent. "I smell peppermint—Jules has been here, hasn't he?" We nodded, and he looked over at Kayce and smirked, running a tongue along his bottom lip. "You come here to finally join my group of girls?" Lucien had been trying to get Kayce to strip ever since the two first met.

"Yeah, I was thinking of starting next week—right after you go fuck yourself."

I stepped between them, my hands up like a crossing guard. "Okay, you two. Could you settle this another time? I have actual problems here."

"That makes two of us, Monica," Lucien said quietly, and ran his hand through a head of damp hair.

I paused, taking in the fact that Lucien looked more stressed than I'd ever seen him. His eyes drooped, and his olive skin lacked its usual luster. "What's going on? What was the meeting about?"

He sighed. "I can't tell you too much—just, well, you know the missing succubi I mentioned?" I nodded as Kayce looked on in confusion. "There's quite a bit more to it than that. They aren't missing—they're dead. Some sort of serial killer here in Vegas is putting all his effort in killing *my* succubi."

"They were murdered? How do you murder a succubus?" I'd never thought of it. I mean—we were *immortal.*

"It's not easy, but there are ways. The main way is to strip the soul from the body." He cleared his throat and shook his head. "You know, I really can't tell you any more. Sorry, ladies. Thanks for stopping by, though." He walked to the door and held it open for us.

Both Kayce and I stood there, our eyes narrowing. "We came here for a reason, you know," Kayce said, daggers in her voice.

"Oh, right," he said, eyes rolling. "I forgot—your 'problem.' "

"Look, asshole." Kayce went nose-to-nose with Lucien. I sat down in the chair by his desk, my brain starting to throb like something I hadn't felt since my mortal days. "Monica lost her powers. She can't teleport, no shapeshifting, and no extra strength. She can't even sense other immortals. And based on the fucking blood dripping down her finger and stitches in her leg, I'm guessing that she could be in some danger here. We could use a little help from our ArchDemon asshole."

Lucien's face softened and he walked over to where I sat. "You lost your powers?"

I nodded and pulled up my jeans to show him the stitches.

"Shit." He stood abruptly and paced around the room. "Shit, shit, shit." He just kept muttering profanities under his breath. "I just assumed when Drew called that you were blowing off work last night."

Kayce was one step behind him with each pace. "Lucien—it's nice to know you're concerned, but the bad language isn't offering her any solutions."

"Just shut up!" he yelled, and put a hand in Kayce's face. His voice boomed, the blow of power knocking her back, reminding her just who the boss was when it came down to it.

He knelt back down in front of me. "Monica, listen to me.

You have to be very careful. This is the trend with the murders—a succubus gets her powers taken and her mortal body is murdered. It's as close to death as we can get."

I swallowed. "Where does the soul go?"

He shook his head back and forth. "I don't know. So far, it just seems as though the girls cease to exist."

"Who's powerful enough to pull off such a strong spell?" I asked.

"That's the problem. We can't find this guy because it has to be an immortal with extreme power to create a vessel to strip an immortal soul. But based on the crime scenes, we're having a lot of trouble linking the actual murders to anything arcane or immortal. Once the soul is stripped, the murders themselves could be committed by a human."

I sat there in silence for a moment. I could feel Lucien's eyes burning my skin. I knew he was watching my every move.

"So—I might die?"

"No." He spoke firmly, and when I looked over at Kayce, she had her face buried in her hands. "No," he repeated. "The difference is, with the past succubi, the transition happened fast. They lost their powers and within twenty-four hours, their bodies were dead. There was no time to protect. No time to assess who was around them. How long have you been without powers?" His eyes were like two stones, unblinking.

"Yesterday was when I first noticed something was off. But it mostly felt like I was just low on energy. This morning was when I woke up completely drained."

"Okay, so we're at the first-day mark." Lucien shook his head and placed his hand over mine. "You're going to be safe. I'm going to keep you safe."

He stood up and walked over to his desk, grabbing his phone. "I need you here immediately." That's all he said into the phone, nothing else. Within seconds there was a *crack* and Jules stood before us again.

They stared at each other. An immortal staredown. It was like a spaghetti western, only the men were much more beautiful. And they showered regularly. I expected them to draw any second—only instead of guns it would be a pitchfork and a halo.

Lucien was the first to speak. "You know the situation." It was a statement, not a question.

"I do," Julian said.

"And are you able to help?"

Julian paused and looked over at me. "I must clear it with the counsel first."

"I understand." Another pause. "If it helps—she has no more succubus powers. She is mortal for all intents and purposes."

"Almost mortal. She retains some succubi traits still." Julian's eyes flitted over to my breasts, and I rolled my eyes, giving an audible sigh.

"I'll need an answer as soon as possible."

Julian gave one sharp nod, and with one last crack, he disappeared. Again.

"Kayce," Lucien called. When she looked up from her hands, her eyes were red and her cheeks streaked with tears. "I'm going to need your help with this, too. We're going to have round-the-clock surveillance on Monica. Can you take the first shift?"

She sniffed and nodded.

"Take your balls out of your pockets, Kayce. We need you to be on your A game."

Kayce stood, swiping an arm over the last remnants of tears, and walked over to Lucien, pupils flickering like a flame. Her stride was fast, and as she reached him, she grabbed Lucien's balls tightly. He squeaked and his face reddened. "She's my best-fucking-friend. You better believe I'm on my A game." She released her grip and Lucien adjusted his clothing.

"Excuse me," I chimed in, "do I get any say in this?"

"No!" they said at the same time, not taking their eyes off of one another.

"Take her home," Lucien continued. "But let her go about her days as normal. In fact, try to keep your tail on her a secret. You're her friend, so for the most part it won't look weird, you hanging out at the coffee shop and at her house, but we don't want the perp to be scared off of the target."

I swallowed. "And . . . I'm the target, right?" I wasn't used to all this covert operation shit.

Kayce shook her head. "I don't like this, Lucien. Monica shouldn't be used as bait."

For a brief moment, Lucien's face softened. "I can't say I like it much, either, but we have little choice. If this guy knows we're wise to him, he'll just back off and find another victim. We'd be sacrificing another for Monica's life."

"I'm all right with that," Kayce said.

"Of course you are. You kill for a living." Lucien rolled his eyes.

"Newsflash, dipshit. I'm a succubus. You're a demon. We *all* kill for a living."

"Enough!" I couldn't take their bickering much longer. They were like the Hellspawn equivalent to the Ropers. "I'll do it. I'll be the bait. But I'll be safe, right? We'll have people constantly watching and maybe you can get me some sort of weapon so I'm not just a sitting duck?"

Lucien nodded. "I can arrange that. But, Monica, you can't tell anyone you suspect you're a target. We have no idea who this person is—who he knows or how he's listening. I know we're safe in here because of my enchantments. But other than me, Julian, and Kayce—you can't talk about this to anyone. I will keep you posted if I add any more security to the team."

I nodded, gulping back the fear that was making my ears ring. "Should I come in to strip tonight?"

Lucien thought for a moment. "Not tonight. Those fucking stitches are disastrous. Here." He touched my leg, and a pins-and-needles sensation coursed through my body. "That should help it heal within a day or so."

Kayce had her hands on her hips and was looking at the ugly carpet. "We should put enchantments on her apartment, too. I can put a basic ward on it, but for anything more intricate, we'll need your skill."

Lucien nodded in agreement. "I'll do that tonight when I take over for you. How long are you available today?"

"I can be on duty until nightfall. Then I have a—er, another assignment. It shouldn't take long, though."

"No problem." Lucien waved her off. "I'll take over at eight p.m."

"I have a thing tonight thanks to Drew," I chimed in. "It's at a church."

Lucien lit up. "That's perfect! You should have no problem entering a sacred place since you no longer have succubi powers."

"Are you *sure*? If you're wrong about this, the consequences could be awful."

"I'm sure."

"How sure?"

He paused, thinking. "Eighty-five percent."

My eyebrows arched. "You're playing Russian roulette with fifteen percent of my life?"

"Oh, calm down." He rolled his eyes and went back to his desk. "You'll know before you actually enter if it will hurt you or not. Just touch your finger to the door. If it sizzles, you know not to go in." His mouth curled into a playful smirk.

Nice to know he still has his humor in the face of danger, I thought, glaring at him.

He went over to the row of cabinets lined up along the wall and hovered his hand over the paneling. He was muttering under

his breath, lifting an enchantment. After a few seconds, he lowered his hand and opened a cabinet door pulling out a .38 Smith
& Wesson and a box of bullets.

I jumped out of my seat to get a better look at it.

Lucien held the gun's grip out toward me. "This is for emer-
gency use. The bullets were blessed with holy water. It will
make it so that the wounds of any demon or Hellspawn won't
heal. After that, it will be up to Saetan if he wants to revive who
is shot. And if the murderer is human, it can certainly be used
against him. You ever shot one of these before?"

I nodded, still staring at the glistening gun. It had been a
while, but if I remembered correctly, it was like riding a bike. A
deadly, dangerous bike.

He exhaled. "Great." He put on a pair of protective gloves
and loaded the gun, careful not to touch the blessed bullets to
his skin. "Just, please"—he slipped the gun into my purse—
"don't blow your toes off."

"That sounds like a euphemism."

"Monica, I'm serious."

"Yes, yes, fine. I won't shoot myself." I picked up my purse,
which was suddenly a few pounds heavier. "Isn't it illegal to
carry a concealed weapon?"

Kayce rolled her eyes at me. "Please. This is Vegas. We make
our own laws."

"All right, you two, get out of here." He turned and sat
down in his desk chair. "I've got some work to do keeping you
safe."

Kayce linked her arm in mine, and we turned toward the
door.

"Oh, and Monica," he called without looking up from his
phone, "I'm gonna want that Newton's Cradle back after you
get your powers restored."

I couldn't be sure, but I thought I heard him chuckle a little.
Demons are such bastards.

9

"Slow down!" Kayce cried as I accelerated to forty miles an hour back in my Toyota. Her face was ash gray, hands clenching the interior.

"Kayce, breathe, darlin'."

"We're going to get in a car wreck and you're going to end up dead, I just know it!" Each word connected to the one before it, as if she were not even breathing between.

"We're not going to die. My senses are still really strong—stronger than human, for sure. I'll be fine."

"Just slow down. I can easily protect you from everyone else, but I can't protect you from yourself." Her voice was slower and calmer than seconds before, but I heard something in the last word—a catch in her voice that sounded like she might cry.

Taking a hand off the steering wheel, I reached across to hold her hand. Though my gesture was meant to be comforting, she shrieked in my ear; I swerved into the lane next to mine, shocked by her sudden outburst. Horns blared from all sides.

"Put your hands back on the wheel!" she screamed.

"Oh, my fucking Hell! If you don't calm down, I swear to Lucifer, I will make you walk home!" I put my hands on the ten-and-two position and slowed down to only thirty-two miles per hour despite the honks and middle fingers as people sped past me. "There. Better?"

Her breathing returned to normal, and I saw the cool, calculating succubus return to my side. "Yes," she said, her voice barely above a whisper.

The rest of the trip was silent with the occasional *thunk* as Kayce adjusted the gun on her hip. As we entered the more happening area of Las Vegas, the streets grew more and more crowded. A man and woman both went for the same cab and got into a screaming match. Horns blared; lights flashed and blinked. On the corner near Circus Circus, I saw my incubus friend, George, wearing tight, hip-hugging jeans and a button-down short-sleeved shirt with suspenders. It was hard to tell based on the outfit if he was hunting men or women today—it tended to vary from night to night. Though, he prefers the boys.

Out of habit, I pulled into the coffee shop parking lot. "Is that Mia?" I asked Kayce, who was already leaning her head out the window to have a better view.

"Yep, that's her."

What the Hell is the Succubus Queen doing in my Vegas coffee shop on a Saturday afternoon? She has stations all over the world. Vegas seemed so dull in comparison to Greece, Italy, and Paris.

Following close at her heels was her minion, Lexi. Okay, maybe Lexi was a bit more than just a minion—more like an executive assistant. But, man, I hated that bitch. She's had it out for me from the day I fell to Earth. Lucien said that she was insanely jealous not only of my relationship with him but also of the fact that I was famous for being an angel. Or being a fallen angel. Whatever. Apparently she's been in love with Lucien for centuries. She thinks *I'm* the reason he won't be with her. Yet, I've heard what Lucien has to say about her—the feeling is definitely not mutual, and I can guarantee it has nothing to do with me and everything to do with the fact that she's a cunt. Needless to say, it certainly didn't illicit strong feelings of friendship between her and me when Lucien took me under his wing. It simply offered the perfect outlet for her bruised ego and anger.

I parked my little Toyota, swinging wildly into the first available space. A car horn blared and a deep voice yelled obscenities through my open window. Maybe Kayce was right—I should drive a little more carefully now. At least until I was immortal again. *If* I were to ever be immortal again. If I stayed mortal, I could have a normal life. Normal relationships. A family even. The thought made me smile, as unrealistic as it was . . . if only for a moment.

"This is actually perfect," said Kayce. "I can run home and grab some of my other weapons as well as this new incantation spell I learned. You'll be safe for the time being with Mia at the shop."

I nodded. "That's true. But what the Hell is she *doing* here?"

Kayce shrugged, her bony little shoulders rising to her delicate earlobes. "I don't know. She's probably just making her rounds."

The first thing to hit me was the overwhelming smell of rosewater again. The same smell that had lingered at Hell's Lair. I walked in, and standing at the counter ordering a latte was Mia, Queen of the Damned. She wore a perfectly tailored blue business jacket with a skirt that came midthigh. Her long red hair sat perfectly coiffed in a French twist on her beautiful head.

Ruby lips matched her red accessories for the perfect color pop. I looked up realizing she was speaking to Drew. *My* Drew.

Calm down, Monica. You cannot piss off your Queen. Especially on a day when you have no powers whatsoever.

Standing slightly behind Mia was Lexi. She was three inches taller than me and two sizes larger with curves that looked simply ridiculous. Her suit was buckling at the seams around her hips and bust, and she wore no shirt under her waist-hugging jacket. Prostitutes would envy her cleavage, and her skirt was so short, you could almost see two ass cheeks hanging out the back. Her dark brown hair was straight and fell to her shoulders, bangs sweeping just below her eyebrows, tickling her eyelashes.

"Could I get that latte with extra *cream?*" Mia's voice was husky and she leaned into Drew as she spoke.

"Of course. Latte, extra foamy, comin' up." Drew somehow tore his eyes away from Mia's smoldering gaze and smiled at me, still standing in the doorway. "And here's Monica now." He gestured at me with a rag he held in his right hand, then tossed it over his shoulder, turning to make the latte.

"I know." Mia spoke so softly that no mortal ears could hear. "I could smell her come in."

I walked up to two of the most powerful succubi in the world, grabbing a couple napkins to stuff into my purse—I needed something to quiet down the damn Newton's Cradle that was going nuts at the bottom of my bag. The clicking quieted down significantly but was still present.

"Hello, Mia." I slightly bowed my head. Succubus Rule #1—*Never* piss off your Queen. Always show appropriate respect. No matter how much disdain you might feel for the bitch.

"So." She looked around my coffee shop as though we were in a dirty, public bathroom. "*This* is where you spend your days. How . . . quaint." She wrinkled her nose as though smelling something foul.

"Yes." I swallowed my uncertainty and tried to replace it with confidence.

"I presume that you use it to find some strong fixes." She glanced around at a few of the tables. "There seem to be a lot of good-souled men and women in here." She leaned in closer, her ruby lips so inviting—sexy and alluring. "Must be so . . . tantalizing."

I cleared my throat. "Yes. This place is filled with the kind of people Hell seeks."

"She's lying." From behind Mia, Lexi growled. "She doesn't sleep with the men she meets here. Only at her strip club."

My initial plan was to try to ignore anything Lexi said or did. Avoid eye contact. Ignore the jabs. But trying to brush off Lexi is like trying to evade an ex-lover who isn't ready to let go of you. And one moment you're standing there sipping your morning coffee and the next you look out your window and he's standing in your driveway carving *FUCK YOU* into the hood of your car with gasoline in one hand and a book of matches in the other. That's Lexi. Insane. Dangerous. Unhinged.

Mia raised a smooth, waxed eyebrow in my direction. "Is that so? I thought you got over your 'ethical' hang-ups decades ago."

I spoke carefully—I needed to tread lightly with such powerful demons. "I did not lie." I shot a menacing glance at Lexi. "I have slept with a couple of men from here. In fact, I stole a man's soul I met here just the other night. And he was married."

Mia smiled; this seemed to please her for the moment. "Good. We have our eye on you, Monica. You need to kick your duties up a notch. And I think a good way to start would be with your boss over there." She peered at Drew with a side glance, not moving her head. "If you don't, I just might."

I could smell Mia's sex drip from within her panties. There

was a tug at my core—Mia wanted Drew. I panicked, and in a sharp breath I blurted out, "He is one of my targets." I just couldn't stand the thought of Mia claiming Drew for herself. At least with me, he'd only lose a small portion of his soul—if it were up to Mia, he'd die at her kiss, perish at her touch, decay from deep inside her.

"Really?" She tilted her head, reading me. "How very . . . interesting." Although she didn't sound all that interested.

"Is that why you're here? To check up on my work progress?"

Lexi scoffed, a guttural laugh that rang out with disgust. "Don't be ridiculous. We are far too busy to come down here simply to talk with such a lower immortal."

Mia held up a hand to silence her assistant and smirked. "Now, now, Lexi. We all know Monica is more than your average succubus. Both in strength and history." Both of which I had heard before but never quite grasped why. Kayce was older, stronger, and more successful than me, yet she was constantly overlooked by our Queen.

Lexi's mouth snapped shut in response. Even if she wanted to defy Mia, it would be almost impossible. The bond between a Queen and her minion was extremely hard to sever. When the Queen requested something, all of us had little choice but to comply.

"We are here," Mia continued, "to investigate the murders that have occurred in this section and to meet with Lucien. I believe I smelled you enter Hell's Lair during our meeting. Clearly he is having trouble keeping his sector in control. We can't have sloppiness in any location."

"There is no way this is Lucien's fault," I interjected. "These murders happened under all our noses."

"Oh, I know." Mia looked at a perfectly manicured nail. "And you are all to blame. But Lucien gets paid well to be in his position, and the burden falls on his shoulders. If he doesn't sort this all out soon, I will have to bring someone in who can. And . . . *dispose* of Lucien properly."

Lexi breathed in sharply at the mention of Lucien's disposal. "My Queen, that might be a little harsh. Perhaps, let me stay behind. I can help gain an understanding of just what we're dealing with now. It might be as simple a solution as bringing in a mind reader."

Mia sighed, seemingly bored with the conversation. "Very well, Lexi will stay longer to sort out the details and run the investigation."

Lexi smirked from behind Mia—a twisted, sadistic grin. At least with Lexi looking into things, someone would be looking out for Lucien's best interests.

I suppressed a groan and simply stood there as Mia went on. "We are touching base with all lower immortals to ensure that you all understand the danger here in Las Vegas. Be on the lookout for anything suspicious, and if you feel anything strange, make it known to your superior."

I wasn't sure if Lucien had told Mia of my lack of powers, yet. Based on how bored she seemed with me, I assumed not. I didn't want to get Lucien in trouble for not alerting them, but even more than that, I didn't want to get *myself* in trouble, either. "Well, I'm not sure this has anything to do with the murders, but this morning I lost most of my powers."

Mia's head snapped up, eyes suddenly wide and interested. "You've lost your powers?" I nodded and looked over at Lexi, who stood there, showing no emotion. On one hand, she was probably elated at the fact that my life was being threatened. On the other, her job was now to help protect me. "This is very interesting, indeed," Mia continued. "I'm not sure how much of this case Lucien revealed to you, but up until now, the victims have been very low-powered succubi. Usually a succubus that just recently came into existence. Immortals who did not know how to use the full capacity of their powers yet. You may be the first target over fifty."

"He's upping the game," I said.

Mia raised her chin and looked down at me with slanted eyes through the feathers of her long lashes. "You realize this being wants to kill you."

"Yes." I squared my shoulders toward her.

"And that you might very possibly die in our attempts to catch this outlaw."

I stared her in the eyes, unblinking. My knees quivered, and I knew she could sense the fear. I kept my voice steady. "I understand."

"And by death," Lexi continued Mia's thought, "we don't mean just losing your mortal body, being sent back to Hell. You will cease to exist on either plane. Your entire entity will be gone."

I nodded, feeling my throat wad up like cotton. Something about Lexi's smile when she explained succubi death made my skin crawl.

"And there's no trace of any arcane magic at the crime scenes?" My Newton's Cradle was still clicking, and Mia's eyes glanced down at my bag, smirking with a knowing grin.

"We have found no hint of magic at the crime scenes. But that doesn't mean the acts themselves weren't carried out by an immortal. It simply means no magic was used in taking their lives."

Drew walked up with a latte in a to-go cup. "Here you go— one extra-creamy latte."

Mia took a sip, running her tongue along her lips. "It's perfect," she purred.

Drew's eyelids drooped at her scent—impossible to resist. He leaned into Mia, intoxicated by her presence. She leaned into his listless, loving gaze and parted her lips. I wanted to scream out—I had declared him as my target. Our Queen, for all her faults, was always good about keeping her word and abiding by the rules set by Saetan. I bit my tongue, pleading with whatever God would have me to save Drew from Mia. His lips parted, millimeters from her poisonous mouth. Just as I thought she was going to touch her lips to his, she looked over at me. "I'll be watching." She turned and swayed her hips out the door, disappearing with Lexi at her side.

Drew snapped out of Mia's trance almost immediately. "What was that all about? Looked like you all were discussing something pretty serious."

"They work at, uh, the strip club. I mean, they're from the corporate offices—like the CEOs. Not sure if you've read the paper, but there's been a string of . . . um, disappearances lately. Some of our strippers are missing."

Lines around Drew's lips and eyes deepened. "Oh, my God. Do they have any idea where they are? Have they been abducted?"

A sob rose in my chest, but I swallowed it down, shrugging my shoulders. "No one knows where they could be. They suspect some sort of kidnapping or—or maybe even . . . something worse."

"Worse than abduction?" Realization flickered across his face. "Oh. Are they doing anything to protect the rest of their dancers? Are you safe?" Concern pinched at the creases around his eyes and his mouth straightened with seriousness.

I smiled at his concern, resisting the urge to lift my hand to his face. Instead, I squeezed his arm in what I hope was a not-*too*-friendly way. There was a tingle as I touched him. It was as though my body was trying hard to steal life from anything it could. It craved it, needed it, and yet could do nothing to satisfy itself. But there was no sizzle at our touch. No sweet relief of soul within my body. The tingle was not me stealing any of his life—simply an attempt to do so. "I'll be okay, Drew." But I knew this was very much a lie. I had no idea if I would be okay. In fact, it was very likely that I would *not* be okay. I pulled my hand back and tightened my hold around my purse. "I should go."

"Why?"

"I just—I'm not here working. You have stuff to do. I should go home."

"Why don't you just hang out for a while? I'll make you a caramel mocha latte."

I turned away from him and wiped my index finger beneath my eyes.

"Monica?" His voice was soft.

My eyes filled with tears and I didn't say anything more; just stood there, lowering my chin so that he wouldn't see me cry.

"C'mere." Drew took my hand, leading me to his back office.

"But the register," I said through sniffles.

"Genevieve can handle it," He made a gesture toward the other barista working and then lead me to the back. Sitting me down on his desk, he placed a tissue box in front of my nose.

I snatched the top tissue and dabbed my eyes. "Sorry." It was all I could manage to choke out. I crossed my legs, suddenly very aware of the fact that I'd never looked such a mess in front of Drew. *Ever.* My hair was always smooth and well kept, my makeup never ran, and my clothes never wrinkled. But today—today I was a mess. I could feel the mascara streaking down my face and saw the results of black smudges on the tissue. My hair was frizzing around my face, and for the first time ever, my jeans didn't fit exactly right. I had forgotten about all the ways being human sucked.

"It's okay." Drew put his arms around me, his muscular chest pressed against my cheek. I raised my hand to his bicep, and my body trembled at the touch. He sighed as he held me. "Your boss at the club—what's his name?"

I reluctantly pulled away from his grasp. "Lucien," I said while attempting to daintily dab at my eyes, knowing the effort was pointless.

"Right, Lucien. Is there anything he can do to help? Can they hire bodyguards or something for you all?"

I shrugged. "He's sort of going to be my bodyguard, I think. He mentioned something about staying the night with me."

"Oh." Drew's voice dropped. "I didn't realize . . . I mean, are you two . . . friends?" There was a note of hesitation in his voice.

I paused to look up at Drew before answering. "Yes. We're friends."

"Oh."

"But not lovers."

"Oh . . ." *Was it me, or did his voice lift slightly?* "Good."

My tears had almost stopped. The relief in his voice made me smile. "Good?"

"Well, yeah," He took a step back from me and put his hands on his hips. His white Hanes T-shirt wrinkled beneath his fingers. "It would be hard for him to remain levelheaded if you two were more than friends." His eyes darted around the office uncomfortably, trying to find any spot to focus on other than me. "It might put you at more of a risk."

I stood up from Drew's desk and took a step closer to him, closing the gap he had created. I was all too aware of my body. My lack of succubus powers felt amazing for the first time all day. "Or it could have worked in my favor. The passion and adrenaline of having a lover protect me could make him stronger."

He swallowed, his breathing shallow and heavy. "Yes. But— you're *not* involved with him."

I slowly rotated my head from left to right, shaking it to say *no*. "Not like that." I took another step and Drew's back hit the wall behind him. My nose came to his Adam's apple. I flicked my tongue out to taste the soft skin at the hollow of his neck.

He groaned, and I pushed my pelvis against his, feeling his firmness pushing through the denim of his jeans. Nibbling his neck I traveled up to his jaw, exploring his skin—the taste of salt and flesh on my tongue. When I reached his mouth I paused. We stood there, lips millimeters apart, looking into each other's eyes. I breathed in as he exhaled, drinking his breath like water. I brushed my lips gently across his, their softness like rose petals, velvety and smooth. I had never allowed this indulgence before. Never walked this tightrope of emotions. There was a flutter of excitement deep in my core, like I had swallowed several butterflies. It was a nervousness I hadn't felt in years. Decades.

"Monica, I don't think we should . . ." I put a finger to his lips to stop his words.

"Shhh," I whispered, and slipped my arms out of my back-less shirt, letting it fall away to the floor. His body tensed beneath my hands, and I lowered them to his waistband, running a fingernail along the edge. He closed his eyes and his head fell back against the wall. I let my lips trail down his jawline, across his neck, and I peeled his shirt off of him, throwing it to the ground.

"No," he said, suddenly loud. With two big hands, he pushed me away, holding me at arm's length. "No," he repeated softer this time. "I can't, Monica. I'm sorry. I can't do this to Adrienne."

I didn't move for a moment; I stood completely frozen and slowly rotated my head up to look at him. *Well, this is new,* I thought. "You two have only been dating for a couple months." When you're a few hundred years old, two months was nothing.

He scoffed. "What difference does that make?"

I opened my mouth to speak and then shut it again. Nothing I was going to say right now would change this situation. Yes, Adrienne was cheating on him—but he didn't know that. Yes, he and I had a much stronger connection. And we had known each other for much longer. But to Drew, that wasn't enough to justify cheating on his girlfriend—a fact that made me both love and hate him all at once. My stomach twisted. I'd *never* been turned down before. Not for sex—not for a date—shit, not even for a small favor. I thought about what I must look like—the messy hair, the smeared makeup, my puffy eyes—my chest grew tight and I turned away from him. I couldn't allow him to see me cry again.

"Monica, please don't be upset. I just—" His voice dropped out.

"You just can't do that to her. I know. I get it." I snorted and wiped my eyes as secretly as I could. "It's fine, Drew." I shrugged but didn't turn around, slipping my shirt back on over my head. From the rustling noise behind me, it sounded as though he was doing the same. It felt as though a hippo had sat down on top of my chest and refused to move, the weight of it slowly crushing me.

A hand rested on my upper arm in soft, reassuring strokes.

I couldn't turn around yet. It hurt too much. I didn't want to see his pitying stare. "I'm sorry—" My voice was slowly becoming more steady. I didn't want to give up on Drew yet. Not when we only had a limited time to be together. One of two things was going to happen—either my powers would be restored or I would die. Either way, I wouldn't get the man. And that bitch, Adrienne, sure as Hell didn't deserve him. And maybe I didn't either, but I would not rest until he knew the truth about her. "I didn't mean to make you uncomfortable." I pushed my sadness aside to make room for a new calm, assertive energy. "And I definitely don't want you to regret something that could be so amazing." I turned to face him, not caring as much about my splotchy cheeks anymore. "Because it would have been. Amazing."

He nodded. "I know." His knuckle brushed across my jawline, picking up a stray tear that had fallen. He held the tear up to my lips. *"Kiss your tear. And forever it will disappear.* Something my mother used to say to me long ago."

The hint of a smile curved my lips and I lowered them to his finger. My tear was wet and salty. Its taste lingered on my mouth like a ghost.

"Know what you need?" His voice perked up, putting on a happy face for me.

"A glass of wine and a strong vibrator?"

He laughed at that. "Well, maybe," he said, "but I was thinking more along the lines of an evening out at my church's event. There will be dancing and drinks. It'll be fun."

It was my turn to laugh. "You are all about getting me laid tonight, aren't you?"

"Not laid. I just want to see you happy."

Sighing, I couldn't help the small moan that escaped from my mouth. "I think I'll stick to my vibrator. I never have to worry about lulling conversations or awkward mornings after with her."

"Aw, c'mon." He sat down on his desk, crossed his feet at the ankles, and nudged me with an elbow. "It would be good for you to be around people tonight." Another pause. "Besides, what about Wills? Could he come, too?"

Shit. I totally kept forgetting about Wills. Probably a bad sign, right? "Right. Wills. We're supposed to meet for drinks tonight."

"Bring him along to go dancing. It'll be fun."

I smiled, getting up to head toward the door. "We'll see."

"Monica?" he asked. I paused but didn't answer him. "We're okay, right?"

I nodded before opening the door and slipping out. I only had a few hours to find Adrienne and prove to Drew that his girlfriend was a lying, cheating bitch.

10

There were only a handful of things I knew about Adrienne.
(1) She worked as a cocktail waitress at a Hooters-like pit
downtown. It was known to be a meeting place for a certain in-
famous Latino gang. (2) She loved to shop at Toyland Gifts—
the cheapest adult toy store in town. Believe me, there were
high-class places to get your bedroom accessories—Toyland
was not one of them. (3) I knew she was cheating on Drew . . .
but I had no idea with whom.

Not only this, but I had no more invisibility—no more
powers to disguise myself—and had little choice but to find
these facts on my own.

As I exited the coffee shop, the Newton's Cradle in my bag
started going nuts, clicking with fury. As I got closer to my car,
I saw Julian leaning against the passenger side door. I smiled—
Jules could always make me smile. Though the feeling was not
always reciprocated, as I could tell by the grim expression
on his face. "Back so soon?" I tucked a frizzy stray hair behind
my ear.

"I wanted to see you again"—a smile flickered across his eyes—"as your friend."

I crossed my arms, pressing my breasts together. "Friends? Since when are you back to being my friend?"

He pushed off my Toyota and stepped closer to me. "As a mortal, you're technically no longer a succubus. It's easier to be your friend when you're not . . . 'feeding' off my Heaven-bound souls." He used air quotes to emphasize the word.

"But I *don't* feed off of moral men. I leave your people alone."

"I know." His eyes twinkled and he stayed silent, watching me in a quiet regard. After another moment, he continued. "But it's still hard to watch. Even though I know you're trying to be as good as you can, your behavior is still . . . painful for me to see." His crystal blue eyes glistened. Blue like ice. Eyes so deep, I could swan dive right into the center of them.

The lump in my chest shifted to my throat. "So . . . you came to tell me . . . *what* exactly?"

"I just wanted to remind you that your slate has been wiped clean now that you're back to being mortal."

"*Sort of* mortal," I interjected.

He ignored my interruption. "But if something were to happen to you—that is, if you were to die, there's always the chance you could be forgiven." He put two hands on my shoulders. They were sturdy and reassuring. "Monica the succubus's soul was scarred. Monica the mortal is not yet tainted."

I shifted my feet, a little thrown off by his sudden change of attitude. The way he stared through me sent a chill up my spine. I shrugged his hands off of me despite their reassuring touch. "Are you telling me that if I die, there's a chance I could go back to being an angel?"

He looked as if I had struck him across the face when I moved away from his touch. "Not exactly. I don't know if they'd allow you to be an angel again . . . but they may let you back into Heaven." He took another step closer and rested his forehead to mine. "You could come back to me."

I wrapped my arms around him, allowing the embrace; letting it warm me, encompass me. "But Mia said that death would mean a complete lack of existence."

Jules scoffed at that. "Mia has no idea what would happen to you if you were to die now. Nobody knows, really, what happens to the souls of immortals when they perish."

I pushed away from him for the second time in only a few minutes, my eyes searching his for answers. "So what are you telling me? Should I end my life here on Earth as a chance to get back into Heaven?"

"Of course not." He chuckled at the absurdity of the suggestion. Heaven 101 is that you cannot take your own life. His eyes remained closed and he pulled me back into him for another small embrace. It was in no way sexual—a rare feeling for me to be held by a man whose erection wasn't pressing into me. "That would be a sin. But keep your soul clean. In case you do pass—you'd at least have a chance for salvation."

He was the one to pull away this time. His hand still in mine, he turned to leave.

"Wait!" I clenched my hand around his before he could disappear. "You said you can be my friend while I'm no longer a succubus, right?"

He paused before answering. "I could always have been your friend. I chose to stay away."

Ouch. "Then stay with me today. Help me do a little sleuthing. It would be nice to have the company."

Eyes narrowing, he studied my face. "What kind of sleuthing?"

"Drew's girlfriend is cheating on him. I need to find out who with."

"Why?"

"Because Drew is a great man. Too good to be wasted on a

woman who doesn't appreciate him." I knew he could see through my slim reasoning.

"And you're the woman who would appreciate him, right?" His face was soft despite his pain.

I nodded. "You said yourself, God doesn't punish love."

"How do you know she is adulterous?"

I made a noise like air escaping from a leaky tire. "Have you seen Adrienne? Of course she's cheating." He said nothing, ignoring my petulant tone. "Okay, fine. Her aura was red."

"That could be any number of things. It could be adultery. It could also be that she was around death that day. Or maybe she's a stripper like you. The lust from the men around her could be the aura you saw."

Damn. I knew he was right. "But—but usually, most often, you see the red aura when someone has cheated."

"Yes—usually."

"Right. So—will you help me today?"

He shrugged. "If you promise me that you will not pass judgment on Adrienne. And instead of searching for evidence of adultery, I ask that we search for the truth. Whatever that may be."

I swear I almost vomited in my mouth a little. "Yeah. Sure. The truth." *Which is that she's fucking around on Drew.*

With one hand, I hesitantly ran my fingers through his long blond hair, soft as feathers, brushing it back from his face. He grabbed my hand, stopping my touch sharply.

"Wait," he said, and walked toward the back of the lot. It was then that I saw Kayce's car parked there. He leaned down and said something to her, after which her engine purred to life. Finger to forehead, she saluted while driving past.

"Calling off the protective detail, I see." I smirked as he approached me.

"There's no reason for two of us to be around. I gave her the afternoon off."

*   *   *

Toyland Gifts was even tackier than I remembered. Cheap, plastic, battery-operated toys lined the walls. The kind of toys that break after two uses.

Julian jumped back, startled as we turned the corner and walked directly into a fake, silicone vagina. His face twisted, horrified, and he spoke through gritted teeth. "When you asked for my help, I had no idea it would involve *this.*"

"If it makes you that uncomfortable, you can wait in the car."

"It's too hot outside." His voice was reminiscent of a grumbling teenager.

"I'm not going to be too much longer. Just go"—I glanced around the store—"go . . . stand over by the piercing section. Not a whole lot over there to make you uncomfortable."

Hands shoved deep into his pockets and shoulders slumped, Julian sulked over to the piercing area.

Down the aisle from where I stood was one of Toyland's workers. An older man, maybe midforties, burly and covered in tattoos. I tried smoothing my hair with my palms before walking over to him.

"Hi there," I said with a cheeky smirk. "I'm looking for someone. . . . I think she comes here quite often."

He didn't return my smile but didn't walk away. "Oh yeah?" His voice was gruff.

I nodded and raised my chin confidently. "Yeah, her name is Adrienne. She's about this tall." I held a hand over my head. "Blond hair, usually wearing a ton of makeup." I tried not to, but I had the feeling my sentences were tinted with my annoyance of the woman.

His eyes narrowed at me. "Yeah, I know Adrienne. What 'bout her?"

"She's my sister." I rolled my eyes at him as if saying *you know how that is,* but his gaze didn't change. He maintained that cold, steel look. "I've been trying to find her all day. Do you know where she'd be right now?"

"If you're her sister, why don't you just call her?"

There was a long pause where we maintained eye contact. Finally, I returned with, "Because we had a fight. I don't want to make up over the phone."

His narrowed eyes softened, if only a little. He nodded, scratching at his goatee. "Let's see. It's Saturday, which probably means she's at the karaoke dive with that guy she's seeing."

Bingo. "Um, which guy is that?"

He looked confused at the question. "Same guy she's been seeing for months. Damien. They always meet here, stand in the back corner chatting quietly. I don't give them shit about it, since they always purchase something."

"Right, right. Damien. So he'll be at karaoke with her?"

He shrugged, bringing two bulging, inked shoulders up to his earlobes. "Probably. They were here not too long ago. They usually come in on Saturdays, before she sings, to pick up . . . stuff."

Thank Hell he didn't elaborate on what they bought together. Ick.

"Thanks a lot. Is the karaoke bar close?"

"Take a right out of here and go straight. It'll be on your right. It's called The Shak."

I thanked him again, and before leaving I picked up a black wig in a bob cut. Walking to the checkout counter, I caught a glimpse of Julian, still standing next to the piercing counter, arms folded. Next to him sat a peroxide-bleached woman with tits larger than my head. She had her shirt off and was chatting to Julian as a man pierced her nipples. She had the most atrocious southern accent I'd ever heard.

"Well, I just don't even have no feelin' in my titties since the surgery! I just thought to myself, what a perfect time to get me that piercing I'd always wanted!"

I grabbed Julian's elbow and pulled him away from the visual that would no doubt haunt him for the rest of his existence. After paying for my wig, we hopped back into my car, where I adjusted the black bob.

Starting the car, I looked over at Julian and raised an eyebrow. "How do I look?" I gave him a crooked smirk.

He sort of smiled back and leaned over to adjust the fake hair. "I like the blond better, but I suppose this will do." He pinched my nose before pulling away.

It was only a short drive to The Shak, but as I pulled into a parking space, the reality of my lack of preparation flooded me with insecurities. Turning the car off, I let my head drop onto the steering wheel in defeat. "I can't do this. Not without my powers."

"Yes, you can. All we need is a game plan for going in there. Think. Where is Drew going to be tonight?"

"At some sort of church party." I spoke without picking my head off the wheel.

"Okay—do you have the address for that?"

I nodded, sat up, and reached into my pocket to retrieve the scrap paper he gave me this morning.

"All right," Julian continued. "So, we essentially need to keep you away from Adrienne because she might recognize you. But whoever her man is, that's who you have to convince to come to the couples event. With Adrienne. Drew will have to see them together with his own eyes to believe it."

The plan itself wasn't so bad. "But it's not like this dude of Adrienne's is going to want to go to a *couples* event at a *church*." Wow, I hope I wasn't this dense when I was an angel.

It was Julian's turn at an eye roll. "Monica, c'mon. Seriously? You *lie*."

Wow, was I dense or what? "Oh. Right. Maybe I could say it's a swingers' party or something. . . ."

"You're on your own there."

"And you could tell Adrienne about it while I convince her man—this Damien guy—to go."

"You expect an angel to lie for you?"

"Damn, I forgot." It's been a while since I'd hung out with an angel. I could see him flinch out of the corner of my eye at my language. "But you can flirt with her, right? That's not against any sort of moral angel guideline, right?"

"As long as the flirting is not a lie."

"If that means that you have to legitimately be attracted to her to flirt, then we might have a problem." I got out of the car with as much confidence as I could muster. "Let's go."

Inside The Shak was about as dirty and dusty as it was outside on our Vegas roads. My heels slid across the gritty floors, and I stepped in a very questionable puddle at the far end of the bar. I could hear Julian's breath quicken beside me. The dank bar was definitely not his scene. I felt a sudden rush of gratitude for all that Julian was putting himself through just for me. I grabbed his hand and squeezed, stealing a sideways glance in his direction. He was staring at me in that thoughtful, sad way.

Resting one elbow on top of the bar, I kept Julian's hand in mine. "What would you like?" I asked, slapping the counter. "Club soda? Water with lemon? Virgin rum and coke?"

"I'll have a glass of pinot noir, please."

I raised my eyebrows and he tilted his head in return with a smug smile. "Jesus drank wine. Lots of it."

"All right, then. Two glasses of red coming up."

While the bartender poured, I scanned the room, the black wig itching at the base of my neck. Then I saw her. She sat next to a tan, dark-haired man—her hand on his knee. She had her legs crossed, and her other arm was wrapped tightly around his neck like a boa constrictor locking in her prey.

"There they are." I nudged Julian and gestured across the room.

He looked utterly repulsed by their display. "Charming," he sneered, taking a sip of his freshly poured wine. "So now we just wait for them to split up for some reason. Then you go plant the seed in his mind about tonight's party."

There was something familiar about his wavy, dark hair. His Mediterranean skin tone. His eyebrows, so prominent they casted a shadow over his eyes—and it hit me. He was the guy I had seen at Hell's Lair the other night. The night I met Erik. The night Wills came back to me. My head was spinning, and I took a large gulp of my wine, drinking half the glass in one swallow. He looked over in my direction, making eye contact with me for just a moment. My heart raced.

Julian's face creased as he watched me. "Everything okay?"

"Oh, just fine," I said, seething. *Had Adrienne sent him to the club to check up on me?*

It took about twenty minutes—just long enough for Damien to finish his beer and for Adrienne to need to use the bathroom. "Okay," I whispered to Julian, "you go wait by the bathroom and intercept her when she comes out. I'll talk to Damien."

Julian reluctantly skulked over to the bathroom as though I were his mother sending him to the corner for a time-out. I, on the other hand, put on as much charm as I possibly could sans any power. I saw Damien out of the corner of my eye waiting to place his drink order—he was very striking. Beautifully sculpted bone structure—the perfect rigid nose and square jaw. Not to mention a deep chin dimple (the kind that I'm an absolute sucker for). How in the Hell does Adrienne keep snagging such gorgeous men?

I leaned into him and knocked his empty pint glass with my elbow just enough to warrant an apology but not so much that it would fall over and break. "Oh, my gosh, I'm so sorry! I'm such a klutz!" I brushed my fingertips over his forearm.

He angled his body toward me in an arrogant manner, breathed in deep, and let the air escape gently through his lips—it was almost as if he'd been waiting for me to make the first move this whole time. His arrogance made me almost gag. Either that or straddle him right here at the bar. "Hey, gorgeous. Think nothing of it. I saw you when you first came in—you're hard not to notice. That your boyfriend with you?" His eyes flashed with a spark of humor.

I bit the inside of my cheek, feeling the rush of his compliment. The very nature of being a succubus immediately warrants me to feel competitive with other women. I loved the fact that he noticed me even though he was with Adrienne. I shook the thought away—it was petty and I should be above that. I cleared my throat and spoke in the most husky voice I could manage. "Not *really*. We're together . . . but we like to switch it up a lot. If you know what I mean."

He raised an eyebrow and ran his hand along my waist to the outer edge of my thigh. I could feel the sweat gathering at the nape of my neck, threatening to drip down my back. "Oh yeah?" he said. "Maybe you and I should grab a drink tomorrow night, then."

I looked up and saw Julian catching Adrienne as she exited the bathroom. She melted under his attention, and the two chatted as though they were old friends. If I didn't know Julian better, I would have thought that he actually was flirting with her. As if there was some sort of angel-redeeming quality in that girl. The thought alone made me inwardly snort. I knew I had Damien for only another couple of minutes. I touched his chin dimple with my index finger and trailed my nail down his Adam's apple, chest, and muscular abs until I reached the waistband of his boxer briefs. "I was thinking maybe tonight? Your girl could even come with . . ." I flashed my eyes toward Adrienne, still under Julian's romantic spell. Whatever he was saying to her was definitely holding her attention. "We love to . . . swing." I tugged at his waistband and let it snap back onto his stomach.

"So, like a swap party? We might be into something like that." He glanced over his shoulder at Adrienne talking to Julian. "She certainly seems to be enjoying your *golden* boy over there."

Something in the way he said *golden* struck a chord with me. Had he heard of me? Did he know my nickname? I searched his eyes for a hint of recognition as to what Julian and I were, but he simply stood there, eyes unbudging. I nodded. "Yes, Julian is—*very* gifted. As I'm sure *you* are, too." I leaned in closer to Damien, so close that I could smell the musk of his aftershave. While I don't condone cheating, I could see how this guy would be a temptation for any girl. It's like being on a diet—if you're going to cheat, it might as well be with gourmet ganache . . . not a candy bar you can buy at any gas station.

He groaned and squeezed my hip. "You're hard for me to read. You walked in and I thought you looked like such a good girl—an angelic glow surrounded you. Now"—he leaned down, lips inches away—"you remind me of the devil. In disguise." He tugged gently on my wig, just enough for it to slip slightly.

I gasped, straightening the wig before anyone could notice. Was the wig *so* obvious? It had been expensive and made from real hair. . . . It should have been hard to detect. Feeling a bit unsettled, I grabbed a pen, wrote the address on a napkin—making sure to omit the part about it being at a church—and handed it to him. "And, uh—when you arrive don't be deterred by the unusual location. We're just really kinky."

He pocketed the address. "We'll be there—both of us." After throwing down some money and picking up his new pint, he leaned in close to my ear again. "By the way, your bag is clicking." Then, with a small flick of his tongue, he licked my ear—just enough to make me melt.

11

Eastern Europe, mid 1700s

I stood for hours outside of a random church I had found, tears cascading down my cheeks. The stones beneath my feet were sharp, and the thin slippers I wore did little to protect me from their jagged edges. How long had it been since I was an angel? An hour? A day? There was an itch burning from my loins. A need that I didn't understand. I knew I was no longer a creature of Heaven. Did that make me a demon? With the little that I had been taught of demons, I knew that traditionally your maker is supposed to become your mentor. Teach you the ways, introduce you to the rules of the underworld. Where was my maker?

All I knew was what I had been taught as an angel—and back then, I had learned that if you pray and ask forgiveness, He will forgive. Because I am His daughter—He loves me.

The sight of the enormous wooden cross on the outside of the church was the most beautiful sight I had seen since falling from grace. I fell to my knees at the sight of it and called out to God, arms outstretched toward the Heavens. I crawled to the double doors and reached out with my right hand to grab the handle. Heat shot through me, as though a fire were on the other side.

The handle was scorching and seared my palm. I fell backward, screaming, writhing on the stone walkway. I lay there crying. When I opened my eyes, a priest stood above me. An older gentleman with kind eyes and silver hair. I gasped for breath and looked around the area, unsure of how long I had blacked out. The courtyard was empty besides us—I mustn't have been lying there for long. Otherwise, he would have called for help.

The burning on my hand was still painful, but his eyes, his kind eyes, were a distraction from the pain. They were the eyes of Christ. Helpful, loving.

"My dear child. What has happened to you?" He didn't touch me, just knelt over my body in concern.

And I didn't dare move. I lay there staring at him, crying. Gasping through my sobs, I choked out some words. "I just wanted to find my way back to God."

He nodded. "Pray with me." He reached out wrinkled fingers and grabbed my hand that had not touched the church door. Once again, searing pain rippled through me. And this time, the Father could feel it, too. I screamed and pulled my hands into my body.

He stumbled backward, frightened. How could he not be? This writhing woman, dressed in hardly anything, had just burned his hand with a simple touch. "Heavenly Father," he whispered, staring at his hand.

"Leave me! Leave me be!" I wailed.

I thrashed around, an attempt to frighten him away. But before leaving, he stood over me once again and said a prayer. He signed the cross over my body, careful not to touch me for both of our sakes.

12

"But how could he even *hear* the clicking, Jules? I couldn't hear it in the loud bar and I still have my strong succubus senses."

Julian was staring out the window with one hand raked through his hair. "Okay, okay, calm down." He dropped his hand into his lap. "Maybe he just has very good hearing for a mortal."

"No." I shook my head, keeping my hands on ten and two of the steering wheel, "He made mention of other things. He called you a 'golden boy' and he said that I was angelic before he realized I was a 'demon in disguise.' Then he tugged on my wig. . . . He *knows* something."

Julian crinkled his nose without answering.

I hesitated a moment before continuing. "Julian—you haven't been very talkative. I can't sense immortals anymore, but *you* can. Is he immortal?"

"No," he said curtly.

Julian doesn't lie. But he doesn't always tell the whole truth, either. "Okay . . . but you could sense something, right?"

"Yes." It was just as curt an answer as before.

"Why won't you tell me?" I threw one hand up, exasperated, keeping the other on the wheel.

"Because I can't."

I exhaled in a disbelieving way. "I thought you were here to help me."

"I am." He looked at me with sweet eyes. "I am here to help you find the truth about Adrienne and to protect you. That is all. I cannot interfere in any other area of your affairs."

Affairs, nice. "Jerk."

"Okay, maybe that was a poor choice of words."

"So you can't tell me what Damien is?"

"No. You have to figure that out yourself." There was a moment of silence that surrounded us like a thick fog. "May I make a suggestion, Monica?"

I grunted a response.

"I think you should let Drew figure out about Adrienne on his own."

I snorted at that suggestion. "But he won't. He's too damn trusting."

"You need to have faith in your friends. Drew is smart; *if* there's anything to know, he would figure it out eventually." There was another long pause. "Besides," he said, "your efforts could be put to better use in finding the murderer who is currently looking to kill you."

"Please, Julian. I have no powers. How could I possibly be of any use in that investigation?"

"You'd be surprised. They could use someone like you on the case."

I wanted to roll my eyes but resisted the urge. My hands clenched around the steering wheel.

As if reading my thoughts, Julian continued. "Oh, the demons they've got investigating the case are good. Kayce and Lucien—even Lexi," His jaw tightened with her name specifically. "But you must have some sort of link with the killer that

you do not know. And if *you* do not know the link, then surely
the rest aren't going to know what it is. You're an integral part
of this investigation, whether you choose to admit it or not."
He rolled down his window and stuck his head out of it, blond
hair blowing in the breeze as if he were a golden retriever. "Besides, I don't think Mia and Lexi necessarily care about your
life. They care about restoring order to Las Vegas. That's their
number one goal. And currently, Lexi is excited over the fact
that if Lucien loses his position here, he might be brought into
Mia's offices to work as a minion."

I pulled over to the side of the road. This was too much to
digest while also focusing on driving. Putting the car in park, I
turned to face Julian. "Well, why do *you* care? He's not a good
guy. He's not on your side. What would it matter to you if Lucien goes off to the underworld as a file clerk?"

He sighed and his blond hair fell into his eyes. "Lucien takes
care of you. And he loves you as much as he is capable of loving
another. For all I care, he could be Saetan himself so long as he
looked out for your best interest."

The raw truth of words caught in my throat and tears welled
up in my eyes for what felt like the millionth time today. "Shit,"
I whispered.

Julian winced. "Monica, please. Shhh." He put his thumb to
my lips, and I lightly kissed it. He smelled like peppermint—
fresh with a cool spice. It was a smell that up until now had
been fading fast from my memory.

"I have received word from counsel. I am allowed to aide in
keeping you safe. Not because it's you," he added, "but because
there is a killer on the loose, terrorizing this sector."

"Is Damien some sort of clue? What does he have to do with
all of this?"

"Start driving, Monica. We're going to be late." He leaned
across, grabbed my seat buckle, and clicked it in for me.

* * *

I still wasn't quite convinced that I was the right person to find the murderer. Surely *someone* else was better equipped to find this being. The only powers I had were heightened senses. That certainly didn't leave me with much confidence in myself. But I wasn't left with many options. However, whatever choice I made, I ran the risk of dying—*and maybe being sent back to Heaven.* But then again, Julian might be wrong about my current mortal state. Mia could be right in assuming that I would cease to exist in death. I just couldn't see Julian playing fast and loose with my life like that. And how the fuck did Adrienne's lover factor into all of this?

"You're awfully quiet over there," Julian said, curiosity flooding his ocean-deep eyes.

"Just thinking," I stated while pulling into the church's parking lot. It was a little before eight and I had told Damien to come around eight thirty. I hoped they wouldn't be early. I needed to time to prepare myself.

I unbuckled my seat belt, then pulled on the handle of my door. Julian's touch on my elbow stopped me from exiting. "Julian. It's too late to back out now—I might as well see the plan through. Then I'll figure out what to do about my . . . situation."

He smiled at me, suppressing a chuckle. "That's all great, Monica. I was just going to ask if you planned to keep the wig on for the rest of the night."

Shit. "Oh. No, of course not." I slipped the black bob off my head, and a tangled mess of blond came falling past my shoulders. I sighed and tried to fix it with my fingers. It was relatively hopeless. "Damn," I said, looking at my reflection in the rearview mirror.

"May I?" There was a glistening in his eyes—a longing for permission.

"Please. Do what you can." I turned my head to him and his fingers twisted around my strands. It felt amazing—like the most delicate and beautiful scalp massage I've ever had. I moaned and leaned into his hands, tilting my head back. His touch is hard to explain; it's firm, but there's a beautiful tenderness to it. He tugged at my hair just enough that the pull tingled, but not so much to cause pain. It was . . . Heavenly—for lack of a better word.

Minutes passed and I leaned into his cool, hard body across the parking brake. He kissed my forehead, lips lingering with a cool, tingly sensation. "There." He tilted my body up and out of his lap, where I had collapsed in a relaxed heap.

When I looked back into the mirror, my hair was gorgeous. Shiny, sparkling, as if I had shifted it myself, except it was glowing like it used to back when I was an angel. His kiss on my forehead glittered and shimmered in the moonlight. Only angels and ArchDemons would be able to see the mark. The thought warmed my insides. The blessing would last only for as long as I was mortal, but such a tender moment wasn't going to slip from my memory anytime soon. "Thank you, Jules."

"It won't keep you safe from all danger," he said, touching the kiss with his forefinger, "but I'll know if you're hurt."

"Man, you angels are a tricky bunch," I said through a smirk.

He smiled back at me. "*You* should know that better than any of these other demons."

I stared at him in my passenger seat, sitting there so perfectly with beautiful golden hair that tumbled down to the middle of his neck. I realized how much I needed Julian. I needed him in my life whether I was succubus, angel, or mortal. I leaned across the car, unable to stop myself, and wrapped my arms around his neck, pressing my cheek next to his. I held him tightly in the embrace, and when I pulled away there was a moment's hesitation as we sat there nose to nose. "What would happen," I asked, "if a succubus kissed you right now?"

His breathing grew heavier and he cleared his throat. "You're not a succubus." I pressed my body slightly more into his chest. His skin was cool to the touch and felt amazing in contrast to Nevada's balmy spring evening.

"Monica." He spoke with his lips still only a breath away. "No. We can't." He firmly lifted me off of his body and back into the driver's seat.

It was the second time in one day that I had been rejected by a man I loved. Okay, well, one was an *angel*—not a *man*. But still. This whole mortal thing was not all it was cracked up to be. "I'm sorry. I was just—"

"I know." He cut me off. "It's okay, Monica. It is your nature to seduce."

My face flushed. "I miss you, Julian."

"I know that, too."

His voice was so stern and cold. I nodded, unable to say anything more. The tears were rising, welling up in the bottom of my eyes. I blinked them back, sitting there saying nothing more.

"Maybe I should wait here." Julian's gaze was fixed in a firm scowl.

"What? *No*, I need you in there with me, Jules. I can't do this without you."

He huffed a sigh, slumping his cheek into the palm of his hand.

"No, seriously, Jules." I touched his hand, "I *physically* cannot go in there without your help." I gestured to the church, knowing that even though most of my succubus powers were gone, entering a church might be painful. Having an angel by my side would surely negate any demon burn.

He said nothing and just sat there staring out the window. After a minute, he gave my hand a tight squeeze. "Ready to go?"

We walked in together, linked arm in arm. I looked at him to my left, and his presence was an immediate comfort. He was rigid, standing stick straight as though he had a rod shoved up his—well, you know. Our almost-kiss really seemed to have shaken him up quite a bit. Mental note: Never attempt to kiss the angel again. At least not without permission. And let's face it—that would never happen. Not if I returned to being a succubus.

The event wasn't in the sanctuary of the church itself—more like a recreational area. We stood outside the double doors of the rec center, waiting to go in. Above them stood a giant cedar cross, carved ornately with some sort of ivy design. Even though it wasn't the sanctuary, it was still intimidating as all Hell. The cross looked almost identical to one that stood out in my memory from long ago. And here I stood inside a church. There was no pain. No burning. Just me and Jules—our arms still linked.

When I first fell from grace, I had a few aimless days on my own. Soon after, Lucien sought me out though it was outside of his call of duty. I was never quite sure how or why he knew how to find me. He showed me the ways of the succubi, had taken me to my Queen, and had even tried to locate my maker—mostly so he could berate him for his lack of responsibility. And here I was doing nothing in return. Julian was right—it was my turn to save Lucien. And if I managed to stop my own murder while at it, even better.

I leaned into Julian so that he could hear my whisper. "Okay, I'll try to find the murderer. But, honestly, Jules, I don't know where to even start. And I still need to do this tonight. It's too late to turn back now." I shrugged and let my free hand fall to my side, slapping the outside of my thigh.

Julian smiled at me, his rigid demeanor relaxing slightly. *I knew you would come around.* His voice boomed in my thoughts.

I jumped at the sound of his voice—I completely forgot that an angel's kiss has the potential to connect our thoughts. My eyes narrowed at him. "Wait—can you hear *all* my thoughts now? Even the naughty ones?"

He laughed. "I can read all of *your* thoughts. You can hear only what I allow you to hear."

"So say something. Let's test this puppy out." I raised an eyebrow and waited.

He stared at me some more, looking down with his chin angled away from my body.

Wiejfdisy.

Wiejfdisy? What the Hell is that? "Wait a minute—gibberish doesn't count, Jules. Think something real." I did a mental eye roll at his childish response.

He sighed. "Fine." Pressing his lips together, he looked to the ceiling, formulating the exact thought he wanted to share. *I'm sorry I pushed you away so aggressively.*

He lowered his eyes from the gaze at the ceiling and glanced back down at me, a look of regret washed over his face.

The corners of my mouth curved into a small smile. "I'm sorry, too. I should have known better than to make advances on an angel. More than two hundred years of not having to control my impulses—it's hard to start now."

Even though you are mortal, your succubus instincts still control your body. You have nothing to be sorry for.

I nodded, though I didn't entirely believe him. I sure felt like I had a lot to be sorry for. "Could you do me a favor?"

"I suppose that depends." His stance became rigid once again, fearing the worst.

"Don't eavesdrop on *everything* I think. Leave me some privacy, please."

He nodded, just one sharp movement. "Very well. I will do my best to leave as many of your thoughts alone as I can."

"Thank you," I whispered, and swayed to bump his arm with my elbow.

He shot me a crooked smirk and bumped me back.

As Julian and I were stealing playful glances, the double doors swung open and there stood Drew. I took in his look—well-fitted jeans, a button-down plaid shirt with opaque buttons, and slightly scuffed brown leather shoes. His eyes grew wide as he realized it was me standing before him, and a giant smile spread across that glorious face of his.

"Monica? You made it!" He ran over and picked me up in a giant hug.

It happened so quickly, but I managed to rest my cheek momentarily on the soft cotton on his shoulder, breathing in his cologne mixed with the smell of coffee that consistently permeates his clothing. My feet lowered back down to the floor, and when I opened my eyes, I saw the two men staring at each other. Julian's body language was still rigid and his eyes were unmoving, assessing Drew. Drew shot me a sideways glance, unsure of how to react to this scrutiny.

"Hi." Drew stuck out his hand ceremoniously. "I don't believe we've met."

"No. We haven't." Julian raised a hand to Drew's, eyes not leaving his face.

Drew looked over at me, his forehead crinkling with concern, no doubt curious about where Wills was.

I screamed out Julian's name in my head—hoping if I thought forcefully enough, he'd be able to hear me. *You're creeping him out, Jules!*

Julian grunted—whether it was aimed at Drew or in response to my thoughts, I wasn't sure.

On an exhale, Julian finally let his mouth twitch into a smile. "Julian," he said quietly.

Drew shot an unsure glance back at me. "Julian, pleased to meet you. I'm Drew, Monica's boss. Are you two—uh, together?"

"Does it *look* like we're together?" Julian smirked, taking my hand and wrapping it around his elbow as if I were a debutante about to be presented to society. "We arrived together."

I rolled my eyes, pulling my arm away from his. "We are not *together* together. Though, yes, we did come here together." I scowled quickly at Julian before returning my gaze back to Drew. "We've known each other for, like, centuries. I just wanted to have the comfort of a *friend*"—I glanced again at Julian, whose mouth was turned upward into a serene smile—"here tonight."

Drew looked relieved. "Oh, phew! I was afraid I had offended you, man, when I hugged our girl, here."

Julian puffed a laugh. "Of course not. I'm happy to see Monica has friends who influence her for the better." He looked over at me, a bemused smile on his face. "You should come to more of Drew's church functions, Monica."

I put my arm around Julian's back, pinching him as hard as I could. "Yes, well—we all know my work schedule makes evening functions a bit difficult." I spoke through gritted teeth hoping Julian was reading my angry thoughts at that moment.

"Right, right. I'm sure both Julian and I have heard all your excuses, Mon." He winked at Julian, his smile creating creases that framed his mouth. "I'm just glad you could come tonight." Drew extended his hands toward the rec room and mocked a bow. "There is food and drink inside. Please help yourself to anything." He looked directly at me. "And have fun."

My stomach growled again at the mention of food. This whole eating thing really gets in the way of your day, doesn't it?

13

The room was decorated rather plainly. There was a bar area serving beer and wine as well as some nonalcoholic beverages, and a small buffet had a variety of potluck items that people from the church had no doubt whipped up themselves. Several tables had long tablecloths that had seen better days. The lighting was low, and candles sat clumped on every table and in every corner. Must have been Drew's attempt at romantic lighting.

I went to town on the buffet, loading a plate with mac and cheese, potato salad, little mini cheeseburgers, and every other homemade goody sitting atop the dollar store serving platters. When I looked to my right, Julian stood there, staring.

"Slow down, Monica. Gluttony is a sin, you know."

"Yeah, well, so is jealousy, mister."

"What's that supposed to mean?" His eyes looked hot as he turned to face me.

Between chewing, I answered him. I wasn't about to put down my food for this conversation. "You don't fool me. You usually regard people so warmly—particularly churchgoers. But with Drew, you held back. Jealousy." I emphasized the word by poking his chest.

Julian shoved two hands into his black flat-front pants. "I was *not* jealous."

"Well, what would you call that little display, then?" I didn't tear my eyes away from the potato salad. Man, what did those little church ladies cook these in? Holy water? I'd never tasted anything so delicious in my life.

"I'm protective of you. That is not a sin."

"So there was no jealousy whatsoever?"

"None."

I lowered my eyes at him.

He stared right back at me, his eyes softening. "I promise you, Monica. I was just getting a read on Drew. And I have to admit—I like him. He's a good person to be in your life. I can see why you don't want to pursue him. His soul is pure."

I sighed and dug into the mac and cheese. No arguing that.

"Julian!" Drew's voice boomed as he walked toward us. Next to him stood a curvy, brunette girl. She looked about twenty-five and was wearing a black skirt, cardigan buttoned up to the middle of her throat, and pantyhose. *Pantyhose.* In the middle of Vegas in spring. Crazy bitch.

Drew approached us, and the girl looked shyly at the floor. "Julian, this is Annie. She's been part of our parish for a couple years now. I thought the two of you might have a lot in common."

Sheesh, he was right about that. She looks wholesome enough to be an angel on Earth.

Jules smiled at the girl with the warmth and exuberance he normally showed in a first meeting.

"Hello." Julian took Annie's hand. "You Make Me Feel So Young" started playing on the iPod speakers. "Would you like to dance?" Julian didn't wait for a response. He swept her into

his arms and fox-trotted her off onto the dance floor in one
fluid motion. Damn, that angel was smooth.

I heard that. His voice rang in my brain.

Well, shit, I thought back.

Drew looked over at me. "You look beautiful tonight." His
eyes flicked down to my feet, taking in my entire look. Obviously, I was dressed the same as earlier, but with the fixed hair
I'm sure I looked a hundred times better.

I flushed. "Thank you."

"I'd ask you to dance, but I'm sort of on duty here tonight."

Julian's voice entered my head again. *He's lying to you. He
doesn't want to dance because he* can't *dance.*

"Shut *up,*" I said, clenching my jaw.

Drew looked shocked. "Excuse me?"

Shit. Shit, shit, shit. "Not you! My phone . . . it won't stop
buzzing."

Drew nodded. "Ah. Probably Wills. Don't you two have a
date tonight?"

Double shit. "Yep, it's probably him checking up on me. Be
right back."

I grabbed my phone and headed outside into the vestibule
area to dial Wills's number.

"Hello, Pocket," he said, ever so cheery. Clearly he did not
know of the Hell that was my day.

"Hey back at ya," I said, trying desperately to match his
tone.

"I'm going to see you tonight, right? Not backing out on me
again."

"Nope, I can't wait." I was smiling. It was the truth, even if
I did keep forgetting about him. Things were so easy with
Wills. Of course, I knew that Lucien or Kayce would be a step
behind us monitoring me. They'd just have to deal with it. I
needed the human touch—or demon touch . . . whatever. And I

was getting it tonight. Despite whoever would be listening. "I just wanted to check in and say hello."

"Your *hellos* are always welcome."

At that moment, a familiar high-pitched, high-maintenance voice echoed in the rafters as the front door swung open. "What in the world is this about, Damien?"

"Wills, I gotta go!" I spoke in a hoarse whisper and snapped my phone shut. I looked for an escape, a place to hide, but it was too late. Damien entered with a blindfolded Adrienne. He flipped the blindfold off her eyes, and I was seen before I had even hung up my phone.

"What are *you* doing here?" Adrienne put her hands on her hips, her acrylic nails digging into her cheap jersey knit dress.

"I met your lover earlier today. I told him this was a swingers' party. It seemed right up your alley."

Damien stood behind her and stifled a laugh, just a slight quirk of his lips upward revealing his amusement.

"A what? A swingers' party?" Adrienne put two fingers to each temple and rubbed in circles.

Her voice lowered, the squeaky girly tone to it completely disappearing. "Look—I'm not messing around here, Monica. What is going on here? Where are we?" Her collagen-injected lips were pressed into a straight line. Her hair had been recently bleached again and stood tall and teased. She looked ridiculous and slutty in her strapless dress.

"I'm kinkier than you think, Adrienne."

Damien's half smile turned into a whole smile. "I'd believe that." His eyes glistened with lust, and I couldn't help but smirk back at him.

Adrienne's jaw just about fell out of its socket, and she glared at Damien, her eyes wide, exasperated. "Not *you*, too." She rolled her eyes and took a step closer to me. "I see it constantly—every man falls all over himself to get to you. Back off."

"All except one." My voice was quiet.

"Don't be so sure," she whispered. She turned away, and her heels clacked toward the door. "I'm leaving. You're coming, right?" She held open the door, gesturing to Damien.

At that moment, Drew poked his head out from the party area. *Triple shit,* I thought.

"What's going on out here?" He looked around, first noticing Damien and me, and then he saw Adrienne at the front door.

She shut the door and turned as though she had just walked in. "Drew! Hi, baby!" She squealed and ran toward him on her toes. Guess it proved too difficult to run in her heels. Amateur. But there on her face—outside of the shock of seeing him—I saw happiness. And love. She nuzzled her nose into his neck, kissing him. She was actually happy to see him, even caught red-handed with her lover.

"Adrienne? What are you doing here?" Drew hugged her back, though looking absolutely confused. He looked over at me still standing there in front of Damien. "And who's this?"

"This? Um, I don't know . . . must be a friend of Monica's." Adrienne looked at me, her eyes pleading.

I looked at Drew, the poor schmuck. He planned this cute little event and here I was about to ruin the entire night for him. Julian was right—it was a terrible idea. Drew will learn that Adrienne's wrong for him, eventually. I shouldn't be the one to bring him to the conclusion—he needs to get there himself. "I've only just met him today." I sighed. It wasn't even a lie— Jules would be so proud.

Damien pulled me into his body in an embrace, and I pushed myself off his chest, trying to wrench myself from his grasp. "Damien, this is Drew. Drew, this is Damien." Damien gave a crooked smile and held out a hand to Drew, not releasing my body in the process. Drew took his hand hesitantly.

"Nice to meet you," Drew said, flashing a wary eye at me. "Mon, can I talk to you a second?"

I slipped out of Damien's grasp and we stepped away from Adrienne and her boy toy. "Monica, I don't know what is going on here, but you have a nice guy waiting to go on a date with you tonight. And if I'm not mistaken in reading Julian, I think you have another nice guy inside pining after you. I'm trying not to read too much into this third man you've invited here—"

I held up a hand to silence Drew. "I met him briefly. Julian was standing right near me when I invited Damien to this event. I didn't invite him *with* me. He's actually dating a— *friend*—of mine." I said the word *friend* through gritted teeth, hoping he wouldn't notice.

"Oh." Drew nodded, but his eyes narrowed, still skeptical. "I just assumed by the way he was looking at you." He glanced back over at Damien. "Just be careful—he looks like trouble."

I nodded, and Damien was looking at us, his eyes glistening as though he could hear our every word. "He sure does, doesn't he?"

14

London, 1939

Wills *showed up exactly on time. His pocket watch chain was draped from his suit vest. His initials were scrolled in ivory script at the end of the chain that clipped to his vest. He wore pinstripe pants and wing tips with a fedora perched on top of his head. I saw him enter when I was peeking out from behind the curtain. I could see his erection from where I waited behind the stage—he must have already been anticipating me, remembering the little preview I gave him in the park.*

I sang a Gershwin tune that night, and he sat in the front row smiling from ear to ear. It was as though he barely noticed the fact that I was half undressed or shaking my body around as I sang, tassels flipping in the patron's faces. He just smiled and clapped eagerly as I finished my number.

Afterward, we went to a late dinner. "Do your parents have any idea where you are or who you're out with?" I asked as I took a bite of the meat pie.

He laughed. "Of course not. My parents only ever care about what I'm doing when they consider it wrong."

I nodded. That was me, I thought. Wrong in every sense of the word. It made sense, I guess. A good boy betraying his parents' wishes with me. "So, I'm a sort of rebellious phase, I guess?" I gave him a wink, though the disappointment at this realization weighed heavy in my voice.

Wills's head tipped to the side, his eyes thoughtful. "Not exactly. I just—I like you."

"You like how I make you feel." I pushed around some carrots on my plate.

"Well, yes. But I also think you're funny, smart, and talented—quite the canary. Not to mention beautiful."

I smiled at that. "Smart, huh?" It was rare any man saw through to my mind.

His mouth quirked and he returned my smile. "Indeed. The girls my mum chooses for me are always proper. Educated, but not necessarily intelligent."

He was a good soul. I could see that in him so clearly—even from our very first meeting. I still wasn't sure if he was a virgin, but he was definitely of strong moral standing. Heaven-bound for sure. And he seemed to genuinely like me, not just for my body or my sexuality. Just one night, I told myself. I would allow myself pleasure with him for just one night. A night to enjoy sex for once. One night wouldn't kill him. Maybe take a week off his life at most. What could one night hurt?

"Wanna get out of here?" I crossed my arms over the table after pushing my plate away.

"Go where?"

"Show me London—your London." I knew only the seedier places of the city.

We didn't get far, though. Within moments of exiting the bistro, his hands glided around my hips, which back then I used to shift slightly curvier to fit the times. I pulled him into an alley. A cat mewled from the garbage and ran as he pushed me against the brick siding of a building. His fingers slid down over the linen fabric of my skirt and cupped my ass, pulling me in for a kiss. He hesitated the moment before our lips touched.

My body itched for the fix. The ache pulled from inside of me. I knew from experience that my skin was flushing and that itch, that damn itch, was practically gnawing at me from inside.

He pulled back just slightly, his hands moving from my ass to cup my face. He stared at my eyes, his own flitting back and forth from my right eye to my left, and his eyebrows drew together. "This is going to sound ridiculous," he said, "but I could swear that your eyes just got bluer. I thought they were more of a greenish blue, but now—now, they're electric."

I swallowed. The pull to devour his life force was shifting me. I grabbed his lapels and pulled him into my kiss. I could feel how good his soul was, and though I wasn't stealing any of it yet, I imagined it filling up inside me. It would be stronger than anyone I'd had yet. It was that rush that kept me kissing him, deeper and longer, wrapping my tongue around his. I pulled away abruptly. The itch was still there, even stronger than before. To experience the force of his soul, he'd have to come. He'd have to come by my touch for me to feel any relief.

"Wow," he said breathless. "Just, wow." He picked me up and spun me around the street, running down the alley with me in his arms.

I threw my head back and laughed, holding my arms out, feeling the wind rushing past my face. I knew his adrenaline was just a side effect. An evolutionary effect that ensured our conquests wouldn't tire on us before we acquired their souls. It would wear off in a minute. He was high on me. I enjoyed the energy, his excitement while I had it. Soon it—and he—would be gone. A man like Wills doesn't stay with a woman like me for long. It made me feel better about this one night. There was no way he'd risk his reputation in a relationship with the likes of me. Just one night.

He lowered me, and we now stood deeper in the back of the

alley. "Wills," I said, "have you ever been with a woman before?" The question was out of my mouth before I had the good sense to stop it.

He cleared his throat and looked to the ground. "Is that something you really want to talk about this moment?"

I nodded and brushed my lips across his.

"Very well." His voice took on a business-like tone. As if he were discussing a property he was looking to acquire. "Once before. At university."

"I bet you two didn't have a chance to get too . . . adventurous, did you?"

His brow furrowed, uncertainty washing over his sweet, boyish features. "Well, we weren't in an alley, if that's what you are suggesting."

I closed my eyes, shifting away my panties from beneath my garter and thigh-high stockings. I lifted a knee and rested it on the wall behind him. "Run your hand up my leg. See what you find," I purred into his neck.

His fingers were tentative, trembling as he traced the inner area of my thigh. Up he traveled, tantalizing, tickling. I wasn't sure if he was taking his time on purpose to torture me or if it was newbie nerves. He pinched the garter and snapped it back against my skin, the sudden sting causing me to whimper. I pushed my pelvis against his, urging him to move faster.

When his touch finally reached the V between my legs, he gasped. "Monica," he said on an exhale, "where are your knickers?"

I couldn't help but chuckle at the innocence of the question. "Do you care?"

His head fell back against the brick, eyes closed. His fingers once again moved in circles over my sex. I was swollen and ready for him. With a free hand I opened his pants, grasping his hard length with a firm grip. He grunted and kissed me again, lips urgent. His kiss was perfect—a delicious mixture of gentle

*and rough with just the right amount of tongue trailing my lips
and teeth.*

*He flipped us so that my back was now against the wall.
Body heat radiated off of him, and his erection brushed against
my moist folds. Both of his hands wrapped under my backside,
and he lifted my feet from the ground with a naturalness that
took my breath away.*

*I locked my legs around his waist just as he entered me. He
was big enough to stretch me, mold me. I cried out, tugging on
his hair to bring his lips once again to mine. He glided in and out
in slow, controlled strokes, and using his thumb he rolled my
clit. An orgasm waved through my body, and he held me closer
until the tremors ended.*

*Beads of sweat formed along his face, and his lips pressed into
a line. "C'mon, baby," I said, bracing my arms on his shoulders.
I was able to bounce on him in faster thrusts. "Let go. You're so
close, aren't you?" The fact he had held out this long was note-
worthy for a man with such little experience.*

*His thrusts grew harder, more frantic, with less of a rhythmic
pulse and more of an animal lust. He groaned and fell onto my
body, elbows around either side of my head. His member pulsed
inside of me, and I felt warm liquid flow into my body. The itch
immediately subsided, like aloe on a burn, and the tingling sensation chilled me to my fingertips. His life flipbooked before me,
very similar to the vision I had seen the other night. A dull life;
he would go to war, come home with an injury, and live his life
working a dull job. His death was slightly different than the last
vision, but he'd still live to be an old man.*

*He lowered my legs to the ground and stroked my face with
gentle fingers. Handing me a handkerchief from his pocket, he
muttered an embarrassed apology.*

*I pushed it back to him. "I don't need that. I love the feel of
you dripping between my legs." With a finger, I gathered some
of his juice from my inner thigh and licked it away.*

His face turned pink and his mouth dropped. "Good heavens," he said. "I think I'm ready again." I put a hand on his member and sure enough, he was at attention once more.

With a smile, I took his hand. "Now, now, I wouldn't want to tire you too much on the first night."

"So there will be a second night?" His eyes were wide and hopeful as he followed me out of the alley, adjusting his pants.

A lump formed in my throat. Oh, how I wanted there to be a second night. He had plenty of years left. Wasn't I entitled to some happiness in my existence? One more night couldn't hurt, could it?

15

According to Lucien, no one else was allowed to know about my situation. Meaning, I had a secret to keep from Wills on our date. And this was like the mother of all secrets. Because when your life is being threatened, all you want to do is crawl into someone's embrace and let them hold you and say everything is going to be okay.

I had to rush over to the bar right after Drew's church thing. I had already canceled on one date with Wills this week—I could not cancel twice in two days.

Julian and Lucien must have made contact at some point during the night. As Julian and I left the church, I saw Lucien parked across the street—as far away from the blessed area as he could get.

I rolled my eyes when I saw him, growing more and more annoyed at needing a bodyguard. Julian flicked a glance at me but said nothing. I guess Lucien's better at handling my temper flares.

"Shut up, Monica," Lucien said as I approached him. "This

is for your own good. Even if you're too fucking stubborn to admit it."

"Yeah, yeah," I huffed.

Lucien looked at Julian. "I see you've given her the kiss." There was a pause as Julian gave one sharp nod and something silently passed between the two men. "So much for not interfering, huh?"

"The counsel has given their blessing." Julian looked over at me and wrapped one of my blond curls around his finger. "Have a good night, my friend." He checked over his shoulder, and with a *crack* he was gone.

"Why does he always talk like he's in a fucking Jimmy Stewart movie?" When I didn't offer an answer, Lucien moved on to the next important matter. "Where to now?"

Lucien followed me to the bar so that Wills wouldn't see us arrive together, and I sent him into the pub first to get a table close to us . . . but not so close that he'd be spotted. He was reluctant to go in first, to leave me out in the parking lot alone, but I reassured him with the fact that it was not late yet, the parking lot was still fairly crowded, and I would come inside within five minutes of him or he could send out the SWAT teams.

I saw the front door to the pub swing open and looked at my clock. 9:24. I had to enter those doors at exactly 9:29 or Lucien's head might explode. I leaned my head back against the driver's seat and closed my eyes. To my left, there was a tap at my window. I jumped at the noise and turned to see a large, shadowy figure standing outside. "Go away." I tried to sound tough, but my voice sounded squeaky, even to me.

"Not a chance." His voice was gruff—it was familiar but I didn't recognize it immediately.

The figure leaned down and rested both elbows on my car; his forearms crossed one over the other. He pulled the hood of his sweatshirt down and Damien stared back at me. I looked at the clock. 9:25.

I exhaled and unclenched my hands from the wheel. Damien was mysterious, but I doubted he was dangerous. "What do you want?" I said, rolling the window down.

"Well, hello to you, too. Is that any way to welcome a guest?"

"You're not a guest, you're an intruder."

There was a hint of a smile behind his eyes. He didn't seem like the kind of guy who smiled much. "I'm a guest. Because of you, I'm going solo tonight."

"What *are* you? You're not a demon. You're not an incubus. You're not an angel, that's for sure. And I think you've been following me even before today. I saw you at my club the other night."

The corner of his mouth twitched. "I'm not an angel, huh? What makes you so sure?" He was leaning into my window now, his face inching closer and closer to mine.

"I know angels. I just . . . I *know*, okay?" I looked at the clock. 9:27.

He nodded. "Okay. You're right—I'm not an angel. An angel would never do this." He leaned all the way and pressed his lips to mine, wrapping a large hand around the back of my neck. His tongue twisted around mine like a ribbon, and his hand traveled down to my breast and gave my nipple a hard twist. I shoved his shoulders away from me, and he finished the kiss with a bite to my bottom lip. I tipped forward in my seat, falling into the steering wheel. My pocket was warm and I touched a hand to it, remembering the stone Erik had given me earlier that day. I reached my hand in and felt the smoothness of it against my fingertips and the same tingly sensation that I experienced with Drew earlier this morning.

"Seriously. What are you?" I asked, breathless.

He backed away from the car. "I'm no angel."

"Yes, I think we've established that," I said, clutching my shirt around my breasts.

His mouth curved into a smile. "You better get inside. Your ArchDemon and your *date* are waiting." He said the word with a sneer. "And as for the club—I wasn't following you. I just like to watch beautiful women dance."

I walked in just as the clock turned to 9:30. To me, that meant I was just barely on time. To Lucien, I was sure it meant that I was late. I saw Wills sitting at a little, circular high top table by a window. I didn't dare look around for Lucien. I knew he was there somewhere; that's all that mattered.

Wills smiled widely at me as I approached. "Hello, Pocket. Beautiful, as always. What else should I expect from a succubus, though, huh?" His accent gave me a gooey, warm feeling in the pit of my stomach. He stood and pulled me in for a kiss. "Hmm, you smell different tonight—like peppermint. Not your usual lavender scent." His eyes traveled over my face, lingering for a moment on my forehead where Julian kissed me.

I nodded and kissed him again. "New shampoo," I said.

"Ah," He stood and pulled out a chair for me. "What can I get you to drink?"

"Gin and tonic, please."

He gestured to a waitress and placed an order for our drinks, then turned back to me, still smiling. "Monica, we have so much to catch up on."

I nodded. He obviously knew that I was a succubus back in the thirties when we were an item. And now that he knew the terms of being a succubus, he probably understood that the reason he had died before his time was quite possibly a direct result of me. "Look, Wills." I started to give my apology as our drinks were set down between us. "I feel like I need to explain . . ."

"Yes, yes, yes," He cut me off in a very British manner and held up his pint. "But first a toast. To reconciliation."

I held up my glass, a sad smile splayed across my lips, and

clinked it against his. After a sip, I continued. "Wills, I don't know how much you know or understand about the succubus lifestyle, but there are things you should know about me. I'm not the typical succubus."

That seemed to get his attention a bit. "Oh?" he asked, eyebrows raised.

"I was an angel. An angel for quite some time. Most succubi are made directly after their human lives end—they're recruited, much like you were. They trade something for their souls. I, on the other hand . . . I'm more like a fallen angel–succubus hybrid. I'm still not sure exactly what happened, it was so long ago. Lucien took me in almost immediately, taught me the rules and took care of me. Most succubi don't have a conscience. But the fallen angel in me has regret. With each soul I steal, I hate myself a little more."

Wills was nodding, his eyes soft and eyebrows creased together. "Why are you telling me this, Monica?"

"Because I'm sorry. Back in London—I fell for you. And I stayed with you longer than I ever should have. And I'm sorry. I'm sorry that I took your soul." There was a catch in my throat as I apologized.

"Oh, Monica." He grabbed my hands across the table, "Don't apologize. I loved every minute of it. If I had to do it all again, I would. You remember our first date?"

I nodded. "You came to see me dance, then we went to dinner."

"Well, you're half right." Wills leaned back in his chair, "I came to hear you *sing*. Then we went to dinner." He paused. "Why don't you sing anymore?"

I shrugged. "There's not exactly time for it. And to be honest . . . singing isn't the turn-on for men as it was back in your day."

"Our day," he corrected.

"Whatever."

"But you were beautiful. Your voice was beautiful."

I didn't answer and played with the stirrer that rested across the edge of my drink. Lifting the glass to my lips, I drained the remaining clear liquid, ice clinking against my top lip in the process.

"Care for another?" Wills gestured to my empty glass. I nodded and forced a smile.

He ran off to get us another round and I heard my phone buzzing. I grabbed my purse and dug in. Somewhere at the bottom, tucked under Altoids and the stupid Newton's Cradle, I grabbed my phone to find a text message from a private number.

You think you're good enough to make an angel fall? Think again, dear succubus. You are good—but not that good. Most angels are not quite so pathetic as you were.

My hand trembled, and I dropped the phone onto the table. I turned and looked at Wills, who was actively engaging the bartender with ordering our drinks. My eyes darted around the bar trying to find Lucien. *Where was he sitting, damn it?* Maybe he shifted to be invisible. Isn't he supposed to be watching me?

With the phone still in hand, I pushed the redial button. Since the number was private, I couldn't see the area code or anything. My eyes darted around the bar while I waited for a phone to ring. Maybe the person was here and I'd see them pick up their phone. On the other end of the line, an operator's voice came on stating that the number had been disconnected. Shit. I didn't know what I had expected, but I was both worried and relieved that the call hadn't panned out.

My outer leg felt so warm. Not hot, like dangerous hot, but just a natural body warmth. I pulled the stone out of my pocket and rolled it around my fingers, letting the smooth rock comfort me. I set the stone down and forwarded the text to Lucien. Maybe he had a way of tracking the number.

"What's that?" Wills's voice startled me and I jumped in my

seat, hiding my phone from him quickly. It wasn't until I saw him looking at the stone that I realized he wasn't talking about the text message. He set another drink down on the napkin in front of me.

"I'm not exactly sure. It's, um, some sort of stone. A . . . friend gave it to me. Not exactly sure what I should do with it."

"A *friend*, huh? The kind of friend who pays you for your time?" He paused for just a second before I could answer. "Never mind. Don't answer that."

"Wills, I—"

"Why don't you turn it into a pendant? I know a guy. Could do something really beautiful with a piece like this." I ignored the fact that he cut me off. Best to let that subject pass without a fight.

"Yeah?" My voice rose at the end of the word. It was so beautiful, it would make a gorgeous necklace.

Wills pocketed the stone. "Sure. I'll have him do it tomorrow for you." He leaned down and kissed me sweetly on the lips. "In the meantime, why don't we finish these and then go back to your place." He kissed me again, less sweetly this time.

It only took twenty minutes to down our drinks and go back to my apartment complex. It didn't take long before we were making out in front of my apartment. Wills leaning against my door—me leaning on Wills, with my arms above him against the doorframe. "We should probably go in, huh?" I said, taking a deep breath in between kisses. He had his hand up my shirt and was caressing my breast.

He leaned in for another kiss before answering, swinging me around so that my back was against the apartment door, switching places with him. His hands traveled down to my waist and tugged on my low-riding jeans. He pulled back, lips red and swollen, and his thumbs hooked into my pants. "Ever since you, all those years ago I have this affinity for doing the risqué in public."

"Oh yeah?" My one eyebrow twitched into a devious arch and I half smiled at him. "Well, allow me, then." I undid the top button of his pants and wrapped a leg around his waist. That's when I heard it—a tearing sound coming from my jeans.

Wills pulled away and looked at me curiously. "Did your trousers just *rip?*"

My face grew hot and a blush rose from my breasts up over my neck, creeping onto my face. I did *not* just rip my pants. Fuck. How much did I eat today? Humans don't really gain weight this quickly, do they?

"Monica?"

I was standing there like a fish with my mouth wide open. I snapped out of it, remembering what Lucien said about no one else being allowed to know about my missing powers. I debated telling him. He was Wills. My—well, he wasn't my boyfriend yet, but we were headed in that direction. I couldn't lie to him, could I? Then again, Lucien had given explicit instructions.

"I shifted myself to look a bit curvier in the ass—I remembered how much you liked my soft curves back in the day. I guess my clothes just didn't fit this new body well enough." I shrugged and gave my best innocent eyes. The kiss mark on my forehead burned at the lie, but I ignored the sensation and kept looking into Wills's eyes.

"Oh. Okay." His face relaxed, but those eyes of his gleamed with skepticism.

I needed to take his mind off the lie. I grabbed his suspenders and pulled him close to my face. His pocket watch chain clinked against my belt buckle. Our noses brushed and I flicked out my tongue, running it along his bottom lip. He moaned and parted his lips. I pushed my tongue slowly into his mouth and pressed my lips to his, moving my hips against him. His hands once again found my breasts and alternated between massaging them and scratching my back. He moved his mouth down my neck and pulled my shirt down over one breast, licking and sucking at it. My head fell back against the door and I groaned, tugging at his full head of sandy brown hair. I opened my eyes, and off in the dark I saw Lucien's SUV parked, the driver's window directly facing my door. I squealed when I saw it and pulled at my shirt to cover myself.

"What?" Wills looked up at me, startled.

I squealed again in the same way and pulled Wills's head toward me, acting as though it was a cry of pleasure. "I just—I need you. Now. *Inside.*"

He kissed me again, copping one more feel before I pulled out my keys and stuck them in the door. I let him walk in first. Before I entered, I turned and flipped Lucien the bird.

I shut the door behind me and Wills grabbed me into his arms, throwing me roughly to the ground. Usually such a gentleman, I loved when he got rough.

His hands wrapped around the waist of my shirt and ripped it off my body, not caring that a few of the seams came apart and stretched as he tore it off me.

I raised an eyebrow at him. "I could have taken it off."

He growled and lowered his mouth to my breasts, running a tongue along my tight nipple. His hands were already tugging my pants down, and I pulled his shirt off over his head. He ran his hands along my smooth thighs and I made a mental note to remember to shave in the morning. His hands landed at my knees and pushed my legs apart. He hovered above me, breathing in my scent, making me wait for it. I moaned from the ground and ran my fingers into his hair, tugging at him to get his mouth closer to me. He didn't move.

"Not until I say so." His voice was dark, gruff. He leaned down and planted a soft kiss on me, gently running his tongue up the length of my sex. My body shivered, and I wrapped his hair around my fingers, tugging even more. Tortuously slow, he continued those long laps until I was writhing on the floor. Finally, he nipped at my clit and used more pressure with his tongue. He alternated between fast and slow, light and firm pressure. He'd move slowly over my lips and then dart a firm tongue inside me. Back and forth he continued like that until I thought I would explode. I lifted my hips, trying to push myself into him and fulfill my yearning. He moved into a steady pace, lapping at me firmer with each stroke. Using a finger, he massaged me from the inside. Quickening the pace, pumping first one, then two fingers in and out of my wet sex while his tongue flicked quickly over my clit. When I finally came, I thrashed around the floor, screaming wildly. There was no itch. There was no life force to steal. Just satisfying, luxurious orgasms. He pinned me down as I came, still licking at me through my spasms.

The two of us stripped him down until he was naked and he lay on top of me, skin on skin. I could feel his erection pressing against my body, though he had yet to enter me. I slid my hands down over his chest. He had new bumps and raised scar tissue along his skin, and I dusted my fingers over them as though I were reading Braille. My hands ran past his stomach with just the slightest amount of a happy trail, and when I finally reached his shaft, I gripped it firmly. He grunted and sighed as I stroked him. He was long and hard, just as I had remembered him. I cupped his balls with my other hand, gently rolling them around. His hips pulsated with each stroke, and I guided him toward me, sliding him inside. I spread my legs wider, welcoming him, and he filled me entirely. Maybe it was because I was human again and could be hurt, or maybe it had just been so long since Wills and I had had sex—but there was the slightest amount of pain around his length that felt simply delicious.

He moved in and out of me with skilled, fluid movements. My wrists were pinned to the floor, and Wills watched my face, smiling as I moaned and bucked with each thrust. With hands clamped around my wrists, he kissed me as though it might be the last kiss ever. His movements grew more fierce, more animalistic, as we each got more excited. Releasing my wrists, he grunted as his hips rotated, sweat rolling down his boyish face. Harder and harder he pumped himself, and I screamed with pleasure as my body tightened around him. I wrapped my legs around his waist and lifted my ass into the air, shifting the angle at which he entered me from. The tip of his cock hit me deep inside, and somehow it still wasn't close enough. I wanted more of him. I clawed at his arms, pulling him down to me once more. My mouth found his and I pressed my breasts to him, holding his body tightly to mine while bucking against him. He closed his eyes and threw his head back. With one final, hard thrust, he held himself in place inside me and trembled with pleasure.

He rolled away and landed on the floor beside me, sweaty and happy. We lay there next to each other in silence.

"What happened to your leg?"

Shit. "I fell. Drew saw, and I had to keep up appearances that I was hurt. Couldn't have a deep gash healing within seconds of him seeing it. He drove me to the hospital, and you know the rest. He called you, right?" I inwardly cringed at the lie. It was for his own good, though. The more he got involved in this murder business, the more dangerous it would be for him. I sat up on an elbow and ran my fingers over his stomach and up through the little bit of chest hair he had. I trailed my hands across the small scars on his arms and chest, finally landing on the large one that ran horizontally across his stomach. The scar tissue was coarse and angry. He grabbed my hand, darting it out to stop mine from touching him. I cleared my throat, searching for a happier topic. "Looks like you've been working out lately, huh?"

He looked at me out of the corner of his eyes and smiled. "Yeah, well, a century of being alive will make one take care of himself." I continued running my fingers over his body, avoiding the scars this time.

I had never in my life stepped foot inside a gym. If I was going to be mortal for a while, I should probably consider a membership. I thought back to my ripped pants and cringed.

He leaned up on his elbow this time, eyes raking over my body, taking it all in until he finally stopped at my face. He nodded slowly. "You're a legend of sorts among the demons. You know that, right?"

I shrugged and rolled my eyes. I definitely knew that, but I didn't want it to become a weird source of contention between us. Especially since Wills was such a lower immortal. "It's just because no one knows why exactly I came to be."

"Word on the street is that you were tempted by a vampire. He had sex with you and bit you—which would normally turn a human into a vampire. But with you, the angel, it turned you into a succubus."

I swallowed and looked at Wills, thinking of the two "birthmarks" on my leg. His voice sounded hollow. As if he was reciting a story in front of a campfire—not about the woman he made love to only moments ago.

"Is that what they say?" I held his gaze, not daring to look away. "What other 'legends' are there about me out there?"

He nodded. "It's said that you're powerful. Extremely powerful. You should only be a lower-level succubus, but if you harness your powers, you could defeat the Queen. You might be stronger than your Queen."

I laughed at that one. I had seen Mia's power firsthand. I was nowhere near her level.

"And then, of course," Wills said, "there are the stories of you not fulfilling your quotas for the underworld. Demons and succubi admire it about you in their own weird ways. The fact that you stand up for something you believe in. Most of us don't believe in anything anymore . . . but not Monica. Somehow, despite the evil you see daily, you manage to stand up for the ideals you once had as an angel. It's remarkable." He leaned over and kissed me, deep and slowly this time. There was a sizzle in the air, a similar sound to putting raw meat in a hot skillet. The power inside me crackled and my heart skipped a beat. It was a small hint that somewhere inside me, I still possessed some magic. Wills looked at me curiously, obviously feeling the power surge, too. I kissed him again quickly, to distract him. It worked. Within seconds he scooped me up and walked us over to my bedroom, dropping me onto the bed, where we proceeded to have an encore of earlier—in a bit more civilized manner. Our bodies twisted around each other, finding nooks and crannies neither of us knew existed.

Sometime in the wee hours of the morning, I fell asleep nestled against his chest. My ringing phone jolted me awake. Based on the faint and cloudy light creeping in through my curtains, I guessed it was around six.

"Mmph," I said into the receiver.

"Monica? You there?"

It was Drew's voice. Not a bad sound to wake up to, but at this ungodly hour no one's voice would make me feel chipper. "Mmph," I said again. I figured this would get my point across.

A chuckle came from the other end of the line. "Good morning, sunshine. How's the leg feeling?"

"No," I said.

"No, what?"

"No, I'm not coming in early today."

"How did you know I was gonna—"

"It's six-fucking-a.m. What else would you be calling about? You know better than to call me this early to simply inquire about my health."

He sighed, and his pleading was palpable through the phone line before he even began speaking. "Please, Monica. Genevieve called in sick. I tried everyone else first and no one can make it." I didn't say anything, waiting for more. "I'll make you breakfast. Please?"

"And lunch. Something nice. Some griddle eggs and a bagel isn't gonna cut it this time."

He huffed a breath. "Fine, breakfast and lunch. But you have to enjoy both in my company." I could hear his smile.

"Deal." I hung up, and as I threw the covers back, an arm snake around my stomach, pulling me back to bed.

"Where do you think you're going?" His voice was deep, gravely. Rough like old cobblestone streets. He rolled on top of me, and I could feel he was already excited. He pushed his erection into me with a thrust, and I threw my head back in pleasure. I only lived a few blocks from the café—an extra fifteen minutes wouldn't hurt.

Exactly twelve minutes later, I was stepping into the shower and rinsing off yesterday's grime. I looked down at my stitches, careful to keep them out of the stream of water. They were almost healed thanks to Lucien's touch. I wondered how I'd explain that to the doctors. I wrapped a towel around me and peeked out at Wills, who had fallen back asleep in my bed. I shut the bathroom door and swept eyeshadow across my eyelid. He would definitely get suspicious if he saw me physically getting ready for work. Another eight minutes passed and I decided that I looked good enough to make it through the day. I threw some of the makeup into my purse and, still wrapped in a towel, went to my closet for something to wear. I tiptoed past Wills and chose low-slung jeans and a white fitted T-shirt. I stepped out to look in my full-length mirror, hung on the closet door, and there, taped to it, was another note.

Genesis 1:27: When the Almighty created the first, solitary man, He said: It is not good for man to be alone. And He fashioned for man a woman from the earth, like him (Adam), and called her Lilith. Soon, they began to quarrel with each other. She said to him: I will not lie underneath, and he said: I will not lie underneath but above, for you are meant to lie underneath and I to lie above. She said to him: We are both equal, because we are both created from the earth. But they did not listen to each other.

Did you enjoy your tryst last night? I bet you didn't like being pinned down during sex. . . .

"Is that what you're wearing today?"

The sound of Wills's voice made me jump. I crumpled the note and shoved it into my purse.

"I planned to, yes."

"To work?" His lips were pressed together and he was still naked, with just the littlest bit of a sheet covering his most impressive parts.

I nodded and took another look in the mirror. Jeans. White T-shirt. Pumas. Nothing spectacular or weird about it that I could see. I nodded, looking at him with a shrug.

"Dressing sexy for your boss, I see." He flopped onto his back with a dramatic sigh. "Next thing I know you'll be shifting your hair to platinum blond and brittle."

I almost laughed, but his pained expression made me stop. I looked down at my shirt, which was thick, was not see-through, and showed absolutely no cleavage. "Are you kidding me? This is so not the kind of outfit Adrienne would wear."

"Sure it is. On an off day."

I narrowed my eyes at him, steam rising from my ears. "Are you implying that I look like Adrienne on a *bad* day? Is that a challenge?"

His eyebrow shot up. "If the tacky shoe fits."

I looked down again at my Pumas. Pumas are so *not* tacky. Jackass. I had completely forgotten how jealous Wills was.

Even back in his human days. I raised an eyebrow back at him and waited. We stood there locked in each other's gaze, waiting for the other to crack.

Finally Wills exhaled. "Will you please just change."

My eyes lowered to slits and I could feel my nostrils flaring with each breath. I pivoted on my heel and went back into my closet. "*Sure,* darling. What do you propose I wear for the day? My June Cleaver dress? Some Mormon underwear? Oh, oh, I know—I'll just put on my Amish bonnet." Before he could answer, I slammed the door behind me and ripped off my clothes, throwing them in an angry heap on the floor. I found the tightest jeans I could squeeze into and pulled my black thong up high on my hips so it came out of the jeans. I slipped an abs-bearing T-shirt over my head—this one was sheer—and wore a black bra underneath. My cleavage popped up to my chin. I switched my Pumas for peep-toe kitten heels and stomped back out to the bedroom.

"Is this better?" I had my hands on my hips. "At least now I look like Adrienne on a *good* day."

Wills opened his eyes groggily, and his jaw clenched when he finally got a good look. I saw the sheet over his region rise up like he was pitching a tent. I grabbed my purse and hustled out of the room before he could jump up and stop me. My purse was a lot heavier than normal, and I had to use two hands to hike it over my shoulder. I remembered the Smith & Wesson and took a look to make sure the safety was still on. With my head down, I almost ran directly into Kayce, who stifled my scream by covering my mouth. She put a finger to her lips and we scooted outside quickly.

"What the Hell are you *wearing?*" Her eyes traveled down my body.

"It's a revenge outfit." I rolled my eyes and walked with her down the stairs.

Her eyes flicked to my door, recalling Wills. "Ah."

"Anything happen last night? Were you inside the whole time?"

She nodded. "I was invisible all night. I saw nothing. I mean, I *heard* you two. I even had to slip out of your bedroom as unnoticed as possible before he threw you down, but overall it was quiet."

I stuck my head in my bag and pulled out the note and handed it to Kayce. "Then how did this end up taped to my closet door?"

She was quiet while she read it. "I-I don't know. Monica, honest. No one was in your house. I would have sensed them."

"What if they were invisible too?"

She shook her head. "I still would have sensed something. Someone's presence." She paused, thinking, her eyes glancing back to my apartment where Wills lay fast asleep. "What if . . ."

We made eye contact. "No. Not possible."

"He was in your apartment all night, Mon. It's the only explanation."

"I'm telling you, it's not possible. He's an infant demon. And not a very powerful one, at that. Lucien said to perform these incantations you need a very powerful immortal. Wills is not. Besides, I got a text message last night, too." I pulled out my phone and scrolled to the text. "And as I got it, Wills was at the bar ordering—no phone in hand. It's not him, Kayce."

She read the text, and with a sigh handed the phone back to me. "Let's just—I dunno. Let's not rule him out yet."

I nodded, still not liking where her mind was at. "Lucien can mask his power sometimes. Couldn't a higher immortal have done that?"

She looked thoughtful for a moment, chewing that over. "Yes. Maybe. I don't know." Her head dropped into her hands. "You know, that fucking Newton's cradle thing was going nuts all night. I thought it was moving because I was in the apartment—but now, I-I don't know." She rubbed her eyes and ran a hand through her raven hair. "Shit. I should have paid more attention to it."

A tremble coursed through my body. The thought of some stranger, particularly one who wanted me dead, watching us have sex was disgusting. "It's okay, Kayce. It's not your fault. I mean, if anyone with the slightest bit of immortality enters, it goes nuts."

She nodded. "I almost forgot. Lucien wanted me to give these to you." She held up a small device. "This is a GPS tracker." She tucked it in my purse. "Make sure you keep your purse on you at all times. It's just in case we lose your tail. And this"— she held up what looked like bulky new age necklace—"is a panic button. If you get in trouble, squeeze the center of the necklace. It's also a GPS in case you lose your purse in the process of being murdered."

"Nice," I muttered. The necklace was hideous and the kind of thing fucking Adrienne would wear. Combined with the outfit, I *was* actually starting to look like her.

"I know, it's gaudy." She smiled and turned invisible. "So! Off to work we go. I'll be with you until lunch. Not sure who's taking over then."

I grunted in response. I opted to walk to work today since it was only a few blocks and not too hot outside. The threats were becoming much more real than in the beginning. Something about this person watching me have sex was entirely too unsettling. It was early—especially for Vegas. Not too many people out yet. But the ones who were out—were they just going about their day? Or were they following me? I shivered and clutched the ugly necklace in my fist.

16

The café was already open and serving a few customers when I arrived. I whispered to Kayce as quietly as I could. "You don't have to be invisible, you know."

"I know. I don't want to spook our man, though."

Drew looked up as I entered, and his eyes became wide, looking up and down at me. "Um." He stuttered a few moments, finding his words. "Wow."

I slipped behind the coffee counter and tied a headband around my hair. FDA regulations.

Drew cleared his throat and forced himself to look at my eyes, not eight inches lower. "Not exactly the outfit I expected after dragging you out of bed at six a.m."

I shrugged. "I was trying to annoy Wills."

He nodded, allowing his gaze to drop to my thong strings sticking out. "I'm in favor of that." He nodded, and his fingers traveled to the strip of skin not covered by my jeans or shirt. He ran his rough hands across my stomach and hooked a finger into the thong strap, snapping it back against my skin. "I especially like these." His face split into a grin. "Exactly how much does this little bit of floss cover?" His breathing was deep and labored. From where I stood, his jeans looked tight in the front.

"Too much as far as I'm concerned." Goose bumps traveled across my flesh at his touch. His hands were warm and gentle. He looked up at me over his nose, and I felt my chest rising and falling quicker than normal. Behind us, a ceramic mug fell into the sink and cracked in two pieces with a loud crash, breaking our trance.

"Breakfast," I said quickly, looking over at the broken mug. The hungry gaze in his eyes all but disappeared. "You make breakfast, I'll clean this up." I headed toward the sink and picked up the broken shards.

"Right," he said, and snapped his fingers. All the customers were taken care of for now. I was sure we'd have another rush of people soon enough. I wanted my food before that happened. "How about some chilaquiles for breakfast?"

I grinned. "Look at you, being all ethnic."

"My mother was half Mexican," he said matter-of-factly.

"What? No way. You're like, the whitest white guy I've ever met."

He laughed at that, starting to mix the eggs.

"I never knew that." I spoke more to myself than to him.

He stopped mixing and looked up at me. "There's a lot you don't know."

I nodded, not knowing what else to say.

I used the time it took him to cook my breakfast to stock the front with coffee beans and grind up some espresso. Only one other customer came in during this time, so I made myself a caramel mocha. I wrapped my fingers around the steaming mug and raised it to my lips. With a sigh, I took my first sip. Heaven. I closed my eyes and savored it. *Coffee is a lot less messy than orgasms and relationships,* I thought as I took another drink.

"Is it that good?"

I opened my eyes to find Drew standing there with a plate of chilaquiles in hand.

"Better than sex."

He huffed a laugh. "Clearly you're having sex with the wrong men."

I leaned on the counter and held the mug out to him. "Wanna sip?"

He shook his head. "No, thanks. I'm not a fan of all that sugar."

I laughed and rolled my eyes. "You'll never achieve the sort of bliss the caramel mocha gives without a little sugar. It could induce multiple orgasms."

His face creased into a smile. "You're flirting with me, aren't you?"

"No, I'm not." *Of course I was flirting.* I guess I was still getting even with Wills.

"*You are such a bitch.*" Kayce's voice was quiet enough that I don't think Drew heard her.

"Well, here's your breakfast. As promised." Drew set the plate in front of me. "Go sit for a bit. Enjoy it. It's still slow here. I can cover until you're done."

I grabbed the plate and inhaled the scent of cilantro, eggs, and spice.

"Oh, and Monica?" I turned to face him. "If you get a refill, be sure to use protection. Those caramel lattes are a slutty bunch."

I smiled, walking to an empty table and lowered myself to the chair.

"*Psst!* Over here!" came from one of the empty tables to my left. I stood back up and followed Kayce's voice over to the area I thought she was. I hovered over another empty table. "Nope, one more over." I went to the left again and saw an empty table with the chair pulled out just enough for one person to comfortably sit.

I set my plate down and lowered myself into the chair next to Kayce. "So?" I said, quietly holding my coffee mug up to my lips. I felt a bit silly talking to an empty chair, though I was certain no one could hear us.

"Someone cast a spell in here. I could sense the incantation coming from somewhere—for all I know it could have been cast from miles away. It was weird. It didn't feel like a demon necessarily. Whoever it was did not like you being close to Drew. The spell broke the cup."

I nodded. I don't know why I didn't assume that before. It was weird that it just *happened* to fall.

The door to the café opened and in walked George, my favorite incubus. He came over, a bright smile stretching from ear to ear. "Hello, my love." He bent down and kissed each of my cheeks. George was the oldest incubus known to man—he was also Merlin's father. Yes, *that* Merlin. Like from King Arthur's Court. He lowered himself just above Kayce's lap and looked behind him. "Who the fuck is sitting there?" He looked at me, still half squatting over the seat.

I laughed. "Kayce. She's undercover."

"Damn, girl. You could have said something before I stuck my ass in your face."

"What can I say?" Kayce voice had a mischievous edge to it. "I liked the view."

George smirked and shrugged one shoulder to his ear. "Well, what can I say. My ass is perfection. Too bad you're not sixty pounds heavier with a dick. I'd be all over your Asian ass."

George was wearing his typical look. Slate gray slacks tailored to perfection. Blue short-sleeved button-down shirt, tucked in. Black belt, black shoes. Newsboy hat with coarse, curly hair popping out from all sides. Clear skin the color of my mocha latte. Downright delicious.

He slanted his eyes at me. If he could see Kayce, I'm sure she would have gotten the same look. "What's going on here?"

I widened my eyes and blinked innocently. "What do you mean?"

"You're dressed like a whore—very uncharacteristic for our little angel. And Miss Thang there has her invisibility cloak on. I'm not an idiot. Something's up."

"Kayce's avoiding a guy she slept with last night." I was bluffing. My earlobe itched and I refused to scratch it. It was my tell.

George narrowed his eyes and looked around. "And who exactly was her target? The sweet old man sitting next to his seventy-year-old wife? Or the thirteen-year-old boy sitting with his mom and sister?"

Shit. I looked around and he was right. There were only two guys in the room. One was lined up for Social Security and the other couldn't yet *spell* Social Security.

George leaned back in his chair, arms crossed and smiling. Kayce's voice cackled beside us. "I'm babysitting Monica, okay? You can't tell anyone, though."

"And why exactly does Monica need a babysitter?"

No one said anything. I sighed. "Kayce, you're to blame for this. Lucien's going to have your head."

"What-the-fuck-ever. I'll squeeze *his* head."

"Amen to that." George looked over at me, eyes turning serious. "So? What the Hell is going on?"

"Uh, Monica?" I looked up to see Drew standing over me. "Is everything okay?"

I smiled. "Yep. I'm almost done eating. I'll join you soon. Sorry it took so long. Just catching up with George."

Drew put a hand on George's shoulder. "Hey, man, how's it goin'? Haven't seen you around in a while."

"Fantastic, as always." George held out his hand and Drew took it, slapping him on the back as well.

"Well, it's always good to see you here." Drew looked back at me. "Take your time eating. Just wanted to make sure things were okay. You were sitting over here alone talking to yourself for a bit, I noticed."

I crinkled my nose and George laughed. "Just a—habit I picked up from living alone, I guess."

Drew grabbed an empty mug from the table next to us. "Maybe it's time to get a cat then, Mon."

I shuddered as Drew turned and went back to the counter, wiping down a table on his way. My head snapped back to George. "If I ever end up as the crazy Siamese-owning succubus, please just put me out of my misery."

"Awww, your mister is so protective of you. It's cute." He pouted his bottom lip out.

I ate another couple bites of my breakfast and pushed the plate to the middle of the table. "Either of you want the rest?"

George didn't answer, but already had a forkful halfway to his mouth. "I can eat while Kayce explains what's going on."

I rolled my eyes and went back to work.

By one o'clock, I was ready to curl up back in bed. This work stuff wasn't as easy when you don't have people's souls fueling you. Somewhere in the midmorning, I hit my stride. George had left hours ago and I knew that Kayce was switched out with someone. There was a brush against my cheek somewhere around noonish, which I'm guessing was either a good-bye from Kayce or a hello from Lucien or Julian. Either way, it was a comforting gesture—but it made me uneasy not knowing who was around. The café filled up somewhere around ten with the after-church crowd, so I couldn't even find a moment to ask who was watching me. At one point I thought I smelled peppermint, which would have meant Julian was there—but it could have been the mint tea we carry at the shop.

"Still wearing that outfit, I see." I turned to find Wills standing stiffly behind me.

"Of course I am," I said in an equally staccato voice.

He sighed. "Can you please shift into something else?"

My angry facade broke down, face softening. "At my next break, I'll find something else to wear." I had a blazer in my locker I could cover up with. Shifting was, of course out of the question. To be honest, the stupid outfit was completely uncomfortable.

His lips tipped into a small, defeated smile. "Thank you." He reached into his pocket and pulled out a leather cord. It had knots with small onyx stones tied in a line and at the center dangled my mysterious blue stone from Erik. "Here. This is for you."

"Wow, that was fast." I took the stone in my hand, and it was warm as always. I always imagined stones to be cool to the touch, and this one almost never was. "It's amazing. I love the leather cord. Thank you." I reached an arm around his neck and pulled him in for a kiss.

He also pulled out two little studs with the same matching stone. "A piece of it chipped off when he was setting it in the necklace. Instead of throwing it away, he made these."

I had a few holes in my ears and put the little studs in my second piercing.

He held the necklace as I finished putting the earrings in. "Here, let me." He reached around my neck to remove the panic button necklace Kayce gave me.

"No!" I shouted a little too emphatically, and he coiled his hands away from me. "Um, I'm sorry. I just think they're both so beautiful. Look, they go together well!" I held up his necklace next to the long gold chain that was already around my neck.

A brief look of annoyance flashed over his face. He clearly wasn't happy about sharing my neck space with another piece of jewelry. Undoing the clasp, he slipped the leather cord around my neck. His fingers brushed my clavicle and down my chest to the edge of my low-cut shirt. He pressed a kiss into the crook of my neck. "Wear it always?"

I nodded. "Definitely."

He smiled again. "Okay. Well, I'm off. Have some demon business to take care of out in Reno for a day or so. I'll be back Monday night."

I nodded. "Business? Doing what?"

He rolled his eyes. "Essentially glorified clerical work. I have a meeting with your Queen's assistant." His eyes drooped in a bored kind of way.

"Lexi?" I suppressed a shudder.

He nodded. "I've had to work with her before—balancing budgets and whatnot. She's not so terrible, so long as you do as she says."

I put my hand to his cheek. He was about twelve hours past a five o'clock shadow, and his stubble scraped my palm. I rubbed my thumb in circles over his jaw. "Well, you're the sexiest finance demon I've ever met." I pulled his chin in for another kiss and touched the stone on my neck. "Thank you again. It's lovely."

He smiled and wrapped an arm around my waist, pulling me in tightly. "I want a real kiss." He pressed his lips to mine and our tongues touched hungrily. He released me, backing away a step, and I steadied myself against the table. He smiled. "I just can't resist when I'm close to you. Dinner Monday?"

I nodded, and he chucked me under the chin before leaving the café.

"Well, that was cute." Lucien's voice was so close to my ear, he must have been standing inches away from me. I turned quickly, but no one was there. Invisible. Fucking demons. "Aw, disappointed? Expecting . . . someone else? Don't worry. Your angel will be taking over later."

I cleared my throat grabbing a napkin, and whispered as quietly as I could into it. "I can't talk to you here. You know that."

He chuckled. "I know." I rolled my eyes and bused a table.

A brush against my arm made me jump, and I nearly dropped the half-full coffee mug I was cleaning. Drew held his hands up, palms out. "Whoa, sorry."

I shook my head. "My fault. I'm a bit jumpy today."

"Ready for lunch?"

I looked over to the counter, and sometime between George, Kayce, Wills, and Lucien's visits, two of our other baristas had shown up. I blew a gush of air up to get my hair out of my eyes. "I am so *very* ready for lunch." He took the dirty plates I had in my hands and flashed me a perfect smile.

"But first," I continued, "I *have* to change. This stupid outfit is so uncomfortable."

He laughed and arched his eyebrows. "Just don't dress too casually. I have a special lunch planned."

I felt a hundred times better once I covered up with the blazer. The whole time I could hear Lucien outside the bathroom door taunting me about the outfit. "The one time your sexuality won't benefit me and you go around dressing like *that*."

I opened the door and brushed past him, feeling his presence without seeing him and went to my locker. "Would you please just *shut up*. You're not going to come to lunch with us, are you?" I'd never hear the end of it if he listened in on my and Drew's date. *Shit.* Not date. Just lunch. *Keep reminding yourself of that, Monica. He has a girlfriend. And you have a . . . Wills.*

I put in the combination to my lock and swung the door open. "Shit." I exhaled. "Oh, fuck." I backed away from the locker and brought a hand to my mouth. Whether my goal was to not vomit or stifle a scream, it worked on both. There hanging on the inside of my door was another note. A knife pierced the note, keeping it in place, and hanging at the bottom of a dirty piece of twine was a decaying nipple.

17

The nipple smelled of rotted flesh and fluid.

34:14 Wildcats shall meet hyenas, / Goat-demons shall greet each other; / There too the night monster shall repose / And find herself a resting place

I covered my nose and mouth. It smelled as if the whole corpse was before me. I grabbed my stuff and slammed the locker door closed.

"Sit down," Lucien whispered in my ear, and I felt his hands on my elbow guiding me to a chair. "I'm calling Kayce now to take over watching you. I'll take care of your locker and get it cleaned out."

Drew popped his head in from the front room. "You almost ready?" He examined me sitting there, no doubt paler than a vampire. "Everything okay?"

"Go," Lucien said. "Kayce will catch up with you."

I nodded and stood, straightening out the blazer. I somehow

had to pull it together. "Yes, everything is fine. Where should we go for lunch?"

"How about L'Atelier?"

"Well, well, well." My eyes widened and I swallowed, my throat feeling extremely dry. "Someone's feeling a bit fancy today." I grabbed my purse, flinging it over my shoulder. The heavy gun hit my back, and I grimaced. Another wave of nausea hit as I thought about the rotting nipple.

"Kayce will meet you there," Lucien whispered.

The drive to L'Atelier seemed to take forever. There was an Audi that I swear had followed us the whole way there. I even asked Drew about it at one point. He glanced into his rearview mirror. "Well, we're going to a very nice place—it makes sense that a nice car like that would be going as well."

I nodded, not feeling reassured at all.

Our lunch passed quickly with me saying very little. Drew wore the concern on his face for all to see. I couldn't stop assessing the people around me—not even to try to reassure Drew that I was okay. Was it the waiter who kept glancing at my necklaces as though he knew what the panic button was? Was it the wealthy-looking woman at the table next to us dining alone? I glanced at Drew, stealing a quick look at the man I had known for two years. Could it be Drew? Someone I knew and trusted, maybe a bit too much?

I shook the thought from my head. Not Drew—but maybe someone I knew.

"Monica—" Drew touched my hand from across the table, his eyes creased with worry. "You're not acting like yourself today. You sure everything is all right?"

I gave a fake laugh—shrill and high-pitched—and we both knew the absurd sound was not genuine. "It's these disappearances." I sighed. "I guess they've just made me a little more jumpy than normal."

Drew opened his mouth to say something in return when our server came over and placed the check down between us. Then he handed it to Drew and looked over at me—his eyes once again making contact with my necklaces.

I narrowed my eyes to slits, a breath escaping my parted lips like a hiss. The waiter backed away from my gaze and scurried over to his station. Again, I looked up to meet Drew's eyes and he was frozen, staring at me with his wallet in hand. I broke eye contact first. "I'm sorry—but, did you just *hiss* at that man?"

I cleared my throat. "What? No—I, of course not." I stuttered. Oh Hell, I was really starting to lose it. "I just, I think I need some gum or something." I opened my purse, shoving my hand deep inside searching for anything to keep me busy.

A knowing smile etched across Drew's face. "You quit smoking again, didn't you?" He pushed his chair back, got up, and walked over to my chair. "That's why you're so jittery today, right?"

My ear itched again. "Yep. That's it. You got it." I angled my eyes back down into my purse. "Now if I could only find that damn gum."

"Here," he said, taking the bag from me. "Let me."

"Oh, no, Drew—I've got it . . ."

But it was too late. The gun was at the top of my bag, resting on my wallet and a bunch of other crap I had been storing in there. He had my purse in his hands and within a moment his face dropped, mouth hanging open in shock. His jaw snapped shut and he dropped the heavy purse back into my lap. He threw some cash down onto the table, grabbed me by the arm, and escorted me out of the restaurant like some sort of prisoner.

When we got out to the car, he swung me around so we were face-to-face. "A gun? What the hell are you thinking?"

I raised my chin defiantly. "I decided to protect myself."

He laughed at that—and not in the playful, jovial way I was so accustomed to.

"Protect yourself? Guns kill people, Monica. You're not a murderer." He raked a hand through his hair. "Shit. Why didn't you just take one of those little self-defense classes where they teach the girls to kick a guy in the nuts?"

My eyes lowered. "You might not want to say things like that when I have a gun in my hand."

"Please. Do you even know how to shoot that thing?"

"Of course!" I said, the snark oozing from my pores. "This gun was actually made just for women! It came in a pink box with tampon bullets and a bedazzled instruction manual," I said in my best Daisy Mae voice. I grabbed the gun out of my purse and aimed it at a tree stump at the edge of the parking lot. "Would you like me to round off a few shots? Because I guarantee I could hit the same spot three times."

"Do not fire that gun in front of me, Monica. I mean it. Do you even have a permit to carry?"

I ignored the question. "Maybe I *have* murdered someone. Have you ever stopped to think just how much there is about me *you* don't know?"

He grabbed the gun from my grasp, put the safety on, and stuffed it back in my bag. He pointed a finger in my face, his voice low and dangerous. "Don't you ever pull a fucking gun out in front of me again."

It was one of the few times I'd heard Drew say the word *fuck*. I stepped closer and slapped his finger away from my nose. "Don't threaten me. I'm scared and I'm protecting myself." I laughed a husky grunt. "And if I have to blow someone's fucking head off to do so, I will." And then, a thought so ridiculous entered my mind, I almost didn't want to admit it. "Unless, of course, you don't want me to be protected. Maybe there's a reason why you want me to be so defenseless?"

"What?" His face scrunched, confusion flickered along his features. "What the hell are you talking about?"

Icicles shot through my veins, the sudden fear sobering. "I'm talking about *you*. What is this really about, Drew?" The past few days flicked across my brain like a slideshow. Almost every letter—every cut and injury—came around a time when Drew was present. My cut shin, the greeting card that was left on my nightstand, the nipple in the locker. Drew had access to all these places. I slowly pulled the gun back out of my purse and held it down by my side. I wasn't exactly pointing it directly at him, but I was a quick draw. "Why don't you want me to be able to protect myself, Drew?"

"Stop, it, Monica." He held a hand out in front of him. His voice was trembling and his hand shook. "Guns are really fucking dangerous." He held my gaze, eyes wide, breath short. His eyes were assessing. Studying. Seeing just how serious I was.

He took a step toward me and I clicked the safety off. He froze, now raising both hands in the air. "Monica." His voice was softer, and I recognized the emotion. Fear. Desperation. "What are you doing?" His voice cracked. "It's *me*. I love you. I am not your enemy—I know you're stressed. You're not thinking clearly."

My lip quivered and I could feel the tears rising in my throat. *Love.* It was the first time either of us had ever used the word in reference to the other. He took another step toward me. "Give me the gun, Monica. I'm not the bad guy here." My hand trembled and a sob escaped from my lips. I dropped the gun, and Drew caught it before it hit the ground. He put the safety back on and I crumpled into his arms, crying.

"I'm so sorry. I just—I-I don't know what I was thinking. I'm so scared. I think someone's after me."

Drew held me as I cried, but there was a stiffness to his body. Once the tears stopped, I pulled away and looked into his eyes. They were cold, emotionless. "Drew?" I asked, blinking away the few remaining tears.

He cleared his throat and pulled out his car keys. "This is exactly why you shouldn't have a gun. You get paranoid. You get emotional. And you pull it on the wrong people." He unlocked his car and opened the door. "Get in the car. I'm taking you home."

"I'm sorry," I whispered. "I don't know what I was thinking. I just . . . I'm—"

"Scared. I know." He interrupted, his voice still void of emotion.

I swallowed and swiped the remaining tears from my cheeks. I was angry again despite the tremor in my voice. "I'm sorry, okay? I'm sorry! How many fucking times do I need to say it? We could drag this out for another month or you could just go ahead and forgive me, like we both know you're gonna do, anyway." I threw my hands wildly in the air, my voice becoming shrill.

His laugh at that comment was an angry sneer. "Maybe it won't be so easy this time."

I got in the car and slammed the door shut. He came in soon after. I clenched my jaw to keep myself from crying again. "I don't need your permission. I'm not even asking for your blessing. But a little understanding would be nice."

He exhaled a breath. "You've got some nerve. You stick a gun in my face, then ask for a little understanding after accusing me of—what is it exactly you were accusing me of, by the way?"

I didn't answer him, and he didn't comment anymore.

For the rest of the ride home, silence fell between us like a third, unwelcome passenger. Drew's face was solemn, a scowl carved in stone. He pulled up to my building and sat there with the engine running, waiting for me to get out.

"Drew—I don't want to leave things like this."

"Thanks for filling in today." His voice was short and curt. He reached over my body and pulled the handle of the passenger side door.

I snorted. "Wow. Someone really did a number on you when you were younger, huh? Who was it?"

His lip curled, making his scar look more ominous. "Let's just say that wasn't the first time I had a gun in my face."

I got out and just barely had time to slam the door before he peeled out of the parking lot.

I slung the heavy purse over my shoulder, and I walked up the stairs to my doorway. I grasped the railing as an overwhelming sense of nausea and dizziness took over my body. The metal was hot from the Vegas sun beating down on it, but I grasped it anyway, letting the heat burn my skin.

Thrashing. I could see thrashing—and water. Hands grasping for anything to pull her head—my head—out of the water. Feet kicking, nails clawing. And fear. Gut-wrenching panic. My left breast ached, and when I glanced down, open, angry flesh was there in place of a nipple. I felt a hand on my head, fingers tangled roughly through my hair. The air was sucked out of my lungs as though I was the one being held underwater. The hands shifted from my hair to around my throat. My fingers were entwined through the attacker's, attempting to wrench them away from me. But as the air escaped me, my lungs convulsed, aching for any sip of breath my body would allow. My arms quit fighting, my feet no longer clenched. And then peace. A relaxation like none I've ever known, and I was floating, looking up at a copper tiled ceiling.

My face burned and stung. When I opened my eyes, I saw Kayce's almond eyes, her hand raised to my cheek, slapping me. "She's awake!" I looked around. I was on my couch, my head cradled in Kayce's lap. I groaned and sat up on an elbow.

"What happened?" I put a hand to my head. This whole fainting thing was getting old fast.

When I looked around, I saw Jules, Lucien, and George all sitting in my living room staring at me intently. Lucien was the first to speak. "How the fuck would we know? Kayce saw you collapse on your way up to the apartment, and she said you fought her. Were clawing at her face."

Kayce looked as close to tears. "And your mouth—it was gurgling. Almost foaming, like you were, I don't know . . ."

"Drowning." I finished her sentence. I looked around the room and made eye contact with each person. "I was drowning." George was using a silk scarf to cover his mouth in shock. Julian looked thoughtful and assessing—as always. And Lucien looked downright pissed.

"Monica, that's the most ridiculous thing I've ever heard." Lucien stood and paced across my living room. "Drowning," he huffed, "outside on your stairwell."

Julian leaned his elbows onto his knees. "You sure it wasn't just heat stroke, Monica?"

"*No.*" I looked directly into his eyes. "I was drowning. With all the crazy shit happening here, why is that so difficult to believe?" I stared at all the people in the room and raised a hand to my throat, the skin around it raw. "Someone was choking me. Underwater."

Jules and Lucien met eyes for a brief moment and their eyes landed back on my neck. "She does have marks on her neck, Lucien," he said in a resigned way.

Lucien snorted a half-disgusted laugh. "She probably got those marks from Wills last night. We all know how rough she likes it." He glanced at Jules, and I swear I saw a moment of regret as he watched Jules's face drop at the mention of my tryst.

What if the murderer was someone close to me? I'd already accused one friend—I had to be 100 percent certain before accusing another. Kayce? I looked into her wet, coffee bean eyes. No way she could fake being this upset. She's not that good of an actress. Lucien? Could the man who treated me like a sister all these years turn on me? He continued pacing around the room. He was a demon, after all. Not the most trustworthy man to have on your side. My eyes met Julian's, his blue eyes sparkling. Couldn't be. Sure rogue angels existed—but not my Jules. His mouth twitched into a smile. Then I looked at George. He sat in my red velvet brocade chair fiddling with his scarf. His eyes wouldn't meet mine. He stared at the ground, shuffling his Armani loafers.

"Monica," Julian said, "leave the judgment calls to Lucien and me."

Damn. I forgot he could read my mind. That same tiny hint of a smile tugged at the corners of his mouth. Well, I was glad to see my deductive reasoning was so amusing.

Lucien's cell phone rang. He stopped pacing and answered it, stepping into the other room.

"What were you doing last night, George?" I tried to make my voice sound light and playful. As if I was just a friend asking another friend about his weekend.

George looked up at me, dropping the scarf from his hands. I saw his mouth tip into a frown, his bottom lip quivering just barely. "What do you mean?"

I shrugged, finally seeing the sadness in his face. Maybe that's why he was covering it—he didn't want to seem like the only emotional guy. Lucien was the angry one. Julian was thoughtful. And George was clearly distraught.

I shrugged my shoulder. "Just curious what you were up to last night."

"I was . . . out. Clubbing." His eyes shifted to Julian. "Met a guy. You know, the usual. Why?"

Julian's eyes flashed with something.

I shook my head. "Nothing. I was just trying to make conversation—something not so depressing as me almost drowning." I gave him a small smile, which he didn't return. Guilt tugged at my center. George seemed genuinely distraught. I inwardly sighed. I was going to have no friends left if I kept going at this rate. "So, who was the guy? Hot?"

He smiled a little more, the concern still evident in the creases along his forehead. "You know I wouldn't have it any other way."

Lucien entered the room again, his hands on hips. "That was Lexi." His gaze met mine. "We had another succubus attack. She was in some sort of meeting with your boyfriend when she heard of the murder."

I sat up straighter. "And?"

Lucien sighed. "The succubus drowned." His eyes met Julian's, his mouth pressed into such a tight line, all the blood was drained.

My eyes narrowed. "What else are you not telling me?"

Lucien's eyes darted from Jules's to mine and back again. Finally, he said, "She was missing a nipple."

18

Julian stood, moving beside Lucien. "We should go to the crime scene." The demon and angel held eye contact as if they could communicate without words. Hell, maybe they could.

Lucien sharply nodded, his shirt collar crinkling with the movement. "Kayce—George, stay here with Monica. No one leaves this apartment."

We all sat there, stunned. He must have taken our silence as an agreement, because within seconds a *crack* sounded through the air and he and Jules disappeared.

I got up and went to my bedroom to dress, putting on a short-sleeved, light knit turtleneck to cover up the red marks forming along my neck. Kayce and George followed behind me. Though only April, it was still hot as fuck outside, and I looked like an idiot wearing a turtleneck.

"Where are you going?" George demanded, then seeing the shirt I picked, he crinkled his nose. "And what in Hell's name are you putting on?"

I rolled my eyes. "It's a turtleneck—do we really want evidence of my strangling displayed on my neck for all to see? Besides," I mumbled, "I can't just sit around here waiting all day. I'll lose my mind."

"Good," Kayce said, her face lips curling into a smirk, "we're not." She pulled a file out of her bag and threw it on my bed. "I spent the latter part of the morning doing some research down at our little Vegas precinct. Made copies of the murders on file."

George and I stared at Kayce—the force to be reckoned with. My gaze shifted to the file sitting on my bed. It called to be opened. I thought of Jules, how he wanted me to be more involved. I leaned toward the folder and George grabbed my wrist, stopping me. "Maybe you should leave the dangerous stuff up to the angel . . . and Lucien and Lexi. What are we going to do? Go walk around the crime scenes?"

Kayce smiled even larger. "I think that's a great idea. What else is there to do this afternoon?"

George sighed and released my wrist. "Just—for the record, I think it might be a bad idea."

I reviewed the file on the drive to the first crime scene. Her name was Savannah. Lifeless eyes peered at me from her last photos ever taken. Her red hair was caked with dried blood, and her body had cuts and gashes covering it. Her lifeless form was twisted on the floor, pools of blood surrounding her like a shadow. I quickly slid the pictures back underneath the notes.

"Detective Kane" apparently had been the first to arrive and had taken various notes on what was found at the crime scene. Blood splatters beginning in the bathroom, ending with the body in the bedroom. A broken hand mirror, shards of glass.

I closed the file just as we pulled into a parking space in front of a small, one-story house in a medium-income, blue collar neighborhood. I flipped a page over within the file, reviewing her assets. "So, she owned this place?"

Kayce nodded. "Yep. And no one has bothered to clean it up or clear it out since her death."

I scrunched my nose. "She didn't have any friends? Three weeks seems like a long time for this to go just sitting here."

George did a one-shoulder shrug. "She was a prostitute, hun. LVPD tends to put their efforts into more high-profile cases."

I knew he was correct, but that thought sent a hollow shiver to the pit of my stomach.

The entrance to the house had a screen door in front of the older, heavier wooden one. Yellow "Do Not Enter" ribbon was taped haphazardly to the doorframe. Kayce and George disappeared with a crack into the house, and moments later the front doors creaked open for me.

With a quick glance around the neighborhood to ensure that no spying eyes were watching, I took a step inside, careful not to disturb the tape.

We entered through a dark hallway, which opened into a kitchen on the left and a sitting area straight ahead. To the right was another hallway. I could smell the faint, lingering scent of blood, and I followed my nose to where the murder happened.

A light, feathery touch brushed against my arm. I shrieked, startled by the contact. Leaning against the wall, I caught my breath.

Kayce held her hands out in front of her. "Sorry, sorry," and she touched my arm a second time in a more reassuring way. "I was just going to ask if you prefer that I go first."

I gestured in front of me in a sweeping, grandiose way. "After you."

I focused my eyes on the back of her head and could feel the death surrounding us. At first glance, it just looked like a bedroom. Nothing too unusual. Most of the gruesome details had already been documented and cleaned. "Hand me the folder again." I stuck a hand out to Kayce, who passed the paperwork my way. I pulled out the crime scene photos, holding them up against the layout of the room.

The bed looked like it hadn't been touched since the night of her death. If I looked closely enough, the rumpled bedsheets had little bits of dust settling between the creases. There was dried blood on the dresser across from the bed and between the cracks hardwood floors. Next to the dried blood droplets were burn marks—they almost looked like acid burns along the floor. Little yellow markers were scattered across the room, noting where the detectives had found bits of evidence. I held up the photo of Savannah's lifeless body. I had seen her a few times at various underworld meetings, but I had never known the girl. I held out the picture and squinted one eye shut, imagining that her body was on the ground before me. Her body was so human-like. If a succubus goes long enough without sex—essentially starving herself—she will in essence die. But she dies a beautiful goddess. The life sucks out of her, but her body will still be compensating. Trying to attract a soul to feed on. And in the case that she runs across a necrophiliac . . . well, she would be brought back to life the second he came.

George bent down, his elbows rested on his knees. After running a finger across the hardwood floor as though he were checking for dust, he held it up to his nose. "Scales."

I dropped my arm to my side. "What?"

"Look." He stood and put his finger under my nose. "Scales."

I grabbed his hand and looked closer. They were dry and brittle, but I'd be damned—he was right. Within the dust on the floor, there were scales. Motherfucking scales.

Kayce shrugged. "Maybe she had a pet snake?"

George brushed his hands on his pants. "Pretty giant snake, wouldn't you say? This scale is bigger than a quarter."

"Why didn't they bag this as evidence?" I muttered a curse under my breath. LVPD. Useless as always.

"Maybe they didn't see it as being evidence?" Kayce offered. "They only take what they see as being important to the case."

A sudden sharp pain cut across my knee. I screamed, falling to the ground clutching my leg.

Kayce and George dropped to my side, and I grasped for their hands, squeezing. My pain subsided as quickly as it came, and I rushed to pull my pant leg up. Had I been bit by something? My tight jeans wouldn't allow themselves to be pulled above my kneecap. George took the fabric between two hands and yanked until they ripped at the seam.

"Fuck," he whispered.

At the back of my knee there was a scar that I had never seen before. I crawled over to the picture, rushing to get it back in my hands, and sure enough—there on Savannah's body was a giant gash behind her knee. I looked from it to my scar and back again. "Fuck is right."

"Does it hurt anymore?" Kayce's eyes pinched with concern, and I shook my head no. She grabbed me under the arms and lifted me to my feet. "We're getting you the fuck away from the crime scene. First you experience the drowning, now you're developing scars that should be on the victim's body—not yours."

I clasped my hand around hers. "Wait!" Under the dresser, there was something catching the light. I crawled under and stretched my arm out until I could feel it, hard and cool beneath my fingers. It was stuck between the cracks in the floorboards. Using my house key, I wedged it out and held it up in front of the group.

It was a tooth—a *fang*, to be more accurate.

Kayce and George's faces crinkled. Kayce spoke first. "Demon tooth?"

George shook his head and took the fang from me. "No—a demon in his true form has small, sharp teeth. It looks more like it's from a vampire."

I exhaled—I had seen vampire fangs up close once. I knew they did not arch in the same way this one did. "No," I whispered. "This is the fang from a reptile. A giant reptile." I closed my eyes and knew. I could see it in a foggy sort of haze. "She fought back—shifted into a serpent with her last remaining powers."

"How do you know?" George's hand on my arm felt warm and reassuring.

I shrugged, staring vacantly in the mirror on top of her dresser. "I don't know how I know it. . . . I just do. Maybe all the targets have some sort of connection."

Kayce laced her arm through my elbow and let her cheek fall on my shoulder. "I think we've seen enough for one day— don't you think?" She tugged me toward the door.

There was a rustling sound coming from the front room. I shushed everyone. We had all heard it and froze. A tiny pop came from either side of me, and when I looked, both my friends were gone. Invisible.

I rushed the window, lifting it as quickly as I could. I had one leg out when I looked up, staring straight into the barrel of a gun. "Freeze!"

19

It was a slightly chubby, out-of-breath police officer, and he shouted in such a stereotypical way, it took a lot of my energy to not laugh in his face. Perhaps I should have been a little more nervous—but man, humans could be funny. I could see this guy sitting at home, munching on salt and vinegar chips watching *Law & Order: SVU* reruns practicing the day he himself could be as big a badass as Stabler.

I put my hands in the air in a surrender sort of position. "Okay," I said, "Don't shoot." The latter was tough to say with a straight face. "I'm going to crawl back into the house." I assumed he wanted me with my feet firmly planted to answer questions and not straddling the window frame. "I'm unarmed," I added as an afterthought, which was entirely untrue. But I was counting on Kayce and George being able to get me out of this mess before a strip search took place.

"Move slowly." He kept his gun pointed at me.

I nodded, and as slowly as I could I swung my leg back over inside the house. As my back was turned, still bracing the window, I whispered in a voice that only my immortal friends could hear. "Okay, you assholes. What is the plan now?"

They were quiet for a few seconds before I heard Kayce's voice. "We'll distract him at the right time and you make a run for it."

"Turn around so that you're facing me. I want to see your eyes," the cop stated in a cool voice.

"Ew," George whispered, "this guy is creepy. He wants to stare lovingly into your eyes while shooting you."

I gritted my teeth. "Now is not the time, George."

Putting my hands back up in the air, I turned slowly to face the cop. We stayed there staring at each other for a moment. He made no movement to approach me. "You know," I started, "my arms are getting a little tired. I'm not armed. I promise."

He squinted, eyes not leaving mine. "What are you doing here? Did you not see the yellow tape? The signs that say *Do Not Enter: Crime Scene?*"

I took a deep breath. *Anytime now would be good, guys.* "I saw the signs. I was"—I paused—"a friend of the victim's. I guess I just had a morbid desire to see her house one last time." It seemed believable enough, and I could have sworn I saw his eyes soften. If I played up this friendship business, he might even let me go.

Just as he was beginning to show me empathy, the bed shook as though we were in the middle of an earthquake. The cop's eyes darted around the room.

"What the hell . . . ?" He took a hesitant step closer to it. Kayce's voice rang out in shrill cries.

The cop jumped back, his gun drawn again—pointed at absolutely nothing. I edged my way closer to the entrance of the bedroom, acting just as scared. He bumped into the dresser, and George picked up a ceramic thimble from the nightstand, the kind you get on vacation. It had Savannah's name scrawled in cursive at the bottom. He carried it, allowing it to "float" over to the cop, stopping for a moment in front of his face, white with fear. George drew back and threw the thimble into the mirror behind him, causing the glass to shatter.

I took off running, full speed, slamming my shoulder into the cop as I passed him. He fell to his ass, courtesy of my 120-pound frame. Okay, maybe 125 now thanks to a few days of eating like a human. I ran out of the bedroom down the dark hallway toward the front door. Even if the cop caught me, I could just claim I was terrified by the display. When I looked behind me, the cop was following at my heels. Whether he was running to catch me or simply get the fuck out of the house, I wasn't sure.

I should have been paying more attention to the direction in which I was running. Because I was looking behind me, I ran flush into a wall of muscle. Two strong pectorals stood in front of me, and when I looked up, I stared into Damien's gray eyes. A bemused smirk spread across his face and his eyes stared at me with authority. He had his hands on my bicep, holding me at arm's length. A wave of lust—carnal desire—swept over me and my knees quivered.

I opened my mouth to speak, but no words came out. A rough hand grabbed my arm and spun me around, slamming me into the wall. I could smell the cop from before as he cuffed my hands. "What kind of an evil trick was that, huh?" He slammed my body into the wall again, harder. My cheek was pressed against the ugly floral wallpaper, and my eyes shifted to look at Damien again.

He approached the two of us and put a hand on the cop's shoulder. "What's going on here, Doug?"

"This bitch tricked me—made me think the damn place was haunted. Then took off." I could feel the waiver in his voice. As though he wasn't sure whether to believe his own story.

"Is that so? And how exactly did she do that. Some kind of 'magic'?" There was an amusement in Damien's cadence that simply infuriated me, and I humphed to make it known.

Through the corner of my eyes, I saw his mouth tip ever so slightly into a smile. "Doug, why don't you leave the young lady to me. I'll question her and figure out what's going on at our crime scene."

Our crime scene?

"Go back to your route, Doug. I've got this covered." His voice was so reassuring—so business like.

I could hear the handcuffs clicking behind my back and the release of the metal against my skin. I sighed, thankful that I might just get out of this situation without Lucien being the wiser. An arrest was no sweat—we can get out of those easy enough with all the demons tucked into the ranks of the police force. But there was no escaping Lucien's punishment for interfering in the investigation.

Doug was gone—out of the "possessed" house in a flash. I glanced back over at Damien, that amused little half smile still splayed across his face. I wanted to smack it off. He was even better looking than that first day I saw him, a fact that pissed me off to no end. He wore black dress pants and a charcoal gray silk button-down shirt that glimmered like his eyes.

"Well?"

"Well, what?" I snapped back.

"Well—what are you doing here?"

"It's like I told Doug. Savannah was my friend. I came to see her house one last time."

"She was your friend, huh? Why didn't I see you at her funeral?"

I crossed my arms over my chest and didn't answer. Mostly because I didn't *have* an answer.

He grabbed my wrist, pulling me back into the bedroom. "C'mon."

I wasn't sure if Kayce and George were still in here. His hand around my wrist softened and his fingers were gentle on my skin.

His head dropped when he saw the bedroom. Dust bunnies were flying in the air from when Kayce stirred up the settled dust on the bed. Broken glass was covering the floor, and some of the other furniture was turned upside down. He rubbed a hand across his forehead. And looked back at me. "You did this?"

"No—" I was pretty sure he was adept at seeing through bullshit, but I tried, anyway. "It was, um, haunted. Or something."

He exhaled loudly. "Haunted. Right." He put a hand to the wall, closed his eyes, and there was a buzzing sound all around me. After another minute, he opened his eyes and pushed off the wall. "Okay—where are they?"

I shifted my weight. "Who?"

He rolled his eyes and stalked around the room. "Your friends. The succubus and the incubus."

"Wha—how? How do you know about *them*?"

"I know they're still here. I can sense them."

"What *are* you?"

Kayce and George turned visible, looking rather defeated. Their faces hung slack-jawed, staring at Damien.

He sighed. "What the fuck did you do to my crime scene?"

"*Your* crime scene?"

"Yes," he snapped, "mine. I'm the lead detective on the case."

I narrowed my eyes at him. "And here I thought you were just a sleazy boozehound wrapped up in some adultery."

His mouth twitched. "Can't I be both?"

"You're an elemental," Kayce said from over near the bed.

George's eyes grew wide and he looked as though he wanted to drop to his knees and bow to the man.

Damien nodded and scowled at Kayce. "Ding, ding, ding. What have you won, succubus?"

"Don't call her that," I said, eyes narrowed.

"Don't call her what? Succubus?" His hand gestured toward her. "It's what she is, isn't it?"

"He's got a point, Mon. We are succubi."

I shot my glare over toward Kayce. "It's *how* he's saying it. Like it's an insult."

His hands clenched on his hips. "The elements can speak to me—stone, air, water. I just have to tap into them."

"It is one of the rarest and invaluable forms of ancient magic we have." George's voice was deep. Almost unrecognizable, as though he were speaking in an ancient tongue.

"Um, okay," I snapped at George, "and it's fucking creepy."

"Creepier than killing a man by fucking him?" Damien retorted, still standing so close to me that I could feel the buzz of his energy between us.

I shot him a look that I hoped showed my hatred. "So you just *spoke* to this house? And it told you what we were doing here today?"

He shrugged, bringing a shoulder to his ear noncommittally.

Kayce stepped closer to Damien. "Elementals' identities are kept very quiet. Their services are invaluable, and most of the time they go their entire lives without fully utilizing their abilities." I stared at her in wonder, and she shrugged in return. "I worked with one once."

"Brava," he said sarcastically, glaring at Kayce. His eyes narrowed, and he pointed a finger in her direction. "Hey—don't I know you? You once did a job for my chief . . ."

"Nope," Kayce said curtly. "You do not know me." She spoke in short, sharp staccato. And I felt the same seething anger I always did when she had to hide her career.

"My mistake. *Succubus.*"

I clenched my fists to stop myself from punching him. "Don't be a dick to her."

"Are you kidding me? She fucked up my crime scene!"

"Oh, calm down. We'll clean it up. It's not like you've made much progress here, anyway."

We held eye contact before he squared his shoulders, facing me straight on and closing in on what little space remained between our bodies. What was left of the air between us sizzled with static—something intoxicating and electric. "And you thought you could do better waltzing in here with no training whatsoever?"

"Tell me something," I continued, raising up on my toes so I could be closer to eye level, "if the walls can talk, why haven't they given you some sort of description on the perp? How come you don't have a character sketch?"

"If you must know, there was some sort of enchantment placed on the house before the murder. Either it can't or won't talk to me about those events."

"So what *do* you know?"

He slumped onto the dresser, leaning against it looking suddenly exhausted. "I know that the attack first started in the bathroom. From the pattern of blood spatter, she fought back—she wasn't the only one bleeding. She ran out here, stopping in front of this dresser, like this, where she was killed."

"What was the exact cause of death?" My eyes settled on the acid burns on the hardwood floor.

"Well, considering her throat was slit through past her jaw, I'd say that's probably the best bet."

"What are these?" I pointed to the burns.

He shrugged. "I don't know. This is the sloppiest crime scene of all of them yet. They get cleaner with each kill."

I nodded. "So he was still perfecting it."

Kayce handed Damien the fang we found under the dresser. "Here. We found this—maybe it will help."

Damien looked at it closely, holding in front of the window light.

"I think she turned into a serpent of some sort with her last ounce of energy."

He nodded. "Well, that would explain the scales. We also found a little bit of venom at the corner of her mouth. Had the coroner completely baffled." His eyebrows acted as a dark hood over his eyes, casting a deep shadow. "I couldn't exactly explain my theory to most people on the force."

"Well." I raised my chin haughtily. "Aren't you glad we came along, then?"

He rolled his eyes and pulled out a cell phone. "Yeah. Thrilled." He dialed a number, then spoke into the phone, "Yeah, Kane here. I'm at crime scene SV713 and I need a cleanup crew." He paused. "No, I'm not exactly sure what happened, but it looks like maybe some kids broke in and trashed the place." He covered the mouthpiece and whispered to us, "You better get out of here."

I nodded and looked at Kayce and George briefly before turning to leave. "Thanks," I mumbled.

"Oh, and Monica." His eyes met mine. "If you want to see the other crime scenes, all you gotta do is say *please.*" He handed me a business card, a smug grin on his face. I slipped it into my purse before scurrying home.

20

Kayce and I had been sitting around, watching bad daytime television for hours. She was sprawled out on my couch with her feet perched on my mahogany coffee table.

"Could get your smelly feet off my furniture?"

She rolled her eyes and with an indignant sigh let her feet fall to the floor. I went back to picking at my cuticles—an old habit. I caught Kayce watching me, her lips curled back.

"Do you have a problem or something?" I raised my voice louder than the television.

"That's disgusting." Her gaze shifted down to my hand. "You're going to have no skin left on your fingers."

I dropped my hands to my lap while Kayce went to the kitchen to scour the fridge. "You've only got one beer left!" she called from the other room.

"So, go get some more."

The fridge shut, glass jars on the shelves clinking as it closed. Kayce stood in the doorway to my living room. "You know I can't leave you unsupervised."

I shrugged. "Fine. Then do without."

"We could both go."

I shook my head. "Not a chance. I'm in for the night." I was already in my flannel bottom pajama pants and my favorite supersoft cotton T-shirt. I had taken off both necklaces—assuming it was okay to do so since I had hand marks on my neck that needed to heal. I was sure that Wills would forgive me—or maybe I just didn't have to tell him. And with my guardians around, the panic button didn't seem necessary.

"It's only six o'clock!"

"Exactly—no one is going to attack me at six p.m." It was a weak argument—I knew that. I looked closer at Kayce's face, and . . . she looked tired. Worn down and ragged. "Hey, Kayce, when was your last energy fix?"

She exhaled a small puff of air and crossed her arms. "Why?"

"Because you look—"

"Careful, Monica—"

". . . tired." I smiled. "You seem tired, Kayce. Low on energy."

She shrugged and sat back down in my recliner. "It's been a few days, but I'm all right."

I started to pick at my cuticles again and forced myself to drop my hands to my lap. "You don't seem 100%, though. Why don't you go out—go get yourself a man. I'm not going anywhere tonight, I swear."

Kayce hesitated, considering her lack of energy and need for a nightcap. She shook her head. "No. I can't leave you. It's too dangerous."

"Who's taking over the next shift?"

"Julian." She looked at her watch. "Probably in an hour or so."

"See? C'mon. I'll be fine for an hour. I could really use a little alone time, to be honest."

After an inner debate, she finally sighed and shifted into a sexy, strapless dark blue dress. The shift itself left her breathless, and she leaned on the wall to collect herself before grabbing her purse. "Do not answer the door for anyone. Do not leave this apartment. Keep the doors and windows locked."

She had her index finger in my face, and I kept my eyes on the TV, only half listening.

"Monica! Do you hear me?"

I huffed an exhaled breath and turned my head toward her. "Don't leave. Doors locked. Got it."

She shook her head. "You're so stubborn sometimes." She turned to head to the door, her deep blue dress hugging her tiny ass.

"Wait, wait." I jumped up, my fuzzy slippers sliding across the hardwood floors. "I'm sorry, Kayce. I'm just—I'm used to being alone a lot. And I've gone from living alone to having someone by my side every second. It's exhausting. And I'm cranky." I gave her a half smile, hoping she'd accept my apology.

She smiled back. "I understand."

I grabbed the necklace Wills had made for me. "You should wear this. It matches perfectly. It will look stunning with that dress."

She smiled and slipped it on, clasping it behind her neck.

"You want the earrings too?" I lifted a hand to undo the back of the little studs.

She scrunched her nose and shook her head. "No offense . . . little button earrings aren't really my style." She shifted two large gold hoops into her ears. "Now, *these*. These are my style." She did a twirl, and for the first time in hours I felt like I had my best friend back. Part of me wanted to hug her, but the mysterious Kayce wasn't necessarily great with public displays of affection.

She checked her enchantments on my apartment one last

time to ensure that no one other than Lucien or Julian could teleport inside and then slipped out my door, giving me a flirty wave good-bye.

I exhaled. I hadn't had the apartment to myself in a couple days—it felt glorious. If even just for a few minutes. Just as I was settling into my favorite nook in my rocking chair, there was a knock at my door. I hesitated, not yet getting out of my spot—Kayce's warning rang in my ears. *Don't answer the door for anyone.*

"Monica? Are you home?"

It was Drew's voice—and he sounded upset. Anger mixed with something else resonated in his voice. I jumped up and rushed to the door, fumbling with the various locks Kayce had installed, cursing how annoyingly intricate they all were.

"Just a minute, Drew." I swung the door open, making sure to plaster an annoyed look on my face. Inside, I was happy to see him, but I knew I should still be pissed about our fight. The man who stood before me looked nothing like my friend. Drew's hair was sticking out in all places. His eyes—those emerald eyes—were rimmed with red and creased as though he had slept on a plastic bag. His nose was raw and he sniffed, placing both hands on his hips. He raised his gaze to mine.

I reached for his hand. "What—what happened? What's wrong?"

He stood there a moment, drinking me in with his eyes. "Me? What the fuck happened to *you?*" His eyes dropped to my bare neck and he reached out a hand, running his fingers along the bruise.

Shit. I had completely forgotten about the strangle marks. "I did this little B movie horror shoot for George. I was . . . a murder victim."

Drew's hand retreated, pulling back, and his body language shifted back to confrontational. "Movie makeup"—I shrugged—"doesn't really come off easily."

His hands rested back on his hips. "Can I come in?"

I held the door open for him and he entered cautiously, keeping an eye on me as he walked into my foyer. I shut the door behind him and locked the various deadbolts.

"What's going on?" I asked.

He clomped his way into my kitchen and paced around in a half circle a few times. "I never thought you'd stoop so low, Monica." His voice was a low grumble.

"What the Hell are you talking about? Sit down. I'm going to make you some coffee." I put a kettle of water on the stove, and Drew just continued to pace, his eyes wild like a caged animal's.

"I know we had that fight"—he stopped pacing and looked directly at me—"but we would have worked that out." Drew sat down at my table. "This is inexcusable."

I sat down next to him, resting a hand on his knee. He flinched at my touch, and I pulled back as though burned. He eventually looked up, a mixture of anger and hurt swirling in his eyes, and threw some photographs down onto the kitchen table. "Did you do this?"

I looked at him, puzzled. Then down at the photographs. I swallowed. There in the first picture was Damien—and Adrienne. They had their tongues in each other's throat, standing in front of a cheap motel room. Damien's eyes were open, and he was looking to the left. For a brief moment, my body felt hot, my mouth went dry. Jealousy tugged at my core, and there was a slight pulsing between my legs. Damn my succubus nature. Even as a human, it still lingered.

"Well? *Did* you give these to me?" he asked, his eyebrow twitching once with the question.

"No." It came out as a whisper, so I said it again louder. "No. Of course not." I reached out and flipped through the other images. The next was Adrienne opening the door, one hand behind her holding onto Damien. The next was them talking in front of the window. And the last image was Damien drawing the curtain closed. I dropped the pictures back down on my table, disgusted. "I would never do that to you."

He put both elbows on the table and wrung his fingers through his hair, nodding. I scooted my chair closer. "Drew— I'm so sorry. Have you talked to Adrienne yet?"

He shook his head, allowing one hand to rub his face down to his stubble. "It's the guy from the church—the one you were talking to. Did you know about this?" He pointed to the pictures, his face hard and accusing.

I swallowed. "I suspected, yes."

He laughed in a bitter way. "I tried calling her, but she wouldn't answer. She said she was working today, but when I found the pictures, I went down to her bar and they said she wasn't due in until tomorrow." He leaned back in the chair. "She was probably with *him*."

I thought back to my day. "What time was that?"

"Around three, I guess."

I knew she wasn't with Damien at that time since he was with me. I decided to leave that part out.

"Well—what's your plan? What are you going to say to her?"

He snorted in disgust. "What do you think I'm going to say? I can't be with someone who has cheated on me." He stood up and started pacing around my kitchen again.

"Drew, I know you're upset." I stood as well, trying to halt his pacing. I grabbed his hand in mine. "But just sit. Try to relax. Let me get your coffee."

He stopped walking, but his chest rose and fell with deep, heavy breaths. "I don't want a fucking coffee." He pulled his hand from my grasp, neck muscles clenching. "I need a drink. Whiskey, preferably. You got any?" He opened a few of my cabinets, moving around various items stuffed inside.

I shook my head. "Don't let years of sobriety go to waste over her, Drew."

"I just can't believe she did this." He grabbed the pictures, taking another look at the two kissing.

I swallowed a lump in my throat. In a small voice, I asked, "Is it really so surprising? Think about her. *I'm* not surprised."

"I'm telling you, she wouldn't do this to me. She loved me. This"—he held the pictures up—"is not who she is!"

I sneered. *Love.* They were only together for two months. "The evidence suggests otherwise."

He threw the pictures back down onto the table and stalked over to me. "You don't know her like I do."

"You're right. Apparently, I know her *better* than you." Why he was defending a woman who cheated on him was beyond me. My eyes flicked back to the pictures on the table.

He grunted in frustration and ran both hands through his hair. "Why are you like this? You are infuriating sometimes." His hands gestured wildly around my head.

I laughed at that. "Me? Newsflash, Drew. I'm not the one who cheated on you just now! This"—I gestured between the two of us—"is just you misdirecting your anger."

"No, no." He threw his hands in the air. "You don't cheat on me. How can you cheat on me when you refuse to ever go out with me?"

I stood my ground firmly and crossed my arms over my chest. "It's for your own good."

"Well, why don't you let *me* choose what's for *my* own fucking good." He wrapped an arm around my waist and brought the other hand to my face, pulling me in for a kiss. His lips pressed against mine—hungry, devouring.

I melted into his arms, opening my mouth around his, my tongue tickling against his teeth. He lifted me onto my kitchen table, tugging his own shirt off. I was suddenly very aware of the fact that I had on a sheer cotton shirt and no bra paired with my flannel bottoms and lack of panties. Once he had rid his body of his shirt, he lifted mine over my head, my nipples hardening into two small peaks.

He lowered his face to my breasts, running his tongue softly around the edges of my nipple. I moaned and arched my back, hoping he'd take more into his mouth. He grunted, throwing an arm around my waist and pulling me closer to his body as if he feared any space between us. Teeth grazed against my sensitive skin and then—a cool breeze. When I opened my eyes, just barely, I saw his lips puckered and blowing lightly against my warm skin. He moved to the other breast, repeating the same technique.

I lay down on my table, the cool wood pressing against my back. His rough fingers tucked under the waist of my pants, sliding them down past my knees until I heard the soft rustle of fabric hitting the ground. I kept my eyes closed—not knowing what was coming next was arousal enough. A belt buckle opened, and there was a louder thud as his jeans fell.

A featherlike touch pressed against my clit, and my body responded in a shudder. The touch grew firmer, fingers circling my wetness. It wasn't until I felt his tongue on my ear that I even knew his face was up near mine. He kissed his way down to my neck, licking softly as he traveled, all the while teasing me with playful fingers. I opened my eyes and turned to look at him as he pulled away from my clavicle. We made eye contact, staring at each other as he stroked me. I raised a hand to touch his face, running a finger over the little scar that ran along his top lip. He entered me with two fingers and my body bucked, lower back arched at the sudden force.

A guttural, urgent noise escaped from the bowels of my throat. I managed to maintain eye contact as his fingers moved in and out of me. He lowered his face to mine, lips hovering a moment, electricity buzzing between our bodies, and then he finally kissed me. His lips were soft this time, moving around mine, and with his other hand he cupped the back of my neck, pulling me closer into the kiss.

I reached my hand out, quickly feeling his arousal. Running a fingernail along its length, I wrapped my hand around him. He grunted within our kiss and responded by placing a third finger deep inside me.

I pulled away from his lips, kissing his jawline up to his ear. "I want to taste you," I whispered.

He chuckled in a sexy way. "Only if I get to taste you, too."

I sat up from the table and he lay down, taking my spot. I straddled his face, my glistening sex hovering above his lips. He opened his mouth, licking my length. I lowered myself onto his tongue and it entered me, in long strokes. Falling onto my hands, I allowed my mouth to come into contact with him. Drew was a large man. And even though I had a big mouth, the size that stood at attention before me was enough to make even me a little nervous. I positioned my hand around the base of his shaft and wrapped my lips around his head. I took as much of him as I could.

He grunted, grabbing my ass and squeezing, continuing to pleasure me. My sex tensed, and as his tongue moved expertly around, I knew it wouldn't be long before I came on his face. The spasms began, and my cries were muffled by his dick still in my mouth. This seemed to turn him on more, and his cock twitched against my tongue.

"I want to be inside of you. Now." He kissed my sex once more before I climbed off of him, turning around. His lips glistened with my juices, and I couldn't resist bending down to kiss him. Using a hand, I guided him toward my entrance. Both of us were wet with our own fluids and saliva and he entered me slick and easily.

He rolled his hips as I pumped myself up and down on top of him. Positioning my hands behind my body, I arched my back to allow even deeper access. His hands lifted to cup my breasts, his thumbs circling over the nipples.

"My God, Monica. You are so beautiful." He cupped my face and pulled me down for a kiss. My breasts pressed against his pecs, his warm skin glistening with perspiration.

"Drew." I moaned his name with our lips entwined. The realization dawned that I was finally able to be with Drew. Nothing stood between us. Adrienne was out of the picture. I had no soul-stealing powers.

Wills. I was still with Wills. My body froze, and Drew immediately noticed the change in my body language. "Wills," I whispered to Drew. "Oh, fuck, Wills." I started to pull away, but Drew held my body close.

His eyes, which had been glazed, flashed with momentary anger. "Monica, wait," he growled. He was still inside of me, and I could feel the panic rising in my throat. He held me in place over him. "You two are exclusive?"

I shook my head. "No, not exactly. But I doubt he'd be okay with this."

Drew flipped me over so that I was again on my back on the kitchen table. He propped himself over me on both elbows. His erection, still raging strong, pressed against my belly. He ran a hand over my hair to smooth away any frizziness. "I've wanted this—wanted you—ever since that first day that you walked into my café and created your own crazy, diabetes-inducing caramel mocha latte."

I shook my head and closed my eyes. Trying to break the spell. Break the contact between us. "I can't do this to you. I can't promise you anything beyond tonight. And I really don't want to hurt Wills either—"

He covered my mouth with his thumb. "I don't want to worry about those things right now. You want me, too. You do, right?"

I swallowed and let the silence answer for me.

"Then I'm not letting you get out of this because you have a sort of quasi-boyfriend excuse waiting in the wings."

I lay there shocked for a moment. "You arrogant son of a bitch." I tried to get up, but his body weight against me kept me pinned to the table. "Let me up!" I punched at his chest.

His eyes lowered, a smirk still tickling his lips. "No." It was almost a grunt.

"I'll scream."

The slightest hint of a smile tugged the corners of his lips. "You might." He kissed me ferociously, still not letting me up. He stopped the kiss, pulling his face back to look at me. I panted from below him. "Admit it. You want this."

My breasts heaved, and I was even wetter between my legs than moments ago. "Of course I want this."

He kissed my neck, biting the soft flesh just below my ear. "Then let's finish it." He pushed his erection against my sex, entering just the tip.

A grunt escaped my lips and the anticipation was dizzying.

He kissed the other side of my neck. "Even if it's just for tonight." He pushed into me a little deeper, his hip connecting with my clit, sending electricity coursing through my body. I cried out again, louder.

He stared at me, his green eyes piercing like emeralds. "Say yes, Monica. Tell me you want me. If you say no—if you can honestly tell me you don't want this—I'll stop. I'll put my clothes back on and I'll never try to seduce you again. Ever." A pause. "So—do you want this?"

"Yes." My voice was barely a whisper.

He chuckled. "Yes?"

I whimpered. "Yes, please, Drew."

He kissed me. "Say it again. Louder."

"Yes," I cried out, the frustration of my impending orgasm getting to me.

He slammed his cock into me hard, pounding with a burst

of energy. I screamed out in absolute bliss, grabbing him behind the neck and pulling his face down to mine. I drank in his kiss. He leaned back on his knees and threw my legs over his shoulders. With two fingers, he put pressure on my clit, circling it with skill. The waves of orgasm rolled over my body, each one hitting like a lightning bolt.

He was growing harder inside of me, close to finishing any second. His body tensed, and as he came inside of me, his body collapsed onto mine.

I saw a flash. It was happening. I was stealing his life. I screamed, trying to push him off of me. I tried to stop it. It wasn't supposed to happen—I had no powers. How can I be stealing his soul? He grabbed me around the shoulders, mistaking my screams for cries of lust. And there it was—for just a brief second, I saw his future. I saw the life I had taken from him. He was old—a much, much older man. He clutched his heart, fell to the ground. And there beside him was an equally older woman catching him in her arms as he fell. If I wasn't mistaken—I could have sworn that that older woman looked a lot like me.

21

We both lay there in a sweaty pile for a few minutes. My body trembled at the sight of myself as an old lady. I shook the thought from my head. The chances of that flash-forward showing *me* were slim to none. Someone once told me that though coincidences were strange, the world would be a stranger place if there were none at all.

How much of his soul had I taken? Did I have my powers back? I had felt a small tingle of dormant power yesterday, but I never thought for a moment that sex with a good soul would have brought them back. I could feel my hand trembling. I sat up and looked down at my toenails. A little test. That's what I needed. I looked at Drew. He was running his fingers up and down my back, his eyes closed in postcoital bliss.

I focused on my toes, put all my energy and thoughts into changing the polish. *Red,* I thought. *Turn red, turn red, turn red . . .* There was a tingle of magic in my feet. My big toe's nail turned red. The rest of my toes remained neutral. *At least it's something.* Furthermore, I don't think I could have stolen all that much of Drew's soul if all I got was a lousy uneven polish job out of the surge of power. I exhaled a sigh. It was a small comfort, but at the moment, I'd take it. I lay back down and rolled onto my side toward Drew. His face was relaxed, and he opened one eye to look at me—the other remaining closed like some sort of reversed wink. "You all right over there?"

I kissed him lightly on the lips. "Never better." I rolled off of the table. "But this is not exactly the most comfortable accommodations I have." I could feel the indentations on my back where the table had left marks. I slipped my pajama pants back on and found my shirt at the other end of the table.

"Awww." Drew sat up and grabbed my hand, pulling me toward him before I could get the shirt over my head. "No clothes yet." The words ran together as he kissed me.

I gave him a playful push. "I have company coming soon," I said, and put my shirt back on.

His face darkened. "Wills," he said grimly.

"No." I ran my hand through his light hair. "Not Wills."

Relief washed over him and he hopped up, putting his jeans on. He bent down and gathered the pictures that had scattered across my kitchen floor. The image of Damien and Adrienne kissing rested by my foot, and I crouched down, taking a closer look as I picked it up. There was something odd about the photo. Damien's eyes—they were open. Looking around during a kiss? Damien didn't seem the type to blink at the thought of participating in an affair. So what was he watching out for?

"You really didn't take these?" Drew held a hand out.

I shook my head. "No. I definitely did not."

I stood up, face to face with Drew, and handed the photo over. He took it with a sigh and tapped the stack of pictures against the palm of his hand. "So, will I see you at the café tomorrow?"

I nodded. The guilt sat heavily in my stomach. "I'll see you tomorrow."

After I let Drew out and locked the deadbolts behind him, I

slipped into the bathroom. Water flowed from the faucet, and I splashed the stream over my face. I looked into the mirror, and my forehead still glistened with the mark of Julian's kiss. It was becoming a comfort to see. I leaned in closer to get a better look at my face. A few fine lines were forming around my eyes. The slightest evidence of life's wear and tear on my body. I tried to imagine what those lines would look like deepened, with creases around my mouth and blanketing my forehead. After a few centuries of always being beautiful, would I even be capable of letting that go?

My mind switched over to Drew's face. He had smile lines. Creases at the corners of his eyes. His teeth were by no means perfect . . . but he was beautiful with a personality that radiated warmth and integrity. I pulled on my pink, fuzzy robe and walked into the kitchen. For Drew, I could grow old. He wouldn't see wrinkles and sagging breasts; he would see me.

Oh Hell, did I really just think that? I might have just vomited in my mouth a little.

"You and me both."

I screamed, wrapping the robe even tighter around my body. The smell of peppermint hit the back of my throat immediately. Jules sat at my table, a glass of red wine in his hand and a second sitting in front of the chair across from him. He swirled the scarlet liquid, and it clung to the edges of the glass like thin blood.

"Don't *do* that!" I shrieked at him.

His mouth tilted, but his eyes stayed on his glass. "Wine?" he asked without looking at me.

"Thanks," I said quietly, and sat down across from him. My forehead tingled and that guilt at the pit of my stomach deepened even more with an added flavor of embarrassment. I could feel the flush rise from the top of my breasts up around my neck and cheeks. I cleared my throat before speaking. "So, when did you get here?"

He took a slow sip, savoring the flavor of the cabernet, swishing it around his mouth in a thoughtful way. "I've been here for—a while."

I nodded. I didn't need to read his thoughts to know what he saw. Or heard.

"I waited outside. In the future, if you wish to keep your indiscretions private, might I suggest the bedroom. Or at least a sock on the door." His lip curled back.

"I'll keep that in mind." Our eyes caught for a moment and he held my gaze. *My mind is blank, my mind is blank, my mind is blank,* I kept thinking over and over.

He exhaled and set the wineglass back down on the table. "Okay, Monica. You win. No mind reading tonight, I promise." He leaned back in the chair and took a less calculated sip of wine.

I raised my glass in the air and tilted my head to the side. "Well, I'll drink to that." I mustered up a little more courage before asking him the question that plagued me. "So, what was the crime scene like?"

"It was . . . informative."

I sighed. "That was pretty much the elusive answer I had expected from you."

We sat in quiet, sipping our wine for a few moments longer. I looked up, making eye contact with Jules. He broke the silence. "What would you like for dinner?"

I shrugged. "Want to order a pizza?"

His mouth twitched at the corners. "I had something a little more creative in mind."

"Oh?" My head tilted. Lately, it seemed, food was the fastest way to get my attention. Food and sex. Though the latter was nothing new.

He stood, taking our empty wineglasses to the sink. "I'll whip up some dinner. Why don't you disinfect the table?"

*   *   *

I didn't even realize I had enough ingredients in my fridge to make mac and cheese—let alone the gourmet broiled chicken and vegetables in a béchamel sauce that Julian had magically "whipped" up.

I cut into the meat, so tender it barely needed a knife to separate. Julian didn't eat much, just sort of shifted his food around. A few bites here and there, he chewed without taking his eyes off me. It took all my energy not to moan as I swirled the asparagus around the cream sauce and slid it into my mouth.

Jules's eyebrow arched in amusement. "Good?"

He knew the answer already. Just goes to show that even angels enjoy validation. "Very. Thank you."

I swallowed another bite and took a sip of wine, the alcohol starting to take effect. "You know what would make this meal even better?"

"What's that?"

"If you would tell me what you discovered at the crime scene."

He sighed ever so slightly. "I can't."

"Why not? You're the one who wanted me to get involved in the first place. I thought we could compare notes."

His arms crossed over his chest. "Notes, huh? And what exactly did you discover today?"

"Nuh-uh. You don't get my observations if I don't get yours."

He stayed in his same position, an intense heat simmering between us. "I could just read your mind."

I smiled and leaned forward, resting my arms on the table. Sticking my knife into the last piece of chicken, I pointed it at him. "I don't think so. You made a promise—no mind reading tonight." Triumphantly, I ate the last piece, chewing happily.

His mouth opened to say something but hung slack-jawed, no words coming out. Finally, he said, "A promise is a promise."

I used a piece of bread to mop up the remaining sauce on my

plate, and when I met Julian's gaze—those eyes burning into me—I put the bread down, feeling suddenly hedonistic.

He laughed quietly. "Would you like *my* plate?"

I hesitated. Part of me wanted more. The other part felt as though he was mocking me with the question. "No, thank you. I would much prefer to hear about any evidence found at the crime scene."

He sighed and gathered the plates. "I can't tell you, Monica. I'm not allowed. Lucien made it clear that I could not share any information."

"Since when do you abide by a demon's rules!?" My voice grew shrill. The only reason I agreed to this whole investigation was because I thought Jules would be helping me the whole time.

"I have a few loopholes when the time is right."

"Of course you do," I huffed. Angels. Tricky little fuckers.

Later that night, we curled up on the couch and watched *How to Steal a Million*. Julian rubbed my feet, gently kneading my muscles. I dozed off somewhere around the time Audrey Hepburn was dressing up like a maid. When I woke up, light was peeking through my curtains. At some point during the night Jules must have wrapped me in a cocoon of blankets and moved me to my bed. The left side of the bed was rumpled and messed as well—indicating that he probably slept beside me. See? Deductive reasoning. I could totally do this detective thing.

I slipped into the bathroom still in my groggy morning haze and splashed some water on my face. After brushing my teeth, I followed my nose to the kitchen. It smelled like pancakes. And bacon. Oh Hell, that smelled good.

"Don't curse. There's an angel present." Jules was standing over my stove, spatula in hand.

"Stop reading my mind," I grumbled, knowing that my pleas were a lost cause.

I could feel Jules's smirk even though he wasn't facing me. "You had a whole night off. Today you're free game." I made a noise that sounded something like a *humph* and poured myself a cup of coffee, our bodies so close to each other that my shoulder was brushing his bicep. "Lucky for you," Jules continued, "I'm off duty for at least the next eight hours." He leaned over and tweaked the tip of my nose with his finger.

I forced myself to take a step away from him. Letting the hot coffee warm my hands, I remembered last night with Drew. How I saw the flash of his future—his future with me in it. Jules was eyeing me from the stove.

"Why didn't you tell me?"

"Tell you what?" I widened my eyes innocently.

"Don't play coy, Monica. You don't wear it well."

I sighed. "It just—I didn't want to talk about the events of last night. Especially with you."

"You have your powers back?" His eyes glistened.

I thought for a moment. "Sort of. Not entirely. Watch." I set the mug down and closed my eyes, willing my body to shift out of my robe and into today's clothes. I felt the tingle sensation— a feeling not unlike someone running their finger along the length of my spine. When I opened my eyes, Julian was staring at me, mouth agape. His eyes were about eight inches south of my face, and when I looked down at my body, the robe was gone. In its place were panties and no bra. "Oh Hell!" I grabbed Julian's white button-down shirt that was thrown over the back of a chair and wrapped it over myself. When I looked up, Julian was still standing over the stove, spatula in hand, staring at where I had been.

He swallowed hard and cleared his throat. My eyes dropped to his jeans. Lust. His pants were definitely tight around the crotch. I looked away, my face burning. He turned, still flustered, and looked at me. His mouth opened, then shut again as if searching for the right words. A few stutters came out, and I interrupted his nonsensical sentence.

"Julian, I never pegged you as the guy to get flustered over a little nudity. But, for the record, that wasn't what I was trying to shift into."

He nodded. "It has been a long time since I've seen a naked woman." He turned back to the pancakes.

Sadness washed over me. Seeing me with Drew must have been torture for him. "Jules, about last night . . ."

"In terms of your powers," he interrupted, "I will tell Lucien when I see him today. Other than from him and me, I think this should stay a hidden fact. Let the murderer think you're still helpless. It will give us the edge if he does make his move. I don't even want you telling George and Kayce."

"I still think we should talk . . ."

A knock at the door cut me off midsentence. Jules smiled, the grin slicing across his face. Eyes still sad, the smile all a ruse. "You should put your robe back on." He leaned in and put a hand on my waist, his mouth coming dangerously close to mine. "That shirt is rather sheer. I can still see"—he exhaled a deep breath—"almost everything." He pushed himself away and put a plate filled with M&M's pancakes on the kitchen counter. "That's probably Kayce," he said. "I'll get the door."

After sliding back into my robe, I sat at the table with my plate of delicious pancakes and my steaming cup of coffee. From down the hall Jules's voice rumbled, and I heard two people walking into the kitchen.

"Hi, George," I said as he came in and sat down next to me. "Want some pancakes?"

He cautiously looked over at mine with a look on his face that suggested I offered him sewage. "Did you make them?" His nose crinkled.

I spoke on my exhale. "No, Jules did."

Julian bowed his head ceremoniously at me and went to the sink to clean. George grabbed a fork and scooped two of my pancakes onto his own plate. "Well, I'm not gonna say no to angelic pancakes, now, am I? They weren't made with holy water, were they?"

Jules brought George a cup of coffee and sat down across from him to my left. "Where is Kayce today? She's supposed to take over detail."

"She called this morning. Hungover. Asked me to fill in."

"Hungover? *Kayce?*"

George shoveled a forkful of pancakes into his mouth and shrugged. "I popped in to check on her this morning. She seemed all right, just out a little too late." Bits of pancake sprayed from his mouth as he talked.

"Damn, dude." I grabbed a napkin and wiped up the remnants of food he projectile spat while talking. "Where are your manners?"

Jules watched, not smiling but also not frowning. "So, you'll be watching Monica today?"

George leaned back in the chair. "Yep. Figured we'd do some shoe shopping or something." He winked at me.

Julian stood from the table. "Well, then, I guess I'll be off." He bent down and kissed my forehead again in the same spot, the cool tingly sensation washing over me. Then he whispered, "That one was just for me."

Crack. He was gone. The only trace that he'd been there was the slight smell of peppermint in the air and his gourmet M&M's pancakes on my plate.

22

I cleared our plates, putting them in the sink and rinsing. "So, shoe shopping, huh? Sounds good to me."

George stood and carried his almost-empty coffee cup over to me. "I figure it will be pretty easy to keep you safe in a crowded shopping mall."

I nodded, squinting my eyes at him. "And we could check in on Kayce in the afternoon. Make sure she's feeling better. Let me go put some clothes on." I scurried off to my bedroom and threw on a pair of jeans. I examined my neck in the mirror. The bruises were still there but almost gone. I decided to go with a short-sleeved fitted turtleneck again, just to be safe, and slipped the panic button necklace back on over my head.

I did what I could with my hair for only having five minutes. Scrunched some mousse in and fluffed it at the roots. I tapped a little concealer under my eyes, brushed a bit of blush across my cheeks, and put on a coat of mascara. I stepped back and checked myself in the mirror. Not quite so put together as I usually look, but not bad for a succubus with next to no powers. I definitely didn't want to waste what little energy I had superficially.

I walked back out to the kitchen, dressed and ready to go.

"Oh, I almost forgot." George pulled the pendant I had lent Kayce from his pocket. "Kayce wanted me to give this back to you." I turned around, lifting my hair, letting him clasp it behind my neck. He then took my hand and twirled me around the kitchen. "Lovely as always." As he raised my hand to his lips, giving it a soft gentlemanly brush across the knuckles, there was a knock at the door. We both froze and stared at the door.

George slid a glance to me. "You expecting anyone?"

I shook my head. "No. But I've been getting a lot of unannounced visitors lately."

George headed for the door. "Stay here."

"Hell, no!" I followed after him, peeking around his shoulder. "Let's just not answer. They never have to know we're here," I whispered.

George sighed and turned to face me, putting both hands on my shoulder. "I may not be an overt badass like Kayce or an angel or even an ArchDemon, but I am one of the oldest known incubi in existence. I think I can take whomever this is. Now, at least stay *behind* me, please."

George swung the door open and coming up the stairs was Damien. He wore black dress pants and a royal blue button-down shirt. He had a light leather jacket on and looked positively delicious. He looked so put together that I instantly regretted not taking the time to apply another coat of mascara.

I peeked out from behind George. "What are you doing here? How did you find my apartment?"

He gave me a *duh* look. "I'm a detective. I can find anyone."

"Except for the murderer, huh?"

He put a hand to his heart. "Ouch." He gave a nod to

George. "Nice to see you again. I hope I'm not interrupting anything."

George shook his hand and scoffed at the idea. "Hardly. I'm her bodyguard today."

"Bodyguard? Got some stalkers, do you?"

I nodded. "Something like that."

He looked back at George. "I'd say you need to boost your security a little." He pointed to the outside of the door. George and I had both been so paralyzed by Damien's presence, we hadn't even noticed the knife sticking out of my door, piercing an envelope with my name on it and a sprig of lavender. The word *WHORE* was written in big red letters underneath.

"Holy shit!" My hands raised to my mouth. "Do you—do you think that's *blood?*"

Damien perked up at this remark. "Blood? Why in the hell would it be written in blood?"

"What will the neighbors think?" I rushed to the kitchen and grabbed Clorox—the only cleaning solvent I owned—and paper towels.

I ran back to the door, where Damien intercepted me, catching me midrun around the waist. "Are you crazy? You might destroy evidence. Now someone explain to me—why would this possibly be blood? What would make your mind go there?"

"Monica's been having some *intense* stalker issues lately." George shrugged.

"With notes made in blood?" Damien asked.

We both nodded, and Damien stepped closer to the door, examining the writing. He put a hand to the door and closed his eyes. I could hear a slight buzzing, and the hair on the back of my neck stood at attention.

"It's not blood," Damien said after a minute. "And *whore* was not written by the same person who knifed the note and lavender to the door."

"So now can I wash it off?" I could not stand the thought of my neighbors, Mr. and Mrs. Libschticky, going on their morning walk with their poodle and seeing this graffiti strewn across my door.

He laid his hand to the door again and nodded. "Whoever did this, both actions just happened recently. Within the hour." He pulled a gun out of his waistband and peered to the left and right outside my front door. "I'm going to go look around a bit. See what I can find."

I spent at least thirty minutes scrubbing the damn door before Damien came back into my home. He was panting slightly, and a small sweat had broken out across his hairline. "The area is clear. I don't think whoever did this stuck around." I heard him walk back to the kitchen and open my fridge.

I looked over at George, who was still standing guard at the door. When I looked back over, Damien was now drinking one of *my* beers. In fact, it was my last beer, with his feet up on my kitchen table. "A bit early for a drink, isn't it?"

His mouth tipped into a crooked smirk. "It's never too early for a beer."

I turned back to scrubbing my door. "By the way," Damien continued, "your door tells me it hardly ever gets cleaned. It feels neglected."

I muttered some curses under my breath. When it was faded enough to where only people up close would see the word, I figured it was good enough for now. Until I could get some paint, at least.

George reached up and grabbed the knife and the envelope while I closed the door. "Would you like to do the honors or should I?"

I gestured to him. "Please. Go right ahead." I walked back into the kitchen and slapped Damien's leg. "Get your feet off of my dining table." I was in a really bad mood, and I had a feeling my day was about to get worse.

"Okay." George slid another greeting card out of the envelope. This one was a Valentine's Day card with a glittery heart on the front. "Roses are red," he read aloud, "lavender for you." He swallowed before continuing, eyes shifting back and forth between Damien and me. "I will not stop"—his voice cracked—"Till you're dead, cold, and blue."

A nervous giggle escaped my lips. And then a full-out laugh. And suddenly, I couldn't stop laughing. I was laughing so hard that tears were spilling from my cheeks and my stomach hurt. "I'm sorry," I said, gulping for air. "I just can't believe the big, bad stalker resorted to a 'roses are red' poem."

George was looking at me with concern, and Damien was now leaning forward, forearms rested against his knees. He stared at me like I was an escapee from a mental institution.

My laughter faded, and as I wiped my cheeks my muscles shook. An uneasy gnawing at my gut made it feel like my insides were twisting. My knees were trembling, and I used all my focus to not pee my pants. I didn't trust myself to say anything else just yet.

George rushed over just as my legs turned to Jell-O and caught me in his arms. "Maybe we should forget shoe shopping. Staying in and watching some movies sounds pretty good right about now."

"Sounds to me like there's a little more to this story than an overzealous stalker." Damien stared at us, still sitting at the head of my dining table.

"You!" I pointed at Damien. "Elemental! What did the guy who dropped this off look like?"

"Damien," he said. "My *name* is *Damien*."

I knew that, of course. My body was humming his name. "Right. *Damien*. Sorry. So, *Damien*, what does this guy look like?"

He rolled his eyes. "It doesn't work like that. I don't *see* what happens in some sort of ethereal flashback. The door just sort of—*tells* me what it experienced." He exhaled and ran a hand through his hair, massaging the back of his neck. "Christ. That sounds just as ridiculous, doesn't it?"

"Well, could you please *ask* the door to give us a description of him?"

He smirked and leaned back in the chair, crossing his arms. "I could." He continued to sit there, doing nothing.

"Well?" My voice was starting to shriek. Not an attractive quality, I realized, but these threats were getting really old. My tolerance had long been surpassed. "What are you waiting for?"

He sucked his teeth and slowly got up and strolled over the front door. He put his hand to it, and once again a low buzz rumbled around the apartment. After another minute or so, he pulled away and stuffed his hands into his black trouser pant pockets. "Mm, yes, that's very interesting." He leaned casually against the kitchen doorway.

"You have a description of him?"

"Oh yeah." He shifted his muscular shoulders and raised his eyebrows arrogantly. "Him and a few others who've been in and out of the apartment in the past couple days. Sounds like you had quite the interesting night last night."

I could hear the blood rushing around my brain, and my heart pounded against my chest. With gritted teeth, I answered, "*That's* not any of your business. Tell me—what does he look like?"

"Oh, I'm getting a strong gut feeling that there's more to this stalker. And I have even stronger suspicions that it relates to my murder case." He pushed off the wall and walked toward us. "I'm happy to help you. *If* you help me in return."

He was very tall and towered over me, my heels doing nothing to balance out our height. He flicked a glance at George, who still had a protective arm around me. "Is there a reason we need a chaperone?" He jerked his head in George's direction.

I tilted my head and snaked my arm around George's back.

"It seems like a good idea to keep a bodyguard with someone like you around."

His eyes raked over me from head to toe. "In a turtleneck? Hardly the sort of look that requires a chaperone, babe." He said one thing, but there was something in the way he licked his lips that made me want to call bullshit.

My eyes narrowed and George answered for me. "I don't trust you." He squeezed me closer to him. In actuality, I don't think Damien was a danger. At least not to my life. Now, to my pants—that's another story.

Damien slipped off his jacket, pulled the gun back out of his waistband and a knife out of his sock, and placed them all on the counter out of his reach. "On second thought . . ." He took the gun, pointed it at himself, and passed me the grip. "There. If I attempt anything—she can shoot me." His dark eyebrows arched. "Can we have a minute now?"

George looked at me for approval, and I gave a little nod. He released my shoulder and headed for my bedroom. On his way, he muttered, "You are bat shit crazy to give that woman a gun."

The door to the bedroom shut and Damien held my gaze. "Well?"

I lowered my eyes. "Well, *what?*"

"Are you going to tell me what the hell is going on here, or am I going to have force it out of you?"

"And just how would you go about doing that while I have a gun pointed at you?"

His eyes twinkled. "I have my ways."

"You're seriously not going to tell me the description of a man who clearly wants to harm me? You're *that* stubborn?"

"I will tell you. As soon as you update me on the situation, I will happily give you any and all information that I think will help."

I sighed and put the gun on the counter. It might have been my imagination, but I thought I saw him relax slightly. "I can't tell you. My . . . superiors have instructed me not to tell anyone."

"Ah yes, Lucien, if I'm guessing correctly. Nevada's good ol' ArchDemon."

"Exactly." I paused, looking again into his dark eyes. I thought back to our kiss in the car. It was unwanted, I reminded myself. He pushed himself on me. *Yeah, right,* I thought, inwardly rolling my eyes. *That's why your nipples are pushing through your shirt right now.* I cleared my throat and fiddled with the gun on the counter. "I could ask Lucien. When I see him next—tell him you have information you would be willing to share. That's the best I can do."

His breathing grew heavy and he stepped closer to me. "Don't play with that." He pushed the gun away from my grasp, backing me against my cabinets, and placed his hard thigh between my legs, applying just the right amount of pressure. "You've had a lot of men in this house the past few days." The tip of his nose touched mine, and his hands were wrapped around my rib cage, his thumbs brushing the underside of my breasts.

I swallowed. "It's my job."

He shook his head slowly. "These visits weren't work related." His eyes flicked to the kitchen table. *Great! Of all the doors in this city, mine has to be a fucking gossip!* He brushed his lips across mine, a light and feathery touch and I felt a sudden surge of annoyance that he thought I would just add him to this list. In a swift movement, my hand rose, as if it had a mind of its own, and slapped him across the face. A loud *clap* sound echoed through my kitchen. He smiled, and as I thought he was going to lean down and kiss me again, he paused, taking notice of my necklace. His head cocked to the side and he looked closer at it. "Where did you get this?" He moved to touch it and I slapped his hand away.

"A . . . client."

"How long have you had it?"

"Not long," I answered honestly.

He seemed to mull that over for a second, and then finally he pushed off of the cabinets, away from my body. "George," he called, "come on out." He turned to gather his weapons, putting them back in their appropriate holsters.

George entered and looked at me carefully. I sent him a smile. I felt much better after slapping Damien.

"So," Damien said after suiting himself back up. "You two want to see the other crime scenes?"

23

I felt pretty safe with Damien by my side. Maybe it was the fact that we now had another supernatural man on our team. Maybe it was because not even my *house* felt safe anymore and being outside was a relief. Whatever the reason, I was glad to have the extra muscle around.

Damien drove one of those giant luxury trucks with four doors and leather seats. I sat shotgun and George rode sprawled out across the backseat. We drove toward the north end of town, and Damien pulled into a swanky luxury apartment complex.

Putting the truck in park, he said, "Well, here we are. Victim number two."

"Does victim number two have a name?" I searched my purse for a stick of gum. With the amount of men kissing me lately, I needed to ensure fresh breath.

"She does, but I don't recommend calling her by it."

I let my purse fall into my lap, pointedly. "She was a *person*. Not just some victim."

"She was a succubus, not a person. Besides, the more you

connect the victim to humanity, the easier it is to mix fact with emotion."

"Just tell me what her fucking name was." I found my gum at the bottom of my bag and popped a piece in my mouth. "And succubi are people, too, you know," I said more quietly.

He tossed me a file, which landed in my lap on top of my purse. "Not *human* people, but sure. Why not? Succubi are 'people,' too." His tone was quiet and snarky. It made me want to slap him again.

I pushed the desire to inflict pain on Damien aside and instead opened the folder. The crime scene pictures weren't anywhere near as gory as Savannah's, but they *were* more disturbing. The top of the file had her name. "Lyla Swan," I said aloud. "The porn star?"

Damien tapped his thumbs against the steering wheel. "Yep."

George perked up from the backseat. "No shit!" He leaned over my shoulder to examine the file with me. She was naked when she died. Her hands were tied behind her back, and she was lying stomach-down on the bed. Her face was turned to the side, lifeless eyes staring into the camera lens. She looked more gorgeous than she ever did on camera. Her skin a flawless porcelain, her hair dark blond. The only signifier that she was dead was a small trickle of blood dripping from the corner of her mouth, down her chin. I shivered and shut the file. "How did she die?"

Damien looked at me from below his dark eyebrows. "It's all in the file."

I handed it back to him. "I don't want to read. I want you to tell me."

He smirked, tucking the file under his arm. Without answering me, he pulled his keys out of the ignition. "In that case— let's walk and talk."

* * *

We stepped into the dingy elevator and Damien pushed the button for the third floor. Damien had his hands in his pockets again, leaning against the marble elevator walls. "We know that Lyla had sex more than once on the day she was murdered. And we think that the murderer might have tried to rape her—it's a major inconsistency from the other crime scenes. A postmortem rape kit confirmed tearing and bruising around the vaginal walls."

"Ick." George scrunched his face.

"Gross," I said at the same time as George. We looked at each other. "You sound like a doctor or something."

Damien sighed and unbuttoned the top button on his shirt, pulling it away from his neck. "This is why I don't bring civilians to crime scenes."

"The last thing either of us wants to hear from a hot guy are the words *tearing, bruising,* and *vaginal walls* in the same sentence. Ugh." George looked at Damien, whose eyes narrowed.

"Why would it matter to you?" Damien asked. His eyes roamed over George, and for the first time since I met Damien, I saw a look of surprise cross his face. "Oh." Recognition hit as he soaked in George's style. Skinny black jeans, a plaid button-down shirt with the sleeves rolled to the elbow, and a striped tie tucked into a gray suit vest. Paired with his bowler hat and hipster (nonprescription) glasses, it's a wonder it took Damien this long to realize. "You're gay," Damien said matter-of-factly.

I took a protective step in front of George out of instinct. "Seriously? You couldn't tell?" I gestured up and down George's outfit.

Damien shrugged. "I just thought he had a great sense of style."

"I *do* have a great sense of style," George said, arms crossed in front of him.

"As do I." Damien smirked. "I guess I didn't realize that was a prerequisite to being gay." George and I continued staring at him. The elevator chimed and opened on the third floor.

Damien sighed and stepped off, holding the door for both of us. "Calm down, you two. I just gave him a compliment and you're acting as if I have a white cone hat on my head and a firebomb in my hand."

I stepped off the elevator, my eyes still skeptically on Damien. George followed behind me. I saw his face soften, which made me immediately relax, too. "I just always expect the worst out of habit," George said.

Damien gave a nod of understanding and unhooked the crime scene tape. We entered Lyla's apartment with much less fanfare than with Savannah's home. The dark mahogany hardwood floors were pristine—waxed to perfection. We walked in; a large marble kitchen was to the left and straight ahead was a spacious living room.

"Damn," George said. "You should change careers, Monica."

I considered this for a moment—porn isn't respectable by any means, but I would have access to men who were deserving of losing their souls. I shook the thought from my mind. No way. I can barely stand taking my clothes off for money. I'd never succeed in porn.

Damien leaned over, speaking close to my ear. "You were considering it for a moment, weren't you?"

"No," I lied.

He chuckled as I walked deeper into Lyla's apartment. "So, I'm guessing based on the picture that she was found in her bedroom?" I entered through French double doors, and the bedroom, too, was large and luxurious. Though not quite as clean as the living room and kitchen.

The boys followed behind me as I walked over to the bed. There was an imprint of what looked like a body in the duvet. "However, we think she tried to run. Was actually poisoned here"—Damien pointed to a different taped-off area on the floor near the doorway—"then placed back on the bed in the sexual position you saw in the picture." I looked over at George, who had barely entered the bedroom.

"And what did the elements tell you?"

He shrugged. "Not much. Either this guy had prior knowledge of elementals being involved in the Las Vegas Police Department or he's really careful. He made sure to put enchantments on everything. There's very little they can tell me about the evening in question."

I crouched down to the floor where she was assumed to be killed. "Was there any hint of magic?" I asked.

Damien shook his head. "Unlike the first crime scene, this place held no traces of the arcane on the night she died. He most likely did it by hand. Could have even been a human. The first time, the magic we felt could have only been her magic."

"So Lyla didn't even use magic that evening?" I asked.

"Nope," he answered.

That meant Savannah hadn't lost all her powers yet but Lyla's were entirely gone. He somehow messed up Savannah's murder. I thought of the night before and how a twinge of power purred through my body. *Like he maybe messed up mine, too.*

I stood up and circled the bedroom, doing two more laps before I stopped in front of Damien. I crossed my arms over my chest. "This is the most boring crime scene ever! There's nothing here to see!"

His gaze settled on mine. "Because most of the time, evidence has already been bagged." He shoved the file back toward me. "Hence the reason you have to *read*. And look at the pictures."

"Well, fine. Just tell me what I missed."

He pulled out one of the pictures from the file. "You should have noticed the condom wrapper in the trash can."

Crap. "Well—maybe I did see it in the picture. She is a porn star. I didn't really think that much of it." I paused, holding his gaze.

"So, the murderer used a condom?" George asked, still standing in the doorway.

"Maybe." Damien started pacing around the room. "All corpses associated with the case so far are essentially human for all intents and purposes. They all had either very little or no magic left in them and were all some form of a sex worker." He took a moment, hesitating before using the phrase "sex worker," glancing at me.

"Savannah . . ." he continued. "Our first victim had consensual sex within a few hours of her time of death. However, with a succubus, I hardly see how that's much of a clue." He said it with a smile. As if speaking only to piss me off.

"So the murderer was a human. If he was immortal, he wouldn't have needed protection," I said.

"Perhaps." Damien put his hands on his hips and stopped walking around the room. "But the man she had sex with using the condom might have been someone other than the murderer. If it was our killer and he was a human, he still must have known she was a succubus in order to successfully carry out these murders. Which means he would have known condoms were unnecessary." He turned, looking directly at me and licked his lips. "And trust me—no man would wear a condom if it wasn't needed."

"Or," George continued for Damien, "it could have just been some random person she had sex with prior to her death."

Damien nodded. "Exactly."

"So—if so far all the murder methods are different, what is there even connecting them?"

"You mean other than the fact that both victims were succubi?" George sneered.

"LVPD doesn't know that. From an outsider perspective— why would someone think they were connected?"

"Now you're thinking like a detective." Damien pointed at me with his forefinger and then allowed it to rest on his lips. It was weird seeing him in business mode. He took on a different demeanor . . . still a dickhead. But a more professional dickhead, at least. "Obviously, we have more information than your average cop. We know the link is that they are both succubi. We know that they both were stripped of their powers. Victim number—uh . . ." He shot a glance at me and put both hands up in front of him in a surrender stance. "Lyla more than Savannah. Lyla was most likely stripped entirely of her power. She had filmed a scene earlier in the morning, and it was pretty obvious that she wasn't able to shift herself to look good. When we talked to the makeup artist on set, she said that for the first time in her career, Lyla did not arrive camera ready."

"You watched the porn from the day she died?" A pang of jealousy stabbed in my chest at the thought of him watching another succubus at work.

His lips twitched. "*That's* what you took from all that information?"

I ignored his smug smile and shrugged. "So, if I was an LVPD cop, why would I think these were linked?"

"That was a bit tricky." He slumped against the wall. "My partner and I had to convince our captain that two women within twenty miles of each other were killed by the same man. We went for demographic—both women were in the sex industry. Savannah worked for an escort service, Lyla was a porn star. They were brutal murders, worked out to punish the victim. It was a stretch, but we were supported by the chief, so no one really questioned it."

I stared at the bed a few moments, and I swear that I could still see the outline of her body weight on the bedspread. I could see her torso, the curve of her hips, waist, ribs . . . I felt a stronger urge to sit down on the bed. Breathing was becoming suddenly harder. It felt as though something was on my chest, sitting there.

A sharp pain pierced my bottom lip. I could feel his tongue lapping up my blood, running along the edges of my bloody mouth. I was tired, groggy. I could taste the coppery tang of an open cut somewhere on his lips, and I sunk my teeth into his tongue as it slithered inside my mouth. His blood pooled between my lips and he howled in pain, slapping me across the face. He was inside of me—I didn't know for how long he had been thrusting into me. He pulled out just as he finished, his seed dripping down my bare leg. Two large hands descended on me, framing my jaw. My neck snapped, twisting unnaturally 180 degrees. I screamed out in pain, falling onto my knees.

The heaviness faded away, and when I came to, I was resting in someone's lap. I opened my eyes and Damien had both hands cupping my face. He was crouched in front of me, worry lines digging deep around his eyes.

"This happened last time. . . ." George's voice sounded far away, and I looked up to find him cradling me in his lap, rocking me gently, stroking my hair while talking to Damien.

I touched the side of my face, a trickle of blood sliding out of the corner of my mouth.

His eyes studied me a moment longer. "You're connected to the victims?"

I didn't answer, but let's be honest, he didn't need me to. Instead, I pushed myself off of George's lap and stood. They both scrambled to help me up. "Did I mess up your crime scene again?" I said as he placed a large hand on my elbow.

He shook his head, a placating smile on his face. "Not so bad this time."

I rocked forward, away from George's comforting arms. "She was dead." I rubbed my palms over goosefleshed arms.

George and Damien shared a look. A look that said I needed to be committed. "Um, yeah. No shit, Monica. Why do you think we're here?" George's lip curled whenever he was being snarky. It was never attractive.

"No. She *was* dead. He was having sex with her *after* she

had already died. I guess it gave her enough power to wake up. He snapped her neck to kill her again. Apparently he didn't give her enough power to heal her wounds."

Damien nodded, his finger to his lips in thought. "That would explain why we found poison in her system as well as the broken neck. The official report was that the broken neck was the cause of death. Initially we just thought he enjoyed the kill, and used the poison to simply sedate her, but this makes a lot more sense."

"He fucked a dead woman?" All color drained from George's face as he stared at the picture in her open file. "You know, Monica . . . she sort of looks like you."

I took the picture from him and peered at it closer. We had similar coloring and features. We both had our hair cut in layers just below the shoulders. George was right. The one succubus he ended up having sex with after death was the one who looked the most like me.

Damien put a hand on George's shoulder and sat him in a chair. "You okay?" George shook his head, beads of sweat breaking out along his forehead. "Put your head between your knees." George did as instructed with no protest. "So,"—Damien paced around the room, talking more to himself than to us— "the killer has to be human, right? Succubi can't get energy from immortals."

"Not . . . necessarily." George spoke from between his knees, breathing slowly with each word. "We can steal energy from other immortals. Usually not through sex, but through blood. We can all gain power by consuming various magical blood."

Both their heads snapped toward me. "Was she bleeding?" Damien asked.

I thought back to the horrible memory. "They both were."

"But life force is taken only when orgasm is reached?" Damien looked back at George again.

"Mostly, yes." I answered for George since he seemed so out

of breath. "If we're starved enough and close to death, though, something as small as a kiss can induce an orgasm in most creatures."

"Hmm." Damien grinned at me. "You turned out to be more valuable than I thought you would."

I rolled my eyes. "Are we done here?"

He gave a single nod and then looked down at George. "Let's get her home."

We stepped out of the apartment and Damien locked up behind us. Shielding the late morning sun from my eyes, I squinted, seeing a silhouetted figure walking in our direction.

"Oh great," George murmured.

The figure continued walking toward us, her breasts leading the way. I saw her clothing before I saw her face—and there was only one person who could make Prada look slutty. Lexi.

Her brown hair was cut bluntly at her shoulders, and long, straight bangs tickled her eyelashes in an annoying way that left me wanting to rip them out by the roots. She stopped close to me—too close. I was breathing the air she exhaled, but I held my ground firmly. I would *not* be the one to step back.

"Well, well, well." She put her hands on her hips. "You're looking—*homely* today."

I gritted my teeth. My Queen might not have been present at the moment, but it's still never a good idea to piss off her right-hand woman. "I'm sure it's better than anything you could do with that straw you call hair. Gee," I said, dramatically placing a finger to my chin, "it must just kill you that even with no shifting and my tits fully covered, Lucien *still* chooses to spend his time with me over you."

Her breathing grew intense, and her chest rose and fell in angry heaves. I leaned in closer, mocking a whisper. "You should be careful. Inflate those babies much more and they're likely to pop." Okay, so maybe I needed a little work in the anger management department of my life.

Lexi's teeth were clenched. "Why you ungrateful little bitch. I'm stuck here working to save your life and you insult me?"

"*You* ambushed *me*," I countered.

She sneered a smile. "That's not what my notes to Mia will say."

My breath stuck in my throat and a small surge of panic caught me right in the chest. Mia was downright terrifying when she was normal. I'd hate to see her angry. "So—what exactly are you doing here? Following me?"

"Hardly." She snorted a laugh, telling me exactly what she thought of that idea. "I suppose I'm here doing exactly what you were. Checking out the crime scenes."

"Not in my crime scene, you're not." Damien spoke from behind me, stepping forward.

Lexi looked him up and down, devouring him. She arched an eyebrow. "And you are?"

"Detective Kane. This is my crime scene."

She stepped forward, moving me aside with the back of her hand. "Oh yeah?" She licked her lips and pushed her breasts into his chest. He stared down at them, mesmerized. I didn't know if I wanted to clothesline her or *him*. I had no claim over either of them, but jealousy itched over my skin like poison oak.

"I'm sure I could arrange something with you, right?" Her lips were close to his, and she glanced over at me as she flicked out a tongue to his lips.

I looked at George, my eyes wide and panicked. He rolled his eyes and grabbed Lexi by the elbow, pulling her away from Damien. "I'll take you up to see it." He held a hand out, palm up to Damien. "Keys?"

George was dragging her into the building.

I crossed my arms over my chest and glared at Damien. He smirked and leaned against his truck. "What?" he asked innocently, eyes wide.

"It would be nice if you could keep it in your pants. For once."

"Ah. Jealous?"

"Of Lexi? Hardly."

"What do you care? I'm not your concern."

I rolled my eyes so far back into my head, that my neck actually mimicked the movement. "I *don't* care. But even scum like you should have higher standards than Lexi." I laughed at myself as I said it. "But what am I saying? You're the 'other man' in Adrienne's life. You clearly just have terrible taste in women."

He turned so that he was facing me and put a hand on my hip. His head tilted in close to mine. "Is that so?"

I smacked his hand away from my body, but it just stayed right there on my hip like a bug that wouldn't leave me alone.

"Yes. It is."

"And if I told you that *you* were my type? What would you say to that?"

I swallowed, and a flutter of excitement spiraled in my stomach like a twister. "I'd say that you're a liar. There's no way someone could be with Adrienne and seriously claim that I was also his type."

"You mean like your coffee shop man?"

I opened my mouth and then snapped it shut again. *Damn.* "That's different. Drew's just . . . naive."

He gave my hip a tight squeeze. "If you give me a good reason to stay away from Lexi, I will. Otherwise, she's easy with big tits. And fair game—considering you're spoken for already. I keep forgetting . . . who is it you're dating today?"

I stepped away from him, shoving his hand back toward his

body. "She's a succubus," I said simply. "You sleep with her and you'll lose years off your life."

He lit a cigarette and held out the pack to me. I shook my head no. The cigarette dangling from his lips combined with him leaning against his car in his black leather jacket—he looked like he belonged in the cast of *The Outsiders*. The smoke blew from his nostrils as he exhaled a small laugh. "Nope. We elementals are immune to your poison, succubus." He held the cigarette out for me to take a puff. "You sure you don't want just one drag?" The smell was so bitter and sweet. One drag wouldn't hurt. I wrapped my lips around it and inhaled the sweet and spicy smoke. "I'm a lot like this cigarette," he said. We stood farther apart now. I squeezed my thighs together in an attempt to make the throbbing between my legs stop. He continued, "You know I'm bad for you, but you just can't seem to bring yourself to throw out that last pack."

24

Malta, 1942

The medic tent was filled almost entirely. We had more wounded soldiers coming in than we had beds. Most of our supplies were in the hotel that we had taken over, but we set up the tents even closer to where the battles were in order to get to the men faster.

"Nurse! We need a nurse over here!" a doctor yelled from across the room as they rushed in a new patient. I was on the other side but quickly taped off the wound I was dressing and rushed over. My heart pounded; a tightness in my chest consumed me as I ran to the new soldier.

The memory flashed into my mind. Wills and I having sex the last time before he shipped off to France for the war. His death splashed across my memory. Blood. Lots of it. A battlefield. Bombs and guns still going off in the distance. And Wills drifting off into the unconscious in someone's arms. A part of me hoped that someone would be me, but deep down, I knew it wasn't meant to be. The only sounds other than explosions were his fellow dying soldiers.

I shook the thought from my mind. If I could just find him. I knew from the countryside that the battle was somewhere near

France. And it was probably sometime soon. I ran to the newest soldier, holding my breath as he came into view. A bloodied face—barely recognizable. Legs blown off at the knees. I leaned in closer to get a better view. Not my Wills. Too burly.

I wasn't sure whether to be relieved or disappointed. A breath I didn't know I was holding escaped through my parted lips.

"You going to just stand there? Get some goddamn gauze!" The doctor yelled at me, and I rushed to the rolling cart, coming back with medicines, gauze, and wraps for his open wounds. Everyone here was being pushed too far. Especially the doctors. As much as I hated being yelled at, it was almost excusable during such an unbearable time. We all had our coping mechanisms.

"Take him into the private tent and get him cleaned up. Holler for me when ready and I'll stitch him up. Think you can handle that?" I gritted my teeth at his condescending tone and nodded. Dr. Yells A Lot opened a flask, threw his head back, and took a gulp of something that smelled like motor oil. He pulled me aside by the elbow. "And don't waste the morphine. This one's probably not going to make it." He patted my rear end before clomping away to his next patient.

I looked over at the dying soldier. He wasn't my soldier— but he was somebody's. And the doctor couldn't care less about saving his life. The soldier gurgled something and I rushed to his side, taking his bloody hand in mine. "Save your energy," I whispered to him. "It will be all right, I promise."

He gurgled again and in a raspy voice, I heard one word. "Beautiful."

I smiled at him. "Let's get you cleaned up."

Two other nurses helped me carry the patient into a private tent that was unused, then hurried off to attend their own cases. Dried blood was still on the edges of the table from the last injured soldier. I dipped a rag into a bowl of water. "This might burn." I washed away the blood, taking my time. Burns cov-

ered a lot of the left side of his body. I cut his clothes away from him. After cleaning as much of the blood as I could, he reached up, hand trembling and touched my face.

"Angel," he whispered.

I stepped back instinctively. "No."

His eyes were drifting off. Staring at me, but also through me. As if he could see something that wasn't actually there. "Seraphina." He barely got the word out before his head flopped to the side and vomit mixed with blood projected from his cracked lips.

"Oh Hell," I cried. The doctor was right. He was too far gone. He was in pain. I had to do something. If he hadn't been vomiting, I would have offered him some whiskey to dull the pain.

"You're going to die." I stood there frozen, and the words escaped from my barely moving lips. This was nothing new. I'd seen numerous men die. But for the first time, a realization dawned on me. I may no longer be a Heavenly angel, but I could be their angel of death. I could offer him peace. I could end his suffering.

I looked down at his body. He was still breathing. No longer vomiting, though blood trickled out of his ears and mouth. I pulled my knickers off and tucked them on the table with supplies. Gently, I climbed on top of him—careful not to put too much weight on the injured areas. His body twitched. His eyes widened ever so slightly as if he knew on some level what was about to happen.

I rubbed myself against him, his body reacting despite his mind's unawareness. What little blood was left in his body rushed to his nether regions. When he was firm enough, I slipped him inside of me. His eyes fluttered and he grunted. Some of his juices dripped into me, and the tendrils of magic started. It was like liquid gold being absorbed into my body. The pins and needles coursed through my veins.

I rode him gently, circling my hips carefully over his. His hand rested on my dress, and his eyes met mine one last time. "Angel," he whispered again as his eyes rolled back into his head. I leaned forward and closed his eyelids. A light fluttering of a pulse was still present. I squeezed my muscles around him as he climaxed, and I felt his soul leave like a chilly whoosh. The flash of his life lasted for less than a second. It wasn't a scene as much as it was a feeling. Peace. And pleasure. I had given him a send off better than choking on his own vomit. I climbed off of him and cleaned each of us up quickly.

I kissed his forehead and covered him with the dirty sheet. As I exited the tent, I saw the doctor up ahead, smoking. "He's gone," I said as I approached him. "He just passed."

The doctor was finishing a cigarette and flicked it to the ground. "Good," he said. "Poor man would have had a hell of a time if he had survived with those wounds."

When I glanced up, his eyes flitted up and down my body. I quickly looked away, keeping my eyes down, not meeting his. He cleared his throat. "I'm sure you did all you could."

I looked up again, this time meeting his eyes. He held my gaze and swallowed. It was as if he knew the soldier perished at my touch.

"I need another nurse over here! Gotta live one!" a voice called from inside the main tent. My heart jolted to my throat, and I swiveled around to get a look.

"Well," he said, "don't just stand there. Go. There's plenty of men who are still alive and need our attention."

I nodded and rushed off. Wills's face popped into my mind, and as I ran to the newest soldier, I held my breath again.

25

Within seconds of being home, I rushed to take a shower. I'd neglected to do so in the morning and I needed to pick up my paycheck from the coffee shop. I wanted to look my best considering it was the first time Drew and I were seeing each other since our night together.

The hot water pelted my skin and muscles, feeling like a tiny massage. I groaned and dropped my head against the shower wall. *Wills.* I had a date with Wills tonight. It seemed as though every time I found myself thinking about him, I was always wishing I were with someone else or doing something else. That's probably not a good sign, huh? But then I thought back to that dry, witty sense of humor he has. How gentlemanly and polite he always is. The way his chestnut hair falls into one eye when he laughs. My heart caught in my throat. I turned the water off and bent at the waist, drying my hair. *We just need more time,* I thought. *And I can't keep dwelling on Drew, as much as I want to.*

I flipped my head back and wrapped the towel around my

body. I spent a little extra time on my hair and makeup, blow-drying my locks straight and lining my eyes darker than normal. I stood back from the mirror and smiled at what I saw. I was getting pretty good at doing this without any magic. I hung the towel up and wrapped myself in my fuzzy robe.

I opened the bathroom door into my bedroom and screamed when I saw a figure lying across my bed. I pulled the robe tighter around me. "Julian! Damn, you could have let me know you were in here. Shit."

He winced slightly at my cursing. He was eating popcorn and threw a kernel into the air, catching it in his mouth. "Just doing my job. You know, protecting you. *You're welcome.*"

I walked to my closet and picked out a pair of low-rise jeans and put the turtleneck back on. I changed in my closet, and a shiver of fear ran through me as I remembered finding one of the notes in here. Nowhere was safe, it seemed.

I came out fully dressed, leaned over, and grabbed a piece of popcorn from Julian. "Get your shoes off my bed." I slapped at his ankles and he followed me out to the kitchen, still munching on the popcorn.

"I was thinking," he said, "about your restored powers."

"You mean, you were thinking about what you *saw* of my returned powers?"

His eyebrow arched, and one side of his mouth slid into a smile. "That, too. But—I was also thinking that, as much as neither of us wants you to, you should find a target tonight. See if you can store any more of your energy."

I fell into one of my kitchen chairs. "You want me to sleep with someone?"

He sat down next to me. "If it means bringing you to safety—then, yes."

"I can't believe I'm hearing this." I looked up, meeting Jules's eyes. "There's something I'm missing here. You initially told me to keep my nose clean while I was human. You said there was a chance that if I died, I could go to Heaven. Why do you now, all of a sudden, want me back to being a succubus?"

He leaned back in the chair slowly, watching me. "Okay"— he sighed—"here it is. I had thought maybe that's where the girls' souls were going after death. In my off time from watching you and investigating with Lucien, I've been researching the three—well, four women now—who've died. Their souls aren't in Heaven. Which leaves two options: They're either in Hell being tortured, or they've simply vanished."

"And," I finished his thought for him, "you'd rather have me as a succubus than not have me at all."

He nodded. "You can protect yourself if your powers are restored."

The tightness in my chest was back. I could feel the tears in my throat, and I swallowed them down. I'd done too much crying this past weekend as it was. "But—but, those other succubi . . . they weren't as good as I am. I'm a good person! Jules, I-I still play for the angel team. I only steal Hell-bound souls." My breath was ragged and I was having trouble inhaling despite the fact that I was sitting down. "Maybe those other girls were mean, bad people. Maybe they deserve Hell. But *I* don't!"

He came over and held me. An instant calm wash over me like a salty wave on the beach. It was sudden and peaceful. "Shhh," he whispered while stroking my hair. His angel magic was beautiful—like a cocaine fix, only not as addictive. "You *are* a good person. You're a beautiful soul. But the politics of Heaven and Hell are tricky. This isn't your time." He pulled back, hands still on my shoulders, and looked into my eyes. "But you will be an angel again. I'm not giving up on you."

"Does this mean you'll stay my friend? Even after I'm back to being a succubus?"

"I can't jeopardize my angel status. I'll do my best to maintain some sort of contact with you after. But I promise to always love you."

Another slow tear descended from the corner of my eye and traveled down my cheek. I didn't bother to wipe it away. It fell off my chin like a large raindrop.

I looked away from his burning gaze. "I hope that's good enough."

Something in me itched to look at him again, but I resisted, swallowing a sob. I wiped the tears from my face and mustered up a smile. "I have an errand to run at the café. You up to it?"

He shrugged noncommittally. "I guess I have to be, don't I?"

"So it seems."

"I also have a couple of people for us to talk to about the case. Feeling up to some detective work today?"

"I guess I have to be, don't I?" I echoed him. "How are you getting around Lucien's orders?"

He sat back down in his chair and lounged back. "I promised specifically about the crime scenes. Not other interviews." He smiled proudly.

I didn't know exactly what Jules meant by that—but I trusted him to know what he was doing. I mean, by his very nature he absolutely could not lie. If I asked him if these pants made me look fat, he would *have* to answer truthfully. There's something dangerous and powerful about knowing this about him.

A soft chuckle came from deep in his chest. He leaned over and brushed his lips just below my ear where skin is soft and tender and full of delicious nerve endings. "Those pants definitely do not make you look fat."

The parking lot of the café was fairly full, with only a few spots left at the back.

"Are you coming in invisible?" I asked.

"No," he said, "but I'll mask my powers. Only those with predisposed knowledge of my status will know I'm an angel."

See? Angels are wily little things.

"I'm going to be tapped into your thoughts for most of the afternoon. I would appreciate it if you kept them—well, on the PG side of things."

I nodded at him.

The bells stationed at the front door chimed like a welcoming song as they always do each time someone enters. The thick smell of espresso sat like a heady fog around the café. If I ever got to Heaven again, I would make sure it would smell just like this.

"I have to find Drew," I said, not seeing him behind the bar. "You sure you want to come with?"

His expression darkened just ever so slightly, shoulders slumping, throwing off his center of gravity. "I have to. I am your guardian today."

I exhaled a breath and stifled a yawn. "Very well." Jules followed me as I said hi to Genevieve and Marissa, the other baristas. "This is Julian," I said, introducing him to each.

Both women stared slack-jawed at Jules as he gave them each a warm smile and a genuine greeting. "Genevieve," he said. "Named for my favorite saint." He took her hand and brushed his lips across her knuckles. "San Genevieve" he said, standing back up, "the patron saint of Paris was accredited for saving the city from Attila's Huns."

Genevieve faltered for a second, stuttering. "My mom spent time abroad in Paris and named me after her." Her eyes widened and she looked back at me. I gave her a one shoulder shrug and what I hoped was an innocent smile.

"That's Jules for you. A walking encyclopedia." I elbowed him "C'mon, Britannica."

I dragged him to the back where Drew's office was. *Sheesh,* I thought, hoping Jules was listening. *Could you be any weirder around my friends?*

She seemed to like it.

I rolled my eyes.

Drew's office door wasn't shut entirely. I raised a fist to knock when I heard crying. A girl's shrill voice sobbing. I recognized it immediately as Adrienne. "Drew, you don't understand!" she said through sniffles.

"Just get out, Adrienne. We're done." As Drew's heavy footsteps approached, I backed away from the door quietly.

"No! I'm not leaving."

"Do you have an explanation for the photographs?"

"Yes!"

"Are you going to tell me what it is?"

"I can't!" Her whiny voice was a lot to take. I turned and pushed Julian's chest to retreat. They'd be finished soon enough and then I'd get my check. We could wait a few more minutes.

He nodded and we got all of three steps away when I heard the clomping of her heels behind me. *"You!"* she screamed. When I pivoted back around, a long acrylic fingernail was pointed in my face. "You! You did this! You *whore!* You've wanted me out of the picture since the beginning."

The way she said *whore* made my blood freeze. The word painted on my door flashed into my mind. *"I* didn't do anything, Adrienne."

"You did! You must have! You saw me and Damien together. . . . No one else knew who we were, but all of a sudden you popped up and *Bam!* Drew dumps me!"

"Nothing *'Bam!'* happened to you. *You* cheated on Drew. And *you* got caught. Even if I had been the one to take those pictures—which I wasn't—it still would have been *your* fault."

She stepped close to me, invading my personal space in a major way. Her voice dropped, and it was suddenly low and husky. "You don't understand." It wasn't the voice of the Adrienne I knew and hated. She sounded like an entirely different person. Her voice faltered, the words catching in her throat as if she could just barely get them out. "I didn't cheat on him. You have to believe me."

Her sudden earnestness caught me off guard. And I found myself standing there staring into large, tearful brown eyes. "But—the pictures . . ."

"Aren't what they seem," she said, her jaw muscles so clenched that I could see them protruding from the sides of her face.

"Adrienne!" Drew's voice boomed from behind her. She closed her eyes tightly and a tear dropped from one corner down the side of her nose. "It's time for you to leave. Stop harassing my employees."

Her head dropped, but her eyes shifted up gazing intensely into mine. "Please." She mouthed the word, barely a whisper. I opened my mouth to answer but realized I had nothing else to say to her. A noise caught in my throat. She squinted her eyes shut as a jagged breath escaped her lips. Without another word, she pushed past my shoulder and ran out of the café.

Drew came over, concern etched into his creased forehead. "Are you okay?"

I cleared my throat and nodded. "Yep. I'm sort of getting used to people yelling at me for no reason whatsoever."

A small smile flickered across his face. His gaze moved over my shoulder to where Julian stood, and a momentary flash of jealousy darkened his chiseled features. It was gone before I could even be sure I actually saw it. "Julian, right?" Drew held out a hand again.

Jules nodded and took his hand. "Nice to see you again, Drew." His voice was quiet and assessing.

Drew's eyes crinkled at the corners, sparkling with a smile as they returned to mine. "How are you feeling today?"

"Oh, I'm fine." The conversation was strained and uncomfortable. Drew and I had certainly had our fair share of uncomfortable silences, but this one felt different. Awkward. Like two middle schoolers after a make-out session.

He leaned forward, his hands still in his pockets. "Can we— can we talk alone for a minute?"

I looked back at Jules. He rolled his eyes and gave me a barely noticeable nod. *Scream if you need me.*

"Sure," I said to Drew, then turned to Jules. "I'll be back in a minute."

Drew put his hand on the small of my back and I entered his office. It was tiny—in fact, I think it had previously been a storage closet that he cleared out. It held a desk, filing cabinet, and a bookshelf. That was about it.

I pulled myself up onto the edge of the desk and sat on it. "What's up?"

He rushed to me, cupping my face in his hands and kissed me urgently in a way that made my heart sweat. Our foreheads touched as the kiss ended. "Drew . . ." I whispered.

"Shhh," he hushed, and kissed me again.

I shook my head, my lips still connected to his, and groaned. I put a hand to his chest and pushed him off slowly. "Drew, I can't. I'm just going to end up hurting you. We're too good friends to be so careless."

"Screw that," he growled, and tucked his hands into the back waistband of my jeans.

I chuckled and slipped my own hands into his back pockets as he pressed his lips to my neck and kissed his way up to my ear. I slid off the desk, away from his grasp. "We shouldn't be doing this. Not right now. Besides, I still need to talk to Wills."

His eyebrows fell. "Who cares? I don't want to wait. I want you and you want me, what else matters?"

I sighed and pinched the bridge of my nose between two fingers. "You said last night—you understood. And that you were okay with the fact that I couldn't promise you anything more than the one night together."

"Yeah—" He paused, and his eyes rolled up toward the ceiling in thought. "Well, I lied. I'm not as okay with it as I thought I would be." When I said nothing in return, he sighed. "I'll back off for now." He took a step closer to me. "But don't think for a second that this is over." He took another step and put a hand on my waist. He leaned in, his full lips dancing just above mine. "Because I'm not going to stop trying."

"Then you're going to make it very hard for me to keep saying no," I said.

He laughed in a low, grumbling way. "That's sort of the point." His thumb brushed the corner of my mouth, and I turned my head to kiss it. "Do I at least get a good-bye kiss?"

I opened my mouth to welcome his lips. To my right, a loud clicking crackled through the air like a thunderbolt. I froze, my lips millimeters from Drew's. When I looked over at his desk, a Newton's cradle I had never noticed there before was rocking back and forth furiously.

26

"How long have you had that?" I whispered, gesturing to the Newton's Cradle. My eyes darted wildly around the room looking for signs of another immortal.

Drew pulled back and scratched his head. "Huh. You know, I'm not sure. I don't even remember buying one of those." He leaned down to look closer.

A knock came from the other side of the door, and Julian barged through without waiting for either of us to let him in. *Someone was in here.* His eyes were wide and his chest puffed out protectively. "We, uh, need to get going, Monica." He swallowed and shifted his gaze to Drew. "Sorry, we have an appointment."

With Julian's entrance, the Newton's Cradle moved even more wildly, thrashing from side to side. I sent Julian a wide-eyed glare. *You're more powerful than whatever was just in here,* I thought.

A knowing look washed across Jules's face.

"Oh, okay," Drew said, looking back and forth between Jules and me. "So, uh—I guess I'll see you later?"

I forced a smile and nodded. "Yes." I took his hand and squeezed it reassuringly. "I'll see you later."

Within a few minutes, we were back in my car, Jules behind the wheel. I ran my fingers along the length of my collarbone, which was still hidden by my turtleneck. My necklaces—the panic button and the one Wills had given me—were still underneath my shirt. I pulled the collar away from my body, and leaving the panic button inside my shirt, I lifted the blue stone out so that it could be seen.

Jules slid a glance over at me. "I noticed that necklace the other day—the day you almost drowned. Where did you get it?"

"The stone was a gift from a client—and Wills had it made into a necklace for me."

Jules nodded. "I can tell it's connected to demon magic."

This made me pause. "Well," I said, thinking, "Wills is a demon. His jeweler contact is probably a fellow demon friend."

Julian shook his head. "No, not the necklace itself—the stone. The stone would be too hot for me to touch. Like fire." He glanced my way quickly before bringing his eyes back to the road. "It probably feels warm to you a lot, yes? Like the temperature of body heat?" I nodded, and he shrugged a shoulder. "Yep. A previous owner was probably a demon. Not surprising around these parts."

"But—but it was a human who gave it to me."

"Not a demon?"

I shook my head, a gnawing fear starting to develop in my stomach. He patted my leg reassuringly, but two frown lines framed his perfect mouth. "I'm sure it's fine. There are far more demons in the Vegas area than most places. But Lucien and I will check into it deeper, just to be sure."

Running a fingernail along the stone, I couldn't push down an uneasy feeling, the kind you get when you walk into an empty room late at night. "Should I take it off?"

Julian shrugged. "Only if you want to."

I didn't really have a response for that. "Wouldn't it raise suspicion with the murderer if I stopped wearing it suddenly?"

His mouth tilted and he put a hand on my knee. "It could. For now, at least, you're probably safe to keep it on if you want to." His mouth twitched upward. "At least with me here, you are."

Using the tip of my nail, I picked at my cuticles again, pushing them back away from the nail. "So where are we off to?"

"A movie set."

"Oh! A movie!" Little butterflies fluttered around in my stomach at the mention of that. "I didn't know they were filming a movie around here right now." Part of me always wanted to be a movie star—as did a lot of other succubi of course. "You know, I was once up for the same part as Grace Kelly. Would've gotten it too if Hitchcock hadn't been so damn obsessed with her."

His lips pressed together in a smile. "Envious of Grace Kelly, are we?"

"Do *I* have my own castle? A princess title?" I was only half kidding.

"No, but you have immortality."

"Not at the moment." My voice dropped. We both remained silent for the rest of the drive.

A few minutes later, we pulled into the parking lot of a mid-size ranch-style home. There were a couple of cars in the driveway—but no trailers. No craft services. No reflectors or giant lights outside of the windows of the home. It looked like no movie set I had ever been on. I gestured palm up to the house. "*This* is where the movie's being filmed?"

He turned off the car. "Yup."

And that's when the realization dawned on me. "No," I said. "No, no, no, *no!* This better not be Lyla's porn company."

When Julian didn't say anything, I kicked my feet around the floor of the car. "I don't want to go in there," I whined.

"And you think I do?" he countered.

That made me take pause. If Julian is willing to step on the set of a porno film in the making, there had to be a really good reason for doing so.

"You think this is important?" I asked.

He turned to face me in the bucket seat of the car. "Would I be here if it wasn't? This isn't an issue of modesty. This is about saving your life."

With a deep breath, I opened the door and got out of the car. "Then what are we waiting for?"

Together, we walked toward the front door. "How are we handling this? Are we pretending to be detectives?"

"You know I can't lie."

"So let me do the lying."

His shoulders slumped with a small sigh. "If you say you're a detective, they'll want to see identification. You're better off going in there looking for some sort of"—he paused, shooting me a sideways glance and grimaced as he said it—"*job* prospect."

"And then who are you supposed to be? My pimp?"

"Porn stars don't have pimps."

I snorted at that. "Oh? How would *you* know?"

We were standing outside the front door by now and talking in hushed tones. He raised a fist and knocked twice on the door. "Wait!" I whispered. "We didn't even come up with a plan—"

But my words were cut off by the door swinging open. A scrawny guy with a patchy goatee and a backward baseball cap stood in front of us. "Well, it's about time!" His eyes widened and he looked back and forth between us. "Well, come in, come in. We need to get started. You're fucking forty minutes late."

I held up a finger. "Um, I think you have the wrong idea."

He grabbed my shoulder and pulled me inside. "Come on, we need to get you into the makeup chair right away."

"M-makeup chair?" My words were stuttered, and there were suddenly several people circling around Julian and me. One guy had his hand on my ribs, and another woman had her hands brushing through my hair. "We're not the talent!" I tried to yell over them, only no one heard amidst the hum of chatter in the air.

"Get your hands off of her!" Julian's voice boomed through the air. Everyone in the room froze, including me. Jules rarely raised his voice. He was much more the quiet and brooding "let's talk it out" type of guy.

The man touching my ribs pulled back immediately, hands in the air as if surrendering. "Whoa, whoa, sorry, dude. We're just preparing her for the scene."

Julian's voice was back to being quiet but still as dangerous as before. The low growl of a jungle cat. "She's not your talent for today." He looked at me, and I still stood there shocked, frozen. *Monica*, he thought, *finish the lie for me!*

I shook my head, snapping out of the trance. "No—I-I'm not." I cleared my throat, nerves shooting up and down my body like electricity. "I just wanted to talk to you about, um, about the process of applying for a job. To be, you know"—I paused—"a *star*." I tried not to sound sarcastic. Julian shot me a look making it pretty clear I did not succeed.

Aren't you supposed to be good at this lying thing? he thought.

I scowled at him before continuing. "So, who would I talk to about the, uh, interview process?"

"Interview?" The scruffy guy in the hat scoffed at that. "Sweetheart, we don't do 'interviews.' We do auditions." I stood there a moment, my eyes wide, mouth agape. "And your pretty boy here? He want to audition, too?"

"Him? No, no, definitely not. He's, um, he's my—" *See,* I thought, pausing midsentence, *this is why we needed to figure our story out before coming in!*

"I'm her bodyguard," Julian said.

"Great," Scruffy said. "Well, let's start the audition, shall we?"

"Oh, I don't know if I'm ready right now. . . ."

"Look." Scruffy took off his hat and ran a hand through his greasy hair. "We're running late. Our leading lady isn't here. We could really use someone right about now. You're hot"—he looked my body up and down—"if not a little prudish, but hey, lots of guys love that sort of thing."

I looked at Jules, who was staring at me thoughtfully, his head tipped to the side. *You could get your next fix here. None of these guys are going to Heaven, I guarantee it. The makeup artist is the only good aura in the room.*

You have got *to be kidding me.* I held Jules's eye contact, my lips pressed into a line. This day was turning out to be a naked nightmare.

You need powers to survive. You're going to have to do it with somebody. I was sure to the group standing around us, we looked like a couple of weirdos just staring at each other like this.

And you're okay with this?

I've grown accustomed to it. I thought I saw his shoulders slump a little.

"Well?" Scruffy tapped a foot impatiently.

I nodded. "Okay. But I have a couple conditions." Scruffy raised his eyebrows, waiting. "I want a wig with black hair. And since this is only an audition, I don't want to have sex with anyone."

"What?" Scruffy threw his hands in the air. "What do you expect me to do with a video of no sex?"

I stood a little taller and put my hands on my hips. "I don't know how often you require your 'talent' "—I could barely say the word without rolling my eyes—"to get tested for STDs. And until I know these things, I'm protecting myself." I slid a look at Julian, who was wearing a soft smile. It must have been a small comfort to him.

"Okay." Scruffy was starting to sound really annoyed with me. "So what *will* you do?"

"I'll . . ." I thought for a moment, thinking back to past porn I had seen. "I'll masturbate. For your male star. And he can masturbate while watching me. He can come on my tits and stomach."

Scruffy mulled that over for a moment. "Done. Get her into makeup and find the girl a dark wig."

The makeup chair was nothing fancy—just a worn-out kitchen chair set up in front of a mirror in the bathroom. Julian stood in the doorway while Mary, the makeup artist, worked her magic on my face. I closed my eyes and relaxed, enjoying the little bit of time I had to rest. Mary was curvy and wore wide-leg jeans and a cardigan sweater over a silk top. She had big, curly brown hair and eyeliner that swept across her eyelids dramatically.

I cleared my throat. "So, where is your usual star? Why didn't she show up today?"

She held up a brush and a palate with various eyeshadow colors lined up in a row. "Close your eyes," she said. "The girl today was just a fill-in. Our previous star"—the words caught in her throat—"is no longer with us."

I stole a quick glance at Julian, who just barely nodded, urging me to continue. I closed my eyes as she asked and leaned my head back in the chair. "She get a better paying gig?"

There was a moment of silence before Mary spoke. The brush swept over my eyelids ever so gently. It was almost a seductive gesture. "No. She—she passed away."

"Oh." I put on my best sympathetic voice. "I'm so sorry. How terrible. Was it unexpected?"

She sniffled, and I wished I could see her expression. "Yes, very unexpected."

"I'm so sorry," I said again. With closed eyes, I didn't have a lot of room to show my sincerity. I just had to make do, I guess. *What else to ask, what else to ask . . . ugh, this is hard!* "Um, you two sounded close. Were you good friends?"

I stole a peek with one eye and saw her shaking her head. "Not especially. It just—I don't know, it was so sudden. I think it made everyone here consider their own mortality." I wanted to tell her that the rest of the people out there had the depth of a petri dish. I doubt they consider what they eat for breakfast, let alone their own mortality. When she didn't tell me to close my eyes again, I went ahead and opened both to look at her.

"So what happened?"

"The cops were crawling all over this place. She had filmed a scene the morning before she died, and they were suspicious of all of us. It was terrible." She wiped her sleeve across her nose, and I resisted the impulse to lean away, disgusted.

"Well, why would the cops care? Did they suspect some sort of foul play?"

She nodded. "She was murdered. And since those of us in the sex industry are all *vagrants*, we were the immediate suspects." She smiled softly at me, her brown eyes crinkling around the corners. "But I guess I don't have to tell you that. I'm sure you know better than any of us, being in the spotlight."

I sort of liked this girl despite her odd sense of style and frumpy mannerisms. There was something very genuine and even—I don't know—sweet about her. I shrugged. "I haven't been doing this for long, but as a stripper I definitely get my share of those looks, too."

She nodded and applied heavy smears of blush to my

cheeks. "It was just the first time I'd ever been called out like that. Looked at like less of person by those cops."

I glanced over at Julian, who was still leaning against the doorframe, pretending to be captivated by *People* magazine. He glanced up, meeting my eyes, and his eyebrows arched in encouragement.

"Was there anyone here who they talked to that they were specifically interested in?"

She stepped back and looked up to the ceiling in thought. "At first it was Max—he was her costar that day. But then they seemed to focus in on Dennis."

"And Dennis is . . ."

"He's the director. The guy you were talking to in the hat."

"Oh, right, of course." *Scruffy.*

"He and Lyla were an item, But he had an alibi, so once they got that from him, they pretty much left. Haven't been back since."

"Well—what about Lyla? Was she acting strange that last morning?"

Mary stepped back, her eyes darkening. "Why are you asking so many questions?"

My breath caught, heart hammering against my ribs. "I-I'm just nervous about the audition. To tell you the truth, I've never done an adult film before." Mary's gaze softened and she leaned forward, painting my lips. "I'm sorry if I was being too nosy. I was just trying to make conversation until I had to perform," I said, trying to keep my mouth still as I spoke.

She nodded, continuing to line my lips in silence. After another minute, she said, "Lyla *was* acting strange that morning. She was always so put together when she came in. Hardly needed me to do any of her makeup or hair. But that morning"—her voice lowered as if she were about to reveal some sort of dirty secret—"she came in with hardly any makeup. Her eyeliner was smeared down her face from the night before.

And she seemed—frazzled. Upset about something." Mary put down the makeup and started pinning my hair up. She ran her fingers through its length in a surprisingly motherly way. "After we finished the cum shot, she cried and ran off the set." She twisted chunks of my hair up to my head, securing it with bobby pins as she spoke, using her mouth to hold them like a third hand. "I've seen a lot of bloopers and my fair share of mental breakdowns on adult film sets, but nothing like that."

She finished pinning my hair and rummaged around in a box under the wardrobe rack. She pulled out a dark wig and placed it carefully on my head. After a little bit more brushing, she turned the chair around to face the mirror. "There! All done!" She had her hands out as if presenting my new look. I smiled, hoping I wasn't grimacing on the outside like I was on the inside. I had glitter painting my eyes all the way up to my brows. Giant hot-pink lips that were lined far outside of my natural lip line. Black eyeliner lining corner to corner like two tiny footballs. And cheeks swept up to my temples. I looked like . . . well, like a porn star. The only small comfort I took away from the look was that no one, and I mean *no one*, would recognize me.

"So"—Mary walked over to a rack of clothes (if you can even call them that) on the other side of the bathroom—"here are your costume choices. Choose whatever suits your 'character' for the day. I'll be right outside. Call for me when you're dressed."

"I think you mean 'undressed.' " My teeth gnashed together.

Mary chuckled at that, and she and Julian quietly shut the door, leaving just me, my slutty reflection, and a pile of clothes that even Adrienne wouldn't be caught dead in.

I chose a simple black lacy push-up bra and a little black skirt with a thong underneath. I called Mary back in, and Julian followed close behind her. He met my eyes, his body stiffening as though refusing to look anywhere below my neckline.

"Oh, very nice," Mary said. "Turn around, let me have a look."

I gave her a 360-degree twirl. "Good, good." She shuffled around, finding some high-heeled platform shoes. "Just put these on and ..." She put a finger to her lips, assessing my whole look. "And I'll just need you to take off your necklaces. Then you'll be ready."

She walked over to the back of me. "Here, let me help you."

I lifted the wig hair up off my neck so that she could undo the clasps. She swung the necklaces off me and inhaled a sharp gasp, which she quickly covered for by clearing her throat. I looked over at Julian, who shrugged.

"What's wrong?" I turned to face her.

"Oh, nothing, nothing." She held up a hand as if shooing my concern away. When I didn't move, her shoulders relaxed and she held up my necklace—the stone from Erik. "It's just—it's so odd. Lyla had a necklace just like this. The stone, at least. I had never seen anything like it before. I even asked her about it, and when I did, she went totally Gollum on me and freaked out that I had touched it." Mary held up the necklace, examining it closer in the light. "She refused to take it off—insisted on wearing it in the last couple of shoots, she loved it so much."

My eyes darted to Julian's. His demeanor was still calm, stoic. "Here," Julian said, holding a hand out. "Why don't I hold on to those for you?"

I nodded, my mouth dry like I had swallowed a ball of yarn.

I handed him the necklace from Lucien first, with the panic button, and then dropped the blue stone into his palm. He winced and sucked in a breath as though in pain, almost dropping the necklace to the floor. He grabbed it by the leather strap, catching it just before it hit the ground.

Mary stared at him, her gaze so wide that I could see veins in the whites of her eyes. "Wow," she said, out of breath, "how'd you do that? I barely saw you move."

He slowly straightened, standing back at full height and cleared his throat. His eyes shifted over to me. *Monica, I need you to lie for me.*

"He, uh, is really good at magic tricks."

He rolled his eyes. *Well, I could have said that.*

"And," I continued, "um, he competes in triathlons. He's superfast."

He nodded and looked back at Mary with a small smile.

Shrugging, she turned back to me, ready to finish up her job. She gave me the once-over, allowing her gaze to travel up and down my body. Her eyes shifted from left to right as if she were reading me like a book—taking in every little detail to ensure she hadn't overlooked something. She seemed quite good at her job; it made me wonder why she was stuck in a porn career. "Well, it looks like you're all ready to go!" she finally said. "Follow me." With a sweeping gesture, she held a hand out, palm up, toward the door.

I slipped into a silk robe before exiting, trying to stay even the slightest bit modest. I turned to give myself a last look in the mirror and used a little of my remaining power to shift the neck bruises entirely away and to make my features look slightly different. Not enough for the cast and crew to notice a change, but enough that my friends would only think it was someone who looked an awful lot like me. Drew once told me he didn't watch porn, but the second the words left his mouth, his aura changed to a dark purple—clearly indicative of guilt. It was sort of sweet that he felt the need to lie to me.

I followed Mary into the bedroom. The crew only consisted of Scruffy—that is, Dennis—and two other men. One was the sound guy, and the other seemed to be an assistant of sorts. He was young with oily skin. I hoped he was old enough to legally be here. Sitting in a chair next to the bed was a decent-looking, fit man. He was in jeans and no shirt. His chest was shaved, and his body glistened as though he had just rubbed baby oil all over himself. Wait . . . he *had* just rubbed baby oil on himself. Gross. Thank Hell I didn't have to touch the guy.

Please tell me I don't have to sit here and watch this. I heard Julian's voice in my head.

Hey, I retorted, *this was your bright idea. Besides, it's your job to stay by my side today.* I smirked at that.

You are evil. His gaze darkened, but there was a twinkle of humor in his eyes.

"Are we ready?" Scruffy asked impatiently. "We're losing daylight here."

"It's two o'clock in the afternoon," I said. "We've got plenty of sunlight left."

He shrugged and sat down in one of those directors chairs that they sold at Spencer's. "It's just a saying," he grumbled, crossing his arms over his chest like a sullen teenager.

I slipped out of my robe and sat down on the bed.

"So." Scruffy clapped his hands together, putting his authoritative voice back on and looking in my direction. Though he was talking to me, he refused to make eye contact with anything other than my breasts. "I'm going to say action, and you're going to start masturbating. Joel will join in soon after. Don't worry about the cameras. We're going to move around you both to get various shots. Don't stop until I say cut."

"Um, right. I think I got it."

"Okay, everyone ready?"

"Oh yeah," Joel said, smoothing his gelled blond hair back with the palm of his hand.

I glared at him. "Mmph."

"Okay, quiet on the set!" Scruffy yelled it out despite the fact no one else was talking. "Action!"

I sat on the edge of the bed with my legs spread wide. I touched myself through my panties and ran a finger over the strap of my bra, down to the middle of my cleavage. Joel undid the button of his jeans and slid his pants down to the floor. He had on no underwear, but in its place were tan lines in the shape of bikini briefs. Dude needed to lay off the tanning bed. I thought of Adrienne and considered for a moment that the two could be perfect for each other.

"Oh, baby." My voice was dry and flat. As soon as the words left my mouth, I cringed.

"Cut!" Scruffy yelled. "Could you at least attempt to make that sound believable? Let's try again. Action!"

"Oh, *baby*," I said a second time. It was an improvement, but still obviously not quite believable. I heard Julian's laugh in my brain. I did my best to ignore it.

I unlatched the bra from the front clasp and let my breasts fall out of it. I squeezed one breast with my hand while my other hand pushed my thong aside to fully reach my most sensitive areas. I was dryer than Red Rock desert down there and licked two fingers in an attempt to get some moisture. Joel came over closer to the bed with one hand stroking his—admittedly large—erection. He reached the other hand out to touch my nipple.

No! Julian's voice boomed in my head just as I slapped his hand away. My slap was hard, and the sound of skin on skin contact echoed through the room.

Joel pulled his hand away and his boner went a little soft. He looked frantically over to the director, who I saw out of my periphery make some sort of "keep going" hand gesture.

I lay back on the bed and raised a foot to his upper thigh. I propped my sharp heel on his body and dug it in just a touch too much. Joel winced, and I smirked at his pain. I didn't need to read auras to know this guy had it coming. I raised my lower body into the air, slid the thong panties down to my ankles, and kicked them up into his face. He inhaled the scent deeply before tossing them over his shoulder and going back to work on his hand pumping. I rested my foot, a bit more gently this time, back on his thigh. There might as well have been sandpaper between my legs. Regardless of how many times I licked my fingers or imagined Drew, nothing was solving my problem. Joel wasn't exactly repulsive, but he just wasn't wetting my whistle. I turned instead to the camera to give it a sultry look. There, standing behind, was Julian. Tall and looming, his eyes fixed on me. My mouth went dry—all the fluid drained immediately to my sex. My finger slid in easily this time.

I held Jules's eyes for a few moments, letting them read me, and bore into my body. I inserted a second finger while my thumb tickled my clit. I closed my eyes and imagined Julian's touch on my body. Those soft, heavenly fingers massaging my sensitive skin. I moaned, and it was the first moan that wasn't manufactured for the camera. Joel grunted and threw out a few of his own *Yeah, baby*s as well—which I ignored. I looked back at Julian and rushed my eyes over his body. He was dressed casually—a fitted heather gray T-shirt and jeans. His Adonis muscles were sculpted, fitting of a fairy tale prince. His jeans were tight around a bulging erection. When I returned my eyes to his, he smiled. A sexy half smile that tugged up toward his eyes. His chest rose and fell with each breath, and he licked his lips.

I sat up quickly, changing my position so I could better hold his eye contact. I ripped the skirt from my body and positioned myself on my hands and knees, peering at him from the side. His hands were now on his hips, clenching, the white knuckles barely keeping him composed. I could feel my body getting close. The tension building.

I stole a secret glance at the clock on the wall—it had been close to fifteen minutes. I wasn't sure how much footage this guy needed. I pumped three fingers in and out of me. Then, pulling out, I put a hand on either side of my ass, spreading my cheeks apart offering Julian a view that he would likely never see again. I could feel wetness dripping from my lips. I ran a fingernail around my slick folds, gathering the juices, and brought them to my mouth, licking them clean. Julian's head fell against the wall he was leaning on.

Joel grunted from my other side. A whisper came to my left, and I looked over to find Scruffy mouthing the words "cum shot" and pointing to my costar. I flipped onto my back with my head hanging over the edge of the bed—making sure I could still watch Jules. His jaw was clenched. I could hear his breathing from the other end of the room. I was spread wide to give the camera the best view.

With Julian's eyes still on mine, I came hard and screamed out in ecstasy. I bit my lip to keep from yelling out Jules's name. Within a second, a grunt came from in front of me, and warm fluid landed on my stomach and tits. I sucked in a breath as his life force entered me—not a very strong fix, but it was more than I had had in days, and it felt glorious. The pins and needles rushed into my bloodstream. I moaned as his death flashed into my brain—he was going to die soon. Very soon— as in within a few weeks from now of an overdose. This fact made me feel quite a bit better about relishing in his soul. It was like glorious tendrils coiling around inside my body—like drinking a warm mug of hot buttered rum on a cold day. Though he wasn't the most moral man and his soul wasn't overly strong or good, it had been so long since I'd had any magic pumping through my blood that it could have been Saetan's life force and it still would have felt heavenly.

"And cut!" Scruffy yelled out.

"Woooo!" Joel jumped up clapping loudly and dancing around the room like an ape. He was clearly feeling the effects of me. Or maybe he was just high on coke. It was hard to say.

I sat up in the bed, feeling an overall ickiness about myself. The cheap comforter scratched the backs of my legs. I stood up and walked over to Julian.

As I approached, his towering presence loomed over me in

an unsettling way. He was my friend. But he was also an angel—an entity that was always inherently good. And yet, he watched me the entire time. Something I highly doubt his God would approve of. I felt meek standing in front of him. He held my robe out and I turned to slip into it, neither of us saying a word.

Mary was back in the room picking up the discarded clothing and tossing it into a small laundry bag. Joel was still dancing around the room, his abnormally large and hairless jewels bouncing every which way.

He bounded over to Julian and me like a Labrador, all hope and smiles. "Hey, hot stuff, I never got your name." I opened my mouth to answer him, but he was so rambunctious, he cut me off before I even got a word in. "Want to grab a beer or something now? Celebrate your breakthrough role?"

Scruffy came over and put a hand on Joel's shoulder. "Put your clothes on, man." He shook his head as Joel bounded off in a quest for his pants. "Sorry about him . . . he gets a little exuberant sometimes." He turned his hat so the brim was in the front. "I have to say—that was pretty great. I had my doubts about a masturbation scene, but you pulled it off. You got the job. We film again next Thursday."

"Oh, um . . ." I stuttered and hugged my robe tighter to my body. "I'll check my calendar and get back to you. I'm not sure I'm available."

Julian put a hand on my waist, guiding me back toward the bathroom. "She's *not*." His voice was a grumble.

Scruffy nodded, shaped his index finger and thumb like a gun, and clicked his tongue at Julian. "Right. Got it." He then handed a business card to me. "Call me. We'll talk money."

Julian followed me back to the bathroom, close on my heels. I stopped in front of the sink and made the subtle shift back to my usual features. I looked up at Jules, meeting his eyes in the mirror. "Sorry," I said, and lowered my chin. Shame crept over my body and I wanted to shrink into the robe. The silk was sexy and soft, but there was still nothing quite like the comfort of my warm and fuzzy robe at home.

"Monica." His voice was as gruff as I'd ever heard it. Rough and pebbly. He had a hand on my hip, and his fingers slid over the smooth silk down my hips. "Don't be sorry."

I turned to face him. His body was a heavy presence, making the air around us thick. "But that must have been awful for you."

He chuckled and took a step closer, his muscular thighs brushing the barely there fabric wrapped loosely around my hips. "Awful? That display was a lot of things . . . but awful was not one of them." He brushed his knuckle across my cheekbone, then pinched the base of the wig and pulled it from my head. Most of my hair was pinned at the top of my head, but a few tendrils spilled out down my neck and over my collarbone. His hands were large and soft, and he moved them to cup my face on either side of my jaw. His thumbs brushed across the corners of my mouth, wiping away the lipstick and I parted my lips. More than anything, I yearned for his lips. I just came at the thought of him on top of me—it was a union that could never be. Just like my Drew. I'm self-destructive in love—only choosing to fall for those that can never happen.

"Does Drew remind you of me?"

The question caught me off guard, and out of instinct I pulled back from his hold. His hands stayed firm, keeping me in place, locked into his gaze. I swallowed knowing that the question was just a formality. He knew the answer. He was in my head. "Yes."

"Is that why you love him?"

What kind of a question was that? "Julian . . ." A nervous laugh escaped my lips, and I playfully pushed his shoulder.

He grabbed my hand in his and kissed my palm, my wrist, the crook of my elbow, and up to my shoulder. He paused at my neck and pulled back, his breath heavy. Our noses brushed, and I wrapped my arms around him, wanting to be as close to Jules as possible. I'd never seen an angel nervous before. He chewed the inside of his cheek. His eyes, usually so comfortable holding my gaze, were now focused on my lips.

"Relax. I'm not going to kiss you, Jules." Even though we hadn't kissed that night at the church, his reaction was enough that I'd never walk that line again. I'd thought this fact would relax him a little. I gave a small smile and squeezed my arms around his waist even tighter.

"*That's* what I was afraid of."

He dropped his forehead to mine and closed his eyes.

He wanted me. He wanted me so badly that he was doing everything he could to *make* me kiss him. "If you want something," I whispered, "why don't you just take it?"

He grunted and his long blond hair tickled the sides of my face. His lips brushed against mine in a kiss that by definition wasn't one—but by judging our reaction to it, it might as well have been foreplay. A whimper escaped my lips and I parted them, inviting more of him in. His lips mimicked my own, parting as well, keeping the contact between us touching and buzzing with anticipation. I slowly let my tongue trace his top lip. As soon as I made contact, I knew it was a mistake. His body tensed, muscles becoming rocks beneath his casual clothes. His lips were still on mine, the moisture sandwiched between making each slick. "I can't," he whispered while pulling away. He moved to the other side of the bathroom, and I had to steady myself on the sink. "Get dressed. I'll be outside." He picked my clothes up from where they were folded on the chair and pushed them into my body. His voice had a gruffness to it that hadn't been there moments before. The lump caught in my throat, and I willed the tears not to fill my eyes. When they didn't listen, I at least waited until he left. As the door shut behind him, I dropped my head and let them spill out over my cheeks.

27

French countryside, 1943

The sound of gunfire and bombs became a sort of lullaby after a while. The nurses all shared bedrooms, each of us given a small cot to sleep on. None of us dared to complain—it was better than the soldiers in the field received.

I lay in bed unable to sleep staring at the white cement ceiling. At this point, I had taken countless lives. Lives that would have been lost regardless, but each of their deaths haunted me night after night. And tonight was no different. Lieutenant Aubert Martine, a leader in the Belgium army, perished at my lips. I could still taste the metallic flavor of his coppery blood on my tongue. "You are doing God's work in the only way you can," I whispered to no one. The other nurse lay in the cot next to me, snoring softly.

"You don't really believe that, do you?" A familiar voice came from my left. I jolted up to a sitting position.

"Julian!" I whispered. He sat on the windowsill and I rushed to him, wanting so desperately to throw my arms around his neck. He put two hands out, stopping me before I crashed into his muscular chest. There was a glow surrounding his body; a *dewiness to his skin that made it look damp like a blade of grass at dawn. He smiled sadly and brushed a curl that had fallen loose from my braid away from my face. I flushed at his touch and immediately shifted my hair into a perfect coif. I even made sure to rouge my cheeks and lips.*

"Silly girl," he said with a sigh, "don't waste these powers on me. Save your energy."

My heart dropped at that. I could think of only one other person worth the vanity of shapeshifting, and he was destined to become an angel soon himself. My chin dropped to my chest, a sadness reverberating through my hollow soul. "I don't think I can save him, Jules."

"You know you can't," he corrected.

My eyes shot up and stared deeply into eyes, so blue they were like the center of a flame. They were a mix of emotions I could no longer read. "No"—I shook my head—"there has to be a way. There has to be a loophole."

Jules snorted and pushed off from the window. "Don't be so foolish. You did your duty for Hell. You took a life for your own selfish reasons."

"It was love. Love, Jules. Remember the emotion? It wasn't selfish." I choked the words out, tears rising in my throat and threatening to spill out over my cheeks.

"You're a creature of lust. Not love." Julian stood tall, looming over me. His chiseled face was stoic and unmoving, casting judgment.

"Well, soon enough Wills will be one of your own. An angel who will look at me with the same unforgiving and hateful stare as you do."

"Don't be so sure about that," he growled.

I gasped, sucking a breath in. I didn't want to think of another one of my loves as an angel—hating me with the same fiery passion as Jules did. Angels weren't supposed to hate. They were creatures of love and forgiveness. And yet Jules stood here before me, the antithesis to what I had believed an angel to be. But if Wills weren't an angel, that left only one alternative. An option that simply couldn't be. Even up until our last tryst, his soul had been pure.

A flash of regret washed over Jules, and his shoulders relaxed into a less aggressive stance. "I don't hate you." He wrapped two large hands around my shoulders. "But we are beings in the middle of an eternal war. There is no place for us anymore."

"How did you do that—you read my mind and didn't even kiss me. . . ."

He chuckled softly and pulled me into his embrace. His skin felt cool against mine, and he ran his fingers through my hair. "I didn't have to. I know you very well." He pulled away and wiped the tears from my face in the gentle way a lover might. "Monica, stop this nonsense with the mercy killings. I am here unofficially to tell you that while your intent is pure, your actions are not."

"But it's the only way I can help these men! Truly help them—"

Jules shook his head and put a finger to my lips. He glanced over at my sleeping roommate. "Shhh. You are a gifted nurse, whether succubus or human. I know your intent is noble, but it doesn't change the fact that you are killing these men."

"But—"

There was a crack, and in an instant Jules was gone. I clomped back to bed and threw the covers back over my body. I am doing the Lord's work to the best of my abilities. These men suffer. They lie and wait for death's reaper to tear their souls painfully from their body. I take it with tenderness and love.

I fell asleep angry and hurt, more resolute with my choices than before the night began.

The next morning I was roused out of bed by a bustling around the hallway. Shouts and cries sounded around me. A fel-

low nurse—a much younger girl with dark hair and wide brown eyes—burst into our room. "Get up!" she cried, her English speckled with an Italian accent. "Get up, we must move out. The battles are getting closer and closer to the tents. We must fix up the patients and move out!"

I ran to the loo and shifted myself into my uniform. I gradually shifted my hair as I rushed to the medical tents. There were twelve new soldiers lined up in various cots. All the men had nurses working on them already. I checked each man—not a single one was my Wills.

"We need a nurse here!" An older gentleman of about thirty carried a young man over his shoulder. I rushed to tend to both. The older man had a gash in his leg, nothing that looked too serious. With three women aiding, we moved the younger man onto a hammock-like cot. His stomach was slashed open, guts spilling out. If I had been able to say a prayer for the boy without the words choking on my tongue, I would have.

A doctor was by his side. "Get him into a room—he needs to be stitched up, now!" There were already three nurses tending to him; he certainly didn't need a fourth. Instead I turned to the older man who had carried him in. "Let me take a look at that leg," I said.

He shook his head, hands on hips. "No, I'm fine. Take care of Daniel."

I took him by the arm and led him to a bed. "Please, just lie down. Let me at least have a look. Daniel is in the best hands."

"Oh yeah? Then whose hands am I in?" He winced as I ran a finger along his wound.

"You, sir, are in equally capable hands." Grabbing a shot of morphine, I ripped his pant leg to give me more room to work with.

"No," he said gruffly. "No morphine. Save it for someone who needs it." I nodded, handing him a flask of whiskey instead. He threw his head back, taking a large drink of the liq-

uid. His English was perfect, but the twang of his accent was one I immediately recognized from my past.

"Talking might keep your mind off the pain, Mr.—"

"Collin O'Malley." He took another swig and winced as I disinfected his leg.

"Well, Mr. O'Malley, I could stitch this up for you. My hands are as steady as any doctor's, I assure you. And you wouldn't have to wait hours for a doctor to become available."

He nodded. "Do as you must."

"Here." I handed him a leather strap. "Bite onto this if you must."

Hours passed since I had finished Mr. O'Malley's sutures. I tended to the wounded as they came in—nobody nearly so fatal as Daniel Doyle, as I learned his name was. I paced around the tents, waiting to hear news regarding his surgery. As soon as he was well enough to be relocated, the entire unit was moving out of the abandoned building.

Julian's words weighed heavy in my head. I didn't doubt that he was right—it was indeed still taking a life. But I would need to find sufficient life force, anyway. Taking it from the men who lay dying seemed like a better way to use my powers. For all parties.

I saw the doctor who had taken Daniel walking down the hall. I rushed to him. "Doctor! What came of the boy? The one you took to surgery?"

He shook his head and mopped sweat from his brow. "That poor soul. I did what I could."

"And?" I asked. A tug at my gut pulled me to him with anticipation. "Will he live?"

The doctor sighed. "He'll be lucky if he makes it through the night." He pulled out a pocket watch, popping it open. "And we'll all be lucky to get the hell out of this building before then." The gunshots and explosions were getting nearer and *nearer. We needed to move out. Daniel was delaying us all. The doctor walked away from me, the sound of his shoes echoing in the halls.*

I found Daniel's room, shutting and locking the door behind me. I pulled the curtain so that peering eyes wouldn't be able to see. "Mr. Doyle?" I whispered. His auburn hair was matted to his head, drenched in sweat and Hell knew what else. I brushed my fingers through it, smoothing it to one side. His face was clammy and his lips dry. A small moan wheezed from deep within his chest.

"Don't you worry, Daniel. You'll be free of pain soon." Pulling down the sheets that covered him, I found access quite easier than past times. I lifted the makeshift hospital gown to reveal his body, and with a hand I started to rub him. Massaging him hard took a while—but the human body is an amazing thing. Biology eventually took over, and soon he was hard enough to straddle. I shifted my knickers away, and with one last glance to ensure the door was locked I carefully straddled him. I rode him gently, hardly moving so not to put any weight on his abdomen. It was taking longer to bring him to climax than I expected, but after a while I felt the familiar hardness growing inside me. He came, and I gasped at the pureness of his soul. It blinded me, like ice-cold water had replaced my blood, coursing through my body like a frozen river. My vision darkened to a tunnel. There was a flash of his life. Only—it wasn't right. His life should end here in front of me. Instead I saw a slideshow of a long life, starting at the end. Him old and in his deathbed. A Nobel Prize. Banquets in his honor. A doctor—a cure for cancer. It kept flashing backward. I pulled myself off of him, falling out of the bed. Tears filled my eyes, and I clamped a hand over my mouth to keep from crying out. With one last wheeze, his eyes opened and rolled to the back of his head.

Bloody Hell, he was supposed to live! He was supposed to live and go on to cure a dreadful disease. I stood and grabbed him by the shoulders—an attempt to shake the life back into him. "Daniel, wake up! Come back." The tears were choked in my throat, and I let my forehead fall to his chest.

"You've just murdered countless people." Through my tears, I didn't hear Jules pop in.

"Shut up!" I yelled. "Just shut up! Even you should recognize I was trying to do a noble thing!"

He shook his head, eyes turned downward like a frown. "We both know better than to believe that."

I pushed off from Daniel's body, rushing to Julian. My heart beat wildly; the blood rushed through my veins like an angry rapid. I shoved him as hard as I could, pushing his chest away from me. I had succubus strength, but he was even stronger. He stayed in place, barely swaying with my rage. I shoved him again, and he grabbed me by the wrists. His hands and mouth were stern, but his eyes—those beautiful, crystal eyes—were soft. "Enough!" He said the word quietly but with an urgency that would have made a commanding officer halt in his tracks.

I broke away from his hold. "Get out," I whispered, looking down at the floor. "Why do you torment us both? Leave me alone."

I looked up in hopes of seeing those eyes staring into mine, but he was already gone.

28

When I stepped out of the bathroom, Julian was already gone. Had left without even a good-bye. Lucien stood outside my door, a snide smirk slithered across his face. He raised an eyebrow when he saw me. "What exactly did you do to our dear angel?"

"I don't want to talk about it," I grumbled, hiking my purse over my shoulder and stalking outside toward my car. I didn't wait to see if he was following me. I thrust open the door and got in the driver's side. Shit. Julian had my keys, too.

"Looking for these?" Lucien dangled my keys outside the driver's window.

I huffed and rolled down the window holding out a hand, palm up.

"Nuh-uh," Lucien said, his head shaking. "You're not driving anywhere. Scoot."

I knew better than to argue with the most powerful demon in Nevada and did as I was told. I didn't actually feel like driving either, nor did I know where the fuck we were.

Lucien slid into the driver's seat. "You'll fucking kill both of us today." He pulled out my two necklaces from his pocket. "Here, put these on."

I held up the necklace from Wills. "But, this—"

"Yes, yes." He cut me off impatiently. "Julian filled me in on the link. Who gave you the stone?"

"A client—Erik. That married guy I was with at the club."

"You mean the guy you fucked right before you started weakening? The guy you were with the night before you split your shin open?"

I shifted uncomfortably in my seat, like a scolded child. "Um—yes."

"Hell, Monica. This never dawned on you earlier?"

I shrugged and clicked my seatbelt. "He seemed harmless. Besides, he didn't give me the stone until a couple days later."

He sighed and started the car, pulling out onto the main street. "I want you to keep wearing the necklace, even though it's clearly a major factor in this whole thing. I don't want the fact that you're no longer wearing it to tip the murderer off that we're onto him."

It took Lucien less than an hour to find out everything on record about Erik. He had just turned thirty-three. Married his attorney wife about eight months ago after dating through law school. She made partner before he did. Two brothers and one sister-in-law. Blah, blah, blah. Nothing about the profile seemed to offer any insight toward him having any knowledge of the arcane.

We were standing outside his office building, looking up at the tall building.

I cringed. "Can't you question him without me in there?"

Lucien's eyes lowered dangerously and he shot me a look, forehead creasing with impatience. I held up two hands in surrender. We entered the office and approached the receptionist. Lucien scooped an arm around the front of my waist, pushing me behind him. He leaned on the desk, his charm turned on 100 percent. The woman flushed under his attention, a blush creeping up her neck to her face. I resisted the urge to roll my eyes. He had her completely under his spell. He was leaning over the desk, entirely in her personal space, and she giggled coquettishly, covering her slightly crooked teeth with a hand over her mouth.

I cleared my throat. I wanted to get up there and finish this as soon as possible. Lucien had her hand in his, cupping it chivalrously as though she were some sort of British royalty.

Her look turned icy cold as she shifted her eyes to me. She pulled her hand back from Lucien's, defenses suddenly rising. "What exactly is it you need to see Mr. Brooks about?"

Lucien shot me a look that had disdain written all over it. When he turned back to the receptionist, he was gentle and sweet again. "Well"—he rolled his eyes in an exaggerated way— "my *little sister* here got herself in a bit of trouble with the law. And as usual, I'm the one bailing her out. We're looking for a good defense attorney and heard Mr. Brooks was the best."

She smiled and leaned forward, her body language relaxing with the mention of our sibling relationship. "Oh, of course. He is the greatest. Let me just call up and make sure he's available."

She buzzed up, and within a minute we were being escorted inside a modern office, slick with black ebony wood and silver accents. The receptionist smiled at Lucien. "Now, don't leave before saying good-bye."

He gave her a tiny wink, the sort that goes by so quickly that you might think it was a blink. "Wouldn't dream of it."

"Have a seat. Mr. Brooks will be with you in just a moment." She shut the door behind her, shooting one last glare in my direction.

Lucien whistled and leaned in to get a better look at the law degree plaques on the wall. "He's not doing too bad, is he?"

I thought back to Erik's wife—her mousy brown hair and dull navy suit. "Lucien, what is the possibility that Erik could be the hand behind such brutal murders?" I picked up a bowling trophy and held it out to Lucien. "He's on a bowling team, for fuck's sake!"

Lucien rubbed his temples, circling around with two fingers. "I don't know anymore. Things just keep getting more and more complicated. Up until you, the murders had been fairly consistent. Now suddenly it's like he's toying with you specifically." He shrugged in a seemingly nonchalant way, but there was a tension about his shoulders. "Which is better for us. The longer he takes, the more time we have to catch the bastard." His lips twitched into a half smile, and he wrapped his large bicep around my neck in a brotherly hug and kissed my hairline.

"All right, all right," I said. "Don't mess up my hair. I can't waste power shifting for vanity's sake."

Lucien released his hold on me as the door swung open. Erik stood before us in a stunning charcoal power suit. He had a cup of coffee in his hand. He looked first at Lucien, and then his eyes bulged as he noticed me, standing slightly behind. "Monica, hi." He turned and quickly shut the door, peering both ways first as if checking to make sure no one was spying on us. "You got arrested?" He looked me up and down, his eyes raking over my body. There was a flash of something as he saw me—disappointment perhaps? Or maybe that was just my insecurity at having to ration the little bit of remaining power.

I shook my head. "No, no. That's just what we had to say to get an appointment with you."

He raised the coffee mug to his lips, taking a sip. I immediately ached for my own cup of java. He walked over to his desk and set the mug down on a coaster before holding a hand out to Lucien. "Erik Brooks."

"This is Lucien," I said. "My, um . . ." I paused glancing again at him. We both filled the pause at the same time. "Boss."

"I'm her brother."

I widened my eyes at Lucien and he just looked coolly on at Erik. "I'm her boss and her brother."

"Her boss at the club?"

I waited until I saw Lucien nod before I smiled in agreement.

Erik's lip curled back in disgust. "You hired your *sister* to work at your strip club?" His eyes shifted back and forth between us, assessing whether this made us just really close siblings or really disturbed.

Lucien didn't miss a beat, "We were raised on a commune. We're very liberal."

Erik's eyebrows raised. "I can see that." He walked to the edge of the desk and sat on the corner, folding his hands professionally in front of him. "So, what can I do for you both?"

"Well"—Lucien glanced at me—"my girlfriend saw this stone you gave Monica, and she just hasn't stopped bugging me about it. I was wondering where you got it?"

Erik took his coffee again, without sipping—just let it sit on his knee. "You came out here to my office—my place of business—to ask where I got a pendant?" His head tilted skeptically. With his mug still in hand he crossed his arms over his chest. "The only thing that reeks of bullshit is bullshit. I'm a defense attorney—I can smell a pile from a mile away."

Lucien stepped in closer to Erik, his face getting aggressively close. Erik just smirked, cocky. Daring him to take a swing. Knowing Lucien, it wouldn't have surprised me.

"Okay," Lucien said. "Yes. Let's cut the shit. The police came around questioning my sister about that pendant. They seem to think it might be involved in some sort of murder case around the city. I want to know where you got it."

"What?" Erik looked at me, panic in his eyes. "This is a

joke, right?" When neither of us said anything, he slammed the coffee cup down, not bothering with the coaster. "A murder? Seriously? I swear to God I don't know anything about any murders. I defend scum, but I've never done anything illegal."

Lucien's eyebrows twitched and he stood there like a statue, staring at Erik in a knowing way.

Erik threw his hands up and used the momentum to stand up from the desk. "Okay, fine, I've done some illegal things, but never murder. Never."

"Okay," I said, stepping in front of Lucien. "Then where'd you get the stone?"

"A woman had a stand set up in the Hawaiian Marketplace. She went into some new age mumbo jumbo about how it was a balancing stone from the Garden of Eden. I just thought it was beautiful. She kept mentioning the previous owner—a woman named Lilith."

"Lilith!" I said louder than I meant to and clapped a hand to my mouth—it was a name almost always associated with succubi.

Lucien grabbed my elbow, giving it a squeeze. "And when did you get the stone? How long have you had it for?"

He gave that a moment's thought. "I think I got it Thursday."

I almost choked on my own spit. "The day we met?"

"Yeah. I had a meeting on the Strip and just slipped it into my pocket. Forgot the thing was there until after we—well, you know."

"Can you give me directions to where the jewelry stand was?" I could tell from the grumble in his voice that Lucien was growing impatient.

"You don't know where the Hawaiian Marketplace is?"

Lucien growled in lieu of an answer, and Erik jumped off the desk. "Sure." He grabbed a piece of paper and wrote down the directions. "It was right on the Strip—in the touristy part of the city." He looked again at me, lust dancing in his eyes. "And how did you get involved in all this?"

My succubus instincts itched at my core. I stole a glance at my reflection in the chrome picture frame on the wall. Sure enough, my skin was subtly more luminous with a dewy nature that was definitely not there hours earlier. The quiet outline of his muscles showed from beneath the expensive suit, and I unconsciously sighed, longing for more of a fix. I shrugged. "It seems as though *you* got me involved in all this."

"Anything else I can help you with?" Erik inhaled, the scent of my raging pheromones no doubt intoxicating him. His eyes flashed, and his mouth, so deliciously plump, curved into the slightest hint of a smile. My nipples pebbled as I remembered what his body looked like beneath me. I took a step closer and Lucien's hand darted out to stop me.

"Yes," Lucien said, "keep the fuck away from my sister."

29

We were back in the car, headed to the Strip in search of a mystery jeweler. There was a giant Coca-Cola bottle and the New York–New York casino, just as Erik directed. "I doubt she'll be here," I said, looking out the window at the various selling stands set up.

"You think I don't know that?" Lucien growled. He swung his head to look at me, his dark ponytail whipping at his neck. He turned quickly, eyes back on the road. With the precision of a stunt driver, he flipped the car in reverse and slithered into a parking spot. "We have to at least try." He cut the ignition and abruptly got out of the car, slamming the door behind him.

I sighed, weary of investigating. More than anything, I wanted to return to the normalcy of my life. Having to steal souls was not a great life, but at least it was consistent and something I could depend on. This week had been utterly exhausting, and my human body ached with fatigue and strain.

We walked out to the center of the Strip where tables were lined side by side. Vendors called to us, trying to sell us everything from massages to hooker trading cards. Lucien took my hand, pulling me along. He moved quickly—I barely had time to process the various tables. Each time I found one with jewelry, I took pause, but Lucien would just yank me along. "Nope," he'd growl, and drag me to the next table.

Somewhere along the outer edge of the market, I stopped to admire some dangly bronze earrings with turquoise stones. They weren't a perfect match to my necklace, but beautiful nonetheless. "Can I help you?" A weathered, middle-aged woman looked at me with kind eyes.

Lucien tugged again at my hand. "No," he grunted. I held strong, tearing my hand from his.

"Yes," I said to her. "These earrings, they're beautiful. May I see them?"

She smiled at me, deep creases framing gentle eyes. Her tanned skin was leathery and I wondered if the years of tanning were worth the battered appearance that resulted from it. "Of course." She opened the Plexiglas case and handed them to me. Lucien huffed a sigh and rolled his eyes.

"Forgive my *brother.*" I slid an angry glance to my right. "He's always in such a hurry."

She continued to smile, meeting my eyes with warmth. "Not a problem. Men rarely understand a woman's desire for jewelry. More often than not, they settle for using it as a way of obtaining forgiveness."

I blinked, staring at the woman who seemed so wise despite her burned-out, new age appearance. "Tell me," she continued, "did you get your necklace here as well?"

Both Lucien and I shot up, eyes wide with attention. "Yes!" I responded hastily. "Well, in a manner of speaking. I know the stone was bought here and I've been looking for the jeweler. You don't happen to know where we could find her, do you?"

The woman's face dropped ever so slightly, perhaps afraid she had lost a potential sale. "She doesn't come by often. Only a handful of times in the past month or so. I had never seen her before that. I've been selling at this market for five years. She's quite odd—a stunning woman, but odd."

I had to stifle my own laugh—this strange, middle-aged woman calling another odd. "How so?" I managed to ask, keeping my mouth set to a straight line.

"She seemed to dismiss most potential customers. People would come by, wishing to see something and ... well, she would act as though they weren't worthy of it. She had all sorts of explanations for the stones and their meanings. The customers who did end up buying something she would call over to the table herself. As if she were there waiting for them specifically." The woman's shoulders dropped and she tilted her head thoughtfully. "It seemed to work so well for her, I even tried it myself. Though, I suppose I would need to be ten years younger with cleavage up to here"—she gestured to her chin—"for it to have worked."

I mimicked her head tilt in a way that I hoped showed empathy. She would have had to have been *twenty* years younger, but I held my tongue.

She opened her mouth to say something else but quickly snapped it shut and fiddled with the fabric of her flowing peasant skirt.

"What was your name again?" I asked.

"Rhea." She held out a hand, which I promptly took in mine.

"Interesting," I said as we shook hands, "Named after the mother of Zeus?"

"You know your mythology!" She stood a little taller.

"Indeed," Lucien muttered darkly from my right.

"What is it you were going to say, Rhea? About the jeweler?"

She dropped her head. "You'll think me clinically insane if I say so."

I leaned forward. "I assure you that *we* of all people will understand whatever it is."

She sighed. "I practice the art of witchcraft. Never for evil. I was born with a gift—visions. And an ability to see some past lives. This woman, she had an aura about her. One very similar to yours." She gestured to me and swallowed, her jaw twitching nervously. "And yours." She looked at Lucien. "They are different than—well, I hate to use the word 'normal.' Let's just say that your auras are anomalies that fascinate me. I knew she was not who she said. There was a power to her." She leaned closer to me and dropped her voice to a whisper. "But there is a stronger power in *you*. Even stronger than him." Her voice trembled as she spoke, and she gestured to Lucien. I darted a look to Lucien, who was scowling at the woman. Rhea leaned away and rolled her shoulders back, standing taller. I admired her fortitude—most cower in fear around Lucien.

I nodded, taking in all she had said. I knew better than to dismiss her observations as crazy human dribble. "Do you have any other information about her? Her name? A number or website? Anything?"

The woman shook her head. "I'm afraid not. I believe she called herself Lilith."

My eyes darted to Lucien. His jaw was clenched shut and his hands were balled into fists at his side.

"Thank you so much," I said. "And, I will take these earrings." I handed them over to her, and her face brightened at the mention of a sale.

"Oh!" she exclaimed. "Let me wrap them up for you. That will be fifteen dollars."

I leaned into Lucien. "Give me twenty bucks," I whispered.

"What?" He glared at me. "Buy your own damn earrings!"

"She gave us information—buying one of her products is the least we can do."

With a sigh, he reached into his back pocket and pulled out his wallet. After routing around for a moment, he held out a fifty-dollar bill. "All I have is a fifty."

"Even better." I smiled and took the bill from his hand before he could tuck it back into his billfold.

I handed her the money and her eyes grew wide. "Oh! I don't know that I can break a fifty!"

"Keep the change." I smiled at her. "Your jewelry is beautiful. No amount of cleavage, *or lack thereof,* could sell it better."

She beamed and grabbed a matching bracelet from the case. "Then I insist you take this as well."

Lucien leaned in close, muttering low in my ear, "You owe me fifty bucks."

30

I swung my car into a front space at the café. Lucien looked around, his face crumpling into a scowl. Which wasn't too different than his normal face. "Why exactly are we back *here* again?"

"Because *I'm* behind the wheel now and *I* need a caramel mocha latte."

"You *do* realize your life is at stake here, right?"

"Yup."

"And that taking a coffee break isn't exactly the best way to take down a murderer?"

"I'm aware of that." I put the car in park and unclipped my seat belt.

Lucien sighed. "All right, well, as long as you're okay with dying over a cup of friggin' coffee."

"You clearly haven't had a cup of *our* coffee. It's worth dying for."

We walked in and ordered two lattes. I sat down at a table and kicked a chair out for Lucien. He stood above me, arms crossed. "Just what do you think you're doing?"

"Relaxing," I said, taking a sip of the steaming latte. "I need a moment to decompress before we go back to reality."

"Let's take these to go. We've got work to do."

I took another long sip and put my feet up, reclining in the chair. "I'm staying," I said, eyebrows arched.

He smacked my feet off the chair and grumpily sat down. After taking a sip of the coffee, his face softened and his expression raised to meet mine. "Not bad," he said, surprised. "Not worth dying for—but not bad, either." He sat there, eyes lowering to half-mast in a lazy way. "What are we doing here, anyway? Your boy isn't even working tonight."

I glanced around the café. Drew's absence hadn't escaped my notice. "Just drink your damn latte."

After another minute of quiet, it became glaringly clear that Lucien was incapable of sitting in silence. "Let me see that necklace," he said.

I slammed my mug onto the table. "Lucien! Can't we just sit—"

"I just want to see it."

I slipped it off from around my neck and handed it to him. "Here. Knock yourself out."

He held it close to his face, squinting an eye shut as if this gave him a better look. Finally he dropped the necklace to the table. It hit, sounding like a marble landing on a wood floor. "I don't even know what the fuck I'm looking for."

"Can demons be diagnosed ADHD? Because you should be tested."

"I'm sorry, kid—I'm just trying to keep you safe." He slumped into his seat and muttered something indecipherable into his coffee mug.

I clipped the necklace back around my neck and grabbed my purse, digging around inside for my cell phone. I had to text George—see if he could take over Lucien's job. He was driving me crazy. At the bottom of my purse, I found it along with

Damien's card he had given me back at the first crime scene. I pulled it out, staring at his name, remembering that smoldering gaze. "I have an idea," I said, quietly at first. When Lucien didn't respond, I smacked his arm. "I *said* I have an idea!"

"Uh-huh. I've heard that before. Does it involve another latte? Because, goddamn, this was good."

"No, seriously!" I slipped the earrings out of my second holes and handed them to Lucien, a smile spreading across my face.

He looked into his palm where the little earrings sat and then looked up at me as though I had lost my mind. "Earrings?" he asked. Finally, a strained smile cracked his face as well.

"Why are *you* smiling?" I asked.

"Because you've lost your mind. And that's what you do to the clinically insane—smile, so they don't know you're judging them."

I rolled my eyes. "Here." I handed him the business card. "This is a friend of mine—Damien. He's an elemental. Give him the earrings—which broke off of the stone the other day— and see what he can get from it. Maybe he can tell us who this 'Lilith' actually is." I leaned back, a sense of haughtiness and pride filling me and I crossed my arms over my chest, waiting for Lucien's apology. "Well?" I said.

"Fine. Okay. That's actually . . ."

"Clever? Brilliant? Ingenious?"

"I was going to say good. It was a good idea. But don't let that admission go to your head."

I smiled. He knew it was brilliant.

"All right then." Standing, he pocketed the little earrings and Damien's business card. "Let's get going."

"I can't go!" I looked at the time on my phone. "I've got a date with Wills tonight."

Lucien rolled his eyes. "Seriously?"

"I can't cancel on him. We haven't seen each other in a couple days. He'll know something's up."

He sat back down, his face once again creased and grumpy. "Well, I guess this'll have to wait. I can't leave you alone."

"Where's George? He can take over."

"He had to work."

"Julian. Call Jules."

"He . . ." Lucien caught my eyes, his expression softening slightly. "Hasn't been reachable for the past few hours."

"Kayce?" My voice was sounding small in my head.

He pressed his lips together, as though sensing my insecurities. "She was sent on some job tonight."

I sat there, an empty feeling at the base of my stomach sending shivers through my body and tingles down my arms. "Everyone gave up on me." I took a sip of my now-lukewarm mocha to give myself something to focus on outside of the emptiness inside. The coffee did little to nullify my suddenly dry throat.

Lucien's hand rested on my knee. "That's not it. Everyone has other obligations as well—even though I'm sure they'd all prefer to be here by your side."

"Not Jules," I said quietly. Kayce and George had jobs, I got that. Their lives couldn't stop and revolve around me. But Jules? Right now, this was supposed to be his only focus. His mission was to keep me safe.

"What about Wills? He could keep me safe. We could finally fill him in on all this."

Lucien shook his head. "I barely know the guy. I wouldn't trust him to work in my club, let alone keep you safe." He drained the last of his coffee with a swig. "Besides, have you seen his aura? The guy's a sorry excuse for a demon."

The bells chimed and the familiar sound of high heels and skin brushing together flooded my ears.

Lexi stopped in front of us, her short skirt allowing us a

view of her pantyless ass. "Well, well, well . . . am I interrupting your little powwow?"

Lucien turned in his seat, giving her his full attention. He ran a hand down her waist and hip, stopping on her thigh. She gave just the slightest gasp, a breath catching dramatically in her throat. And I gaped at Lucien—I was pretty sure I had never seen him touch her before. He'd *been* groped by her, but never the other way around. "Lexi," he said, circling his thumbs over her hip bone tenderly. "How are you, kitten?"

Her moment of shock corrected itself quickly, and she crossed her arms over her chest, eyes narrowing. "What do you want, Lucien?"

"Do I have to want something to touch you? Have a seat— Join us."

She carefully took the seat next to him, her eyes darting back and forth between us. I wasn't quite sure what he was up to either, but I knew he wouldn't spend time with her of his own volition if there wasn't a damn good reason why.

"Can I get you anything? Coffee? Tea? I can vouch for the lattes here; they are indeed quite good." His charm was sickeningly effective. Had I not been immune to him, even I would have been a puddle on the floor at his feet.

"I—I was coming in to get a chai latte."

Lucien leaned forward and took her hand in his, turning it over in his and rubbing her palm. "Monica—please get Lexi a chai latte."

"But—"

"*Now.* Please."

I shoved my chair out from behind me and stalked over to the barista bar. I waited there while they steamed the drink, preparing it for her *highness*. Lexi looked slightly uneasy, but the two sat together laughing and touching. Flirting. As though they were on a date. The taste of vomit suddenly rose to my mouth. I had seen a lot of disgusting shit this week, but this might take first prize.

When it was ready, I carried the chai latte back to the table and dropped it carelessly down in front of her. A bit splattered out the top, landing on the table. "Here you go." I looked at Lucien, full of attitude. "Anything else I can get for you, *sir?*"

He ignored my sarcasm. "No, not right now, thank you." I sat back down and he kept his gaze intently on Lexi. "So," he said, "I actually wanted to ask a small favor of you."

Her gaze turned icy and she wrenched her hand from Lucien's grasp. "I knew it," she said coldly.

Lucien ignored her and continued to lean forward, moving his hand to her knee instead. "I have to run an errand—but we need someone to keep an eye on Monica. Keep her safe while I'm out."

I snapped my head in Lucien's direction. "No!" I said a bit too loud.

She smirked in her bitchy way. "Well, that was going to be *my* answer." She pushed Lucien's hand off her knee. "But this could be *fun*. And please, don't insult me with these pitiful displays of affection. We can all see right through them."

He leaned back smiling, crossing his arms over his muscular chest. "Flirting with a beautiful woman is never pitiful."

She gave him a sarcastic smile. "I'll believe it when it's more than just words. So, you need me right this second?"

Lucien nodded. "Preferably, yes."

"Okay, then. Go on, get out of here. Run your elusive 'errand.' "

After draining the last of his latte, Lucien kicked the chair out behind him, leaning down to land a tender kiss to my forehead before leaving. Lexi's eyes bore into mine, and a slow Cheshire grin spread across her face. "Well, well, well, whatever will we do to keep entertained?"

I stood, grabbing the empty mugs, and brought them over

to the sink. "I don't know what you plan on doing tonight, but I have a date."

She clicked her tongue and tilted her head dramatically to the side. "And you expect me to wait in hiding until Lucien comes back?"

"Basically." I turned to face her, hands on hips.

"You are a terrible hostess." She grabbed her purse. "Come along, then."

We made it back to my apartment in a matter of minutes. As we walked up my steps, she eyed my door curiously. After a moment she chuckled at the script, though faded, still evident on my door. "Whore," she said. "You didn't do a very good job washing that away. You've seemed to piss quite a few people off, haven't you?"

I paused, my key lingering just in front of the lock. "Well . . . there is a psychotic murderer out to kill me."

She clicked her tongue. "This was not written by the murderer, Monica."

I froze, keys still in hand. "What makes you think it isn't the killer who left it?"

I felt a chill from behind me and her frosty lips were on my ear, whispering. "Because, I would have remembered writing it."

31

She clicked her tongue three times. "*Tsk, tsk, tsk.* I've been waiting for this moment for a couple of centuries, now. Waiting for just the right time to rid the world and the underworld of *you*. Hell's own version of a double agent."

A knife pressed sharply into my lower back. I bit back a moan and my hand trembled. I didn't want to turn around and meet her eyes, but I knew I couldn't just stand there in fear. I could open my door; let her into my home—but that seemed like an even worse idea. I could make a run for my car? She has more energy reserves and surely would catch me before I reached the bottom of the stairs.

"Let me guess what you're thinking. . . . Fight or flight?" She cackled an evil laugh that sent a shiver through my bones.

I remembered the panic button hanging around my neck. I slid the key into the lock and cracked the door open slightly. If I can just fight her off until Lucien can respond to the panic button, I might get through this alive. With the other hand, I tried as discreetly as I could to reach it toward the necklace.

Her hand shot out quicker, grabbing it and ripping if from

my neck. The chain snapped. I felt the rawness of the burn on my neck for a moment—but in the next my magic took over, healing it. I clapped a hand over it, hoping she hadn't seen the small burst of energy. If she thought I had none, I could still use it to my advantage. The door was cracked open, and she pushed me through it into the darkness of my apartment.

I fell to my hands and knees, and she kicked me hard in the ribs. A cracking sound rang in my ears and Julian's kiss on my forehead stung. I forced my body not to heal itself. I'd need to preserve whatever life force I had left in me from my stint as a porn star.

She turned on the lights in the house, not taking her eyes off me, and checked the blinds and doors, making sure they were closed to peering eyes. Tears were streaming down my face, and I slowly pulled myself up to a standing position, hunched over in pain. "So this—all these murders . . . it's just some stupid vendetta over Lucien? A guy I've never even slept with?!"

She sauntered back over, the knife still in her hand. "Oh, that was just the icing on the cake." She smiled, the curve of her mouth like the curve of a sharp blade. "I'm not the only one who wants you dead. This is simply a job."

My mouth went dry. "You've been hired? Someone else wants me dead? But—but *why*? I fill my quotas well enough. I stay in the middle as much as I can. I don't ever try to attract too much attention."

"Yes, yes. You're perfectly average. But your potential is terrifying to some of the higher-ups in Hell. Surely you've heard by now how strong your powers are."

"My—my what? I've heard some gossip, but I never gave it much thought."

She laughed again at this. "Well, maybe you should have." She glided toward me with a fury I had never seen before in anyone. She was so fast, I stared in wonder. Faster even than any succubus I'd ever seen. She took my face, pinching it with one hand. "Oh, this is going to be fun." She had me pinned against a wall. I prepared myself for the last bit of fight I had in me. I saw the panic button chain hanging off my entrance side table next to her purse. If I could knock her out in time to get to that, I'd have a fighting chance.

She raised the knife to my throat. I swallowed, not taking my wide eyes off of hers.

"Knock, knock." Wills's British voice called through the door while letting himself in. He held a bouquet of flowers in one hand and a box of chocolates in the other. "Monica?" He looked at Lexi, her knife to my throat, taking in the scene. "Lexi?" He dropped the flowers and the candy to the floor and shut the door quickly behind him.

"Wills!" I shouted. "Run! Get some help!"

"Oh, Pocket," he said, strolling toward us, stopping to check his pocket watch before looking back to Lexi. "A little early, aren't we? I thought we had planned to do this tomorrow evening."

She shrugged. "An opportunity presented itself."

A coldness filled his eyes. They were like two gray stones staring at me. "Very well." He shrugged out of his suit jacket and hung it up on my coatrack, rolling up the sleeves on his pressed, white dress shirt. "Let's get this over with, shall we?"

32

She tossed Wills the knife, and he flipped into the air, catching it between two fingers on the dull side of the blade. He flipped it a second time and caught the handle. "I have become quite skilled with a knife over the past few years." He threw the blade at my wall, and it landed in the center of my face on a framed picture. The glass shattered and fell to the floor like raindrops.

Lexi sighed. "So theatrical." She gestured to the knife. "Well, go get it."

"I prefer to use my own blade." He pulled a serrated knife from his boot and slipped it out of its sheath.

I was still pressed up against the wall, though no hands held me there anymore. "Wills," I whispered, my eyes brimming with tears. "All this time, it was you?" I thought of the bodies I had seen. I remembered their fear, their deaths. The way he consumed their blood. "You had sex with her—she was dead and you had *sex* with her!" My voice was a hoarse whisper.

He propped an elbow against the wall, leaning over me. "You should take that as a compliment, Pocket. She looked so much like you—it was impossible to resist." He ran the flat blade of the knife along my body, careful not to break the skin just yet. "You murdered me. You took my life. I'm just return- ing the favor."

I shook my head. "Fine. I accept that you're angry for what I did. But why all the others?"

He pushed off the wall and flipped the knife over in his hand again, like some sort of new habit. "Killing a succubus is an art in itself. I needed to perfect it."

"So all those women—they were just *practice?*" This couldn't be the man I had once loved.

"In a sense, yes. But they kill, too. Sure they didn't take *my* life per se, but they took numerous others. They deserved it as much as you—though, I have to admit . . . all this talk of your reformation made me doubt myself. You're not quite so thoughtless with your powers as you used to be. You don't haphazardly steal the souls of men you claim to love anymore. I respect that. But, as Lexi made me realize"—he smiled at her and she smiled back—"that doesn't change history. If it weren't for her in my life, I'd just be another corpse on the battlefield."

"You." I looked at Lexi, a hatred flooding inside of me like I had never felt before. "You did this. You turned him to a demon."

"Yes," she said matter-of-factly. "And I explained that none of this would have happened without your interference. I showed him what his life would have been like had *you* shown some restraint."

I pleaded, reaching my hands out to touch his clean-shaven cheeks. "Wills." The tears spilled out over my eyes. "I would have saved you if she hadn't interfered. I heard you calling for me in Bastogne. I-I found your pocket watch chain. I still have it." I could hear the panic in my voice.

His face softened at that, surprise washing over him. He took one step closer. "You have my chain?"

He wasn't reaching out to me, but he also wasn't pushing me

away. "Yes." I smiled at him. "Yes. Would you like it? I can get it for you."

"That was my father's chain. When were you planning on telling me this?" He touched my hand, and I continued to caress his face.

"Wills . . ." Lexi's voice was a low rattle. A warning.

"Quiet!"

His sudden loudness made me jump, and he squeezed my hand slightly. There was still an affection for me; I knew it. I had seen the crime scenes, felt the victim's pain. There was no way I could love this man any longer. But I could fake it until I got to safety.

"Wills," I whispered again, plumping my lips slightly with magic. "Don't you understand? I loved you. I couldn't resist you. I needed you in my life." I leaned in to him, my lips coming closer to his, angling for a kiss. "All of this—this whole thing, it was destiny—and now that you're a demon, we can be together for eternity."

He slid the knife blade over his lips like a barbed wire fencing to keep me out, his eyes full of sorrow. "Come any closer and I'll slice your bloody lips off. "

I backed out of his personal space. "You have to believe me, Wills." I clutched my purse closer to my body. The gun hugged against me within it.

Lexi stepped forward. "Wills, my love, are you ready? Let's drink her blood, absorb her power. We'll both be stronger for it."

Wills stepped back. "I'm sorry, Monica. I don't doubt you loved me as much as a Hellspawn could love another. I'll admit my desire for revenge has subsided in seeing you in your new life. But not enough. You still do the devil's work."

"Newsflash, Wills—your 'beloved' Lexi is a succubus as well. *She* does the devil's work. As do *you*."

"Lexi gets her powers from the blood of other demons. Not from preying on humans."

I laughed at that. "Oh? Is that what she told you?" I clicked my tongue in the same way Lexi had done to me earlier. "*Tsk, tsk, tsk.* You clearly haven't been honest with your beau, *Alexandria.*"

"Don't call me by my full name. I hate that," she said through clenched teeth.

"I guess she also didn't inform you of her undying love for Lucien, did she?"

He looked at me blankly, then at Lexi. "Lucien? The Arch-Demon?"

She shook her head, her eyes calm, but the muscles in her neck were strained. "That was a long time ago, darling. Don't believe her. She's just trying to get out of this alive. Besides, you admitted it yourself—you've had other indiscretions since we became partners." She then turned her attention to me. "And perhaps you should tell Wills about your recent developments with that boss of yours. I was in his office. I saw you two."

"Enough!" Wills yelled, and shoved me up against the wall again. His arm was against my throat, constricting the amount of air flow. "Time to taste your power, *Pocket.*"

He sliced my cheek with his blade, a crimson stream gushing from my cheek like a wall of blood. He licked it, his tongue rough and scaly. With the lack of oxygen, my body's natural defenses took over and the cut healed itself, closing over.

Wills pulled back, his eyes glistening red for a fraction of a second. "Wh-what just happened?"

Lexi grabbed a fistful of my hair and bent my head back to get a closer look at my healed cheek. My neck stretched backward in an unnatural way. "I thought you said you were going to take care of her! Make sure the stone absorbed the last of her powers!"

"I did, I did!" He gestured to me. "Right before our meeting, I arranged for Drew to find out about Adrienne. You said yourself—you saw her with him." His eyes grew wide and he grabbed the back of my head, tearing Lexi's hands away from me. He cradled my face. "You didn't have sex with him, did you? If—if you had, the stone would have absorbed any energy you had gained back. In order to absorb power, you need to have sex in the stone's presence."

The night with Drew rushed back into my memory. The necklace—I had given it to Kayce that night for her hunt. I still had on the earrings, but they must not have been powerful enough to absorb all of Drew's life force—which was why I only got a small fix off of him. I stared into Wills's eyes in as much of a lovingly way as I could muster. There was a flicker of hope in them. Trust. If I could get him to think I was faithful, maybe he would spare my life. I nodded, my teeth clamped down to keep from chattering with fear. "No—no, of course I didn't have sex with Drew. I'm with you. I would never cheat on you." I had some energy left, but not nearly enough to survive a battle with either of these two . . . let alone both of them at once.

He kissed me firmly on the lips, pressing my body even harder into the wall. The taste of my blood on his tongue brought a gag up my throat.

"Well, that's sweet and all"—Lexi sighed from beside us—"but Wills, we still have a job to do. Or do you not remember that this isn't *only* about revenge. There's a bounty on her head. If we don't finish the job, someone else will down the line."

He looked at me, regret flooding his eyes. "She's right."

"Wills, no . . ." I whispered. It was a moot point. He still loved me, I could see that. But he was going to kill me. "One last kiss, Wills. Can I just have one last kiss?"

He looked over to Lexi, who rolled her eyes and nodded yes. His lips brushed against mine, parted, teasing. My heart pounded against my rib cage. I lifted one hand to his face and with the other reached slowly into my bag. Making as little noise as possible, I rooted around for the gun. There was no way to click the safety off without their demon ears hearing. Once I made the choice to shoot, I'd have to do it all in a matter of seconds. As much as I'd rather shoot Lexi, Wills was the only guaranteed hit. With the gun still in my purse, I pointed it at his stomach.

Our kiss was ending. I could feel his lips finishing as he had done so many times in our past. "I'm sorry," I whispered, the tears spilling silently over my cheeks. He tilted his head ever so slightly, a small crinkle at the corner of his eyes. As fast as I could, I clicked off the safety and pulled the trigger. The shot echoed through my small apartment and blew a hole through my purse. Wills crumpled to the floor; the bullets blessed with holy water caused a steam to rise from the wound, and he lay moaning on the floor. Before I could stop her, Lexi was on top of me. The gun fell inches from my hand, just out of reach. I shifted into something rabid, with threatening claws and teeth, and ripped past Lexi, rushing for the panic button. I barely got beyond her before my magic flickered away and I turned back into my normal human form. I grasped the necklace in my hand and squeezed, the button clicking uneventfully beneath my fingers. A heavy weight hit me from behind, sending me sprawling to the ground. Lexi flipped me over and sat above me, knife in hand, sputtering a demon tongue I hadn't heard before.

She stabbed the knife into my stomach and quickly raised the bloodied knife to her mouth, licking the length of the blade. Splitting pain seared through my body, up my spine, and my vision grew dark. The wound healed, and I gasped a staggering breath. I reached for the gun with all my strength, but she flung my arm down by my sides and pinned them there with her knee. "Let's see how long your strength holds up." She stabbed me again in the stomach. And again in the ribs. The kidney. The liver. I could feel some of them healing, but my energy wasn't able to keep up with the wounds. From the ground, things were starting to move in slow motion. Blood dripped from the wounds, gushing up my chest, pooling around the base of my neck. Some blood hit the stone necklace, and it sizzled, evaporating in a steam. Lexi paused, licking some of my blood from her fingers, and her eyes flashed red; veins rippled around her temples and jaw as some sort of dark magic took hold. She once again plunged the knife deep into my core. Sounds were further and further away. I heard distant voices, a group of voices. The stabbing stopped, and when I looked up, Lexi was no longer on top of me but standing, facing off with Jules, Lucien and ... someone else. A stranger's face, so familiar and dark at the same time. He looked at me, made eye contact. His eyes traveled down my body, letting them linger on my bloody, open stomach. He licked his lips, then quickly returned his gaze to Lexi. A shiver tingled down my spine. Not a stranger—I knew him. My maker, Dejan.

"You cannot win here," Dejan said.

Lexi growled and took a fighter's stance. "Even if *I* don't kill her, someone else will."

Another moan came from the floor in front of me. "Wills." I whispered his name. He moaned again, and I heard a rustling.

I closed my eyes. Sleep seemed so close. To sleep would be Heaven.

Heaven.

A stinging on my cheeks woke me. Damien and Adrienne hovered above like two guardian angels welcoming me home. "Monica," Adrienne said. "Stay with us. We're going to get you help." There was a badge around her neck, a detective badge. I reached out for it, running my bloody fingers along the crest.

"You're a . . ." I coughed, and could see the blood sputter out of my mouth.

"I'm a cop." She nodded. "Damien's my partner." She started

chanting incantations that I didn't recognize. I had very little knowledge of witchcraft and spells, but I was mesmerized by the calming tone of her voice. Her eyes swirled like two twisters, and a numbness settled over my body. "There," she whispered, looking up at Damien, "that's the best I could do. I'm not advanced enough to cast a healing spell on such a powerful succubus, but it should at least numb her pain for a little." She and Damien stood, moving in as backup behind Lucien, Jules, and Dejan. It was five to one—Lexi didn't stand a chance.

I could see the face-off, Lexi clutching her bloody knife. She knew she was no match for an ArchDemon and an angel. In a movement so fast I almost couldn't see it, she grabbed a handful of the shards of glass scattered across the floor from my broken picture frame and threw them at the group. The glass sprayed everyone, snipping and cutting into their skin. She turned to me, and in one last ditch effort to not go down without a fight, she lunged. I, on the other hand, had no more fight left in me. I closed my eyes waiting for the pain to come; waiting for her knife to sink into my flesh one last time.

I heard Wills's distinct voice scream, "No!" Lexi's dagger was rushing toward my body. And suddenly like a shield, Wills threw himself on top of me. The knife sank into his back and a gunshot rang through the air. Heavy weight landed on my chest and stubble scratched at my neck. Wills's eyes stared back at mine, blood trickling out of his mouth. "Pocket," he managed to whisper in a raspy voice before his eyes rolled back into his head. His lungs emptied themselves of his last breath.

33

Bastogne, Belgium, 1944

I knew he was here. Somewhere. This was where his battalion was stationed. We found an abandoned school in Bastogne, which was where the medics set up their base. I exhaled in relief that it wasn't another church. Those always proved difficult to navigate around. Constantly sleeping outside in tents, asking other nurses to get me supplies. People grew wary of why I would never enter. But having them speculate was easier than having them see for themselves what would happen.

We didn't have many supplies when we first arrived—and now, only two weeks later, it was so sparse that we were cutting up sheets to make bandages. Dead bodies lined the entranceway to the school.

"Medic! We've got one of our own here!" two men cried out as they carried in a doctor whom I recognized. I rushed over, morphine in hand. He was shot in the throat—not dead center. It must have missed the jugular since he had yet to bleed out. I injected him with morphine as he sputtered and gagged on his own blood. A hand shot up, and I grabbed it in my own. "You're going to be okay, doctor. We're going to take care of

you." His eyes bulged in pain, the veins red and angry. He gurgled, trying to say something. "Don't try to talk, you'll make it worse." I could see it in his eyes—he knew he wouldn't live. He had seen injuries much less severe than his take lives.

A different doctor came rushing over and pushed me aside. "Hendrix!" he cried. A moment of horror crossed his face before he moved into action, putting pressure on the wound. The blood soaked through the rag with no effort at all. They didn't need the extra set of hands, so I kneeled, holding Hendrix's hand and stroking his head.

"Bastards!" the doctor cried. "They are not to shoot medics! They know that."

I gave the medic as much of a genuine smile as I could muster. You'd think we'd have all grown accustomed to death after years of this, but the sight of a wounded soldier dying in pain never became easier. He outstretched one finger and ran it across my lips. Gurgling twice more, his eyes rolled to the back of his head.

"We need another medic to come out to the field with us," said one of the soldiers who had carried him.

The doctor pulled away from the lifeless medic's body and shook his hands. Blood splattered, and he wiped the remaining on his pants. "We're low on men as it is. I don't know if I can spare another." His hands were on his hips and his head hung low in defeat and exhaustion.

I stood, dropping the medic's hand gently across his chest. "I could go," I said. "I'm as skilled as any doctor. And I don't fear being in the barracks." I failed to add that it was because I knew I could not die.

The men looked at me, surprised. One opened his mouth to object. Before he could utter a word, the doctor looked me up and down. "Very well, then."

* * *

December in Bastogne is bitter. The men all suffered from frostbite and trench foot. I sat low in a hole, shivering along with them. One man passed around a cigarette. While the smoke would have offered a small comfort in the midst of this snow, I passed without a drag to the soldier next to me. The men needed it more than I.

They were mostly tentative with me. Unsure if a woman would be willing to run into the line of fire to pull an injured soldier to safety. I felt their assessing eyes as we passed the cigarette. "Here." I reached into my sack and handed out dry socks to the men. "Take off the ones you've got on. Dry them around your necks. Switch your socks every couple of days." They did as they were told. I think some were happy to have a mothering figure instead of yet another man barking commands. Others still seemed wary.

A shot rang out through the air. Then another zoomed over our heads. There was a splat-like sound, then a scream rang out through the air. The men in their holes fired back.

"Medic!" a voice screamed. I secured my pack to my hip and hopped out of the hole. A man grabbed my skirt's waistband, pulling me back down.

"What, are you mad? Don't go out yet! Wait until we can cover you!"

I could see the injured soldier, lying in the snow, clutching his arm. Blood-soaked snow framed him like a portrait. He cried out again in agony. "I'll be fine," I said as I yanked my skirt from the soldier's grasp. I ran, dodging bullets.

I reached the soldier. He was shot in the shoulder. Not the worst injury I had seen, but without being treated it could lead to infection, or worse. I grabbed him under the arms and pulled with every ounce of muscle. In my current body, I wasn't strong enough to pull him to safety. I shifted myself to be more muscular. A change that only someone who had seen me naked would notice. I pulled again and his body dragged in the snow. I pulled until he was out of the line of fire. I shot him with morphine and tied a tourniquet around the top of the wound.

Two soldiers came over to us, wide-eyed, staring at me in wonder. "We called it in. A medic truck should be by soon."

"Well, what are you waiting on? Take him over there to wait. I'm needed here." They nodded.

The days and nights melted one into another. I would go back to base to check on the men we had brought in and get supplies, though there weren't many to be had these days.

It was closing in on Christmas. Morale was low, and I certainly wasn't a lot of help in that department. Every so often, I would sneak over enemy lines, shifting into the Nazi medic uniforms. It was the most guilt-free way to get life force I could think of. While there, I would steal supplies we needed. Bandages, morphine—I even managed to sneak away with some chocolate for my boys one night.

As we moved in on enemy territory, I heard other battalions close by. They were allies, I was sure of it. Each night, I closed my eyes and listened carefully for Wills's voice. Shots rang out once more. I was growing accustomed to them, the sound becoming akin to an adrenaline boost for me. I waited in crouched position behind the battle area, waiting for the soldiers to call me in.

The calls came within minutes. "Medic!" was being shouted from so many different directions, I didn't know where to begin. The men whose injuries didn't seem so severe I left with some morphine and bandages before running to the next screaming voice. One man lay in the center of the field—no cover for him whatsoever. It was no wonder he was shot. I took a breath, and ran, covering my head. A pain unlike any other bit into my thigh, and I fell to the ground. Shot. The fuckers had shot me. A woman medic.

"Medic down!" a soldier cried out.

"Save the medic!" another one shouted.

"No!" I called out to them. "Stay where you are! I am fine!" I lifted my skirt above my knees, reached a finger into the wound, and dug out the bullet. I shifted the wound closed but kept it still somewhat bloody in case anyone asked to see it later. It still stung like Hell, but it was manageable. I crawled over to the wounded soldier, the morphine between my lips so I could inject it as soon as I reached him.

His face and lips were white. "Are you—are you all right?" he asked me, gasping for breath.

"I'm fine. Just a little bullet wound." I smirked at him, and he gave a broken chuckle, his breath pooling in a fog around his mouth.

"M-Me too," he said, clutching the hole in his stomach.

As I dragged him out of the field, the shots died down. Then after a few moments, they stopped entirely. The enemy had retreated. There were bodies lying everywhere. "Medic!" was being screamed in French and English. Another battalion had been involved nearby, as I suspected. Their screams did not subside.

I looked over at the captain. "I need to go help them."

He nodded. "All our boys are accounted for?"

I nodded, my eyes scanning the field. "Those who are alive."

"Go," he said. "We'll wait here for you."

I ran toward the screams. One by one, I found the wounded, patched them up, and pulled them to safety. I skipped over the bodies that had no pulse. I came across their medic, shot dead.

Then, I heard a specific voice above all the rest. "Medic!" he cried in a dignified British accent. Wills. My heart froze, a stabbing pain. I took off running toward the voice, jumping over bodies, ignoring other injured soldiers. I couldn't feel bad about that. I wouldn't feel bad about that. I'd already shortened Wills's life enough. I could save him. I could counteract all the essence I stole.

"Wills!" I screamed out.

"Medic!" I heard his voice cry once more. I ran faster, just barely dodging a wounded soldier who reached out and grabbed at my ankle. I fell to my face in the snow.

"Medic," he whispered hoarsely. I looked into my sack. I had run out of bandages. I ripped my apron with my teeth, tearing off a long strip, and handed it to the soldier along with a morphine shot.

"I'll be back for you," I assured him before taking off running toward my Wills again. But his screams had stopped. "Wills!" I called out again into the empty field. I heard other people's cries, other soldier's voices. Some were calling out for me—others for their mothers. Some for God. I listened carefully. His voice was no longer among the screams. I kept running toward the area I thought the voice came from. I arrived at a different clearing. Several bodies lay dying or dead. I scoured the men, not seeing my Wills anywhere among them. Finally, I knelt by the man closest to me, tearing off another section of my apron.

His wound wasn't so terrible, and I only had a few morphine shots left. I packed his wound with the bandage. "Parlez-vous anglais?"

"Oui, mademoiselle."

"Can you walk yourself to safety?"

He nodded, and I wrapped his arm around my shoulder to help hoist him up.

"Pardonne-moi, mademoiselle, but aren't you Monsieur Wills Brindley's lady? He's shown me your picture on many occasions. A beautiful image of you on the stage."

An icy breath caught in my throat. "You know my Wills?" I grabbed onto the lapel of his coat and pulled his face to mine. "Where? Where is he!" I yelled.

"He was over there. Calling for a medic not far from here."

"Get yourself to a truck. There should be one waiting." I

took off running again until I stumbled over an abandoned gun and a single boot. A large pool of blood stained the snow, and there lying in the center was a broken pocket watch chain. The initials WDB were engraved at the clip. A couple of damp pieces of paper lay facedown in the snow. I picked them up, holding them to my face, only to find an image of myself onstage singing—the photograph torn in half.

34

Floating. Something soft and gentle brushed against my skin, and I was floating. When I regained consciousness, I was in bed. Though the curtains were drawn, I knew it was still dark out. A sliver of moonlight seeped in through a crack in the curtains and illuminated the room like a lit match.

My tongue felt fuzzy, and I swallowed in an attempt to conjure any sort of moisture unsuccessfully. "You're up." Jules was sitting in bed next to me, wiping a cool cloth over my head. I shivered and pulled the covers around me tighter. I felt my upper body—bandages were wrapped around my middle. All I had on was a sports bra and yoga pants.

"Water?" I rasped. He handed me a full glass of tepid water. My head was too heavy to lift on my own, and I whimpered with the attempt. Jules slipped a hand under the back of my head and raised my lips to the glass. I greedily drank the entire cup, bits of water dribbling down my chin. Jules gently wiped them away. He set my head back down after I had finished. "How long have I been out?" My voice sounded foreign. Groggy and deep.

"Not long. An hour or so. Enough time for us to move and change you."

"Lexi?"

"She's been dealt with."

"Meaning what exactly . . . ?"

He didn't answer. Just sat there, his lips pressed into a line.

The pain shooting through my body was almost unbearable. There was an aching that I had never felt before—and in over two hundred years on Earth, I've felt a lot of different types of pain. "Wills?" I asked, his name catching in my throat. Instinctually, I touched my sternum, the stone no longer there.

Julian just shook his head.

"I killed him." I closed my eyes, willing the tears to stay away.

"He would have killed you first. Besides, he chose your life over his. He threw himself over you—Lexi killed him. Not you."

"The knife alone wouldn't have killed him without the holy water bullets." A wave of nausea filled me, and it felt like a walnut was stuck in my throat. I gurgled a noise to which Jules reacted faster than I could regurgitate. A bucket was suddenly in front of my face, and I heaved into it. It was dark in the room, but the vomit looked thick and tar-like—blood. With a shaky hand, I touched the corner of my lips and brought my fingers to eye level. A red smear stained my fingertip. "That can't be good," I whispered, and Jules guided my head back down to the pillow.

"It's going to be okay." He made the sign of the cross over my forehead, chest, and shoulders.

The sight was laughable. A dying succubus with an angel over her body giving a blessing. I remembered the familiar face— the third man, Dejan. "Jules—the other man with you . . . he was my—"

He stared at me thoughtfully, but before I could finish, the bedroom door burst open and light from the kitchen streamed in blindingly. "She's awake." It was Lucien.

Several people came rushing in to my bedside. Kayce pushed past Lucien, then George and Damien, and hanging toward the back, Adrienne. Their horrified faces were all I needed to see. My outlook was not good.

George looked at Lucien. "Can't you heal her?"

He shook his head. "These wounds are far too damaging. Demon inflicted. Even I can't heal them."

"She needs a human—she needs life force," Kayce said, sitting on the other side of the bed next to me and taking my hand in hers. I could feel the clamminess of my damp skin in contrast to her dry, warm hands.

The group stood in silence, their heads hung.

"Well, let's go get her someone," George finally said.

Lucien snorted a bitter laugh. "And just what human is going to have sex with a dying, bloody woman? Besides—the amount of energy she needs to survive would kill any person."

"It doesn't have to be human." Julian's voice was low, almost an inaudible whisper.

"Julian, no," Lucien growled.

"I wouldn't die," he said, his eyes rising to meet Lucien's.

"An angel cannot commit that sort of treason." Lucien's voice was a warning, and his body language looked as though he would tackle Julian if he tried. "You would be cast out. It would be worse than death for an angel."

Jules looked at me and ran a knuckle down my cheek. I shook my head. "I'm not worth it, Jules. Why sacrifice an angel to save a demon?"

"I have my reasons."

Adrienne pushed herself to the front of the group. "Monica, are you still in pain? I can cast another numbing spell."

I nodded, remembering the blissful magical anesthesia from

earlier. "Please, please," I whispered, the pain so unbearable that I could no longer differentiate between tears and sweat.

"Could you two step away from the bed for a moment?" she asked. Julian and Kayce obliged. The group took a few steps back to give her room. She took each of my hands in hers and crawled into the bed to kneel over me. She whispered in a foreign tongue again. A shield formed around us like an impenetrable bubble. I could hear the group shouting, though they sounded far away—faded voices calling for us.

I looked at her, curiously. With all the enemies I'd made, I had no idea whom I could trust anymore. "Are you an elemental, too?"

She shook her head. "No, I'm just your average witch. It runs in the family." She knelt over me, staring in silence. "Drew really loves you," she said, an emptiness in her eyes.

"He loved you, too," I answered.

She laughed in a hollow way. "Past tense."

"He thinks you cheated."

She nodded. "I know. Damien and I had to pretend we were lovers. And we were so close to finding the killer. I couldn't risk coming clean." I attempted to nod, the action causing a coughing fit. I covered my mouth but could feel the blood sputtering out with each cough; my insides twisted. I could feel the bleeding inside me. Organs shutting down. Pools of blood forming in my guts.

"And, I'm sorry." She paused, an embarrassed little smirk playing over her lips. "About your door. You're not really a whore. I was just upset."

If I could have laughed without it being excruciatingly painful, I would have.

She began another incantation, and the numbness soothed my body once again. I sighed, and she wiped the blood from my lips and chin. "Will you tell him? Tell him I never cheated.

Explain it to him," she whispered. Her voice cracked, and she wiped a tear from the side of her nose.

"Why don't you?"

Her jaw stiffened. "Because . . . I'm not going to be around."

I opened my mouth to object, and as I did she pressed her lips to mine, her tears falling to my face. A tingle coursed through my body, tendrils of magic spilling out of her into me. Her soul filling mine. With what little strength I had, I tried to push her off of me, but the soul pulled me in. It was intoxicating, and I got lost in the kiss. In her thoughts. She tasted like honey and cinnamon, and I drank her like a fine wine. Her hands were on my face, and I rolled on top, pressing my body into hers. The power. Her power. She was a good soul, angelic on the inside. Her lip had a small cut from where the glass Lexi threw hit her. I could taste the combination with my blood. I saw her childhood, growing up in South Vegas in a rough neighborhood. Her teenage years, rebellious in the way teens tend to be. The death of an older brother who raised her—gang violence. College, studying to be in the criminal justice department. Her death flashed in my eyes. Her dead body twitching in my bed. I was in this swirling tunnel—I could hear voices around me . . . far off voices screaming my name.

The bubble evaporated. The visions flew out of me like a cold gust of wind. Someone pulled me from her body—Lucien. I was in Lucien's arms. He stroked my hair and held me to his chest. "It's okay," he crooned. "It was her choice, not yours." I looked at Adrienne, pale and cold, lying in my bed where I had been a moment before. I tore the bandages from my stomach—my flesh was tan, glowing, perfect. Not a scratch on my body. The pain was gone. I whispered a shocked expression—only, it was in another language. Something ancient that to my knowledge I had never learned. It was Adrienne's incantation language. I touched the corner of my mouth where her cinnamon blood dripped. Jules stood over her body, offering a blessing, and Damien knelt next to her, head down, shoulders shaking. I buried my face in Lucien's chest, wishing I could hide there forever.

35

Coffee is a lot like people. In many ways, it's deceiving. The sweetness that you smell as it brews is more often than not a fallacy. The scent of a dark roasted coffee bean promises you rich flavors with hints of chocolate and hazelnut, but if you're not used to coffee's deceptiveness, you're left with a bitter aftertaste dangling at the back of your throat. To those of us who are used to it—we've grown a fondness for that bitter taste. It's complex. It's teasing. It reminds us that most things in life are not consistently sweet with every sip. One morning, your coffee might brew mild with just a flirtation of nutty undertones. And the next morning, it might be pelting you in the face with those same nuts, leaving little stinging marks with each sip. It's moody. It's not easy to perfect. But when you get the perfect brew, it's rewarding. And that same perfection is not guaranteed tomorrow just because you managed it today.

I stared into my mug of coffee—its flavor was a lot like my mood today. Muddy. I swallowed another sip, hoping the flavor had improved from moments before. The bitter, acidic sting hit the back of my throat. I looked over at Drew, who was clomping around behind the bar. He was still off his game. It was as though the coffee was brewing angrily, and each sip I took I was swallowing Drew's pain and frustration.

I untied my apron and walked over to the bar. The place was practically empty. Just Drew, me—and one old man sitting in the corner sipping a tea. Drew's rag hung out of his back pocket and swung from side to side as he moved around behind the bar. I set the mug into the sink. "Maybe she's not coming back, Drew."

"Huh?" He grunted while lifting a shipment of baked goods just delivered.

"I said—maybe she's not coming back."

He shook his head. "Her letter said she was."

I sighed and ran my hand over my face. I shifted my makeup so that it didn't smear as I did so. I didn't know quite why yet, but I was given strict orders not to tell Drew of Adrienne's death. They said they would "handle it." Whatever that meant.

He pounded his fist on the counter. "She had an explanation all along and I—I wouldn't even listen. I was too pigheaded to hear her out."

I shrugged, trying my best to ignore the stinging pain in my chest. I didn't want him to love her. I didn't want him to have regret about our one night together. But she saved my life—and he deserved to know just how good she was.

"For what it's worth—I know what you saw . . . *see* in her now. I finally saw her good side, too."

"You did? When?"

"Oh—she, um, came to me before she was sent off on this case. She wasn't sure you'd even read her note. She wanted to make sure you knew the truth."

He nodded. "You didn't tell her about us—"

"No," I cut him off. "Of course not."

The bells on top of the door chimed and Damien walked in, wearing his normal dress pants and button-down shirt with a fitted leather jacket over top. He tucked his sunglasses into his shirt pocket, and Drew gave him a welcoming nod. "Hi," he said, taking the rag out of his back pocket and wiping up the counter. It was a nervous habit of his—Drew was notorious for cleaning when antsy.

"Hello." He nodded to Drew and looked at me, his eyes traveling down my body to my shoes, then back to my eyes. "You look . . . better." There was a hardness to his jaw. Sure, he found me hot . . . but I had killed his partner and friend. That's not exactly something you get over right away.

I nodded and mustered up the faintest flicker of a smile. "I am, thanks." I looked at Drew, who was staring curiously at me. "I had a small stomach bug yesterday. Nothing big."

"Could I get a coffee to go?" Damien asked.

Drew turned his back to fix the coffee and I gave Damien a wide-eyed stare. "Don't get the coffee!" I whispered.

He leaned against the bar, not looking me in the eyes anymore. A hard line was set on his jaw. "Don't tell me what to do."

"Fine. Suit yourself."

The guys exchanged money and coffee, and Damien glared at me as he raised the cup to his lips and gulped back the biting coffee. His eyes grew slightly wider and it seemed to take him a second to swallow it down. Fine, I got it. He was making a point. Men are such dicks sometimes. He pushed off the bar and gave a salute to Drew. "I'll see you around." He didn't say good-bye to me. Didn't even look at me as he turned on his heel and stalked out of the café.

I grabbed my stuff from my locker and headed back out. "Have a good night, Drew. See you tomorrow."

He held my gaze for a second and looked away just as I felt the same lustful sparks we'd had in the past. " 'Night, Monica."

I saw two people waiting for me, leaning against my car. Instinctually, I put a hand to my new purse. The gun still weighed heavy inside it. Knowing there was a bounty on your head makes a girl a bit paranoid, I had to admit.

"Jules!" I sighed heavily, the stress melting from my shoulders. "Oh, my Hell, you scared me!" From behind him, Adrienne stepped out. She was wearing a white flowing skirt that looked like something I had worn at Woodstock, with a brown crewneck T-shirt. "Adrienne?" I wasn't sure if this was some sort of trick. I had seen her soul—I knew she was Heavenbound. I just didn't realize she was angel caliber. But the glow surrounding her body was unmistakable. Her hair was no longer bleached and brittle. It was soft and luscious, cascading down past her shoulders in long, silky curls. Her face was luminous and shimmered. She looked like she stepped out of a L'Oréal commercial, and I couldn't help but stew with envy.

She stepped closer to me, and the smell of cinnamon and honey was taken with the breeze and blown into my face. "You're . . . you're an angel," I said, still dumbstruck.

She nodded and smiled. Her teeth a perfect row of glistening pearls. "Julian's taken me in as a mentor of sorts." Her voice was soft and melodic.

The news knocked the wind out of me. He was *her* mentor? He chose to take her in? That was my position. He was my mentor. She looked strikingly similar to me in her angel form. Without the orange skin and horribly bleached hair—there was a definite likeness. I swallowed and looked at Jules. My voice cracked as I tried to say something.

"I thought it was the least I could do, considering she sacrificed her human life to *save* you," Jules said pointedly. Adrienne turned and smiled at him.

"Well, I wanted—*we* wanted . . ." Adrienne gestured to herself and Julian. *Oh Hell,* I thought, she was "we-ing" me. ". . . to tell you that I was okay. And I needed to let you know that when I died—I was alerted to a lot of things that I wouldn't have known as a human." She took a step closer to me. I was never again going to be able to put honey in cinnamon tea without gagging. "I know about your and Drew's night together, and I just wanted to tell you—I forgive you. And Drew was so distraught that night, I wanted to thank you for keeping him away from alcohol. He really needed you."

I wanted to laugh. And cry. "Great. No problem. I'll be sure to open my legs again when he needs it. You just give the word." I unlocked my car and yanked the door open. "We're done here, right?"

Adrienne looked back at Jules, panicked. Jules shook his head. "She doesn't mean it, Adrienne. Regardless of how brazen she's acting now, she does have a moral code."

"The fuck I do." I slammed my door shut and closed my eyes until I heard the familiar *crack* of the angels leaving. I held out my hands hovering above the steering wheel and allowed Adrienne's ancient Indo-European tongue to whisper across my lips. The car started on its own—surprising even me. I revved the gas and squealed my tires as I pulled away. I grabbed my cell phone from my purse and dialed Kayce.

"Hey girl, how are you?" she answered.

"I need to get laid. Tonight."

"But—you just bagged the good cop. You should be good for days."

"Fine," I said between gritted teeth. "I don't *need* to get laid. I *want* to get laid. By someone good. A church boy, preferably."

Kayce was silent on the other line for a second. I could hear her breathing. Finally, she said. "Does this mean I finally have a hunting partner?"

I smirked. "You fucking bet it does."

Turn the page for a sizzling preview of
the next book in Katana Collins's new series,

SOUL SURVIVOR

An Aphrodisia trade paperback,
coming October 2013.

1

The neon-colored lights were blinding as they swooped around the club like laser beams. First purple. Then green. Now blue. It felt like I was in the middle of a lava lamp, watching them spin around me. With the little stirrer straw, I sipped my Long Island Iced Tea and kept dancing. Sweaty men bumped into me from all angles, each attempting to brush my ass or breasts, in the hopes I might look up and give them even the slightest bit of attention. If only they knew just how deadly my attention could be.

Kayce, my best friend, grabbed my elbow and swung me around, our noses almost bumping in the process. Even with immortal hearing, I could barely make out what she was saying over the thumping of the bass. Grabbing the back of my head, she pulled me in closer, her lips on my ear. "I think I found two!" she yelled.

For normal girls on the town, this could mean anything— two seats, two bucks, two drinks. For two succubi on the town? It meant victims. We prey on the local men and women here in Las Vegas to satiate the raging itch between our legs and sustain our immortal souls on Earth.

With her hand still wrapped around the back of my neck, she turned me toward two college-aged guys, staring transfixed at us while their clammy hands clenched plastic cups, spilling over with cheap beer.

My head snapped back to Kayce. "They're so *young*," I said, noting their auras, silver and sparkling. These two were Heaven-bound for sure.

"I thought you didn't care anymore?" Her gaze narrowed.

My stomach twisted, guilt trying to gnaw its way out as if some little animal had burrowed into there. I pushed the feeling aside. "I don't," I shouted over the music with a nonchalant shrug. I was bluffing. If Kayce knew I was lying, then she chose to ignore it.

"What do you say we give them a little something to look forward to?" she said as a devious grin crept its way across her face. She nestled her body into mine, bumping her ass from side to side to the beat of the music. Running her hands through my shoulder-length blond curls, she sent a wicked glance to the two guys watching, their mouths hanging agape. "C'mon girl," she whispered, "it's showtime."

I moved to the music with her, running my fingers down her open, bare back. We turned in rhythm so that I was looking directly at the leaner college kid; he had surfer blond hair that flopped to one side and full lips. An itch surged through my core, shooting between my legs, and my mouth went dry. A droplet of sweat tickled its way down the side of my face along my hairline, and I quickly shapeshifted it away, making sure to settle my makeup, yet again. Drinking was making me sloppy with my appearance—and I had it much easier than most humans. With one hand, I swept Kayce's curtain of jet black hair to the side and ran my lips ever so gently up her neck to her ear.

My eyes stayed on the college kid as I darted out a tongue that barely grazed her earlobe.

Her fingers splayed against my scalp, weaving into my hair, and she tugged my neck back. "Which one do you want?" she whispered. With my eyes closed, nose aimed at the ceiling, I could feel her kisses as they trailed down my throat. When I finally opened my eyes again, I turned around, still on the beat, dropped myself down the ground, and swiveled my hips back to a standing position.

"Surfer boy. We've been staring at each other," I answered, as simply as though I was ordering mustard on a sandwich.

"Okay, then," she answered, "that leaves me with the mocha candy."

The crowd on the dance floor had parted, and there was now a group of people circled around us, watching. Men gazed hungrily and women scowled, eyes red and angry. Their jealousy surged a bolt of energy into me. Even though I used to be an angel—that bad girl side wins out every time. An angel turned succubus—I was a creature no one in the demon or angel realm could explain. The succubus with a soul.

The song ended and Kayce took my hand, leading me to the two guys. "This is Monica," she said, running a fingernail down the length of the other guy's bicep, which bulged beneath his Hollister polo shirt.

Surfer boy took my hand in his. "I'm Paul," he said. His palm was sweaty, and after the handshake ended I wiped my hand on my slinky, sequined dress, not caring if it stained. That's the beauty of shapeshifting. It took a lot of my focus not to slink away, hoping that none of his other body parts were *that* sweaty.

Kayce already had a leg wrapped around the other guy, pressing herself against him to the beat. I grabbed Paul's hand and pulled him off the dance floor. I wasn't quite the exhibitionist Kayce was. The bathroom was an extremely modern design with clear glass walls that fogged over as soon as you locked the door, so that no one could see in. I tugged Paul inside, locking the door behind me. The glass fogged, encasing us, looking as though the entire club surrounding the glass filled with a mist instantaneously. He grabbed me from behind and turned my hips back to him, his hands squeezing my waist in a way that suggested a carnal need. Our lips rushed to find each other's, and his hands cupped my jaw. Bright blond hair flopped forward into his face, and I brushed it back, my fingernails running through the silklike strands. My tongue found his, and they twisted around each other.

With my eyes closed, it was easy to pretend for a moment the hair was Drew's—my human manager at the café where I worked during the days. I pretended that those lips were fuller, with a tiny scar slicing across the top. Pretended that this college boy's hands were more calloused and weathered from years of hard work as they circled and caressed my body.

An apelike grunt pulled me back to reality. Cool air tickled my puckering nipples, and it wasn't until that moment that I realized he had pulled my dress down over my breasts. A raging erection was poking through his jeans against my belly, and the contact sent a jolt of electricity through my blood. I needed his life—this wasn't about passion or even sex; it was survival. Never mind that I had had sex the night before as well. Never mind that I chose Paul because he had a slight resemblance to the man I loved but couldn't have. Never mind I probably could have gone two weeks without another conquest with all the Heaven-bound men I've been seducing lately. Right now—all that mattered was the life force in front of me. A morality so strong that its power pushed on my gut, causing the air to gush out of my lungs, leaving me breathless.

I shoved Paul against the opposite wall, wrapping my legs around his waist. As I propped myself on his hips, the dress slid up above my ass and I shapeshifted my panties away. One of the glorious things about having more sex than I need—I have plenty of power for superfluous shifting.

A finger slid inside me, and I tensed my sex around him. Again, I captured those pretty-boy lips in mine and drank him in. His soul was glistening, shimmering. He was going to be an amazing fix—the high would be electrifying. Much more so than the assholes and Hell-bound men I used to sleep with. And what's a week off their life in order for me to not be condemned to Hell? A week off their life so that I could maintain a human body and not be a drifting soul in the bowels of Hell. And in exchange, they get a night with me—sex extraordinaire. It's an even trade.

Okay, maybe not even, but it's the closest I can get to justifying my actions. Besides, my broken heart is still on the mend. Anonymous sex speeds up the healing process. Not only did I discover Drew was still in love with Adrienne, but now she was the apprentice to my Julian. My old mentor back when *I* was an angel. I lost both the loves of my life to the same woman.

I shook the memory away, concentrating again on the fix that stood before me. I'm not against falling in love—but I am against getting involved with humans or angels *ever* again. Demon dates only from now on. And the biggest downside to dating demons—they're a bunch of fucking assholes. But Paul was here in front of me. He was hot. And he wanted me. My job is to corrupt souls for Hell and steal their life force. I used to fight my duties . . . but these days, I was becoming friggin' Employee of the Year.

His arms, which had been holding me up by the ass, released me back to the ground. We both scrambled to get his pants off. I tore the pale blue polo shirt from his head and threw it on the floor. His hands entwined through my golden, soft curls and just as I thought he was going to pull me in for another kiss, he grunted and pushed me to my knees.

Under normal circumstances, this sort of overt lack of re-gard for my sexual needs wouldn't fly. But, right now, I didn't really give a shit. If I was training him to be a consistent lover at my beck and call, then I would have taken the time to fight it. But for now, fuck it. I flicked a tongue out and ran it along the tip, then up and down the length of his shaft. His fingers still twisted in my hair, tightening its hold on me. He pulled my face closer to his cock—he clearly didn't want the teasing. Done with the appetizer, he wanted the entrée.

I grabbed his balls, squeezing perhaps a little too tightly, to where pain turned into pleasure. A gust of air whooshed from his lips, the sudden change from gentle to rough proving too much for him. Amateur. I took his entire length into my mouth, wrapping my lips tightly around his girth. My teeth just barely grazed against him as he fucked my mouth. With the skill of an expert, I used my other hand to grip the base of his dick, rotating my head with a swirl as I reached the tip. His head slammed against my throat.

"Fuck me with those stunning sucking lips, gorgeous." He was growing in size; I could feel him getting bigger against my tongue. There was no way I was letting him get away with not doing any work. I lowered his hands from my hair and placed them on my breasts. His thumbs rolled over my pebbled nip-ples, sending shock waves through my whole body. The ache between my legs grew, and I pulled my mouth away before he could finish.

He groaned and tried to pull my head back toward his cock. Slapping his hands away, I stood, bending over the sink. I flipped my dress up past my hips. "Don't you want this in-stead?" I pulled my ass cheeks apart, allowing him a view of my everything.

His eyes grew wide and he licked his lips before approach-ing. Two large hands wrapped around my hips and the sides of my ass. The tip of his finger teased my opening, wet and slick and ready for him. The same hand traced around the curve of my ass and spanked me. It wasn't a hard slap, but I gasped in an exaggerated way. Finally, he pushed himself into me. Reaching around front, he flicked at my clit. My knees buckled with the small but effective motions. I could feel the tension building, and I gripped the sink, my body trembling, an orgasm rolled over my body.

The itch between my legs was fierce, reminding me that though it was pleasurable, this fuck was a necessity. I could come a hundred times for him, but until he spilled his seed on me, his soul—his energy—was safe.

Thanks to my succubus senses and inhuman reflexes, I saw him unlock the bathroom door before the fogged walls cleared. Within those milliseconds, I shifted my face to look like someone else. Modesty might seem silly—being that I corrupt souls by fucking countless men each week—but I didn't like my Hellish duties to cross over into my day job. And even though most of these people here in the club were visiting from out of town, I didn't want to be known and recognized as the girl who was publicly getting it from behind. I did the same thing with my night job as a stripper—shift my looks slightly so that most people wouldn't necessarily recognize me during the day.

The walls around us cleared. See-through. "Oh, yeah," Paul grunted, and slapped my ass, squeezing it hard enough to leave a mark. Grabbing a fistful of my hair, he pulled my head back and pushed into me with one final thrust. Sliding out just in time, he came all over my ass. It dripped down into my folds, and the rush of his life force was like walking into an air-conditioned room after sweating outside on a hot summer's day. It momentarily took my breath away. His life reeled before my eyes, like I was watching an abridged version being projected before me. He'd graduate cum laude, move to Chicago, work in a boutique marketing firm before marrying and settling down in the suburbs. And last, he'd die of a heart attack.

Finally I released the breath I'd been holding, thankful that I hadn't stripped too much of his life. I pulled my dress back down over my ass and looked into the mirror above me. I was glowing, radiant with the new life force. Paul's life force.

I turned to face him, not bothering to shift back into my original features. He was so drunk on cheap beer, he wouldn't even notice I looked slightly different than before. I glanced quickly out at the line of people formed to watch our little performance, then touched his cheek, running a finger down his jawline. "Thanks, Paul."

His pupils were dilated, eyes wide, ready to party some more. Just a side effect of my poison. He was high on me. "Who says it has to be over?" He grabbed me around the waist, pulling me in for another kiss. I could taste myself on him. The crowd of people watching outside whooped and hollered. I let him kiss me a moment longer before pulling away and handing him his pants.

"I do," I said quietly, reaching for the door. "Oh, and Paul?" When I looked back over my shoulder, he still had the energy, but a dejected look was etched on his pretty, boyish face.

He straightened as I turned around, eyes wide and expectant. "Yeah?" he said, hopeful, zipping up his pants. Like a puppy, I imagined two floppy ears perking up.

"Never shove a woman's head to your dick without reciprocating the act yourself." His face dropped, all color draining quickly away. On an exhale, my shoulders slumped slightly. I spoke again, a tad more quietly this time. "And lay off the red meat, okay? I mean . . . it's just, it can be bad for your heart."